PROBE

STAR TREK®

PROBE

Margaret Wander Bonanno

POCKET BOOKS

New York   London   Toronto   Sydney   Tokyo   Singapore

The publisher wishes to thank Gene DeWeese, who made essential creative and conceptual contributions to this book.

POCKET BOOKS, a division of Simon & Schuster Inc. 1230 Avenue of the Americas, New York, NY 10020

This book is published by Pocket Books, a division of Simon & Schuster Inc., under exclusive license from Paramount Pictures.

Library of Congress Catalog Card Number: 90-64064

ISBN: 0-671-72420-7

First Pocket Books hardcover printing April 1992

10 9 8 7 6 5 4 3 2 1

POCKET and colophon are registered trademarks of Simon & Schuster Inc.

Printed in the U.S.A.

Historian's Note

Probe takes place sometime prior to *Star Trek VI: The Undiscovered Country*. The events of *Star Trek IV: The Voyage Home* are also pivotal to this story, and the reader may wish to view it as a referent.

PROLOGUE

☆

In its five hundred millennia of existence, the entity had been given many names. Some had called it Probe; some, Messenger or Wanderer. Some, such as the silicon-based creatures of the Ophane star cluster, whose metabolic rate was so slow as to prohibit meaningful communication with most star-faring intelligences, had called it Traveler.

But its creators had not named it. They did not name machines, even one of this magnitude and complexity, one whose centuries-long building had consumed all their energies and half their world. Instead, they had described it: Seeker, they had called it, for that was its function, to seek another race like their own. Communicator, they had called it, for that also was its function, to communicate not only with others like themselves but with any who might someday become like themselves.

1

Protector, they had called it, for that, too, was to be its function, and Nurturer and Recorder.

But Seeker they had called it most often, for that was its ultimate purpose: to find, somewhere in the galaxy, a race the equal of their own, with which it could Speak in the True Language. When that day came, it would return, bringing with it the message that they were no longer alone in a universe that seemed to favor only the scurrying mites that had, before the Winnowing, dominated the waterless areas of their own planet.

But in its half million years, it had found none. In the waters of hundreds of worlds it had found primitives who held the promise that, in another million years, they might be able to Speak, might become capable of learning the True Language.

The blue world the entity had recently departed had held such primitives for millennia. Time and again it had returned, listening to their evolving story, etching their rudimentary recitations into its crystalline memory, observing, prompting them in the direction of Speech. But then they had fallen silent. No amount of calling, no intensity of prodding, had brought forth a response until, finally, the creators' instructions had said: Prepare the world for new life. Whatever the cause of the primitives' extinction, remove it; insure that it will neither recur on this world nor spread to infect other worlds.

But the instructions had barely begun to be implemented when the primitives had reappeared, had raised their planet-bound voices in joy.

The entity had stopped, considering the puzzle.

Its creators had included neither instructions nor explanation for such a circumstance. Had the primitives made a sudden evolutionary leap? Had they developed abilities even the creators had not possessed, enabling them to leave their world and return, unseen, at will? Or had another race even more advanced than the creators found them, transported them to some other world, and then returned them?

There were no answers. The primitives were still primitives, little different from their ancestors a thousand years before. When questioned, they would speak only of enclosed spaces and chaos and then freedom. The machines that darted through space like the mites that rode them had not the power of Speech, nor did they respond in any fashion to the True Language except to become silent and motionless.

In the end, the creators' instructions, incomplete as they were proving to be, had left no choice for the entity but to move on, to continue its search, continue its monitoring of other primitives on other worlds. But it would return, not in another millennium but in a decade, for that blue world now occupied a special place in the entity's crystalline memory, a place occupied by no other world. There were unanswered questions there, the kind of unanswered questions that implied not the small uncertainties of the position or spectrum of a star but the possibility of danger, certainly to the primitives, perhaps to the entity itself. Perhaps, even, to the creators.

Only once before in its five hundred millennia of existence had such danger arisen. For a few milliseconds the entity attempted to reconstruct the events of that brief period of danger and destruction, but failed. The crystalline memory was damaged—and unlike its physical structure, those lost memories could not be regenerated.

And in their absence, despite the questions—the

possibilities—that circled soundlessly, endlessly in its ever-evolving crystalline pathways, the entity could only continue on its mission.

Unknowing, it moved forward, skirting the edge of the Neutral Zone that separated Federation territory and that space claimed by the Romulan Empire.

ONE

☆

Jim Kirk was glad he'd come home alone. It gave him the chance to fall in love all over again.

He'd been halfway across the galaxy and back, seen more different kinds of cities in a year than most Starfleet officers saw in a lifetime, from metropolises vast enough to swallow the North American continent whole to villages rustic enough to have come out of an old Swiss woodcut—and still, there was no place like San Francisco.

He'd decided to adopt it as his hometown his first day at the Academy, when he and Gary Mitchell went running up and down the rolling hills of the old city. The years he'd spent here, on and off, since returning from the *Enterprise*'s first five-year mission had only strengthened his feelings for the place and its people. The Presidio, Haight-Ashbury, the new city that housed

Starfleet headquarters—there was half a milennium of history here that Kirk liked being a part of. Earlier in the day, he'd walked by his old apartment that overlooked the Bay . . . and been reminded of his days here as Starfleet's chief of operations. It occurred to him that now there were few places in the city he could walk that didn't bring to mind some memory, weren't connected to some person or past event. If Spock and McCoy had taken him up on his offer to spend a couple days here, the last few days would have been very different.

Which was why the sight of Golden Gate Park on this, his last morning on Earth, came as such a surprise.

Everything was so lush, so overgrown, it was like walking into the middle of a tropical rain forest. Rhododendrons leapt out of carefully planted terraces to spring across his path, grass covered the slate path beneath his feet, and (though he knew this must be his imagination) even the trees along Kennedy Drive seemed several meters taller. All residual effects of the monsoonlike rains brought on by the Probe, just a few short weeks ago.

Scientists were saying that growth patterns across the planet would be affected for another few years. The Probe, after all, had almost sent the Earth back into another ice age. Worldwide, many of the immediate effects of its visit had receded—cloud cover and planetwide temperatures had returned to within normal parameters, and floodwaters had receded from all but the most low-lying regions—but the repercussions of the Probe's visit would be felt here, and elsewhere, for a long time to come.

Well, if the repercussions were all like this, Kirk didn't think that would be such a bad thing.

On a patch of concrete before him, a sudden gust of

wind scattered a cluster of sea gulls fighting over a crust of bread. Even the air smelled fresher, he decided, almost as if the rains had somehow washed clean the entire planet. He'd noticed it out in Yosemite, too—a sense of renewal that pervaded the entire park, from the old sequoia forests Spock had been so intent on studying to the top of El Capitan. Kirk was glad for the chance to spend time on his homeworld these last few days—but he could feel the restlessness building up inside him.

All I ask is a tall ship, and a star to steer her by. . . .

And still, that was all he wanted. He'd gotten the word from Starfleet Command yesterday afternoon—a whole new sector of the galaxy was being opened up, and he and the *Enterprise* were being considered to spearhead its exploration. Right away he'd made an appointment to see Admiral Cartwright—*and you'd better start hightailing it if you plan to make that meeting,* he thought, noticing the sun overhead—to persuade him that his ship was the correct choice.

And it was his ship—he'd finally made his peace with that. *Enterprise-A* had done everything he'd asked of it last mission—of course, it wasn't the old *Enterprise,* but then (as Dr. McCoy kept reminding him) he wasn't the old Jim Kirk, was he? Nothing was the same as it had been twenty years ago, and he wasn't complaining. There was a truce now, however uneasy, with the Klingons, and even the Romulans were quiet.

A sudden squawk and a flap of wings distracted him, and Kirk looked up to find he'd walked into the middle of the gulls' feeding session, almost tripping over one in the process.

Talk about having your head in the clouds. Better get your feet back on the ground and over to Starfleet.

Whistling happily (if somewhat off-key), James T.

Kirk made his way out of Golden Gate Park toward the city of San Francisco proper.

The rising sun glinted off the surface of the Coral Sea and sent light splashing among the crystalline waters of the great lagoon that lay between the Barrier Reef and Australia proper. Were he not due to leave within hours, Spock would certainly have taken the time to explore those waters, which boasted a wealth of colorful marine life unmatched in this part of the world. But he would have to leave that for another time.

This last day of his leave, the Vulcan had come to observe George and Gracie—the two humpback whales the *Enterprise* had transported through time from the twentieth century—in their home at the New Cetacean Institute, off Australia's Great Barrier Reef. Other considerations aside, Spock was fascinated by these extraordinary leviathans, who had not their like in Vulcan's shallow, turbulent oceans.

As he lowered himself from the edge of the newly constructed platform at the reef's edge into the water, several hundred meters out to sea George leapt high in the air and slammed back into the water sending fountains of spray and massive ripples in all directions. Spock pushed off from the platform's underwater supports and began swimming, the only sound in the early-morning silence that of his limbs slicing through water.

And then, suddenly, there was whalesong: it held no cadence or melody that Vulcan or human ears would recognize as such, and yet the "feel" of the sound, despite all the logical objections Spock's mind automatically raised, was that of a song.

A saga. George's "voice" was clear and strong: anyone listening, even swimmers as far away as the other end of the Great Barrier Reef over fifteen hundred kilometers distant, would have heard his tones, pure and undistorted. But there were none left who could understand him, none with whom his saga, if such it was, could be shared.

Five hundred years ago, Spock knew, the songs of a thousand thousand humpbacks had crisscrossed beneath Earth's oceans. Before the advent of humans in large numbers upon the seas and more specifically, the invention of the screw propeller, cetacean life-forms had possessed an extraordinary communication network. For millennia the seas had been filled with a complex tapestry of underwater sound, its uncounted strands woven around the planet, each a never-ending, constantly evolving saga. For such they must have been. Enduring anywhere from five to sixty minutes, they were memorized and passed from pod to pod. Old songs were repeated, new songs added, every year. One whale could communicate with another across distances up to twenty thousand kilometers—literally anywhere in the planet's oceans.

Then had come "civilization." By the late nineteenth and early twentieth centuries, Spock's studies had revealed, the incessant background noise of commercial and military steamships—reverberating at the twenty-hertz frequency that lay at the very heart of the massive creatures' vocal range—had made it impossible for them to sing to each other over distances of more than a few kilometers. It was thought this was why so many species had engaged in mass beachings during the twentieth century. They were disoriented, unable to warn each other away from shallow water. The threads of song had been broken, the global tapestry torn.

And then the singers themselves were gone.

Until, finally, two were returned, not out of any sense of rightness or guilt—though the captain undoubtedly experienced those feelings on behalf of his twentieth-century ancestors—but out of self-interest. Self-preservation.

They had been returned, not for their own sake, but to save Earth from the Probe's destruction, and George's song, simple though it was, had done just that. The Probe had left, retreating to the vastnesses of the galaxy out of which it had appeared, never to be seen again.

Or so a relieved Starfleet seemed to want to believe.

Spock, logically, felt otherwise. All the evidence indicated the Probe—or others of its kind—had visited Earth in the past. How else could it have known and produced the whalesong? Its last approach must have been when whales were plentiful, before Earth's science was capable of detecting its presence. Five hundred years ago? A thousand? Ten thousand? He had no way of knowing. But this time it had found a world that had changed. It had found only two of the creatures it had apparently sought, and those two, it must have noted, had appeared out of nowhere. If it had been prepared to destroy an entire planet because of their absence, it was only logical to assume that it would be concerned for the welfare of those two, that it would return not in another thousand or ten thousand years but within months or years, certainly within the lifetimes of the whales themselves.

It was this logic that had brought Spock here, to the two beings on Earth that had communicated with the

Probe, the two beings that might have learned something, no matter how slight, about the Probe's purpose or its plans. He harbored no illusions that his task would be easy, that he would learn everything he wished to learn. There would be no words, any more than there had been words exchanged when, in the tank in twentieth-century San Francisco, he had learned of Gracie's pregnancy. He had said, when questioned about his knowledge, "She told me," but that was not strictly accurate. "I learned it from her" would have been more precise, just as, amid the death and pain of the mining tunnels of Janus VI, he had learned the truth from the silicon-based mind of the injured Horta.

At best there would be images, feelings, none of which could possibly mean the same things to a hundred-kilogram, half-Vulcan starship officer that they meant to a fifty-ton, air-breathing water dweller without so much as an opposable thumb to manipulate its environment. He would have to experience what he could, what George would be willing—or able—to share with him. He would have to interpret. In the end, much as it offended his logic, he would have to guess.

The water heaved in another series of majestic ripples. As if George had sensed not just Spock's presence but his purpose, he had approached, breaking the water less than a hundred meters distant, then submerging and coming to an almost complete stop a few meters below the surface, his great head directly beneath the Vulcan.

Breathing deeply, Spock dived.

Knee-deep in the rubble of a millennia-old city on one of the barrenest of the Romulan Empire's newly acquired colony worlds, Dajan glanced up from his scrutiny of a weatherworn petroglyph to discover a pair of jackbooted feet planted on the rim of the retaining wall above him. The archaeologist had to squint against the dull red sun to discern the true shape of the shadow figure standing in the boots.

It was the sublieutenant from the guardian vessel that had dogged his research ship the entire way here. *Why am I not surprised?* Dajan wondered.

"What is it?" he demanded imperiously in the precise tone his elder brother had taught him to use with sublieutenants and their ilk.

"A summons, kerDajan, from the capital. All scientific missions are herewith recalled."

"For what purpose?" Dajan's glass-green eyes snapped with fury. He had barely begun! He stood, abandoning his perusal of the petroglyph, though he did not yet put away his magnifier. Oh, how he longed to flash it upward into the sublieutenant's eyes, claiming later that it was an accident! But he was not yet that far rehabilitated. And he had to be careful for his sister's sake, for her position was even more vulnerable than his. She was still in the capital, where intrigue and backstabbing and petty revenge constituted a way of life. A whisper was all it would take to send her tumbling back down the slippery slope to un-Orthodoxy.

"I was not told," the sublieutenant answered with a touch of smugness, "therefore I cannot tell you. But your ship departs within the hour. Be on it, or be marooned here."

In his departure, the sublieutenant managed to loosen enough scree from the top of the retaining wall to all but bury the petroglyph.

*   *   *

12

From the bridge of the *Enterprise-A,* Dr. Leonard H. McCoy watched the blue-and-white confection that was his home planet glide peacefully by on the viewscreen. *Very* peaceful, considering what had happened there only a short while ago. There were the isolated food and medical-supply shortages to keep off-planet transports working overtime, and people in certain areas were still advised to boil or irradiate their drinking water until groundwater could be certified pure, but on the whole, things on planet Earth were pretty much back to normal.

As were things aboard the *Enterprise.*

"Awailable twentieth-century selections coming up on-screen now, Doctor." The thickly accented voice belonged to Commander Pavel Chekov, who sat at the science station before McCoy, punching buttons. "A wery important period in the history of Western music. Significant composers include"—he paused the scrolling display for McCoy to read some of the names listed there—"Shostakovich, Prokofiev, Miaskovsky, Strauss . . ." He frowned at the display a moment, then continued reading. "Khachaturian, Volkonsky . . ."

McCoy leaned over the display and laid a hand on his shoulder. "Do I detect a slight bias here, Mr. Chekov?"

"Bias, sir?" Chekov turned back to McCoy, the look of puzzlement so pronounced that the doctor couldn't help but wonder if it, like the occasional thickening of the Russian's accent, was 100 percent genuine and not at least partly the continuation of a "game" that had started in his days as an ensign on the old *Enterprise.* But then, McCoy thought ruefully, there were those who had voiced similar suspicions about himself and his exchanges with Spock. There were even times, after all the years and adventures, when he himself would be hard put to give an unequivocal answer.

"Almost every one of the composers you've mentioned is Russian, Mr. Chekov," McCoy pointed out.

Chekov shrugged. "It is a well-known fact, Doctor. Russian contribution toward twentieth-century Western music is substantial. Concepts of atonality, dissonant harmony, computer-generated composition . . ."

McCoy leaned back against the guardrail circling the bridge's command deck and tuned out the musical-history lesson. Half an hour ago, he'd come to the bridge, planning to take advantage of Starbase One's extensive facilities to update the ship's on-board musical library. Chekov had been on duty and immediately volunteered to aid the doctor in his task. So far, much to McCoy's consternation, their review of Starbase One's selection had produced little that was not tinged with a distinctly Slavic flavor.

"Shall I instruct the computer to initiate transfer?" Chekov asked. "I would suggest a sampling of some of the recent interpretations of Shostakovich's works in particular."

"No, no," McCoy said. "Let's skip ahead, Chekov. I'm interested in more recent compositions."

"As you wish, Doctor." Chekov swiveled back to the science station. "Twenty-third-century works now coming up on-screen."

"Ah," McCoy said. Now that was more like it. He smiled, recognizing most of the names now scrolling by. "Now this is music. Salet of Vulcan, Evanston, Penalt—" He frowned. "Vigelshevsky?"

"Anton Wigelshevsky, Doctor," Chekov said. "Why, he is this century's most famous composer of electronic music. His wariations on a theme by Prokofiev—I cannot believe you have not heard of him."

Before McCoy could give his opinion of "all that
electronic hooting and braying," he was rescued by the
sound of the bosun's whistle.

"Probably Dr. Chapel," he said, stepping quickly to
the captain's chair and toggling on a switch. "I promised
her the five-dollar tour of the new sickbay before we
shipped out."

But it wasn't Chapel.

Instead, the viewscreen before them filled with the
image of a dark-haired Starfleet ensign.

"Starfleet Operations. Admiral Cartwright for Captain Kirk."

Chekov and McCoy frowned at each other. McCoy
spoke first. "The captain isn't here. But I understood he
already had an appointment to meet with the admiral
later this afternoon."

"Thank you," the aide said brusquely. "One moment."

The screen darkened for a few seconds, then the aide
reappeared. "If the captain checks in, please have him
contact the admiral immediately. Starfleet out."

The screen went dark again and stayed that way.
McCoy frowned. "Now what do you suppose that was all
about?"

"Captain!" Sulu called, bounding out of the shadow of
the Sciences building where a maintenance robot was
polishing the structure's transparent aluminum facing.

Kirk smiled as the helmsman caught up and fell into
step beside him. The two strolled across the broad,
sunny plaza of Starfleet Command HQ Central. "Mr.
Sulu, where've you been? I've been trying to get in touch
with you all day."

"Out enjoying the city." Sulu grinned, all enthusiasm. "It wasn't much fun when the rain was coming down, but it's sure had some beautiful side effects. So, ready for the grand tour of Chinatown?"

"Er . . . that's what I've been trying to get in touch with you about. I'm afraid our little outing will have to be delayed for a while. Cartwright's schedule cleared, and I managed to get in to see him early."

"No problem, Captain." Sulu's expression remained doggedly cheerful. "I don't mind waiting out here in the sunshine."

"Why don't you come along?" Kirk paused at the entrance to Headquarters and motioned the helmsman inside. "It certainly won't hurt to have someone else there to support my case."

Sulu paused in the doorway, dark eyes wide. "If you're sure the admiral won't mind . . ."

"He won't mind," Kirk said easily. He felt certain Cartwright had already chosen the *Enterprise* to lead the exploration; it would simply be a matter of the admiral's announcing the fact, and Kirk's thanking him. Cartwright certainly wouldn't have managed to clear time so quickly in order to argue against it. "I asked for the meeting, after all."

They walked briskly to the central turbolift; within one minute, no more, they stood at the outer office leading to Cartwright's. The admiral's door was shut, but an aide rose at the sight of Kirk and Sulu.

"Captain Kirk to see Admiral Cartwright," Kirk announced confidently, smiling pleasantly at the aide.

But the aide—a young human female with dark hair and features severe enough to be Vulcan—did not smile; in fact, she looked decidedly worried. "Captain Kirk, sir. The admiral's been trying to reach you." She pressed a toggle on her desk console. "Admiral, Captain Kirk is here."

The admiral's door slid open.

Cartwright's mellow baritone filtered through the intercom. "Tell him to come in."

Kirk raised his eyebrows in surprise and nodded at Sulu, who glanced uncertainly at the aide, then followed the captain into Cartwright's inner sanctum. The aide's protests were cut off as the door snapped shut behind Kirk and Sulu.

They were greeted by a second surprise: Cartwright was not alone. The admiral sat, not at his desk, but at a nearby conference table across from the white-haired President of the Federation Council. And from their furrowed brows, it was clear that whatever had come up was serious indeed.

"Admiral. Mr. President." Kirk nodded in turn at each man; Sulu followed suit. "I believe you both know my helmsman, Commander Sulu."

Cartwright gave a distracted nod, barely glanced at Sulu; the President looked as if he were about to object to the commander's presence, then changed his mind and released a small smile of welcome.

"Gentlemen, sit." Cartwright motioned for them to take a chair. "I know, Captain, that we were supposed to meet about an entirely different subject, but there's something I want you to hear." He rose, went over to his desk, and stooped to press a control.

A burst of static erupted from the console speakers; Cartwright grimaced. "Sorry. The transmission's of poor quality because we had to hyperaugment the volume, and his voice is distorted because of the scrambling devices used."

Kirk strained to sift the words from the static.

"To friends across the Neutral Zone: I have news. You would know it soon enough through normal channels, but better you hear it now, for it has already changed relations between us. The Praetor is dead."

Jim Kirk glanced sharply at Cartwright, who nodded slowly.

"For a time," the distant voice went on, "there will be chaos in the Empire. There is opportunity amidst this chaos, to be sure: perhaps an understanding between our two peoples can be reached. Bring this news to all among you inclined to work for peace, and be wary of those who would stop its spread or distort its meaning: unfortunately, censorship is one of the many things our empires have in common."

The static increased, gradually drowning out the transmission. Cartwright pushed the control, ending the message.

"How recent is this report, Admiral?" Sulu asked.

"As recent as a subspace squirt from the heart of the Empire received at three this morning," Cartwright answered, his sculpted, dark face looking ashen, suggesting that it had gotten him out of bed and he'd been hounding the decoders from that time to the present.

Kirk shook his head skeptically. "There've been rumors of the Praetor's impending death since Hector was a pup, or at least as long as I've been in Starfleet. I suppose even a Romulan can't live forever, but even so, he's only third in power—"

"Third in rank, but first in power," the Federation President interjected, his tone indicating that he took the report very seriously. "There is no question among those who know but that the Praetor rules the Empire. Or ruled it, while he lived."

"If we can trust that message," Sulu interjected.

"Nothing Romulan can be trusted completely," the President said. "However, we have received information from this same source in the past, and it has always proven out in the long run."

"In any event," Cartwright said, "regardless of personal feelings any of us may have, we have no choice but to assume it *may* be true—and to prepare accordingly."

In the Empire, there was no doubt of the Praetor's death. The press of the crowd in the streets of the capital bore witness to it and threatened to produce deaths of its own as every element struggled to reach and enter the Hall of Columns to view the body and be seen expressing earnest sorrow at the passing.

Jandra herself would soon have to join them, though she would at least not have to endure the physical danger represented by the impatient mob of "mourners" she had seen from the windows of the Citadel quarters she shared with her husband, Tiam. It was possible, she supposed, that for some very few the "mourning" was genuine. For most, it was—it had to be!—the necessary show of Orthodoxy, nothing more. As for her own thoughts, they were occupied—as they had been since she had first been informed of the "honor" to be bestowed upon her—almost exclusively in trying to thread her way through the maze of what the death and the subsequent summons might mean to her. It had come with stunning suddenness, almost as sudden as the "reforms" with which the Committee seemed to be trying to overwhelm the very Empire. For years, her "rehabilitation" had exhibited little more progress than Tiam's career, but now, in a matter of days—

"An official flitter will come for you," Tiam interrupted her thoughts, trying not to posture too obviously in the glass as he arranged the mourning ribands over his uniform insignia. "I've had a place cleared on the roof to avoid the mob."

"What music will they require?" Jandra asked, careful to keep her voice neutral, her hands unclenched in her lap; tension was bad for them and would affect her playing.

"The flitter pilot will bring it." Tiam turned in her direction. Jandra's heart quickened. She remembered when the marriage had been arranged, and how she'd raged and wept for days when told it was the only possible route to rehabilitation for herself and her family. Yet, when she first saw Tiam, her rage had dissipated somewhat. *At least he is handsome*, she remembered thinking at the time. That was before she knew the rest, before she realized that the road back to Orthodoxy was exceedingly slow, that, though her alliance with Tiam allowed her back from the Provinces, she was as much an outsider as ever. "Undoubtedly the Lerma requiem will be required," Tiam went on solemnly. "Lerma has been longer on the Orthodox list than any of his contemporaries."

"Of course," Jandra replied without inflection, thinking: *Lerma is so bland that no one, not even the Praetor, could have objected to him.*

So she had been summoned to play at the Praetor's funeral. Romulans were masters of irony, but this, Jandra thought, was beyond irony. This Praetor, who was a swine and a murderer, who by the most conservative estimates was responsible for a million deaths or "disappearances" among his own kind, not to mention untold incursions against alien citizenries, this Praetor whose own order had sent her elder brother on an impossible mission whose failure required his execution, her parents' ritual suicide, and the un-Orthodox stigma placed upon her and her surviving sibling—this Praetor presumed to reach her even beyond his own death and require that she offer him her music.

"It is quite an honor," Tiam emphasized, not for the first time. "I do not need to tell you there will be— uncertainties—in the coming days. I was made a middle-level administrator by this Praetor's favor. Who knows what I may achieve with his successor, provided he is pleased with me and mine? And I have been told on good authority that several elder musicians were passed over in your favor." He eyed her as if expecting an expression of gratitude. When none was forthcoming, he shrugged. "As for me, I have already been made privy to something that—" He fell silent abruptly, as if realizing that, in his need to boast, he had slipped into dangerous territory.

Jandra held her silence, unaware of Tiam's momentary apprehension. She still reflected on the "honor" he insisted she was being done and wondering how he dared say such words to her. He of all people knew her family's past, knew she had married him solely in order to win rehabilitation for herself and her brother. *How that fact must gall him even now,* she thought with some slight satisfaction.

She looked up from her hands in her lap to see that Tiam was watching her narrowly.

"You're indolent," he accused her. "Have you some— qualm—about the honor assigned you?"

"I will play, Husband." Jandra fought to keep the

21

resignation out of her voice. "More than that you need not know."

Commander Hiran of the bird-of-prey *Galtizh* was the very model of restrained military mourning as he received official notification of the Praetor's passing. Only when he was safely in his quarters did he allow the hint of a smile to soften the lines of his broad, rough-hewn face.

"So they have finally let the news out," Hiran said. "Did they think they could keep it a secret forever?"

He turned to stare directly at Subcommander Feric, who stood in the doorway of his quarters, hands clasped behind his back. His newly appointed first officer shrugged.

"They kept his illness secret for years."

Hiran nodded absently, letting his gaze roam over the *Galtizh's* personnel roster, now displayed on his computer screen. He noted that he and Feric had now been serving together for almost four years—how was it the man had managed to remain such an enigma to him for so long?

Probably because he answered every question put to him as succinctly as that one. Gods, but it was strange to have to ferret information out of your first officer. He couldn't help but contrast the long, silent gaps in his conversations with Feric to the animated discussions he'd enjoyed with Ren. There was no doubt but that he far preferred an honest, heated, exchange of opinion.

But then, there was no doubt he had far preferred Ren.

It was still strange to look at the roster and not see her name, listed beneath his. Still strange to be in this cabin, alone. And—back to the matter at hand—still strange to have to ferret out information from his first officer.

"The next few weeks will be interesting," Hiran offered. "Do you think we will be called back, Subcommander?"

"Anything is possible." Feric hesitated. "Particularly in times of transition. Rumors abound."

Hiran nodded. He supposed that, right now, that was as definitive an answer as he could have expected.

Even from Ren.

"So, Spock," McCoy said as the door to sickbay hissed shut behind them, "did you have another meeting of minds or did you just get wet?"

"Neither characterization accurately portrays the encounter, Doctor."

"I didn't mean— Look, Spock, just tell me what you found out. You did find out *something,* didn't you?"

"Of course, Doctor. George and Gracie are both quite pleased with their new surroundings, but they—"

"About the *Probe,* Spock! The Probe!"

"As I was about to say, Doctor, I was unable to glean anything definitive. At best, I was aware of what humans might describe as impressions."

"The same kind of 'impressions' you picked up back in San Francisco that let you know Gracie was pregnant?"

"Approximately, Doctor. That impression, however, was much stronger, much more specific, in all likelihood because it regarded a natural biological function with which Gracie was familiar. The Probe and its actions, however, were totally outside their experience, as were many of our own actions in bringing them here from the twentieth century. In fact, if my interpretations are correct, the two events are not totally and clearly separate in their minds."

"You're saying they can't tell the difference between us and the Probe?"

"To some extent, yes, Doctor. We are both associated with events totally outside their normal experience."

McCoy frowned, then shrugged. "I guess I can see how they might think the Probe sent our Klingon clunker down to pick them up the way the *Enterprise* sends a shuttle to pick someone up. If they knew about the *Enterprise* and shuttles, which they don't. Do they?"

"Almost certainly not, Doctor. One of the few impressions I was able to uncover that clearly related to the Probe and not to our intercession in their lives was one of a feeling of familiarity, of other beings physically not unlike themselves. But beyond the feeling of familiarity, there was also one of comfort, or perhaps security, not just for the present but for the future."

"Meaning what? That that thing is piloted by some kind of superwhales and it told them it's going to watch out for them?"

"That seems to be how George and Gracie feel. There were also indications of something that might have been anticipation, perhaps for future contact with the Probe or some similar device."

McCoy exhaled audibly. "So it *is* coming back. Or sending for its big brother."

"I do not believe that anyone familiar with the events in question doubted that it would return at some future date, Doctor. My limited findings only move the probable time of that return much closer to the present."

McCoy shook his head, uneasily remembering, first, the unexplained call from Starfleet and then the abrupt summons from the captain to meet both him and Commander Sulu in the transporter room, which was

24

where they were heading now. "You don't suppose *that's* what Jim is so anxious to see us about?"

"I do not believe so, Doctor. My first act upon returning to the *Enterprise* was to avail myself of the latest subspace communiqués regarding the Probe's course and location. It is continuing its outward course in the direction of the First Federation and thus far shows no indication of turning back."

McCoy snorted. "So it's someone else's problem for a while. Well, I wish them luck."

Spock's eyebrow arched minutely, but he said nothing as the door to the transporter room hissed open before them and he saw Sulu and the captain materializing.

The funeral lasted two nights and a day. In that time, thousands upon thousands appeared to sign the Book of Death and pass before the wasted waxen figure in its upright sarcophagus in the Central Septum of the Hall of Columns. In that time, lacking food or sleep, Jandra performed, and almost as many marveled at her tireless brilliance as expressed their grief over the event that gave her the chance to display it.

She alternated among the three instruments best suited to elegiac music—the three-stringed bahtain, the twelve-stringed plekt, and the all-but-impossible one-stringed the'el. She worked her way through the repertoires of Lerma, Talet, and Mektius without missing a note or repeating a single work.

Her person captivated her audience as much as did her music, as the passers spread her history from one to the next. Wife of subCenturion Tiam, some whispered, and twin of kerDajan the archaeologist. A twin! marveled those new to the information. And was she the elder? Told she was, they were pleased: Well, that explains it!

But wasn't there an elder sibling as well? someone asked.

It was a reasonable question, in that clearly neither Jandra nor her twin was in the military. But the silence spread up and down the line of mourners.

No, of course not!

Never!

You must have been mistaken!

And the mourners passed the dais where she played, returning their attention to the motionless figure in the upright sarcophagus, who yet held sway over them, consigning music and musician to the background where they belonged.

Jandra played. Her head buzzed, her wrists and fingers were numb; she was beyond exhaustion. Sometimes she daydreamed, remembering another lifetime when she had been a child prodigy, playing for the great musicians of many worlds.

"Be grateful," more than one had told her parents, "that there is an elder to fulfill the military obligation. For this one is destined to be a musician!"

Sometimes Jandra wept, the tears splashing from her glass-green eyes to bathe the soundboard of the the'el or the bahtain.

How touching! the passers murmured then. See how moved she is, that she weeps for him!

Not for him! Jandra thought fiercely, *save for the fact that he ever existed. Rather, I weep for them—my mother, my father, my brother. . . .*

Among the worlds of the Federation, of course, there was little weeping done for the Praetor. Instead, there was preparation, so that, by the time the official word promised by the static-shrouded voice actually arrived,

Starfleet had already doubled its patrols along the Neutral Zone and ordered its ships to the highest state of readiness. If the chaos in the Romulan Empire was to turn to outward aggression, the Federation would be ready to defend itself.

But then another call came through, a call and an invitation.

An invitation not to war but to peace.

TWO

———————— ☆ ————————

Captain's Log, Stardate 8475.3:

What was once known only to Starfleet Command is now common knowledge: the Romulan Praetor, said by some to have been "third in rank but first in power" in governing the Empire, is dead. The official statement, issued by the Emperor's Legate and sanctioned by the Interim Government, states "natural causes after a long illness exacerbated by the burdens of office." To Romulan watchers everywhere in the Federation—and likely within the Empire as well—the "long illness" implies a slow-acting poison of one kind or another. Too slow-acting, some say. We shall probably never know.

In a somewhat unusual move for a government supposedly redefining itself in the wake of a leader's death, the Empire has tendered an offer of peace toward the Federation. In typically stilted terms that offer little concession, they request a meeting of minds on an uninhabited world of their choosing deep inside the Neutral Zone. While this is viewed

28

by the experts as more of a "feeler" than an actual peace conference, it is hoped it may lead to something on as grand a scale as the ongoing negotiations with the Klingon Empire. I have serious doubts, however, particularly in light of their "official" response to the Federation's earlier attempts to inform them of the fact that the Probe's course was bringing it dangerously close to Romulan space. They denied that it existed, and felt compelled to add that "any efforts to monitor movements of any ships within Romulan territory could be detrimental to the current effort to improve relations between the Federation and the Empire."

Meanwhile, the *Enterprise*, in Admiral Cartwright's words, has been chosen to be the ferryboat for the negotiations. We will bring the Federation's diplomatic liaison to the conference table and stand peacefully by, demonstrating as much goodwill as a Constitution-class starship is capable of. If experience has taught me anything, however, particularly with regard to the Romulans, it is that nothing ever goes as smoothly as the optimists among us would have it. And with a wild card like the Probe in the game, even now making its way deeper into Romulan territory, Mr. Scott's assurance that everything about the *Enterprise* will have been "made right" before we leave spacedock has never been more welcome.

Admiral Cartwright's briefing was originally intended for all of *Enterprise*'s senior officers, but Sulu and Chekov had been working overtime to realign the aft thrusters, and Uhura had already come and gone, after having spoken briefly with Cartwright. Engineer Scott had assured the admiral that, with all due respect, he could be contacted at any time in engineering, providing Cartwright would pardon his French if he were caught under a recycling duct with coolant dripping in his face. Ultimately it was Kirk, Spock, and McCoy who sat across the briefing table from a grim Cartwright and the President of the United Federation of Planets.

"Good morning, gentlemen." The President began to speak before Cartwright could do more than motion them to be seated. "The purpose of this briefing is to clarify your orders regarding the peace initiative to the Romulans, which are already on a computer feed to your vessel."

When there appeared to be neither questions nor objections, the President cleared his throat and went on. "Before we go any further, are any of you familiar with the term *perestroika?*"

Spock pricked up his ears, canted his head slightly, and answered, "A coinage from Modern Russian, most precisely translated as 'restructuring.' First employed, in tandem with the less easily defined term *glasnost*—"

McCoy sighed audibly and rolled his eyes.

"—which can mean either 'openness' or 'publicity,' depending upon the context, by spokespersons for the Soviet Kremlin during the latter half of the twentieth century, to specify a vast and pervasive liberalization of a heretofore strictly hierarchized Soviet government. This liberalization was to include the simplification of an unwieldy bureaucracy, the elimination of corruption among government officials, and increased efficiency and increased production in all areas of industry and agriculture. Whether it would have succeeded given time is still debated, since the failed coup that precipitated—"

"That will be sufficient, Mr. Spock, thank you," Admiral Cartwright cut in. "It is exactly this type of 'restructuring' that is apparently—and I want to strongly emphasize the word *apparently*—taking place within

30

the Romulan Empire since the Praetor's demise. From the upper echelons to the Romulan in the street, our information indicates radical transformations.

"First the prisons were opened and all political prisoners were released," Cartwright went on. "Or all the political prisoners the Interim Government admits to, at least. Free trade has been established with non-Federation worlds on the far borders, and the so-called Banned Lists have been abolished. Philosophers and scientists, artists and writers, formerly forbidden to speak or publish under pain of death, are now considered Orthodox again. . . ."

"Dajan!"

The cry escaped Jandra's lips before she could help herself. She knew Tiam would be watching via the wall comm but did not care. She and her brother had not been permitted to see each other for five years. Let her spouse scowl and add to his store of grievances against her; her emotions could not be denied. She threw aside the bedcovers, where she had been languishing for days, and ran to him.

"Greetings, Little Sister!" He used their childhood nickname, though Jandra was in fact the elder by some six minutes, a significant distinction in a culture infatuated with twins. They embraced, and though they were of a height, he was the stronger and swept her off her feet.

They were both laughing and breathless when he set her down. "What? No cry of 'My hands, be careful of my hands!'? Are we grown so sophisticated, or only jaded?"

"Only so glad to see you that it doesn't matter, Sib."

Delicately Jandra dabbed tears from her green eyes; seeing them mirrored in her twin's, she touched the handkerchief to his face as well. "What miracle permits you to be here? I have been sleeping, for days it must be now."

She glanced at the chrono, which confirmed her fears. "Three days," she went on with a grimace, "while the capital empties of mourners. A 'collapse,' if you please, from 'grief,' if you please, following the funeral and seven public performances thereafter. As if grief were more genteel than exhaustion. Enough! You are here. How is this possible?"

"Don't you read the 'nets for anything beyond news of your recently reexalted self and the ambitious sub-centurion Tiam?" Dajan surveyed the apartments, sniffing disapproval. No doubt decorated in his brother-in-law's preferred stuffy style; he saw very little of Jandra here. "I've been declared Orthodox. Rehabilitated in full in the twinkling of an eye, and 'under consideration for a project worthy of your august talents, kerDajan.' I may gag! Now, of all times, damn the luck! I was *this* close to translating the key petroglyph on T'lekan. Well, but I kept copies to pore over at my leisure. Assuming I shall have any, between fetes. I'd almost rather be un-Orthodox again. Parties—ugh! How do you stand them?"

"I do because I must." Jandra studied her hands. "It seems our fortune ever to be either condemned or coddled, Sib. Would that they would simply leave us to do what we do in peace!"

"So the rumors have proven true, Commander." Subcommander Feric offered his hand in congratulations as he entered Hiran's quarters on the *Galtizh*. "There is to be a peace conference, and you are to be a part of it."

"Perhaps. There is yet opposition to the *Galtizh*, as there is to the conference itself." Hiran shook his head grimly. "No matter how much I favor peace, I cannot help but wonder if those who would do this are not overreaching themselves." He sighed. "But if they do not try, they will not succeed. But neither will they fail, and a failure will bring them down even more surely and more quickly than the actions of their enemies."

Feric nodded, but said nothing.

Tempted as he was, Hiran did not ask his first officer what he made of the proposed peace conference.

"Opinions, gentlemen?" Cartwright asked.

"Admiral, if I may . . ." Kirk took the floor. "It seems to me that change on such a vast scale as we've heard described could hardly have been orchestrated solely to impress us."

"We've given you only the bare bones of it," the President said. "Further examples are virtually endless."

"Examples are endless only when one lacks either the resources or the will to enumerate them," Spock interjected quietly. "I submit, gentlemen, that whether this perestroika is genuine or not is of greater importance to the Romulans themselves than to the Federation. Our most immediate concern, whether the reform is real or counterfeit, is to obtain a reliable answer to the question of who now rules the Empire, and how firm is his hand. It is only logical to assume that the Praetor's death has opened the way for a massive and perhaps prolonged power struggle."

"We have no hard data on that as yet," the President answered. "As always, they present a united front to everyone beyond their borders. There is a so-named Committee that has assumed the Praetor's duties, though we don't know who they are."

"Utilization of an Interim Committee is consistent with past law and precedent," Spock supplied.

"A Committee, gentlemen," the President reiterated. "Names and numbers unknown. And they are our only official contact within the Empire with regard not only to the proposed peace conference but to the accompanying scientific and cultural exchange as well."

McCoy's forehead pursed. "Damned unsociable, if you ask me. Not even a face to respond to."

Cartwright, obviously in no mood for McCoy's facade of public grumpiness, scowled. "Whatever skepticism we may reserve in our private thoughts, gentlemen," he said stiffly, "we are forced to treat this offering as genuine and respond in kind. The stakes—the chances of developing a meaningful peace between our cultures —are simply too high to do otherwise."

"Agreed," the President said quickly, wryly noting Kirk's almost undetectable smile and the darted glance he exchanged with the doctor. "That is precisely what we are here for, gentlemen—to insure that we make the most of those chances."

"Without giving away the store in the process," McCoy added, garnering another scowl from Cartwright.

"Without giving away the store in the process," the President repeated, smiling faintly himself while Cartwright only nodded, his scowl still in place. "Shall we proceed? There are a number of aspects to the agenda the Romulans propose, some of which I'm sure at least some of you will consider peculiar. For one, they appear determined that this will be seen as a full-blown cultural and scientific exchange mission, not just a first-step peace initiative. On the cultural front, they will be represented by a full orchestra, and we are expected to provide the same. Performances, I understand, will alternate between the *Enterprise* and whatever ship the Romulans send."

"An excuse to get a whole shipload of Romulans on board a Federation starship," McCoy opined.

"Precautions will be taken, Doctor, you can rest assured," Cartwright snapped. "As will Romulan precautions doubtless be taken while their ship is overrun with Federation personnel."

"You mentioned other 'peculiar' aspects, Mr. President," Kirk prompted, smothering another remark from McCoy.

The President nodded. "One you may find more offensive than peculiar, I'm afraid. One of their conditions regards the ambassador who will represent us at the conference."

All *Enterprise* eyebrows arched at that announcement. "You certainly don't mean," Kirk said disbelievingly, "that they're trying to tell us who they want our ambassador to be!"

The President shook his head. "Only who they suggest we *not* send."

"That should make it easy enough, then," McCoy snorted. "Whoever they *don't* want is our obvious choice, I'd say."

"Are you quite positive, Doctor?" Spock asked. "I believe there is a human folk tale involving a rabbit and a form of plant growth known as a briar patch—"

"Whether the Romulans have similar folk tales, I don't know," the President broke in, "but it does not apply to this situation. Their demand is not diplomatic posturing. They insist—and we have no reason to disbelieve them at this point—they will attend no conference at which this particular ambassador represents the Federation."

"Have they given a reason?" Kirk asked.

"They have—and I must admit, there is a certain diplomatic logic involved. If talks involving an ambassador of his high level and brilliant reputation were to break down, it would be catastrophic, whereas if a lesser negotiator was involved . . ."

" 'Don't start at the top'," Kirk commented. "If it fails at that level, there's nowhere else to go."

The President nodded. "Precisely. It was a common practice on Earth, where heads of state rarely met each other until lesser lights on both sides had paved the way, worked out all the details."

"And who is this top-level persona non grata?" Kirk asked.

"Someone I'm sure you all know." The President's eyes flicked toward Spock. "Ambassador Sarek of Vulcan."

McCoy blinked, then snorted. "So I was right. They really *don't* want him, and it's easy enough to see why. If anyone could see through whatever schemes they're going to try to pull, it's Sarek."

Kirk had to agree on that point. "Mr. President, the very fact that they refuse to deal with Sarek specifically tells us something."

"That they're not on the level!" McCoy snapped.

"Very possibly. However, as has already been noted, other possibilities do exist. It may be, for example, that while they are ready to deal with the Federation, they are simply not yet ready to deal with their own cousins, the Vulcans. In any event, as has also been noted before, we

have to take the chance. This merely means that we will
have to be even more on our guard, if that's possible."

"So who's the acceptable second-stringer?" Kirk
asked.

"Someone else I believe you also know," the President
said, a faint smile flickering at his eyes, "one of Sarek's
protégés. He should be here any minute. Should have
been here several minutes *ago,* in fact. His name is,
Riley."

In his forties now, sporting a ruffian's salt-and-pepper
beard, Commander Kevin Thomas Riley, Starfleet Diplomatic Corps, could still be as rakish, as brimming with
Irish wit and charm, as his younger self had ever been.
He could, that is, under normal circumstances. These,
however, were far from what he would consider normal
circumstances, and he had never felt less witty or
charming. And to make matters worse, he was going to
be late—late for a briefing conducted personally by the
President of the Federation and if that were not enough,
attended by the senior officers of the *Enterprise.* Of all
the times to have been caught in a traffic jam, just as he
was rushing to the Cairo terminal in hopes of getting
there in time to make use of the transporter slot he had
managed to scare up when the summons had come. And
now this 'lift to the briefing room floor—it was surely
the slowest in the Federation! It did not bode well for his
new assignment.

Not that he had not developed major misgivings even
before the omens had started. Kevin Riley, back on the
Enterprise—the prospect was not a prescription to
soothe his nerves, nor in all likelihood, those of Captain
Kirk.

Never mind that it wasn't the same ship, that it was twenty years later, that he wasn't the same nervous young lieutenant. All the familiar faces would be there —Scotty, Spock, Uhura, and countless others—and that would make it strange. And it *was* still the *Enterprise*— in spirit, at least—so the memories would be there as well, ghosts overlaying the spanking new corridors as he walked them.

But he could deal with that kind of strangeness. What Kevin Riley was *really* having trouble dealing with was his status as the most important person aboard the ship, the man around whom the entire mission would revolve. And if *he* found it hard to deal with, he wondered how James T. Kirk would feel.

After all, Riley had been an eager-to-please ensign the first time he'd met the captain. Kirk had forced him to specialize, gotten him an early promotion to lieutenant. When Malik had died in a landing party under his command, Kirk had nursed him through it. When his career was in tatters, Kirk had picked him up, dusted him off, and gotten him an entirely new one. Saved his life, really, if you thought about it. And now he was to be the representative of the Federation, nominally in charge of Kirk and his entire crew.

That was the kind of strangeness he wasn't sure he could deal with.

But he had survived his apprenticeship with Ambassador Sarek, he told himself firmly. And he had approached that assignment with even greater apprehension, he remembered, none of which had been allayed when his first meeting with the ambassador got off to what Riley considered a less than auspicious start.

"You recount here an incident while you were on active duty," were the first words out of the Vulcan's mouth as he scanned Riley's personnel file. Riley himself, not yet invited to sit, stood and sweated. "You were given charge of a landing party wherein a crewman was killed by an indigenous predator. You claimed responsibility for the crewman's death and retired from starship duty for a time thereafter."

It was not a question, exactly, but the ambassador obviously expected a response of some kind. Riley swallowed and began, "As the officer in charge of the landing party, sir, it was my responsibility—"

"—to anticipate every possible contingency? To know future events in advance in order to counteract them? I think not, Mr. Riley. Do sit down."

Riley sat, but he did not stop sweating. When he'd asked for a transfer to Diplocorps, he'd expected at most the kind of posting he'd had with his former captain—a glorified secretarial job, attached to some commodore's office in the boondocks where he could learn the drill and maybe, by the time he was in his fifties, end up second-in-command at some remote starbase where the natives were mostly female and dark haired. He'd never expected to be assigned to Sarek, and he certainly hadn't expected Sarek to accept anyone less than a Vulcan as his 'fleet liaison.

"Humans have a certain—spontaneity—which I have frequently found of value," was the only explanation Sarek ever gave, and that only once, weeks later, when Riley, after a particularly frustrating day, had suggested that his posting might have been a mistake, the result perhaps of a computer glitch or a bureaucratic mix-up. "If you are uncomfortable with the posting," Sarek had gone on, "you may request a transfer at any time, barring our being in midcrisis at the time."

That first day, though, Sarek had said nothing as he

impassively read Riley's file from beginning to end. After what seemed like hours to Riley, the Vulcan had looked up and contemplated his erstwhile new aide.

"You have no family, Mr. Riley." Again, not a question but a statement of fact requiring something more than a nod as a response.

"No, sir, I don't. With the amount of traveling I do, it didn't seem fair to acquire any permanent attachments. And my biological family—my parents—were killed on Tarsus IV."

"I am familiar with the circumstances," Sarek said. "Do you believe this has any bearing on your choice of career?"

Riley nodded. *Hell, yes,* he wanted to say. But he supposed one didn't use that manner of language around an ambassador. This ambassador, certainly.

"I know I'd like to use whatever skills I have to prevent the kind of incident that gives rise to a monster like Kodos."

The answer seemed to satisfy Sarek, who folded his hands on the desktop and studied Riley in silence.

Riley thought he knew all about Vulcan silences: he'd survived a few under Spock in the early years. What was expected of him, he knew, was to wait, for however long it took—without flinching, fidgeting, looking bored, or otherwise implying that his valuable time was being wasted. He didn't know how long Sarek's silence lasted, although subjectively it felt like at least a year, and it was so complete that Riley occasionally imagined he could hear his beard growing. In fact, he began to wonder if the beard was the object under scrutiny.

He'd started it during his years as Kirk's secretary and become rather fond of it, fascinated with the range of colors it produced, from brown to red to what he still believed was a premature gray. He wouldn't go so far as to say it made him look distinguished, but it made him feel less boyish, and that had to be an advantage to a diplomat, at least among humanoids who associated facial hair with maturity and/or dignity. In any event, he'd hate to have to part with it.

"Vulcans have a saying, Mr. Riley," Sarek said at last. "'A beard more often reveals than conceals.' You will therefore rarely encounter a bearded Vulcan. Do you intend to retain this—growth of yours?" There was, of course, no trace of emotion in either Sarek's voice or his features, nothing to give Riley the faintest cue as to what the correct answer might be.

"It can go if you dislike it, Ambassador," Riley offered at once.

He saw just as quickly that it had been the wrong answer.

"If you are to be my liaison with Starfleet, Mr. Riley, you must understand one thing: I have no patience with indecisiveness. It was one of your own revered philosophers who said, 'Be thou either hot or cold. Be not lukewarm or I shall vomit you out of my mouth.' Not a pleasant metaphor, perhaps, but one with which I hold. You may be unsure, Mr. Riley, but never indecisive. Do you understand the distinction?"

"I believe I do," Riley had said after a long moment.

"I believe you do as well," Sarek had responded. The deal was done, and Riley kept the beard.

And learned. The learning never ended.

Bracing himself, Ambassador Kevin Riley exited the 'lift and after only one false start, made his way toward the briefing room.

* * *

As if on cue, only seconds after the President's announcement concerning the identity of Sarek's replacement, the replacement himself hurried tardily and apologetically through the door. There were handshakes all around, those of Kirk and McCoy perhaps a bit warmer and hardier than the others. Admiral Cartwright, however, cut the greetings and reminiscences short and pointedly brought Riley up to date on what had been covered prior to his arrival.

When the admiral had finished and Riley had quietly taken a seat between McCoy and the admiral, Spock turned to the President. "I believe, Mr. President, you indicated there were other Romulan demands you felt might also be deemed 'peculiar.'"

The President nodded. "'Unusual,' or perhaps 'unexpected' might be a better description. Nor would some be considered as much 'demands' as 'opportunities.'"

McCoy snorted. "Since when have Romulans been known for offering anyone an 'opportunity'? Unless it's an opportunity to die!"

Cartwright's scowl, apparently never far below the surface, staged another comeback while the President smiled faintly as he gestured to the admiral.

"The conference is to take place," Admiral Cartwright said, "on and in orbit around a planet the Federation designates Temaris Four." As the admiral spoke, an orange globe formed and stabilized in the air above the center of the briefing table, courtesy of one of the conference room's concealed holographic projectors.

"The Neutral Zone," Riley said, his eyes widening as he read off the navigational coordinate grid floating alongside the globe. "Why so far out, sir?"

"So they can have us all for breakfast," McCoy said

sarcastically. "I don't know about you all, but the odor of rat is getting stronger all the time."

Admiral Cartwright turned to face McCoy directly. "The odor of what, Doctor?"

"Commander McCoy," Kirk said hastily, glaring at his chief medical officer, "was simply reiterating his suspicion of the Romulans' motives."

"Damn straight," McCoy added.

"Regardless of the Romulans' reasoning, gentlemen," Spock volunteered, "this is a remarkable opportunity. Temaris Four is an archaeological site of great significance to both the Romulans and ourselves, but the fact that it lies within the Neutral Zone has kept it untouched by either side for a hundred years. For the Romulans to suggest such a world as the site of a meeting with the Federation, and for the Federation to agree, can be seen as, at the very least, an important symbolic gesture on both sides."

"Exactly, Mr. Spock," the President said. "However, the gesture appears to be more than symbolic. The Romulans are proposing, as part of the conference, at least the beginnings of a joint excavation. Or perhaps it should be called reexcavation. I understand the remains of an entire city were uncovered before the war forced everyone out."

"That is correct, Admiral, and it would indeed be more than a gesture, particularly if work was allowed to continue after the conclusion of the conference." Though Spock's voice was as even as always, it was obvious to Kirk and McCoy that he was as close to being openly enthusiastic as they had ever seen him. "The Temaris ruins are of great historical significance, Captain," he went on. "According to the records of the original expedition, the city they uncovered was the single largest known remnant of the Erisian Ascendancy, as well as the most recent and therefore perhaps the best preserved. The Erisians themselves are also the object of intense debate and speculation. Several theories have been advanced as to their point of origin, and the reason for their apparent exodus from this part of the galaxy. Some have even conjectured that they did not leave at all but became the distant ancestors of Earthmen, or of Vulcans and Romulans."

McCoy snorted. "Every species this side of Antares has tried to claim the Erisians as kin or mentor at one time or another. It's been kind of hard to prove one way or the other, though, since no one's ever found so much as a toe bone, not even any statues or—"

"Thank you, gentlemen," Cartwright broke in impatiently. "The point is, this joint excavation, whether it lasts an hour or a century, brings us to another of the Romulans' 'peculiar' requests."

"This whole setup is 'peculiar,'" McCoy said, shaking his head, "and that's giving them the benefit of a hell of a lot of doubt, if you ask me. The next thing you know, they'll be trying to tell us what archaeologists to send."

Cartwright frowned, his eyes betraying a flicker of suspicion as he darted a glance at the President. "As a matter of fact," the admiral continued, "that is precisely what they are doing, at least insofar as the team leader is concerned."

"You're joking!" McCoy almost exploded before a dark glance from Kirk silenced him. Riley's face betrayed surprise, but he remained diplomatically silent.

"Dr. McCoy's reaction may have been . . . intemperate, Admiral," Kirk said, "but I can't disagree with the thought. Vetoing a particular ambassador I can understand, but this— How is it the Romulans even *know* of a specific Federation archaeologist?"

"They have had dealings with her before," the President put in, "exceedingly unpleasant dealings. They *say* that their 'request'—and this, unlike the matter of Sarek's absence, is not a demand—is an attempt on their part—and here I quote the Committee directly— 'to in some small way redress her legitimate grievance against those who once acted against her and her colleagues in the name of the Romulan Empire.' There was no mention of the symbolism that will attach itself to the situation, but they are obviously aware of it and will, I am sure, exploit it to the hilt."

"So who is it?" Kirk asked. "And has she agreed to be a symbol?"

"Her name is Dr. Audrea Benar. As to whether or not she will agree, that is what Commander Uhura has been dispatched to learn."

Uhura paused beneath the porticoed facade of Lincoln Center's Philharmonic Hall, realizing yet again that she did not *really* want to do what she was about to do. She was comforted only slightly by the further realization that, if she had not volunteered, someone else would be here in her stead, someone who would do the deed in a far more businesslike way. Perhaps Admiral Cartwright, perhaps even the President himself. Dr. Benar, faced with a straightforward, albeit apologetic, request from the likes of either of them, would be left with little choice, whereas, with a lowly commander making the request, offering to take the heat, even offering herself up as a buffer if the archaeologist was inclined to refuse . . .

Bracing herself, Uhura went inside, hurried purposefully through the chandeliered elegance of the ornate lobby, and pushed through the muffling doors into the concert hall. Abruptly, she was enveloped in the barely controlled chaos that was the sound of a musicians' rehearsal in progress. Beethoven's Seventh, she realized a moment later as her ears adjusted to the hall's acoustics, which of course had been thrown completely out of kilter by the total absence of a suitably sound-absorbent audience. The first movement. Halting just inside the doors, at the top of the plushly carpeted aisle that led down to the airy blondwood stage where the entire string section was having at it, she listened.

There were, Uhura thought with sudden warmth, some things that *never* went out of style, and the works of Ludwig van Beethoven, performed live, were certainly among those things. After more than four centuries, not a year went by that did not see a Beethoven festival somewhere, if not here, then in Salzburg or Vienna, Tokyo or Sydney, not to mention the off-world festivals, some featuring instruments and arrangements that the composer likely never even dreamed of. It was hard to believe there had ever been a time—although, according to the history books, there had indeed been such a time—when the computerized descendants of Moog, with their prerecorded perfection, had been so in vogue that live performances, not only of Beethoven but of *anyone,* new or old, had been in danger of extinction. In the days—the dark days, to Uhura's mind—before the twenty-second-century renaissance of live performance, assembling enough professional musicians for a full classical orchestra such as this one would have been virtually impossible.

Watching the musicians, Uhura found herself marveling at the coordination, the discipline that was needed to weld together all those dozens of disparate individuals and sounds. She knew music, even considered herself a fair to middling performer, but only as a soloist, only as a hobbyist. As a member of a professional ensemble, particularly one of this size and complexity, she would be hopelessly out of her depth.

Finally there was silence, punctuated by a gentle but authoritative tap of a baton as the slender female figure at the podium expressed her dissatisfaction—Uhura could not imagine why—at what she had just heard.

"Cellos," she began in a low, clear contralto that carried to where Uhura stood. "I'm aware of the arduous tempi in this section, but I assure you they can be achieved. May I remind you that the notation for the movement reads poco sostenuto vivace. By no definition I understand could your present rendition be construed as 'vivace.' "

There was a smattering of laughter at her dryness.

"Now again, please." She raised the baton as the musicians readied their instruments. "From the top, and—"

"Isn't she delightful?" someone stage-whispered at Uhura's elbow.

Uhura recognized the small, plump figure with the fringe of silver hair as Maestra Carmen Espinoza, the principal conductor herself, from the larger-than-life holos gracing the theater lobby. She was winded, as if she had run the entire length of the plaza.

"You must be Commander Uhura. But you're early! I was told not to expect you until this afternoon," she chided Uhura with the easy familiarity of someone aware of her own talents and her place in the scheme of things. "Don't you know artists are not morning people?"

47

She did not wait for an answer. "Come. Even I don't dare interrupt one of Audrea's rehearsals; I doubt anything short of the Second Coming could. I'm afraid you'll have to wait in my office, though I can at least offer you a cup of tea."

Uhura accepted the invitation—the delay—with some relief and followed the older woman down a labyrinth of corridors, backstage past the scene shop redolent with wood shavings and paint thinner where a massive backdrop for this season's *Otello* was under construction, and into what was apparently the conductor's office.

"Please excuse the mess," Maestra Espinoza apologized, seeming to address the cello, which had somehow taken up residence in her chair and which she now relegated to a far corner, making room among a clutter of music stands so that Uhura could sit on the divan while she programmed the servitor for tea. "I suppose I must ask what you've come about, though I can guess. Starfleet recently tried to commandeer my entire orchestra, but I was not to be budged. Now, if I have correctly interpreted their latest cryptic message, you have been sent to draft my best rehearsal conductor for whatever secret reason. Before you attempt to take her from me, I must tell you what a treasure Audrea's been."

A small bell on the servitor intoned a perfect A, indicating that the tea was ready; Maestra Espinoza poured, never losing a beat in her monologue.

"As you doubtless know, she came to us under somewhat . . . unusual circumstances, so I suppose it's only fitting she leave the same way." Espinoza smiled and returned the pot to the servitor. "You do know the story?"

"I'm afraid I don't," Uhura replied, more than willing

to listen. Like most, she knew the story of Kalis Three but little else, least of all how someone who was still one of the Federation's premier archaeologists had ended up here, conducting the New York Philharmonic. The media had been full of grossly sensationalized accounts of the year-long captivity of Dr. Benar and her archaeological team, of the "experiments" the Romulans had conducted on them all, of the brutal deaths of her colleagues, of her brother, and of her own final escape. Once she sought refuge on Vulcan, however, she had faded from public view. Her efforts to use Vulcan logic to rebuild her mind and her life were not as newsworthy —read "titillating"—as the events that had nearly destroyed them in the first place.

"Well then!" Espinoza settled back in her chair, unapologetically propping her stockinged feet up on the desk. "About a year ago—or was it two? No matter— the Philharmonic was in the process of planning a retrospective of the works of off-world composers—one performance to be devoted to each of six, as I recall. We had selected a most challenging Vulcan piece by Salet, which required an obsolete instrument—the tlakyrr— and we were on the verge of substituting another instrument because, frankly, finding a virtuoso on the tlakyrr had us stumped. That is, until someone recommended we contact Smithsonian's xeno-archaeology department. They put us in touch with a specialist in ancient Vulcan musicology: Audrea Benar. Such talent, that one! In due course, I also learned that she had recently begun a private study of ancient Earth music, and particularly of conducting. I don't have to tell you how extraordinary a skill that has become even among humans in this push-button synthesized century. And Audrea's field of concentration, fortuitously enough, was Beethoven—no surprise, as he is the one Earth composer Vulcans seem to find most simpatico. Someday I intend to find out why." She smiled. "Audrea's human, not Vulcan, of course—though after years of study there, she behaves so much like one of them I tend to forget."

Uhura nodded, smiling and wondering what Spock would have to say about such generalizations about Vulcan musical taste. His father's favorite composer, he had once confided, was not Beethoven but Mozart. Whether it had always been so, even before the cross-cultural pollination of his marriage to Amanda, Spock had not said.

Maestra Espinoza sipped her tea. "But I'm squandering your precious time with my chatter, aren't I? It's the burden of the performing artist, you see. So accustomed to singing for our supper that we don't know when to shut up.

"But to be concise: Audrea has since become one of our rehearsal conductors—the best of the lot, I might add. The musicians respect her; there's a lot less carping and silliness when she's in charge. You know how musicians can get sometimes."

Espinoza paused as a faint chime, a precise octave above that of the servitor bell, sounded somewhere in the cluttered office. Some of the cheery brightness in her expression ebbed as she glanced in the direction of the door and stood up. "I believe that marks the end of the rehearsal, at least for the moment. If you would like to use my office to speak with Audrea . . ."

Uhura, also on her feet, shook her head. "Thank you, but there's no need for that. This won't take long." *Whichever way it goes,* she added to herself.

But it did. Or so it began to seem to Uhura as soon as, on the now-deserted stage, Espinoza introduced her to

Dr. Benar and then quietly, discreetly absented herself. Seconds stretched into minutes as Uhura expressed her admiration, then her sympathy, delaying, always delaying. Finally they were seated in folding chairs, facing each other beneath a worklight. Benar tilted her head, blue-black brows forming a crease in an otherwise smooth, unlined forehead. Espinoza had been right: it was difficult to remember Audrea's earthly origin. Her manner, dress, intonation, were distinctly Vulcan: cool, subdued, precise. Were it not for the ears, she could easily be mistaken for one, with her dark hair and tall, slender build. Her spine, poker straight, did not touch the backrest of her chair.

"I assume," Uhura said, her soft voice seeming uncomfortably loud on the bare stage, "that you're aware of what's been happening in the Romulan Empire the last few days."

"I know of the Praetor's death, Commander."

"And nothing else?"

"I have sought out nothing else."

Understandable, Uhura thought, but it didn't make her job any easier. Carefully, she explained about the Romulan Committee, the apparent upheaval and reform within the Empire, and finally the general outline of the invitation extended to the Federation.

"I can safely assume," Benar said when Uhura fell silent, "that I would not be the first to urge caution." She spoke in the same dry tone she had used with the cellists, but with a tinge of brittle tension that had been totally lacking earlier.

"Nor the last," Uhura agreed. "The thing is, the Federation can't afford not to at least *appear* to take the invitation and all the rest at face value. If it turns out the

Romulans are even halfway sincere and the Federation balks, chances for a meaningful peace could be lost for decades. Even if this so-called Committee only represents one faction, that one faction needs whatever bolstering we can give it."

"Starfleet suspects a power struggle within the Empire?"

"To the best of our knowledge, there's *always* a power struggle of some kind going on within the Empire," Uhura said with a rueful smile. "The Praetor's death has probably only exacerbated the situation. Not that we have any reliable firsthand information. Everything official coming out of the Empire so far shows a united—and reform-minded—front."

"And my own role, Commander? I assume my experiences with a small contingent of Romulans on Kalis Three are not sufficient reason for Starfleet to deem me an expert on the Empire and to send a representative to consult with me before accepting or rejecting the invitation."

Uhura released an almost inaudible sigh. "That's not exactly the way it happened, but the invitation *is* the reason I'm here. And part of the Federation response is dependent on yours now, Dr. Benar."

And Uhura launched into an explanation, concluding with her hasty assurance that she would understand if, under the circumstances, Dr. Benar felt obliged to refuse. "And I'll do my best to see that Starfleet understands as well."

"That will not be necessary, Commander," Benar said after a moment's contemplative silence. "It would be both illogical and ungracious for me to refuse such an offer."

"Are you certain, Dr. Benar?" Uhura asked, noting the brittle emphasis the other woman had managed to place on the word *ungracious* without so much as a flicker of accompanying facial expression. "Your team— the Federation team—would be working side by side with the Romulans at the dig. You would all be in day-to-day personal contact."

"I understand your concerns, Commander. Do you, however, understand the significance of this offer?" For the first time, a trace of emotion, what Uhura could only think of as a scholarly gleam in her eyes, cracked the Vulcan-inspired mask. "It was the mystery of the Ascendancy that first drew me to my field. I have personally worked on two Ascendancy worlds and have studied the recordings made on all, including those from Temaris itself before the war, before the Neutral Zone cut it off from all study, either Federation or Romulan. As I am sure you must know, Temaris holds at least one entire city, its ruins the best preserved and most extensive of any Ascendancy world, in or out of the Federation. To have access to that site, even under these conditions, is an opportunity that is at least as irresistible to an archaeologist as the opportunity to negotiate directly with some seemingly peaceful Romulans is to a diplomat. And the odds of my achieving some small measure of success, of gaining some new bit of knowledge of the Ascendancy, are far better, I suspect, than the odds of your diplomats' achieving a similar measure of success."

Benar rose from the rehearsal chair with a small, distinctly human sigh and wistfully surveyed the vast empty concert hall as if for the last time.

"I am prepared," she said solemnly. "You may so inform your superiors."

Uhura felt a catch in her throat. *Spock would be proud,* she thought irrelevantly. *I just hope she doesn't regret it—too much.*

"You can inform them yourself," she said. "My shuttle's waiting outside."

Following the briefing, Kirk, Spock, and McCoy retired to spacedock's officers' lounge, where Spock ordered a round of Thirellian mineral water. Kirk smiled as he sipped and half-listened to his friends discuss the logic or lack thereof, the sincerity or lack thereof, of the Romulan proposals and demands. The real object of his attention, though, was beyond the clearsteel window, suspended at the very pinnacle of the spacedock. Luminous, hanging in the antigrav like some ethereal Christmas ornament: *Enterprise.*

Just steer the boat, Cartwright had said. In other words, trust Kevin Riley to fill the diplomat's role. *The role I nudged him into,* Kirk thought, remembering that then Riley had seemed too immature, too undisciplined ever to qualify for the Diplomatic Corps.

But that had been years ago; since then, Riley had not only made it into the Diplomatic Corps, he'd distinguished himself a dozen times over, thanks probably to the on-the-job training he had gotten from his years with Sarek.

Perhaps, Kirk admitted to himself, at least part of his uneasiness was due to a small amount of professional jealousy. He was glad to be the captain of the *Enterprise* again, glad to be out of the diplomatic troubleshooting business. But what a hell of a juicy assignment Riley had fallen into when the Romulans had declared Sarek ineligible—chief diplomat on the first peace conference with the Empire!

Kirk sighed inwardly, annoyed at himself. Jealousy was not, as Spock would point out if given the chance, logical. The important thing was not who got the glory. The important thing was to work together to see there would be glory—not blame—to be had when this was all over.

Taking another sip from the mineral water, Kirk let his attention drift again toward the clearsteel window and the starship that lay beyond it, waiting for him. Waiting for them all. Waiting for the mission.

Commander Kevin Riley—he still marveled at the "commander" now and then, despite everything—had just finished stowing his gear in his quarters aboard the *Enterprise* when he heard the sound of footsteps approaching the open corridor door.

"Kevin?"

Riley looked up, and there was Sulu, the onetime swordsman of the helm.

"Thought you might like to head over to the lounge in spacedock, maybe grab something to eat," Sulu said, smiling his usual incandescent smile. "I think there's even some kind of party—a festival or something—going on tonight."

"Sounds good," Riley said, returning the grin. He started for the door, then stopped. "Déjà vu," he said, eyeing Sulu suspiciously. "This isn't another one of Mr. Scott's surprise parties, is it? Like that one you dragged me to my first year on the ship—what was it called?"

"Robert Burns's birthday," Sulu supplied, clearly remembering the incident—particularly the horror Scotty had insisted against all logic was food, something he fondly called haggis—as well as Riley. "Don't worry about Mr. Scott. He's still busy making sure Chekov's navigation computer talks to the sensors without an accent."

"All right, then," Riley said, clapping the helmsman on the shoulder. "Lead the way."

Hiran eyed Centurion Tiam, newly appointed delegate to the Federation, with less than enthusiasm. The younger man, his back to Hiran, stood at the room's single narrow viewport, making a show of contemplating the slowly moving starfield even though they were still in homeport orbit. Tiam's aide, Kital, old for a subCenturion and almost skeletally thin, stood by the door, hooded, unreadable eyes fixed on a spot midway between Hiran and Subcommander Feric.

Here was a pair, Hiran thought uneasily, that would bear watching.

According to the records Hiran had accessed—coupled with a few rumors and some intuition—Tiam had not only survived the Praetor's death, he had flourished in its wake, apparently through a mixture of serendipity and opportunism. Remarkably, he had never seen combat of any kind, neither border clashes nor the putting down of civil unrest, of which latter there had been more than sufficient under the late Praetor's ruthless policies. Until his recent promotion, Tiam's had been a life of midlevel administrative work, undistinguished work at that, but Tiam obviously meant to make up for lost time. His tone and bearing as he had swaggered into Hiran's quarters—and Hiran had rarely been proven wrong in his readings of such things—had told him as much, and the so-called "briefing paper" the aide had thrust at Hiran had only further lowered the commander's opinion. To the centurion's mind, the *Galtizh* was his battlefield, and whomever the Federation sent as their representatives were to be his enemy. There was no way of telling what his sphinxlike aide thought.

Hiran dropped the paper on his desk. "Delegate Tiam."

The centurion turned from the viewport with deliberate slowness. "Yes, Commander?"

"Delegate Tiam," Hiran repeated, gesturing at the paper, "if there is one thing I do not need, it is a lecture on either the importance of our mission or the untrustworthy nature of the Federation."

Tiam shrugged off the implied reprimand. "I did not intend it as a lecture, Commander, merely a straightforward setting out of the assumptions from which I intend to operate as I conduct these proceedings. After all, if we are to be effective for the Empire, we must have a clear understanding of its . . . adversaries."

Hiran suppressed a sigh, wondering who on the Committee was responsible for Tiam's selection. Another "compromise" no doubt: necessary but nonetheless galling. But there was no point in pursuing the matter. Best to move on to more nearly neutral ground. He was stuck with Tiam, and Tiam was stuck with him. Neither was going to change. He would just have to make the best of it, as Tiam surely would.

"I trust your accommodations are satisfactory? It is not often we have civilian guests aboard, and while the rest of the musicians have been stowed in cadet quarters, we have had to knock out three subsidiary bulkheads to create a suite large enough for you and your wife. I trust she was pleased?"

"She will make do," Tiam answered flatly, vaguely irritated at the commander's presumption to such familiarity. As for Jandra . . .

At this point, he was sure his wife could hardly care less about the accommodations. After the years of un-Orthodoxy in the Provinces and then the years of rehabilitation, followed by years of virtual confinement in the Citadel, she was so entranced by the prospect of going anywhere that she had almost required sedation. A tent in the engine room would have sufficed so long as distance was being put between herself and the Citadel.

"I did intend to thank you, Commander, for providing us with three separate rooms. Her need to practice constantly would drive me to distraction otherwise."

"Mm," Hiran ruminated noncommittally. So that was not neutral ground, either. He had yet to meet Tiam's musician wife, but already she had his sympathy. He stood dismissively. "I shall look forward to hearing her play."

Tiam, no more eager than Hiran to continue, took the hint and departed after a last look out the viewport, his aide following a step behind. When they had gone, Hiran sighed heavily.

"Will there be anything else, Commander?" Feric asked.

Hiran shrugged. He wanted to talk to Feric about Tiam, about the suspicions he had regarding the ambassador, and the Temaris conference. No, strke that. He didn't want to talk to Feric.

He wanted to talk to Ren.

"No, nothing," Hiran said finally. He raised his gaze to Feric's. His first officer's eyes were steely gray and unreadable. "Dismissed."

Nodding sharply, Feric left the room.

THREE

☆

Captain's Log, Stardate 8478.4:

The *Enterprise* and its crew continue to prepare for departure. No one is anticipating any difficulty in keeping to the ordered schedule, which calls for rendezvous with the Romulan vessel *Galtizh* in ten days' time. Spock has been in daily communication with the Starfleet HQ team that is tracking the Probe and attempting to make sense of the masses of sensor readings taken during its near-disastrous journey through Federation space. He has also gotten permission to have a complete record of all such readings transferred to the *Enterprise* memory banks. Unlike the Starfleet team, he appears to have a theory as to the nature of the energy fields generated by the Probe, but he isn't sharing it with anyone yet. "It needs more study," he says, but then, by his lights, what doesn't?

On the diplomatic front, Commander Riley and his staff are already aboard, as is most of Dr. Benar's archaeology team and the musicians. The only major absence is that of the "orchestra's" conductor, one Andrew Penalt, who, according to those who claim to know, has a reputation for grand and last-minute entrances.

The passengers already on board are proving an interesting study in diversity. Both the archaeology team and the musicians appear to have been selected not only for their knowledge and skill but to provide the more homogeneous Romulans with an object lesson in interspecies harmony. Or so the theory goes. There have already been heated arguments in both camps over matters so esoteric that even Spock has been hard-pressed to explain them. I only hope that Dr. Benar, whose abilities as a mediator in things both musical and scientific appear to be almost as great as Uhura predicted, will be able to keep up the good work. And that she will be able to retain her Vulcan-like objectivity once she finds herself alone on Temaris Four with the Romulans.

"Penalt and his staff are ready to beam on board, sir. Commander Riley respectfully requests your presence in the transporter room. And Mr. Scott reports the last of the archaeology shuttles has docked."

"Thank you, Lieutenant." Kirk nodded toward Uhura's substitute at communications—Kittay, he remembered now. "Tell Mr. Riley I'm on my way." Catapulting out of his chair, Kirk inclined his head at the center seat.

"Mr. Chekov . . . ?"

"Aye, Keptin." Chekov took the conn without missing a beat in his intimate dialogue with the computer regarding mainstage flux-chiller status.

In the transporter room, Riley was waiting, along with a pair of ensigns. "I thought your conductor was on his way," Kirk said, noting the empty transporter circles.

Riley shrugged as he signaled to the lieutenant at the

controls. " 'Impresario,' if you please. And he is on his way—now that you're here to welcome him aboard."

Kirk frowned. "I suppose I should know who he is, then. I have to admit, I'd never heard of anyone named Penalt before he showed up on our passenger list."

"You're not alone, Captain. *Symphony for the Nine* is the only composition of his that ever gained widespread recognition, and there are those who credit his wife of the time with more than the 'moral support' he acknowl-wedged the first time he conducted it."

Kirk shook his head. "Sorry, the name still doesn't ring a bell. Not that I'm a musical scholar."

"Suffice it to say, he's a composer, conductor, and pianist, and he's supposed to exercise all three abilities while on board—conduct the orchestra, take a solo shot at the piano, and begin composing some kind of musical 'impression' of the proceedings."

"A real triple threat?"

"So his PR releases would have you believe. There are some, however—including his ex-wife—who say he has more political connections—and ego—than talent."

Before Kirk could reply, the "ready to transport" signal came up from the ground, and Riley hastily assembled his diplomat's expression of respectful wel-come.

Kirk grimaced but followed suit as best he could. Moments later, two figures materialized at last on the platform. One was a broad but not overly tall, bearish hulk of a man who looked, Kirk decided, purposely rumpled, even his expression. Next to him stood a dark-skinned, reed-slender woman—probably half his age and certainly a third his mass. Another musician, Kirk assumed, noting her unconventional attire: a rainbow-colored caftan that seemed to float about her like a mist and shifted colors whenever she moved.

"Maestro Penalt." Riley bowed from the shoulders. "Commander Kevin Riley of Starfleet Diplomatic Corps, at your service. May I present Captain James T. Kirk of the starship *Enterprise?*"

Penalt grasped Kirk's hand in a crushing grip. "Call me Andy," he said with a Midwestern twang that may or may not have been genuine.

Kirk kept from wincing as he returned the grip and made a mental note to see that the man had the opportunity to exchange grips with Spock before the trip was over. "Welcome aboard, Mr. Penalt."

"And this is . . . ?" Riley smiled at the young woman.

"Hm? Oh, uh, my protégé, Anneke." Penalt dismissed her without so much as glancing at her; he turned and set his sights on Riley. "Riley . . . Riley . . . Always considered Irishmen to be common drunks, myself. Even wrote an operetta about it once."

Kirk shot a concerned glance in Riley's direction, but Riley's gracious expression never wavered. *"The Drunken Irishman;* I'm familiar with it. Understand the critics panned it," Riley supplied smoothly. "Have to do our diplomatic best to disprove the theory this voyage, sir."

"A lot of history to overcome there, Mr. Riley." Penalt turned to the two waiting ensigns, zeroing in on the woman, a pretty brunette. "Now, I wouldn't object if someone were to show me to my quarters."

"Ensign Smith will be happy to oblige," Kirk said, nodding at the male of the pair. "Ensign Carver," he added to the other, "you can report to Commander Scott on the shuttle deck. I'm sure he could use some help with the archaeology shuttle that just came in."

"Kirk—"

"Yes, Mr. Penalt—Andy?" Kirk's most disingenuous tone coated the requested short-form name. "Is something wrong?"

Penalt scowled for a moment, then shrugged and seemed to relax. "No, nothing. I look forward to working with you. This has the makings of an interesting tour of duty, wouldn't you say, Captain?" Touching two fingers to his temple in a jaunty salute, he turned from Kirk and strode into the corridor, his "protégé" and Ensign Smith hurrying after him.

Kirk shook his head wonderingly as he and Riley exited the transporter room and headed for the nearest 'lift. "*What* have we done to deserve 'Andy' Penalt?" Kirk asked rhetorically. "Is he at least a good conductor, Kevin? Not that it will make any difference if he insults the Romulan diplomats to their faces."

"We'll have to make sure that doesn't happen," Riley said, but his expression was none too confident.

At least, Kirk thought, the musicians wouldn't be mixing with the Romulans the way the archaeological team would. Though God knows what Penalt might say from the stage by way of introduction to whatever he decided to perform.

Just then the turbolift doors hissed open to reveal Uhura.

"Captain, Commander." Distracted by her work, she looked up briefly from a datapad as they entered.

Kirk acknowledged her with a nod, and glanced over her shoulder at what she was jotting down. "Busy?"

"Oh, um, instrument status," Uhura said vaguely, jotting again. "Musical instruments, that is. Seems the Steinway got a little cranky going through the transporter, so the tuner's given me specific instructions for getting the other pieces up safely. I'm on my way down to the cargo transporter room now to supervise."

Kirk wondered what a Steinway was, but wasn't about to ask. He was having enough trouble thinking of schemes to keep Penalt under control without offending —*too* greatly—whatever Federation officials were responsible for Penalt being on the mission in the first place. And hoping that the conductor didn't have an opposite number in the Romulan delegation.

"Imagine it, Little Sister," Dajan exulted as the *Galtizh* sped toward its rendezvous with the Federation ship. "Not only are we permitted to see each other freely again, we have actually been selected for this voyage together! Rehabilitated, washed clean, deemed pure and Orthodox exemplars of our race, worthy to face the Earthmen and shame them with our brilliance. We have five years' worth of gossip to catch up on. Do you think we shall grow sick of looking at each other?"

"Once we arrive at this desolate rock, I doubt we shall see each other at all," Jandra said bleakly. She and Tiam had quarreled again this morning; the very engine room, several levels below, must have reverberated with it. It was humiliating to have one's private life bruited about the entire vessel, but the bulkheads were not soundproof and Tiam would shout. Naturally, when he shouted, she was obliged to shout as well. Now she was hoarse and irritable, and Tiam was off sulking, or telling his troubles to that provincial Hiran. She couldn't even remember what had started the quarrel, but then, she rarely could anymore. Anything would suffice, it seemed. Once she had merely asked the source of a computer recording she had heard him playing in his quarters one day, a cacophonous blend of thousands of seemingly disparate sounds, yet some of which had seemed to bind themselves to her mind. "Never speak of them again!" he had shouted, almost apoplectic, and she never had, though the sounds still persisted in her mind when she would allow it.

"Surely you shall not be *that* busy," her twin protested. "You must pause at least to allow the Federation players to perform."

But she was not to be comforted. "Then I shall be locked in some makeshift practice hall, playing my fingers to the bone, not because of necessity but because those who watch over us still do not trust in my abilities. It was the same, always the same, during my years of atonement in the Provinces. And you shall be grubbing about in your precious Lihalla ruins, searching for gods know what."

He put a chiding smile on his face. "Temaris, not Lihalla. We have agreed to abide by the Federation designation for simplicity—Temaris."

"Whatever!" Jandra said indifferently, her mind on other things. "I wonder if there will be a piano aboard this *Enterprise?*"

"Tell me what it is and I'll tell you if they're likely to have one," Dajan offered, keeping his mood as sunny as his sib's was gloomy. "Is it one of those un-Orthodox instruments you involved yourself with in the Provinces?"

"More un-Orthodox than you know. From Earth, I was given to understand, a trophy of the early days of the war. The marvel is that it now seems to have been restored to Orthodoxy as quickly and easily as you and I."

Dajan laughed. "They wish to flaunt you, I suspect. It

would not cause me great surprise to learn that this once-illicit ability of yours was high among the reasons you suddenly find yourself once more in favor, once more allowed—even ordered—to perform for your loving public. What better proof of superior Romulan culture than a Romulan who can outperform humans on an instrument of their own design—as I have no doubt you could do, Little Sister. None of this, however, tells a cultural dunce like myself what type of instrument this piano is."

Jandra turned to the terminal, wondering if the computer library was as "restructured" as the society they now lived in appeared to be. She accessed "Music: Alien" and tried to call up *piano* on the screen. The computer balked; Jandra sighed.

"A keyboard instrument," she said, struggling to be more specific, to limn the size and shape of it, perhaps to conjure it in the rarefied air of the bird-of-prey's cabin. "Similar to a tra'am, yet not."

"Ah!" Dajan said, his monosyllable of choice whenever he would not admit that he did not entirely understand a subject. "But if it is, as you were told, a common Earth instrument, there will almost certainly be at least one among the assemblage of Federation musicians this *Enterprise* is bringing to us who will be expected to perform upon it. Therefore they will just as certainly bring one."

"Perhaps," she said, but her voice was lined with pessimism.

Dajan sighed. "After all that has happened, you still persist in gloomily expecting the worst. I know Tiam can be a trial, but he is not here. Only you and I, Little Sister, only you and I and a chance to dazzle the Federation musicians."

"It is not only Tiam," Jandra replied.

Dajan recognized the look. "Still grieving, after all this time?"

Jandra's eyes were baleful. "As should you, unless your loss is somehow less than mine."

"Will grieving bring them back?" Dajan dismissed it. "Life is for the living, Little Sister. While we live, we strive to restore their honor, and that will be done only through deeds, not through endless, unproductive brooding."

The shuttlebay was in chaos. Musical instruments from several worlds in their invariably cumbersome cases vied for space with whole shuttlecrafts of archaeology equipment, while garishly clad musicians chatted with less flamboyant archaeologists in field gear, voices caroming off the bulkheads. A spindly Andorian maneuvering crates that seemed beyond his wiry strength— Dr. Benar's assistant, Sharf—acknowledged Kirk and Riley.

"Morning, Captain, Commander. Dr. Benar had to beam back down, if you were hoping to speak with her. Some piece of equipment that can't be found. The usual. I'll let her know you were looking for her."

"No problem," Kirk said easily. "Just let her know about tomorrow morning's briefing."

"Will do, Captain."

Scotty stood in almost the exact center of the bay, arms folded, overseeing everything.

"Here, now—easy with that, lad. Careful not to unbalance her." Scott rushed over to help the Andorian heft a substantial-looking crate onto a nearby zero-g sled. "There." He slapped his hands together. "That should do you fine."

"The miracle worker, as ever, Mr. Scott." Kirk smiled as he laid a hand on his chief engineer's shoulder.

"Aye, sir," Scotty said proudly. "Commander Riley, good to see ye again after these many years." His eyes gleamed playfully as he and Riley clasped hands. "So, Commander . . . are ye goin' to be gracin' us this cruise wi' a wee song?"

The parts of Riley's face not covered by beard flushed bright pink, but his grin was good-natured. "I hadn't planned on it—though it might relieve you to know I've since taken voice lessons."

"And added to your repertoire, I hope," Kirk murmured, smiling faintly as he remembered the number of times he'd had to listen to Riley's acutely painful rendition of "I'll Take You Home Again, Kathleen."

"Well, if ye *are,*" Scott continued, "I'll warn ye now: I advised the ship's designers about that wee incident with your barricadin' yourself in the engineering control room . . . and they've made it near impossible to do again. I'll not be burnin' through any wall circuits this voyage."

"Foiled again," Riley said easily, and clapped Scott on the shoulder. "Well, Scotty, I'll just have to be more ingenious next time I come down with a disease that causes temporary insanity and try to take over the *Enterprise.* Right, Captain?" He winked at Kirk.

"Not *my* ship," Kirk said, still smiling. "Try someone else's."

"By the way, there was an ensign here a few minutes ago looking for you," Scott said to Riley.

"Handler," Riley replied instantly.

"Aye, that's the one. Tall, nervous type."

"I see him now." Riley craned his neck slightly. "Thanks, Scotty."

The engineer nodded as he moved off to continue his supervision.

Ahead of them, a gangly, young ensign with a shock of corn-silk hair was weaving his way through the jostling civilians like a backfield runner, shielding what looked like a Diplomatic Corps brief against his body as if it were a thrown pass. Riley and Kirk watched as the ensign got caught in a bottleneck, murmuring, "Excuse me, pardon me!" with desperate urgency as the civilians parted like a flock of sheep. Riley grimaced.

"Your new aide?" Kirk asked, trying not to smile.

"Awkward kid!" Riley answered by way of acknowledgment. "Means well, but awkward. If I could get my hands around the throat of the misguided personnel counselor who persuaded him he was Diplomatic Corps material, who then, in their wisdom, assigned him to me . . . !" He sighed and rolled his eyes heavenward.

"Makes you wonder," Kirk murmured, remembering another awkward, well-meaning kid he'd helped steer into diplomacy once.

"Handler, Ryan J.," Riley greeted him as the breathless, sweating youngster skidded to a halt barely ten centimeters from his nose, fumbling the brief into Riley's outstretched hand. "Ensign—as you were!"

Riley keyed in the proper code, opened the brief, and scanned it right there in the corridor while the kid stood by uneasily, avoiding eye contact with Kirk, uncertain what to do with his hands, much less his feet. Riley closed the brief, clearing his throat; Handler snapped to attention.

"You been cleared by sickbay yet?" Riley demanded. "We're less than an hour from departure."

"No, sir, I—the brief was top priority—no time." Handler's voice cracked, and he ran out of words.

"Handler?" Riley asked dangerously; only Kirk could see the fond merriment in his eye.

"Sir . . . ?"

"You're still here."

"Sir!" Handler turned on his heel and started back the way he'd come, though there were at least two shorter routes to sickbay.

"Poor kid's very nearsighted," Riley observed, his tone suddenly sympathetic as he watched Handler's retreating back. "Almost didn't pass the Academy physical because of it, and he needs a Retinax booster every six months. Still, even at Four-A and twenty-twenty, I don't see that as Diplomatic Corps material, do you?"

Kirk hid the twinkle in his own eye. "Stranger things have happened."

Eventually, all stations reported in ready. Handler got his physical, Scotty returned to engineering, Penalt kept a suspiciously low profile, and Kirk found himself on the bridge once more.

The ride out of spacedock was smooth and uneventful beneath Sulu's unerring hand, under considerably less harrowing circumstances than those in some more recent endeavors. There was something comforting, Kirk thought, about having a fully crewed, fully functional ship beneath you and a green light on the spacedoors. He was even looking forward to the mission. Ferryboat cruise it might be, but potentially one hell of an important one, for both the Federation and the Empire.

They cleared the spacedoors, and Sulu skeined her out like silk, under impulse until she was well above the ecliptic, clear of all planets and asteroids, then eased her into warp.

70

FOUR

☆

"'Moderate' Romulans! Aye, Captain, that'll be the day!" Commander Scott rolled his eyes as he glanced toward McCoy and Spock, clearly confident of their agreement.

The briefing room was empty save for the four of them, who had all arrived early for Kirk's mission briefing on this, their second morning out of spacedock. The subject, which they had already been discussing all the way from the bridge, was the latest message from Admiral Cartwright, received only minutes earlier.

"Nonetheless," Spock pointed out, "if we are to believe the admiral's anonymous informant, just such a faction is in control of the Interim Government, holding most of the seats on the Committee."

"Even if it's true," McCoy put in, "it can't last. Cartwright's Romulan pal admitted that. There are a dozen other groups waiting in the wings, and the only reason the reformers have gotten *this* far is a backlash against the recently departed Praetor. He was a nasty customer, even by Romulan standards, and this new bunch is taking advantage of the situation by pushing as hard and fast as they can before they wear out their welcome."

"What are you saying, Bones?" Kirk asked. "That we should have ignored their overture?"

"Of course not!" McCoy said. "I'm just saying what I've said all along—and what Cartwright's pal is saying, too, from the sound of that last message. Even if your reformers are for real, they may be overreaching themselves with this 'conference,' so don't get too upset when it blows up in your face. And don't be too disillusioned if the opposition has slipped a few ringers into the delegation, so that if, miracle of miracles, things start going too smoothly, they can start lighting fuses."

"I'll take your paranoia under advisement," Kirk said, smiling. "Now, Mr. Spock, I believe you were about to let us in on your hypothesis about the Probe."

"I was, Captain?"

"Come on, Spock," McCoy said, turning on a conversational dime. "Are you going to keep this theory of yours to yourself until that blasted thing tries to eat another planet?"

Just before Cartwright's message, Spock had been filling them in on the Probe's movements. After passing within a few hundred parsecs of Starbases Nine and Thirteen, along the edge of the Neutral Zone, it was currently describing a leisurely arc through parts of old First Federation territory. Hyperchannel communiques indicated that the Probe was still behaving itself, content to take the scenic tour of the First Federation. What was interesting was that it now looked like, if the Probe altered neither course nor speed, it would penetrate Romulan space about the time the *Enterprise* and the *Galtizh* were taking up orbit around Temaris Four.

"Bones is right, Spock," Kirk said. "Any theories, even half-baked ones, are better than none, especially if that thing gets ticked off again. And who knows—we might even have a few ideas of our own, once we find out what yours *are*."

"As you wish, Captain. However, I would hesitate to dignify my speculations by calling them a theory."

"Whatever!" McCoy snapped. "Just talk to us."

"Of course, Doctor. As you know, Captain, the team at Starfleet Headquarters has done a thorough analysis of all sensor readings made during the Probe's activities in the vicinity of Earth."

Kirk nodded. "And they haven't figured out how it did *any* of what it did."

"They have not, Captain. In fact, they found no incontrovertible evidence that the Probe is responsible for the phenomena that accompanied its presence."

McCoy scowled. "We all heard and saw—"

"We heard and saw the effects, Doctor. We saw the oceans boiling. We heard the sounds. However, no one saw and no sensor was able to detect any form of energy being projected from the Probe itself."

"That's crazy!" McCoy protested. "Are you saying something *else* is responsible for everything that happened?"

"Of course not, Doctor, although it is a possibility. It is more logical to assume that the Probe is responsible but is using a form of energy that is undetectable except for its effects on the matter at which it is directed. It would be analogous to a phaser beam vanishing at the muzzle of the weapon and reappearing only when it reached its intended target. As a result, sensors in the intervening space could not detect the beam's energy. The energy could only be detected through its effect on the target."

"That means," Kirk put in, "you couldn't even tell what direction the energy came from. Right?"

"Precisely, Captain. Nor could its propagation rate be measured. With electromagnetic and subspace energies, the time between the moment the energy is discharged and the moment it arrives at its target can be measured. With these unknown energies, there was no way of determining when the energy departed the Probe, only when it arrived at its target. However, an analysis of the effects of that energy indicate that they could be most nearly duplicated by some form of tractor beam."

McCoy's eyes widened. "You're saying that thing turned several cubic miles of ocean water into steam with a super tractor beam?"

"In effect, yes, Doctor. The readings indicate that the heating was accomplished by the direct physical acceleration of the water's component molecules, as if by an incredibly complex tractor beam, capable of affecting trillions of individual molecules simultaneously, as well as being capable of reversing polarity thousands of times a second in a seemingly random pattern."

"Sounds damned inefficient," McCoy said, obviously not convinced.

"On the contrary, Doctor, it could be extremely efficient. Heat is simply a measure of the energy level—the motion—of the molecules of a substance. Setting those molecules in motion directly instead of generating a phaser beam, for example, to do the job indirectly eliminates at least one step in the chain and therefore has the potential for increased efficiency. However, the process would be extremely complex."

Kirk, who had been frowning thoughtfully, said, "You make it sound like moving a sand dune with a million pair of microscopic tweezers, each one with a single grain of sand—as opposed to shoving it around with a bulldozer."

Spock thought a moment and then nodded. "Your analogy is basically correct, Captain. In any event, the sounds the Probe transmitted into the water—and into several starships—were produced in much the same way, except that, instead of the air and water molecules being accelerated in seemingly random directions resulting in heat, huge numbers of them were forced to move back and forth in unison, thereby producing sound waves. Computer simulations indicate that, with minor modifications, the *Enterprise* tractor beams could be used to duplicate the latter effect."

"So what's your theory, Spock?" McCoy asked impatiently. "So far you've just made the whole thing sound even more impossible than it sounded before."

"My speculation, Doctor, is that the energy utilized by the Probe is some form of mental energy, analogous to telekinesis. This speculation is based on, first, the thus-far-undetectable nature of the energy, and second, the impressions I received from George about the Probe. If you will remember, one of the few impressions I was able to obtain that was related exclusively to the Probe in George's mind was that of beings similar to himself."

"Your superwhales. I remember," McCoy said. "So how does that lead to telekinesis?"

"If we assume the impression is accurate, and if we further assume that these beings were in fact the builders of the Probe, then we must ask ourselves how such beings would be capable of building it, or indeed, how they would be capable of building anything, lacking as they do any organs capable of manipulating objects external to themselves."

McCoy snorted. "For someone as mired down in logic as you are, Spock, that's a couple pretty big leaps. They never developed opposable thumbs, so they developed telekinetic powers in their place? And what then? They developed machines to amplify those powers?"

"It would be the logical next step, Doctor, just as beings with opposable thumbs developed machines to amplify the power of their own muscles."

"And as we developed computers to amplify the powers of our minds," Kirk put in, nodding. "If you buy the basic premise, it makes sense."

McCoy was working on his next objection when the briefing-room door hissed open and Riley and Sulu entered, both smiling energetically, Riley clutching his morning coffee protectively. Dr. Benar and Commander Uhura followed close on their heels, engaged in spirited conversation.

"There is evidence," Benar was saying, her plain, angular face showing an animation that dispelled much of the Vulcan aura that normally cloaked her, "that the Erisian Ascendancy cultures, so-called, shared some significant traits with certain Earth human cultures, though the Earth cultures were obviously far simpler. In some of his earliest papers on his discovery, Dr. Antonin Erisi himself pointed out a parallel with the Australian aborigines. They believed that when their totemic ancestors walked the countryside, they weren't only mapping it geographically, but musically, laying down trails of song with their footprints, so that if a thousand years later someone learned the songs, he could find his way unerringly across a land he'd never seen. Erisian cities, on the other hand, were designed and built using principles that appear to underlie certain aspects of the music of many cultures, including those of Earth. Unfortunately, despite much rigorous mathematical analysis, no one can yet say they fully understand those principles, or even know precisely what they are. Nonetheless, they produce patterns that humans can learn to recognize, even predict in some rare instances. Those patterns, in fact, were what led Dr. Erisi to first suspect a connection among the Ascendancy worlds."

Falling silent, Benar took the seat across from Spock. As her eyes met his, she seemed to absorb his emotionless facade and restructure her own to match.

"Where do these 'Exodus halls' you mentioned fit in?" Uhura asked, leaning forward as she took her own seat. "I understand every Ascendancy world has one, and that they may indicate where the Erisians went, even when."

Benar nodded, her features threatening to once again take on a distinctly un-Vulcan enthusiasm. "That is at present no more than a hope. No such halls have been found completely intact, but if conditions on Temaris are as reported, it may hold the first. Only ruins have been found prior to this, and the information gleaned has led not to worlds the Erisians may have migrated to but to a half dozen burned out cinders, destroyed tens of thousands of years ago when their suns underwent periods of instability, ranging from major flares to novas. Some of my colleagues have gone so far as to call these structures not Exodus halls but—"

"You're talking about the Erisians, right?" The hardy voice of Andrew Penalt broke in even before the door had hissed shut behind him and a bemused Chekov.

"Somebody *told* me this place we're heading for was one of their worlds once. Who are they, anyway?"

Kirk repressed an urge to roll his eyes skyward. "All right," he said, straightening in his chair. "Now that we're all here, let's get started."

In response, Spock activated the desk viewscreen, but before he could begin, Penalt was speaking. "Good idea. Look, Admiral, I don't want to worry anyone, but I've been checking out the 'orchestra' I'm supposed to conduct, and I'll let you in on a little secret—they ain't no orchestra. Hell, I don't think more than two or three of them have ever even *seen* each other before they were shoveled aboard."

"They're all accomplished musicians," Riley said quickly, "and all have had years of experience in major orchestras. Admittedly, this particular assemblage has never performed as a unit, but for someone of your talents, Maestro Penalt, I'm sure it will be an easy task to fuse them into a coherent, if not brilliant, whole."

A momentary frown was hastily replaced by a jovial smile as Penalt turned to Riley. "Exactly what I was about to say, Ambassador." He glanced around at the others. "I just wanted you to know, if any of you drop in on any early rehearsals, there's a reason for the way they may sound. But I'll have everything whipped into shape by the time we have to face off with the Romulans."

Audrea Benar's lips parted as if to speak, but a moment later she clamped them shut and returned her even gaze to the viewscreen next to Spock.

"Understood, Mr. Penalt," Kirk said. "Now, Mr. Spock, if you'd care to proceed?"

"Thank you, Captain." The Vulcan paused a moment, waiting for everyone to focus on the viewscreen, now displaying the image of a Romulan commander. "What information we have," he began, "has been supplied by the Romulans as part of the initial exchange."

"Which means it could be a complete fairy tale," McCoy put in.

"It is true, Doctor, that there is no independent verification, but that does not mean that some or all of the data may not be true. You are correct, however, in implying that we cannot rely on its accuracy. It is being presented as it was transmitted to the Federation. Its truth or falsity is not vouched for."

McCoy shrugged. "I suppose we should be thankful they're giving us *anything.*"

"This is Commander Hiran," Spock continued, indicating the Romulan face still on the screen. "He is from a military family extending back seven generations to a matrilineal grandsire. Being from the Provinces and without social connections, he has had to make his way solely on merit and without patronage—no easy matter. He distinguished himself recently for his role in putting down a particularly nasty rebellion with negligible casualties. Only one casualty, in fact." Spock's eyebrows lifted. "His first officer. And wife."

Kirk felt a sudden empathy for the man.

"I wouldn't think holding down enemy casualties would lead to promotion for a Romulan," McCoy said skeptically.

"That is perhaps why, Doctor, his subsequent assignments have been largely limited to border patrols and mapping expeditions. It might also explain why he is currently in command of a bird-of-prey rather than a larger vessel such as a battle cruiser."

"I see that his commands have also been remarkably free of intramural bloodletting," Kirk said, skimming the text that had appeared at the bottom of the screen.

"They even list some officers who followed him to the *Galtizh* from his previous command. And no notable advancement through the ranks by the unexpected deaths of superiors in any of his commands. Not that the publicity packet we've been given by the Romulans would include anything of the like, even if it were true." He studied the broad, smiling face on the screen. Odd, he couldn't remember ever seeing a smiling Romulan before. Hiran seemed more heavyset than the average Romulan; a pleasant-enough-looking fellow of Kirk's own age, if his guess was accurate.

"A straight shooter," he said quietly, realizing as he spoke he was developing an inexplicable admiration for his opposite number, the commander of the Romulan ferryboat *Galtizh*. *Intuition?* he wondered. *Or wishful thinking?* After the latest message from Cartwright concerning the possibility of an infiltrated Romulan delegation and a ship's crew of doubtful loyalty, caution was the watchword. And yet . . .

The next image on the screen was a different matter altogether. Nothing worth hoping for there. Harsh features, perhaps considered handsome by another Romulan, but with an imperious, self-satisfied expression, almost a smirk, something that had been totally absent from Commander Hiran's face.

"Centurion Tiam," said Spock, "promoted from subcenturion coincident with his appointment as chief negotiator to the Federation. The promotion would appear to be unusual in that no mention is made of battle experience, which is traditionally considered a prerequisite to becoming centurion."

"Probably knows where the bodies are buried." McCoy, of course.

"Perhaps, Doctor. However, the records we have been given indicate a distinguished academic record, including a degree in political science, prizes for fencing and gymnastics. He also received awards of merit for work in linguistics and etymology."

Spock glanced at the captain as Tiam's image was replaced by that of a startlingly beautiful Romulan woman. "Centurion Tiam's wife, Jandra, considered a premier musician, proficient in an unspecified number of instruments, including the piano."

"Piano?" Several eyebrows shot up, but McCoy was the first to speak, as he often was. "How the devil would a Romulan learn to play the piano?"

"If we are to believe the information given us, Doctor, several Federation musical instruments, including at least one piano, were part of the booty—though the Romulans do not call it that—from either the early days of the war or from before the war. In any event, she is reputed to be a virtuoso on many instruments but particularly on the piano."

There was a snort then, but for a change it wasn't from McCoy. It was from Penalt. Kirk didn't know the Romulan woman, but he hoped she was indeed the virtuoso her biography claimed—and that she would play rings around Andy Penalt.

"And this," Spock continued, bringing up another image, "is Jandra's brother, Dajan. He is the leader of the Romulan archaeological team, Dr. Benar."

Kirk turned surreptitiously to watch Benar as she was given this first look at her opposite number, the Romulan with whom she would be working closely for at least the duration of the conference. Was it his nervous imagination or was there a more-than-normal tensing of her seemingly impassive features as she studied the image?

Betrayal! Tiam would shout if he could read her thoughts. And it was not just her own thoughts that would set him screaming, for it was one of the Citadel's toadying staff who had first planted the seed in her mind.

Unless it had simply been Tiam's way of testing my loyalty. Jandra shivered at the thought. It would be so like him, as if there were not already more than enough to drive them apart, to give him reason to wage new verbal assaults each day.

But no, she would not allow herself to believe such a thing. The man was merely one who, unlike Tiam, understood the importance of freedom, even though he had none of it himself. *That is, in fact, probably why the man appreciated it, and why he recognized the lack of it in me, despite my seemingly "exalted" position. And he feels that I, unlike him, have a chance at gaining it.*

She shivered again.

But what of her dear sib? Their elder brother's actions —and his had not been a betrayal, only, at worst, a misjudgment of his superiors' intentions—had destroyed the family. Could what she now contemplated, whether it succeeded or failed, have any less effect on her brother? At best, he would be driven again into un-Orthodoxy, perhaps killed. If only she dared to tell Dajan her scheme . . .

She shuddered, as much from indecision as from fear. She was a musician, not a politician or a soldier. Nothing should matter but the music, nothing in this or any other world. She should not have such decisions thrust upon her, decisions that could ruin her life or save it, decisions that could send her brother once again into exile, or worse.

Oh, for a return to the innocent days of her youth, when music *was* all that mattered!

Her mind slid back to that first time she had brought her tiny fists thudding down on the keyboards of the elegant tra'am her mother kept in the second parlor (strictly for show; no one in the family could play it or cared to learn), only to be led away from it by the governess Kalih, with stern admonitions about where sticky little-girl fingers did not belong. Was it that very same evening, or only seemingly so because of a child's ability to telescope events in memory, that her father had brought the guests home and one of them knew how to play?

Jandra had hidden herself in the filmy wall drapes, watching and listening for what seemed like hours or only minutes, until Kalih had pounced on her and shooed her back to bed. Later, when all but the serious guests were gone, and those lay about on the divans in the good parlor discussing crop yields and trade embargoes, she had crept down the long corridor from the sleeping quarters and into the second parlor, hauled her small self up to the keyboards, and tottering sleepily but quite determined, reprised note for note every piece the visitor had played, to finish, grimly satisfied, aware of a doorway full of late-night Ministry functionaries, her father among them, staring gape-mouthed at the prodigy.

There followed tutors, lessons, travel and study with musicians, including one who secretly exposed his young pupil to the best of alien music: Bach, Mozart, Beethoven, the legacy of a human smuggler whose ship had crashed on Romulan soil. The pilot perished, but his tape library survived to change Jandra's life forever.

There followed also performance upon performance. She was eight when she performed for her first Great Audience, though the glitterati did not impress her; it was only Dajan's opinion she valued. Long before she understood the importance to her family of playing before the Ministries, the court cliques, the Important Ones, Jandra knew that nothing really mattered but the music.

The music was the music, whether she played it for her own ears and the gods', for Mother and Father when they had time truly to listen rather than be caught up in the necessity of displaying her for yet one more select audience, for Sib when he would pick his head up out of his mole holes and cock an ear for whatever drifted through the open casements.

Most taxing were the official state audiences—jaded, sated functionaries preoccupied with gossip after too big a meal, too many mood-enhancing drugs. Yet she learned to win them over, and as she grew into winsome adulthood, she played for them all, Romulans and outworlders alike—their prodigy, their pride. She had even played for the Praetor, who, hidden behind his mirror screen, sent word that she had pleased him.

That was before the illness, which was to damage first his features and then his hearing. Decrees were issued banning performance on tra'am and all other keyboard instruments—first from public performance, then from private playing. Instruments were confiscated, burned, destroyed. Was it memory or only imagination in which Jandra threw herself across the body of her parents' precious tra'am as it was carried out into the gardens to be burned? She remembered being dragged away, her hair and clothing singed. One wrist still bore the scar.

She was inconsolable for the proper amount of time, then resigned herself to string instruments, per the Praetor's decree, and being Jandra, she mastered them all, domestic and foreign. She owned an Earth cello and a Vulcan ka'athyra and defiant, played them in public performance along with plekt and the'el and bahtain. She was their darling, unassailable. Nothing mattered but the music.

Then came Reelan's disgrace, and her parents' ritual suicide, made even more painful by her and Dajan's being barred from even seeing them in their final hours, barred from saying even the most sterile and perfunctory of farewells. And even before the bodies were cold, her own and her twin's exiles had come, dooming her, she thought at the time, to a lifetime of playing the provinces. She was indeed fortunate, it was impressed on her time and again, that she would be allowed even that. If not for a generous Praetor, she could have been banned entirely, unable to play her music, not even for her own ears and the gods'. And it was there, in one of the unwatched Provinces, that she found one of her greatest treasures, an Earth piano. How it came to be there, no one knew precisely, except that it dated from the war, perhaps before, and stories of lost Federation ships floated about it like the notes as she played. And play it she did, discovering to her wonder that here was the instrument for which the music on those smuggled tapes had been designed. And nothing mattered but the music.

And now there was this! Jandra thought. The wheel had turned yet again; the gods had changed their fickle minds once more. First she had been bonded to Tiam, given partial rehabilitation, and now, suddenly, the rehabilitation was complete and she was specially selected to play before the aliens, the humans and their like. For the moment, at least, even her previously secret accomplishments were being treated as simply a facet of her genius, something with which a Romulan such as herself could impress the humans.

But she knew all too well how quickly, how capriciously her world could be turned on its head again. And she knew that, rather than being her own person, she was expected, like Tiam, to be a creature of the Empire, with no will of her own.

No freedom.

She shuddered again. She would have to decide, soon. Soon, or not at all.

"We want to establish at least the appearance of trust," Riley said, "if not the complete reality." The briefing had moved on from the review of Romulan personnel to a discussion of procedures to be followed once in orbit around Temaris Four. "The first face-to-face meeting will be on the planet's surface. We beam down with communicators only. No weapons. Security team on standby, to be beamed down only on Captain Kirk's direct order or my own."

"I don't like the sound of that, Commander," Chekov objected immediately, obviously recalling Cartwright's message but wisely not referring to it. The officers and all security personnel knew, but not the civilians.

"Me neither, sir," Sulu chimed in.

"That's the way it has to be," Riley said, curtailing debate but with an apologetic look. Kirk, at least, was nodding agreement. "If two starships staring down each other's throats aren't enough deterrent, we might as well turn around and go home. We have to start somewhere. Captain Kirk?"

"My feelings as well, Commander," Kirk said, remembering the smiling face of Commander Hiran, "as long as the Romulans march to the same drummer."

"They have at least unofficially agreed to do so," Riley said. "This first meeting is intended to be strictly introductory. A few handshakes, a chance for the heads of both archaeology teams to have a look around, then we retire to our respective vessels until the conference officially begins the following day. That's to be the pattern at close of day, incidentally. No one from either side remains on the surface after sundown."

"And our transporter chiefs have been instructed to keep a fix on each of us at all times," Kirk added. "I can only assume the Romulans will do the same for their own."

Nodding, Riley turned to the archaeologist. "Dr. Benar, you'll leave your team up here the first time. And you'll instruct them when they do beam down to have their communicators with them at all times."

"Of course, Commander," Benar answered. "We will follow all safety precautions."

"We'll also leave the musicians on board," Riley continued while Kirk murmured silently, *Particularly Andy Penalt.* Both were relieved to see that the composer did not choose to argue the point. Kirk in particular had been half-afraid Penalt would insist that, if the leader of the archaeological team was to go down, so should the leader of the musicians.

"The first working meeting," Riley went on, "will be the following day, on the *Galtizh.* Assuming the wheels don't fall completely off, a second meeting will be held the next day on the *Enterprise.* Meetings will continue, alternating between the ships, until some kind of agreement is reached or one or both sides has had enough. And don't anyone bother to ask what kind of agreement or what might constitute 'having enough.' I can only say that I hope we can avoid the latter and recognize the former when we see it. Meanwhile, the cultural exchange —the entertainment, if you will—will occupy the evenings. Current plans—subject to change, of course— take us through four days. First, on the evening after the handshaking on the surface, Federation musicians will perform on the *Enterprise,* followed the next evening by Romulan musicians performing on the *Galtizh,* followed by Romulans on the *Enterprise,* and finally, our people on the *Galtizh.*"

Riley looked around the table. "Any questions?" When there were none, he turned to Kirk, who, after a surveying glance of his own, stood up.

"That's it, then," Kirk said. "Spock, Mr. Sulu," he added as the others headed for the door. "A moment if you please."

When the door hissed shut behind the last of them, he turned to Spock. "You were watching Dr. Benar when the Romulan archaeologist came up on the screen. Any opinions?"

"About what specifically, Captain?"

"You know what I mean, Spock. Not too many years ago she saw several of her closest friends tortured and killed by Romulans, and she barely escaped herself. She has Vulcan training, but she's human—all human, not half. Will she be able to handle it, down there cheek to jowl with another batch of Romulans?"

"I could not say, Captain. If the training was thorough, if Dr. Benar was fully receptive, then it is entirely possible she will be able to cope with the situation. You, as another human, should be better qualified to estimate her capabilities than I."

Kirk nodded. "You're right as always, Spock." He turned to Sulu. "There isn't going to be much for a helmsman to do once we get to Temaris, Mr. Sulu, so how would you like to be an archaeology sitter?"

Sulu looked blank for a moment, then broke into a grin. "Stick close to Dr. Benar, you mean? My pleasure, sir. As a matter of fact, I've been trying to think of a diplomatic way of telling you I'd sooner be down there grubbing through Erisian artifacts than up here marking diplomatic time with you and Kevin."

"I'm glad the assignment is to your liking, Commander. But try to restrain your enthusiasm for grubbing. Stick close to Dr. Benar, at least while she's mixing with the Romulans." Kirk frowned. "I assume it's occurred to you that the Romulans' insistence on her being in charge could be less an attempt to 'make up' for their earlier offenses against her than an attempt to exploit them?"

Sulu nodded, sobering. "Part of the sabotage the admiral and his tame Romulan are worried about, Captain? Possible, if whoever suggested her was an opposition plant."

"Just what I was thinking. Spock?"

"It is definitely a possibility, Captain. At this point, however, almost anything is a possibility."

"Unfortunately true. Do what you can, Mr. Sulu, without being too obvious. And keep me informed, both of you."

He watched as they left. Dr. Benar, whether she had been selected as a gesture of goodwill or as an act of sabotage, was in for some rough times.

FIVE

─────────── ☆ ───────────

The entity paused and extended its crystal sensor. Data defining the shape and content of the space surrounding it began racing along the microscopically glittering pathways honeycombing its vast interior. Trillions of calculations were made each microsecond, comparing what had been and what was, comparing its own predictions to current reality, adding the results to its near-infinite store of data. Several stars, it noted, were displaced nearly half a stellar diameter from their predicted locations. The energy output of others were minutely greater, their energy spectra even more minutely shifted. And the planets . . .

The refinements to the process would never end, not within the entity's projected span of existence. The interactions of the gravity fields of tens of billions of stars and ten times that many major planets, the effects of the diffuse fields generated by the even greater masses of unseen and otherwise undetectable matter, were too complex for even it to ever completely analyze, and the raging, multimillion-degree hearts of the stars were opaque even to the crystal sensor. All was not known, nor could it ever be known.

Its course modified, as it had been modified millions of times since its journey began, the entity moved on, still unaware that it was leaving Federation space.

Already, at the very limit of the crystal sensor's range, another world was entering its awareness, another world whose primitives, like those on the blue world it had recently departed, held promise. With a special alertness that, in a living being, might have been called both anticipation and apprehension, it sought the voice of that distant world.

Captain's Log, Stardate 8488.7:

Word has come from the First Federation vessel *Guarnerius* that the Probe has suddenly crossed the Neutral Zone and entered Romulan space, abandoning any pretense of being out for a "stroll." Its course went abruptly from the "leisurely" arc it had followed all through the First Federation to a perfectly straight line, and it more than doubled its velocity.

One must logically wonder why.

Whether there are any other significant worlds—or outposts—in its current path is known only to the Romulans, and they aren't talking, even with all the perestroika and glasnost allegedly rampant in the Empire. The *Guarnerius's* information was passed on to the Romulan Interim Government, but the Committee's only response was another curt denial of the Probe's existence and an even more curt reiteration of their warning to keep Federation ships well clear of the Empire.

Scotty eyed the viewscreen image of the *Galtizh* speculatively. At the bottom of the screen, a sliver of the reddish gray surface of Temaris Four was visible. He and Kirk had watched from the conn as the Romulan vessel, uncloaked from the moment it dropped out of warp at the limits of the Temaris system, had approached under impulse, smoothly inserting itself into an identical orbit with the *Enterprise,* then heeling over into its present nose-to-nose position less than ten kilometers ahead.

"Now why d'ye suppose," Scotty asked finally, "they'd send a lesser ship than ours, knowing we could overpower her?" The chief engineer had been looking over his shoulder for gremlins ever since the prickling at the nape of his neck told him "Neutral Zone" a tick before the computer made the official announcement of their entry.

"As a measure of trust, possibly," Riley suggested, watching from beside Uhura's station. "This is, after all, supposed to be a peace conference, not a duel. Or considering the number of concessions we've made, perhaps they're showing us they're not afraid to meet our biggest ship with a smaller vessel."

Scott exchanged glances with Kirk, exhaling under his mustache. *Youth and innocence!* he seemed to be saying. *Trust a Romulan? That'll be the day!*

"On the flip side, you could read it as an insult." McCoy had to put his oar in. "You caved in to all our demands, so what do we have to worry about?"

"Or they may simply be implying that this conference is of very little import to them," Kirk suggested quietly, wishing their clandestine Romulan informant were available for consultation. "In case anything goes wrong, it saves face for them in retrospect. It could be the same kind of reasoning that gave us Riley instead of Sarek." He glanced at the diplomat. "No offense, Kevin."

"None taken, Captain. I'd have to have an ego as big as Penalt's to put myself in the same category as Sarek." Riley straightened and pulled in a breath. "Wish us luck, Commander," he said as he stepped away from the communications station, his fingers lightly brushing Uhura's shoulder.

"Good luck, Ambassador Riley," she said with a solemn smile.

"All right, people"—he gave the two captains and Sulu and Benar a glance—"it's time to go make history."

Kirk and his team—Spock, Sulu, Riley, and Benar—stood facing a group of six stiffly formal Romulans on a rise overlooking the desertlike remains of what had once been a terraced, fertile valley. Immediately below them, in the mouth of the valley, the Spartan assemblages—headquarters for the archaeology teams-to-be—that had just been beamed down by *Enterprise* and *Galtizh* cargo transporters looked like squat, mechanical invaders on this soft-cornered, ancient world. Beyond them, in the valley proper, flanked by what must once have been verdant hills before half the world was turned to desert, the ruins stretched almost to the sandy horizon.

There should be an honor guard, Kirk found himself thinking, *a band—something. This doesn't look like an intergovernmental peace conference; it looks like a wake.* The conspicuous absence of fanfare reinforced Kirk's opinion that the Romulans wanted to imply the conference was unimportant to them, perhaps nothing more than a minor distraction for the people back home, something to keep their minds off the inevitable food shortages and the fact that they had to spend half their time looking nervously over their shoulders while they waited for the fallout from the upper-echelon power struggles.

But at least, he was pleased to note as the introductions were being made, the Romulans were also unarmed, as per unofficial agreement. Perhaps he'd read this Hiran correctly after all.

"And of course, Commander Riley," Hiran, the smiling Romulan, was saying, "it is my honor to present to you Centurion Tiam." Kirk couldn't be sure, but he thought there was a flicker of something other than a smile as Hiran spoke of the "honor" he was being accorded. He wondered if his own face would reflect a similar betrayal—if such it was—when it came time to introduce Maestro Andy Penalt to the Romulans.

Then the introductions, all equally stilted and formal, were over, and Dajan and Dr. Benar, escorted by an enthusiastic Sulu, escaped to "survey" a few square meters of the ruins while Centurion-cum-Ambassador Tiam stood watching, silent and poker stiff next to a seemingly relaxed Riley. Spock and Hiran flanked Kirk, while Hiran's first officer, Subcommander Feric—a steely-eyed enigma—stood a respectful step back.

One of Tiam's aides, a young subcenturion named Jutak, trailed the explorers at a discreet distance, leaving Kirk to wonder if the aide was doing for Tiam or Hiran what Sulu was doing for Kirk, only with notably less enthusiasm. The other aide, introduced as Subcenturion Kital, was far from young and almost anorexically thin. This one remained next to Tiam, standing even straighter and more rigidly than the ambassador. Nothing moved but his eyes, but they were in almost constant motion, systematically darting from one target to another, as if his life depended on knowing the precise location and appearance of each and every participant at all times. *More bodyguard than aide?* Kirk wondered. Whatever the man was, he presented an even more unforgiving aspect than Tiam himself.

Hiran turned to Kirk, as if on a sudden impulse. "It appears there will be precious little to occupy you and me on this mission, Captain Kirk. I, at least, am not trained to diplomacy, nor am I overly well versed in either archaeology or music. Or am I assuming too much about yourself?"

"Not at all, Commander Hiran. I can't say I expect to be completely idle, but I'm more than content to leave the negotiations and the rest to the experts."

"My feelings exactly, Captain. However, I do have my interests, as I suspect do you." When Kirk nodded easily, Hiran continued, "Good. Then I would be honored to conduct you on a tour of my ship, if you will do the same for me."

Centurion Tiam remained silent, watching and listening. Something that on a human face might have been a cold smile shaped the corners of his mouth. His aide Kital had stopped systematically surveying the entire scene and was zeroed in on Kirk and Hiran, but there was still no way to tell what, if anything, he was thinking. It was as if the guy came complete with his own little personal cloaking device, McCoy would say later.

"I'll personally escort you, Commander," Kirk told Hiran, looking him straight in the eye, hoping—feeling —he was not making a mistake.

SIX

— ☆ —

So far, so good, Kirk thought, surveying the mixture of
colorful civilian costumes and regulation Starfleet issue,
all swimming in an unintelligible hubbub of dozens of
voices going simultaneously, drowned now and then by
bursting bubbles of laughter. On the surface, this first
reception, in the most spacious rec deck facilities the
Enterprise had to offer, was a genuine miracle after a
hundred years of cold—and sometimes not-so-cold—
war. Maybe, just maybe, something worthwhile could
come of this meeting after all. Even Dr. Benar, though
she had yet to join in anything as un-Vulcan as laughter,
appeared comfortable—or at least not uncomfortable—
as the archaeologists engaged in what he assumed was
energetic shoptalk. His only moment of fright had come
not from Benar but from a stout, silver-haired Catullan
female who had been repeatedly poking a lanky
Romulan male in the chest to emphasize her point. Just

when Kirk expected the Romulan to draw back in anger,
however, he exploded in laughter instead. Fascinating, as
Spock would doubtless say. The idea of a laughing
Romulan was, at the very least, a pleasant surprise, even
after the smiling Commander Hiran, but it was still
something that would take getting used to.

On other hand, there was Tiam, an iceberg in the
shipping lanes if there ever was one. Even Riley had
given up after uncounted attempts at small talk.

Commander Hiran, still at his observation post immediately to Kirk's right, loosed a sigh. "My pet diplomat
seems to be behaving in a decidedly undiplomatic
manner," he said. "You will excuse me, Kirk, while I
have a word with him."

"By all means, Commander," Kirk acquiesced. "No
one likes a party pooper," he added, wondering what
Romulan equivalent the translator in Hiran's ear would
supply. Whatever it was, it seemed to delight the commander.

"That is priceless, Kirk," Hiran said, laughing. "I shall
remember it at my next staff meeting!"

So saying, Hiran navigated the throng and spoke
quietly in Tiam's ear. The ambassador stiffened, his eyes
flashing, but finally, gritting his teeth, he nodded. As
Hiran ambled back toward Kirk, Tiam looked about the
room, as if casting about for some target to lock onto. As
luck would have it, Anneke, Penalt's lovely "protégé,"
made her colorful entrance at just that moment. Within
minutes, she was hanging, giggling, on Tiam's arm. Tiam
himself quickly developed a smile to rival Hiran's, even
laughed out loud at one of her remarks. His wife, Jandra,
didn't seem to mind; if anything, she seemed relieved to
be rid of his attentions.

On the other hand, Tiam's aide, Kital, seemed less

than pleased as he abruptly turned his back on the pair and seemed to lock in on Hiran, once again at Kirk's side. It was only then, however, that he let something substantial slip through the "personal cloaking device" McCoy had noted: a look of pure venom, directed not at Kirk but at Commander Hiran. But even that was gone in an instant.

Suppressing an impulse to ask Hiran what he knew about the aide, Kirk sipped his ale and turned his attention elsewhere, trying to listen in on some of the dozens of overlapping conversations around him. And as more and more began to register, he realized that, despite the light, almost frivolous tone that predominated, there was an undercurrent of seriousness, a repeated theme of: What if . . . ?

"What if an accord was signed and we were free to stay here?" archaeologists from both teams wondered longingly to each other, Dajan perhaps the most longingly of all. "There are centuries' worth of study on Temaris alone, not to mention the six other known Erisian worlds in the Zone. What if . . . ?"

"What if we were to treat with humans as we have been treating with the Klingons these many years?" Commander Hiran demanded of McCoy, who had had the temerity to suggest it. "Do you suppose the Federation contains our only adversaries? We have as many as we have common borders. What if . . . ?"

"What if humans were to cease to see us as the faceless aggressor, the cog in the vast military machine?" one of the Romulan musicians wondered. "What if they came to see that we have family lives, friendships, greater arts than the art of war, the same as you? What if . . . ?"

Patterns altered kaleidoscopically; groups scattered

and regrouped until finally, it was time for the music. A solo piano recital by Maestro Andrew Penalt.

Originally, the full orchestra had been scheduled to perform, but Penalt had petitioned for a delay. They were not yet as fully "integrated" as he wished, though none of the musicians that Uhura had spoken with felt the least bit "unintegrated." On the contrary, Uhura reported, they had come together almost flawlessly the second day of rehearsals, as if all it had taken was a few musical handshakes that first day to build a sort of collective musical intuition. "It was like the way a collection of starship veterans will become an integrated crew almost instantly when they're assigned to a new ship," she said, trying to put it in terms less alien to the captain, "no matter how many different ships they last served on. The only Klingon in the containment field, so to speak, is Penalt."

None of the musicians objected to the delay, however. They were all still enjoying themselves exploring the *Enterprise,* none of them ever having been aboard the likes of her before. Some few had never been off Earth, and those who had, had done their traveling on standard commercial runs and charters. "Let Andy have his fun," one violinist said, and went on to suggest that "Andy" simply wanted center stage all to himself the first night. "Being the first musician to play solo for a Romulan audience will look great on his political résumé—or he'll figure out a way to *make* it look great."

Riley of course did the honors when Penalt finally stood by the Steinway on its raised platform in the center of the room. To his diplomatic credit, he made it sound almost as if Penalt's solo was what they had planned all along.

Acknowledging the polite applause, Penalt seated himself, signaled for the computerized orchestral accompaniment he had arranged for, and began to play. Thunderously. Spectacularly.

From the rousing opening bars of a twenty-second-century Coulson march to the bravura final movement —allegro assai, "very quick"—of Mozart's Twenty-third Concerto, Penalt seemed to be trying to display his physical strength and dexterity at least as much as he was trying to produce music. There were moments when Kirk wondered if the keys would stand up to the assault as Penalt's rigid fingers hammered down on them. Often—whenever the tempo allowed—his hands would arc up to shoulder level or higher and his whole upper body would aid them in crashing back down. Even when the tempo was too fast for such embellishments, his bobbing head and shoulders kept the action going, as if he were using their motion and the sometimes tortured looks that twisted his features to wring a more stirring performance out of the accompanying computer.

"Liberace Bernstein lives," one of the musicians muttered during a brief lull, but the only nonmusician within earshot who grinned in response was Sulu. The others glanced at each other puzzledly.

As Penalt finished with the Mozart piece—full of pyrotechnics, all sparkle and dazzle and flying fingers— he stood with a flourish and bowed to the applause, which even the other musicians joined in, though not as enthusiastically as the rest.

"At least he's good—isn't he?" Kirk glanced from Uhura to Sulu.

"He has to be *pretty* good," Uhura said with a grin, "to do all that flailing around and still hit most of the right notes."

"Good, but not as good as he thinks he is," Sulu added. "*Nobody* could be *that* good."

As the applause died down, Kirk noticed with sudden apprehension that Tiam was heading for the platform. Penalt looked equally apprehensive as the Romulan bore down on him.

"That's all we need, for those two to butt heads," Kirk muttered, stretching up on his tiptoes and looking around the room. "Has anyone seen where Commander Hiran got to?"

A moment later Kirk spotted the Romulan commander, on the far side of the room, already heading toward Tiam. Belatedly, Kirk got moving, aiming for Tiam's target, Penalt.

But before any of them could close the gap, Tiam was striding up onto the platform, his hand extended, not as a threat but as, they all suddenly realized, an invitation to the peculiarly human ritual of a handshake.

Penalt recovered quickly, restoring his smile and gripping the offered hand. Kirk watched for some evidence of the hand-crushing war that Penalt seemed to like to turn handshakes into, but if a war was in progress, neither combatant let it register on his face.

"A brilliant performance, Maestro, absolutely brilliant," Tiam said loudly, and Penalt accepted graciously, if smugly.

"Thank you, Ambassador Tiam," Penalt said just as loudly. "Coming from you, that's quite a compliment. I understand your wife is a musician as well."

"She is," Tiam said. "In fact," he went on, his voice lowered to a conversational tone now, "she is the reason I have taken the liberty of approaching you."

Penalt, who had undoubtedly noticed not only the green-eyed Romulan beauty but Anneke's off-and-on alliance with Tiam, smiled. "And what exactly is that reason, Ambassador?"

"It is the piano, Maestro Penalt. You see, it is one of her favorite instruments, but it has been years since she has had access to one. Your playing so inspired her that she was wondering if she might . . . indulge herself with this one."

Penalt hesitated, glancing toward Kirk and Hiran, both of whom were now at the edge of the platform. Jandra stood well back, possibly frowning, possibly not. Her brother Dajan stood not far away, watching Tiam thoughtfully.

"I realize it is an unusual request, Maestro," Tiam went on with a touch of apology in his voice when Penalt still hesitated, "but surely—"

"Of course," Penalt capitulated abruptly, cutting off the scattered encouraging applause, mostly from the Federation musicians. Stepping down from the platform, he strode quickly to where Jandra stood and took her arm. For a moment, she nervously resisted, casting a dark look at her husband, but then the scattered applause began again. "Very well," she said, not so much to Penalt as to Tiam, who only smiled as she took Penalt's arm and allowed herself to be escorted to the piano.

"If there is anything I can do to assist you . . ." Penalt's voice trailed off as she sat before the keyboard.

She sat motionless for a moment, then brushed her fingers soundlessly across the keys, then let them rest, pressing down lightly, still soundlessly, as she closed her eyes and leaned slightly forward. For several seconds she sat that way, giving Kirk, for just a moment, the insane impression that she was somehow mind-melding with the instrument.

Then there was sound as her fingers darted up and down the keys. Simple scales, but on the Steinway, under her touch, even they sounded somehow melodic.

Then silence again. She looked up at Penalt, who still stood by the side of the piano. "The piece you concluded with, the final movement of Mozart's Twenty-third," she said. "Would your computer have the accompaniment for the second movement? At a slightly different tempo?"

"Of course. I assembled the program myself. It is designed to follow the lead of the player."

"Ingenious," Tiam remarked, stepping down from the platform to join the audience. "I will leave you to it, then."

Penalt joined him a moment later as the computer accompaniment began.

And Jandra played.

Without a single false start or misstep, she played.

The contrast to Penalt could not have been greater.

Where he had thundered, she whispered.

Where he had thrown his entire body into the playing, as if physically ripping the sounds from the instrument, she remained almost eerily motionless as her fingers, as if possessed of an independent life, coaxed the sound from the keys, delicately shaping each and every note.

Where he had raced, she strolled languidly, poignantly through the adagio movement, letting the sound drift out and envelop her listeners and draw them in rather than hurling it at them in a desperate bid for attention.

And draw them in it did. When she lifted her fingers from the keys at the conclusion, there was total silence except for the inevitable background of the *Enterprise* itself as it labored to keep its five-hundred-plus passen-

gers and crew alive and in comfort. For several seconds
the silence lasted, as if all were holding their breaths,
waiting for her to continue.

And then the applause broke out, starting with the
musicians.

And Sulu, again next to Kirk, laughed as he joined the
others in the applause. *"She*'s as good as Penalt thinks *he*
is."

"I thought maybe she was," Kirk said, relieved to see
that his I-don't-know-music-but-I-know-what-I-like cri-
terion had not led him totally astray. As the applause
died away and the conversations started up again—
virtually all, he was sure, on the same subject—he
looked around to locate Penalt.

If he had looked a second later, he would have seen
only the Maestro's broad smile, but in that first second,
he saw the mixture of fury and humiliation that had not
yet been completely obscured. Kirk was glad he hadn't
missed it.

A moment later, the smile now firmly in place, Penalt
bounded back onto the platform. He took Jandra's hand
as she stood up from the piano.

"That was stunning, my lady, absolutely stunning," he
gushed. Then, turning to the crowd—and Tiam, who
still stood nearby—he raised his voice. "Ambassador
Tiam, your wife's performance has given new urgency to
your mission, at least insofar as a humble musician such
as myself is concerned. You and your colleagues *must*
succeed, if only so that her gifts may be shared with the
worlds of the Federation."

Even Tiam seemed taken aback by Penalt's effusive-
ness, but he recovered quickly. "Jandra and I thank you,
Maestro Penalt," he said with a tight smile. "And we will

do our best in the coming days not to disappoint the Federation."

"And you, my lady," Penalt went on, turning to Jandra, "when the day comes that you are able to tour the Federation, I would be honored to be your sponsor and adviser."

"And her agent, for a healthy percentage," Uhura muttered, sotto voce, bringing a sidelong smile from Kirk, who turned to explain the concept of agents to a puzzled-looking Hiran.

Tiam stepped off the concert platform, beaming—and almost tripped over Subcenturion Kital. His aide was scowling.

"Yes?" Tiam snapped impatiently, preoccupied by thoughts of Jandra's obviously triumphant performance, and the glory that it would no doubt bring him. He was in no mood for whatever problems Kital wanted to discuss.

"Commander Hiran," the aide began stiffly. *Gods, why did the man talk so slowly?* "He—"

"What about Hiran?" Tiam snapped. At the same time, he turned and saw the commander and his first officer apparently engaged in animated conversation with Kirk and a half dozen other *Enterprise* officers. About his wife's brilliant performance, no doubt.

"In light of the amount of time he spends with the Federation captain," Kital said, "I would only suggest that you remind him that you—and only you—are empowered to speak for the Empire."

"I will remind him—when I feel it appropriate, *Sub*centurion." In truth, he had noticed the relationship himself, particularly in the wake of Hiran's admonition to not be a "party pooper," whatever that ridiculous term might mean. "Now, if there is nothing else that needs my attention . . .?"

Without waiting for an acknowledgment, Tiam turned from his meddlesome aide and waded into the swirling crowd.

Later, in her quarters, Jandra drew the curtain before the clearsteel window closed, the image of the Federation starship beyond fixed firmly in her mind.

And she realized that her decision had been made. When had she become certain?

Certainly not when that buffoon Penalt had made his "offer," for she had seen his face as she finished her performance. His anger had been palpable in those moments before he brought his features under control. He would be a human Tiam, interested in nothing but what he could personally gain from any association, willing—even eager—to destroy her if he could only profit from the destruction.

Nor had it been during the spontaneous burst of applause, for she had heard similar outpourings countless times in the Provinces without having her opinion of the Empire or its leaders raised an iota.

Perhaps it had been the crowd afterward, not as they told her how much they had been moved by her performance but as they lingered to talk of other things, to inquire about her life, her happiness. As they treated her, not as a performer or a possession or even as an alien, but as another being like themselves.

Or perhaps it had been the captain, not the aloof Vulcan but the human named Kirk. And the ambassador named Riley, and the commanders named Uhura and

Sulu and Scott and McCoy. There had been a camaraderie among them—including even, once she thought of it, the Vulcan—that she had seen before only among her fellow musicians, and *never* among the Romulan command structure, civilian or military, at any level. It would be unthinkable for a Romulan at any level to treat his subordinates as fellow Romulans, let alone as equals. The only Romulan whose temperament even remotely resembled those of the Federation officers and crew was Hiran, and he was considered—at least by Tiam—a gullible fool.

So, the decision had been made.

But it had still to be carried out. And the first step, perhaps the hardest step of all, would be to talk to Dajan. She dared not simply make her move, leaving him to face the consequences. About Tiam she was not worried. Whatever became of him, it would be his due. He as much as anyone was responsible for her desire, he and a thousand others just like him at all levels of the command structure.

But Sib . . .

She would have to take the chance. He would have to be warned, be given the chance to talk her out of her absurd plan.

Or be given the chance to join her.

Her heart leapt momentarily at the very thought, unlikely as it was.

More likely he would tell her she was a fool, and she wouldn't be able to deny it. He might even—he was a Romulan, after all—betray her. He no longer mourned their parents as she did. He insisted only on restoring the family honor—among Romulans—and what she had decided to do would destroy it for all time.

And as for what it might do to this peace conference, and the hopes of those humans . . .

Bracing herself, she moved down the Spartan corridor to her brother's quarters. Tiam, sated with self-satisfaction, had fallen asleep almost immediately after their return from the Federation ship, leaving her free to slip from their quarters unnoticed and search out Dajan's. Leaving her free to stand outside Dajan's door, fighting the urge to turn and run and unmake the decision.

She knocked—and was startled by the suddenness with which the door snapped open.

"Little Sister! What—No, come in. Come in!" The door clanked shut behind her. "I was right, you see! They wished to flaunt you, to prove Romulan superiority even in such lesser activities as music. And that fool Penalt—"

"I must speak with you, Sib," she said abruptly, knowing that if she delayed, she would be lost. The momentary burst of courage that had allowed her to rap at his door would desert her, and she would never get it back.

"Of course, Little Sister, and I with you. You were the sensation of the evening, and—"

"I have decided," she said, cutting him off again, the words coming out in a rush. "I have decided I will defect to the Federation!"

For a long moment there was only silence. Her brother's face was frozen, his mouth still open with unspoken words.

Suddenly, he laughed.

"I am not jesting!" she protested angrily, but then she was being snatched off her feet, hugged, and whirled about the tiny room, even more wildly than when they had first been reunited.

"And I am not laughing at you!" he said, finally setting her down. "It is just your remarkable timing—just like a musician! I have been pacing the floor for hours, it seems, trying to work up the courage to tell *you* precisely the same thing!"

SEVEN

☆

Captain's Log, Stardate 8489.1:

The first "working diplomatic meeting" is set to begin on the *Galtizh* at 0900 this morning. After the smash the Romulan ambassador's wife made last night at the reception, hopes are perhaps a bit higher than before, but no one is holding his or her breath. Even Penalt, who obviously knows which side his bread is buttered on, has been on his best behavior. If I hadn't seen his face immediately after Jandra's performance, I'd almost believe his offer to her was gracious and altruistic rather than simply opportunistic.

The first working session for the archaeological teams is also scheduled to begin at 0900, although if Dr. Benar and the others had anything to say about it, it would begin at first light. As it is, there appears to have been an "informal" agreement between the teams, and the transporter room has been alerted for traffic to Temaris to commence no later than 0700. If the interactions between the teams are as smooth down on Temaris as they were at the reception, where this agreement was apparently hatched, Mr. Sulu won't have to worry about having his "grubbing time" interrupted by misbehavior on the part of Dr. Benar or anyone else.

"The Federation transmissions are confirmed, Commander," the subcommander of the Romulan vessel *Azmuth* reported, her eyes narrowed above the scanner scope. "There is an unidentified object approaching us on precisely the course their transmissions gave. I estimate it crossed into Romulan space four hours ago."

Frowning, the commander came out of the command chair to peer over her second's shoulder. "Mass? Propulsion? Lifeforms?"

"Unknown, Commander. Our instruments react as if the object were employing some form of cloaking."

"It is Romulan, then?" Sharply. That would at least explain the peculiar denial of its existence issued by the Interim Government.

"No, Commander. It is not cloaking of any form we are familiar with. It interferes with our readings rather than blocks them. It is perhaps the result of the object's drive system."

"How so?"

"As it accelerated, the readings began varying even more widely."

"But this effect, whatever it is, does not interfere with our ability to track the object?"

"No, Commander. It is coming within visual range. Shall I—"

"Of course!"

A dark, cylindrical form appeared on the *Azmuth*

screens. It had to be at least the size of a small planetoid, the commander thought. At this distance, at the limits of visual range, the *Azmuth* itself would be little more than a speck. Whatever this thing was—

"Commander! Another ship—a Romulan ship—is in the object's wake."

"What? What ship?" The commander stopped, her mind racing. "No, belay that! Pull back *now!* Get us out of sensor range of that ship! But don't lose that thing it's following!"

What had she fallen into here? Was that other ship simply another that, like the *Azmuth,* had happened to be in the right place at the right time to intercept the Federation message? Or was it under orders from the Interim Government, or some other, competing power block that already *knew* about this object, whatever it was? But whatever the truth of the matter, it would be wise to keep her own presence undetected—if it wasn't already too late.

A mixture of fear and exhilaration flooded through the commander as she returned to the command chair. Whatever this behemoth was, there was opportunity attached to it, opportunity for anything from vaulting advancement to sudden death. Such opportunities had always existed for those who could seize them, for those who could improvise and not lose their nerve, but never more so than now, in the wake of the Praetor's death.

For years the Praetor had meant power, and the webs of intrigue that existed at all levels almost all centered on him and were readable to those who knew the codes. But now there was chaos as the struggle to succeed him raged. No one's loyalty to *anyone* was guaranteed, from the lowliest junior officer to the heart of the Citadel itself. Orders were still issued by familiar voices, belonging to familiar faces, but for how long? Some had already vanished, she was sure, and more would doubtless follow, to be replaced by those ready and able to seize the opportunity.

In the ancient days of Empire, the bodies of the fallen would be laid out on the cobbles as a lesson, but these were more sophisticated days. Bodies and voices vanished, along with the names they'd borne, in the Praetor's wake even more quickly than in his time; they were simply replaced with newer, different bodies, different names, different secrets, different holds on power.

And this object the Interim Government proclaimed did not exist? Where did it fit in? Was it already under the control of one of the factions? Or was it still a wild card, beholden to no one? What *was* it?

More to the point, how could she find out? Was it something that could be controlled? Directed? Learned from? How, if it was not already under another's control, could *she* gain control of it? And even if it was under the control of another, how could she wrest power from that other?

"We are out of sensor range, Commander. The object, however, is still within range, as requested."

"Acknowledged. Follow a parallel course with the object and maintain subspace silence."

"We cannot match its current speed, Commander. We will lose it within one day."

The commander scowled at the woman but said nothing. At least, she thought a moment later, the other ship, the one in the object's wake, would lose it first, and there would be a brief period during which the *Azmuth,* now well ahead of the object, would be the only ship

within range. For at least an hour, near Wlaariivi, she
would have the object to herself. If she could just figure
out what to do—to *try* to do with it . . .

Audrea Benar and the Romulan archaeologist Dajan
stood next to the prefab "headquarters" at the mouth of
the valley as their teams spread out and began threading
their way as rapidly as practical through the ruins, their
eyes alternating between the sand-filled streets and the
readouts on their shared tricorders. The evening before,
the reception "shoptalk" had led quickly to an agreement to pair off, Romulan and Federation, so that,
during the initial survey, each pair would have the use of
a tricorder, which even the Romulans—the Romulan
archaeologists, at least—readily admitted were superior
to their own devices, and which could in minutes extract
the same information it would have taken the prewar
expedition days or months to obtain. This morning,
everyone had leapt into action virtually the moment
they were beamed down. None of them knew how much
time they would have, and none wanted to waste a
moment. First, a fast survey of the entire valley, with all
tricorder readings transferred to both *Enterprise* and
Galtizh computers at the end of each day. No one yet had
even an estimate of how many days the initial survey
would take, but all were determined to complete it, and
then to concentrate on the most promising areas—
though it was hard to imagine any area here being
*un*promising.

"Lihalla," she said out of deference to her companion,
wondering why the Romulan name for the world was
softer, more melodic than the Federation's. It was a
decaying gray world with a feeble sun, dim and forbid-
ding, but to an archaeologist's eyes, the sight was

stunningly beautiful. Yet Audrea was finding that, if she closed those eyes, it was all too easy to imagine that she stood amid the ruins of Kalis Three, with a different Romulan at her side. . . .

"Temaris," Dajan allowed graciously. Like most Romulans, he was shorter and slighter of build than the average Vulcan, scarcely taller than she. His coloring was lighter: pale, curling hair framed a face set with dark green eyes. A strikingly familiar face: Audrea decided he had to be the fraternal twin, not just the brother, of the musician, Jandra, who had so captivated everyone the evening before.

He was handsome by either human or Romulan standards, although that obviously meant nothing. The Romulan in charge on Kalis Three had been even more handsome, and his clinical torture and butchery of her friends and colleagues—and brother!—had literally stolen her sanity. Only their cousins the Vulcans had been able to help her reclaim her mind. And more: they had taught her the mind rules; she had achieved a halting mastery over her emotions. With the Vulcans' help, she had dealt with the rage, the hatred. Out of both gratitude and necessity, she had sworn herself to logic—insofar as human frailty permitted. She had attained a measure of peace.

It had never been easy, but over the years she had managed to maintain a precarious hold on it. Even during those first moments when the dark-skinned commander from the *Enterprise* had explained her reason for coming, had outlined the unlikely mission to Temaris, she had managed to hold on.

But now, faced not with theory but with reality, she wondered if she was, after all, strong enough, if she had absorbed enough of the Vulcan disciplines in which she had submerged herself. She had thought she could control, or at least overcome, her emotions. Otherwise, she would not have accepted the Federation's invitation, even for an opportunity such as this.

But now, with the Romulan actually standing beside her, close enough to reach out and touch, his features echoing those of that other, she felt it all coming back: the fear, the hatred, the *loathing* that had built up in her during that year on Kalis Three as the deaths, each more horrible than the last, had come, one by one, at the hands of one who could have been this one's brother. The fear she could control: it was an animal reaction, simple stimulus-response, a function of the lower brain and easily dealt with.

The hatred was more difficult. In that year, it had become so ingrained in every fiber of her being, it had become almost instinctual. In all likelihood, the strength it had given her—even the logical Vulcans had admitted it—was the very strength that had allowed her to survive where so many others had died. *I will survive to see you dead!* had been her mantra, and it had worked.

But this was a different world, a different time, and in this world and time, that mantra was one that could destroy her, not save her. It could steal from her the opportunity of a lifetime.

But most of all, it was illogical. Dajan was not responsible for the events on Kalis Three. He was, after all, an archaeologist like herself, not a military tyrant and torturer like the creature on Kalis Three. Not for the first time, she yearned to be Vulcan instead of a weak-willed human, to be free of the emotions that haunted her, although she knew full well that, without the same training and discipline she had undergone, Vulcans themselves could succumb to emotions as easily as any human. It was, in fact, that very weakness that had long ago led to the development of the discipline.

She drew in tepid air and let it go, imagining all emotion was exhaled with her breath. Time to concentrate on the task at hand. This was Temaris, and the exhilarating scientific opportunity that existed here far outweighed the momentary—and completely illogical —agonies that scraped at her mind.

"Come," she said abruptly, turning and striding toward the beginnings of the hills that flanked and protected the valley. "There is a structure I would find before all others."

"Exodus Hall," Dajan said quickly, without thinking.

"Yes, I have found—"

She stopped, cutting herself off and turning to face the Romulan archaeologist. "How did you know? This was not mentioned in the briefing, to my recollection, and I was not aware that my theories had reached the Romulan archaeological journals."

Swallowing, he made his way up the incline toward her. "They have not," he admitted as he drew closer, "but there is an underground we are occasionally able to avail ourselves of, as I would suspect there is in the Federation."

She was silent a long moment, then nodded, wondering. Surely he must know that such information, in the wrong hands, could lead to not only his arrest but the arrest of his colleagues—conspirators. Romulans, she was certain, did not distinguish among types of information when it came to exchanges in either direction with non-Romulans. Archaeology or weapons design, it was all the same to them. What was theirs was theirs, and anyone who communicated secretly with the enemy was himself an enemy—and soon dead. Or was he so confident of the changes in his government that he dared make himself so vulnerable? So confident that this so-called peace initiative would actually bear significant fruit?

"I will not deny it," she said finally, "but it surprises me that you do not."

"It would be inefficient to deny existing truth when new truth is what we are all seeking here."

"That sounds almost Vulcan."

He shrugged. "They are our cousins, after all."

She flinched inwardly but kept her shell intact. That the Vulcans—her saviors—were cousin to the Romulans—her torturers—was not something she liked to dwell upon. The possibility that somewhere deep beneath a Vulcan's disciplined surface existed the potential for the kind of cruelty the Romulans displayed daily was not pleasant to consider, for it carried with it the inevitable implication that, if you dug deep enough, you would find the same horrors in *any* race, in any *being*. Even herself. Particularly in herself, where, after Kalis Three, the digging would not need to be deep at all.

"Come then," she said. "If you know of my name for the structure, you must also know what I hope it contains and how I hope to locate it."

"Not entirely," he admitted. "What I have read has been incomplete and perhaps badly translated. Completeness and accuracy, while highly prized, are rarely achievable when secrecy is most highly prized of all."

She found herself momentarily tempted to smile, remembering the Romulan data on the Dozadi worlds she had once seen, or for that matter, the rumors that still persisted in some circles about artifacts supposedly recovered from the mysterious Talos star group despite Starfleet's rigidly enforced General Order No. 7.

"Very well," she said, "as we walk, you can tell me of your incomplete and inaccurate knowledge, and I can tell you what has been lost in the translation."

"I would be honored."

Together, they made their way higher, the powder-fine sand squeaking softly under their boots as they talked.

"Remarkable, Captain." Commander Hiran managed to tinge the words with an obligatory disdain while his smile indicated only soft-edged envy of the trees and grass and multitude of plants that lined the winding paths of the *Enterprise*'s botanical garden.

"It's just one of the perks of being assigned to a Constitution-class starship, Commander," Kirk assured him. The guided tour had, at Hiran's request, gotten under way early, before his so-far-amicable relationship with Kirk could be "complicated" by Tiam's opening salvos on the diplomatic front.

"And you say anyone in your crew—not just officers —is allowed to make use of this facility?"

"Crew and this time out, passengers." A half dozen of the musicians walked the paths or stood at the viewports on either side, watching Temaris turn slowly beneath them as the *Enterprise* and *Galtizh* continued in standard orbit.

"Remarkable," Hiran repeated, shaking his head, the original trace of disdain gone from his tone, "truly remarkable. You will see nothing to match the like of this on the *Galtizh.*"

"It is a smaller ship," Kirk said graciously. "Less room for the amenities."

Hiran almost laughed. "Amenities, yes. There are a few for Centurion Tiam and his wife, but little for others. But tell me, Captain Kirk, do you hold any hopes for this 'ferryboat ride' we are both on?"

Kirk thought a moment. "Hopes, yes. Expectations, no."

Hiran nodded. "Myself as well." The Romulan paused, eyeing Kirk speculatively, as if debating whether to go on. Finally, he apparently resolved his inner argument. "I will tell you honestly, Federation captain, my hopes were higher at the start of the ride—before I became familiar with Centurion Tiam—than they are now. Does that surprise you?"

Kirk smiled. "Only that you admit it."

Hiran shrugged. "Then I will admit something else, and this just *may* surprise you. It is my secret hope that the archaeologists determine that the Erisians were the ancestors of you humans. Do you know why?"

Kirk shook his head, keeping his expression mild. "No, why?" Hiran had been right. This *was* a surprise.

"Because then my government would be obliged by its own terms to give the Federation access to this world. We will be responsible for carving the first path through the forest of the Neutral Zone. It will be a beginning."

"I hope my own government would see it in the same light if the Erisians prove instead to be your ancestors," Kirk said, wondering if indeed they would, but wondering even more if the Romulans would live up to the obligation Hiran suggested they would have.

"As do I. But tell me, Kirk, now that we are exchanging confidences, how real is this so-called Probe my government denies?"

"*Very* real, Hiran," Kirk said, sobering, remembering. "And very dangerous."

"Indeed? You have seen it personally?"

"I have. And I have heard it. I have seen what it can

do. I could show you the records, as we have offered to show your government."

"And I would be glad to look, but I fear it would not change anything. Tiam will no more listen to me than to you. Nor would those whose orders he follows."

"The Interim Government?"

Hiran shrugged. "The Government never speaks with one voice even in the best of times. In times like these, there are a thousand, and none to whom you can assign a face or a clear-cut purpose."

"We have heard there is a power struggle, but—"

"When is there not? The forces of reform—reform according to the lights of those like myself—hold sway now. Or they did when I last saw the Citadel. But their organization, like all organizations, is doubtless riddled with those who hold opposing views." Hiran shook his head. "Whoever forced the selection of Centurion Tiam was no friend to reform, I will tell you."

Startled at such seeming openness, Kirk suddenly wondered if this Hiran was genuine. His instincts, from the first moment he had seen the Romulan's smiling image, told him he was, but . . .

Kirk looked up to see Hiran tentatively touching a booted toe to the grass at the edge of the path they stood on. "Is it permitted to depart from the paths?"

Kirk blinked as, for a moment, he saw both the paths at their feet and the greater, more restrictive paths that Romulan and human minds so often refused to leave.

"It's not encouraged," Kirk said, smiling, "but it is certainly permitted, particularly for a distinguished guest such as yourself."

Leading the way, Kirk moved off the path onto the grass.

* * *

"Your third formula was missing entirely from the material I saw," Dajan said. "It is no wonder I had difficulty visualizing the overall effect."

They were more than a mile from the mouth of the valley, looking down from one of the highest points in the westward hills. The dozen pairs of Federation and Romulan archaeologists in the ruins below were like insects scurrying through an unending maze. From here, the extent of the ruins was even more apparent than from the beam-down point. It was by far the most extensive Erisian site ever studied, and as such—

"There is more to the visualizing than the formulas," Audrea said, "just as there is more to a symphony than the mathematical relationship of the individual notes. The formulas are simply aids that point out certain essential relationships, pulling them, so to speak, out of the ocean of other, lesser relationships, the way a musician identifies and isolates major themes and structure. The ultimate design of the finished product is still a matter of intuition. Or it is with me at any rate, although I hope someday to have enough data to allow me to develop equations for it all."

"Never allow my sister to hear you speak so," Dajan said, almost laughing. "To her, all music is mystery and inspiration. To analyze it with something as crude as mathematics would strike her as sacrilege."

"Unfortunately, many humans feel as she does."

"But you are human and you do not."

"Humans are not so easily categorized. In any event, I have been subject to Vulcan training. Perhaps some of my humanity has been lost."

Abruptly, she realized she was straying onto dangerous ground. And wasting precious time discussing irrelevancies. "There," she said, pointing toward a segment of the ruins near the far side of the valley, "that is one of the nodes. It is larger than any I have seen, but this site is more extensive than any I have ever seen. Do you see it?"

Dajan followed her finger with his eyes, searching the ruins. "I cannot be positive," he admitted.

"That single wall," she said, "with the others crumbled around it, that is the center. If the others still stood—"

"Yes, I see it now," he said. "Remarkable, Dr. Benar. I would never in a thousand years have recognized that for what it is, even with your third formula."

"It comes with practice, that is all. I have been on two Erisian worlds and have studied the records of all, as well as everything I have been able to find on any culture that bears even a minor resemblance to them. Given time, you will be able to do the same."

"Perhaps. I suspect, however, that you are being overly generous in your estimate, Dr. Benar. But now, if that is one of the nodes—but not the principal one?— then there should be another . . ." His voice trailed off as his eyes scanned the ruins, following its broken patterns, still clear after all these millennia. Not a right angle was to be found anywhere, and even straight lines were nonexistent except for brief spans within certain of the nodes.

"There," he said abruptly, pointing, this time to a collection of broken walls near the center of the valley.

"In all likelihood, yes. And the principal node, in a pattern of this size—"

"Yes, if your formulas are correct, there would be two."

She nodded. "Yes, precisely."

Within minutes, both principal nodes had been located, and a feeling of triumph was coursing through her, almost drowning out the ever more distant cries of Kalis Three. And Exodus Hall . . .

It was there! Double the size of any she had seen before, it was, she realized, the most nearly intact structure in the valley. Maybe, just maybe, this time—

Forgetting even to inform her partner, she began to make her way down the slope.

Entering the *Galtizh* conference room at 0900, Handler, whose preconference nerves had kept him from sleep most of the night, discreetly hid a yawn. Riley noticed and just as discreetly pretended not to. This was Handler's first major conference, and Riley felt sure he knew what the younger man was feeling. He had felt the same way himself more than once. He had not, truth be told, slept all that well himself last night.

On the other hand, Centurion Tiam and his aides, including the ominously unreadable Subcenturion Kital, looked thoroughly alert and rested, without the faintest indication of a need or desire to yawn. Riley couldn't, in fact, imagine Kital yawning under any circumstances. Or sleeping, for that matter, or doing anything other than hovering silently in the background. As for Tiam himself, yawning for him was probably like everything else: he would do it only if he was certain it would prove to his advantage. Riley had watched Tiam the evening before, while his wife, Jandra, had awed the crowd with her playing. Tiam had been neither appreciative spectator nor sympathetic husband. He had been a house counter, so to speak, his eyes darting about, coldly gauging the reactions of the others. Riley had also seen Jandra's face when she had been with Tiam earlier in the evening and again when he had approached Penalt with his request that she be allowed to "indulge herself" at the piano. Those were, in fact, the reasons Riley had made the effort—and a powerful effort it had taken—to transfer his attention from Jandra at the Steinway to Tiam in the audience. And if there was one thing Riley quickly became certain of, it was that it had been Tiam's idea, not hers, that she play then and there. And that there was no love lost between the two. Tiam had put her on display, and she had obliged.

But once she sat down and began to play . . . For those moments, the serenity of her features had told him, she was beyond her husband's reach. Beyond the reach of everything but the music she was producing.

Pushing the memory away, Riley took his place at the conference table, a small tricorder before him and Ensign Handler at his left elbow, a datapad at the ready. Water carafes and both round and square drinking glasses had been set in the center of the table by a pair of the *Galtizh*'s functionaries—the *Enterprise* would provide its own freshly distilled spring water when the talks moved to the *Enterprise* the following day.

If there were to be any talks the following day.

Riley was not so sure. But then, he never was. Despite his numerous and sometimes impressive successes, he was never fully confident that things wouldn't fall apart the minute he opened his mouth. *But it's that very uncertainty and the alertness and thoroughness it engenders that gives you the edge,* Kirk had said years ago. *Always* appear *totally confident, but the day you* feel *totally confident is the day to hang it up because you're bound to make a mistake.*

Riley had spent the last few days filling his head

with Romulan psychology, attitudes, beliefs—and yes, stereotypes—but little of it, he suspected, would prove useful in dealing with Tiam. Such generic studies—of a race, not an individual—rarely did, any more than studying humans en masse would lead to an understanding of how, say, Dr. McCoy would react to any given diplomatic stimulus. As always, Riley found himself preparing to rely on something that, in their own disparate ways, both Captain Kirk and Ambassador Sarek had advised him to rely upon a long time ago.

Trust your instincts, the captain had said.

And Sarek, in paying modest tribute to the sometimes usefulness of "human spontaneity," had confirmed it.

And this time, instinct told Kevin Riley: Start with a reality check. He and Tiam could spout polite or not-so-polite platitudes at each other all day, could even make solemn promises to each other, but none of it would mean a thing unless both sides were operating in the same universe—in the real universe.

And the Romulan Interim Government's initial response to the data concerning the Probe's movement toward Romulan territory was clear evidence that *someone* in the Interim Government was not operating in the real universe. In the real universe, the Probe existed. It had come within a whisker of destroying Earth. It had disabled Federation and Klingon ships. It had been coming from the general direction of the Neutral Zone when it had first been spotted, and now it was returning along that same path.

And the Romulans, presumably with no attempt to investigate the truth or falsity of the Federation's information, had simply and forcefully denied, not once but twice, that the Probe existed. On the other hand, as Kirk

had suggested when they had discussed the latest
Romulan response and Riley's proposed diplomatic
reality check, if it was a case of the Romulans not
needing to verify its existence . . .

"Ambassador Tiam," Riley began, "we have received
only hours ago new data regarding the location and
course of the object we have unofficially designated 'the
Probe.' Are you familiar with that object? Or with our
previous transmissions of data regarding it to your
government?"

Tiam's eyes widened momentarily before he assembled a moderate scowl. "I am of course familiar with the
fiction the Federation is attempting to perpetrate. What
I fear I am not familiar with is the reason the Federation
persists in its attempts."

Riley sighed heavily. "We persist, Ambassador Tiam,
for the same reason I persist in sitting in this chair rather
than falling through it to the floor. The chair exists. The
Probe exists. It has done major damage to Earth. It has
temporarily disabled a number of Klingon and Federation starships. It has demonstrated the capability to
destroy entire worlds in a matter of days, if not hours. It
has now passed through the Neutral Zone and has
entered—possibly reentered—Romulan space. It has
also recently accelerated so that it could reach the
vicinity of your homeworlds in little more than a day."

" 'Reentered,' Commander Riley? Are you now claiming this fiction of yours originated in the Empire?"

"Not at all, Ambassador Tiam. If we thought it
had—if we thought it was something manufactured by
Romulans—I doubt that we would be sitting here today."

"Very well, then, Commander Riley. If you are not

accusing the Romulan Empire of anything in regard to this fiction of yours, I see no point in discussing it further."

"But I do, Ambassador Tiam." Riley slid a paper across the table toward the Romulans. "These are the most recent coordinates, together with a precise projection of its path, assuming it does not again change course. It will soon be beyond the range of Federation ships on our side of the Neutral Zone, so any further tracking will be up to the Empire."

"You wish us to track this fiction of yours, Commander Riley? Surely you do not wish permission to enter Romulan territory to track it yourself!"

"We could not even if we wished and if your government granted us permission, Ambassador Tiam. It is already almost beyond the range of our sensors, and its current speed is such that it would be impossible to overtake."

"So you have turned this fiction over to us? Is that what you are saying, Commander Riley?"

"No, Ambassador Tiam, that is not what I am saying." Riley paused. This was going nowhere. He and Tiam could trade clever—or not-so-clever—assertions and denials for hours, and it would get them nowhere. Or he could accept Tiam's denial and go on to other matters, and *that* would get them less than nowhere.

Trust your instinct.

"What I *am* saying, Ambassador Tiam, is that the Probe—or whatever you choose to call it—is *not* a fiction. It is reality, possibly a very grim reality. In the period since your government was notified of its existence and its course, it has passed well within range of the sensors of at least one of your outposts. Your

128

government—or its outposts—know it is a reality. And until our governments—or at least you and I, officially or unofficially—can come to an agreement on something as basic as the inarguable reality of this very concrete object, I fail to see any point in even trying to discuss any of the countless other issues about which there is ample room for *legitimate* differences of opinion. We would simply be wasting our time."

And with that, Riley stood up from the table and, trailed by an agitated Handler, strode from the room.

"A peculiar game, Kirk," Hiran observed, "hurling a massive ball at a set of distant sticks rather than at one's opponent."

They were on the rec deck now, watching one of the musicians and an off-duty ensign on one of the bowling lanes.

"Humans have many peculiar games, Commander," Kirk acknowledged. "You should discuss the matter with my science officer if you have the chance. He has any number of interesting theories to account for them."

"Ah, yes, Mr. Spock—your first officer as well, is he not?"

Kirk nodded, but Hiran said no more. Ever since the time for the opening of the diplomatic session had come and gone, the Romulan had seemed distracted, noting the time every few minutes.

"Was this always your desire, Kirk," Hiran asked suddenly, "to be in the military?"

Kirk's eyes widened slightly. "To be captain of a starship, yes. To be in the military . . ." He shrugged.

"Are the two not inseparable?"

"In a way, I suppose," Kirk said. "Starfleet is less

military now than it was, and it will be less military yet
in the future. Particularly if these talks are successful." A
platitude, he knew, but true.

"I never wanted a military career myself," Hiran said
abruptly. "My elder sister had already fulfilled the
conscription quota. But then, as now, it was the only way
out of the Provinces. University degrees are still reserved
only for military veterans and the children of privileged
parents—which is to say those close to the current ruling
party. Is it thus in your Federation?"

Kirk shook his head. "I'm the equivalent of what
you'd call a provincial. I came from farm country, a
place called Iowa."

"'Iowa,'" Hiran repeated the untranslated English
word, as if he liked the sound of it, and Kirk absently
noted the similarity to the Romulan name for the world
they were orbiting, Lihalla.

"Our educational system is theoretically based solely
upon ability," Kirk said, "although that wasn't always
true."

"Then perhaps we shall also discover its wisdom
someday." Hiran sighed. "I always wanted to be an
engineer. I wanted to build things. Instead, I am here.
Then again, if I had been an engineer, I might never have
met humans." His mood seemed to brighten at the
thought.

"Have you met many humans?"

"You and your colleagues are the first!" Hiran said
heartily, clapping him familiarly on the back. At almost
the same instant, Scotty's voice rolled from the *Enterprise* PA system.

"Captain Kirk, report to the bridge."

Then Hiran's communicator sounded as well.

As he answered it, the two captains eyed each other,

130

and Kirk was suddenly all too aware of the uniform his shipboard guest was wearing.

Though it was little more than three kilometers from their hilltop vantage point to the structure identified as Exodus Hall, it took Dajan and Dr. Benar more than an hour to reach it. Partly it was because the sand made slow going, but it was also because there was no such thing as a direct route, short of beaming up to one of the ships and beaming back down at the Hall coordinates. Benar, however, would have none of it, and Dajan could not disagree. To move through the ruins as the Erisians must have moved through the undamaged streets and structures was one more attempt to see it as they had seen it, to absorb the patterns not from above but from ground level, a player in the orchestra, not a spectator in the second balcony.

Not that either of them could ever truly be a player. Both could, with the aid of mathematics, spot the patterns. Walking the streets, they could sense that patterns existed, could come around a curve and see some aspect of the ruins the patterns had told them to expect. They could not, however, have devised the patterns originally, could not even devise new, lesser patterns, variations on a theme, nor alter the ones that existed without shattering them into meaninglessness.

We can see and recognize and appreciate, Benar thought as Exodus Hall finally appeared before them, *but we cannot build. That is something only the Erisians have been able to do—so far. But if we can find them and learn from them . . .*

Under ordinary circumstances, she would have spent days surveying the exterior of the hall, documenting it down to the molecular level before even attempting an entrance, but these were not ordinary circumstances. They were highly unusual circumstances, and they gave her a window of opportunity—a window that could, courtesy of Tiam and whoever controlled him, be slammed shut in her face at any moment. After a single survey around the squat, low-domed building, she returned to what the tricorder had told her was the point of least resistance—a small section of curving wall, a tiny, igloolike annex. Extruded and exposed to every sand-laden wind of the last hundred millennia, it was near to collapse.

From her kit, she took a small, short-range, phaserlike device. Normally, it was one of the dozens of the tools used to excavate buried artifacts and organic remains. This particular one was programmed to distinguish between inorganic and organic material, even when fossilized. Its normal use was in extracting fossils from the rock strata in which they were found. Ten careful minutes with this device, monitored moment by moment with a tricorder, could replace dozens of hours with tiny picks, tweezers, and brushes.

Setting it to full power, she brought it within an inch of what her tricorder had told her was the weakest spot in this weakest section of the walls. She pressed the activator, felt the tool hum and grow warm in her hand, heard the faint whine as the wall surface began to react, to peel away, saw the first layer disappear in the greenish glow that coated the area for several centimeters around, heard the sandy shuffle of feet behind her and—

Audrea Benar clamped down on a scream as visions of another time crashed down on her, visions she had thought—had hoped—that the years on Vulcan had forever banished. A similar device was in her hand, but she was inside a structure, not outside, and the footsteps were echoing in the corridor outside her room—her cell—and she knew that Reelan was coming for her once again, and—

Something touched her shoulder, and she spun and saw Reelan's hated face above her and she lurched to her feet, raising the excavating tool and thrusting it at him, screaming her fury and confused terror.

Sulu's first mistake was not in telling the computer to give him everything it had on the Erisian Ascendancy but in neglecting to instruct it to interrupt his studies when the archaeological teams were ready to beam down. As it was, the words *Unfortunately Dr. Erisi was unable to visit Temaris before the war broke out* made him suddenly realize, first, why he was cramming on the Ascendancy in the first place, and second, that he had been at it for over three hours and Benar and Dajan had doubtless been down on Temaris—without him—for at least half that time.

"Computer, interrupt session but don't lose my place," he said, darting from his quarters and heading for the transporter room at a run.

"You have a bead on Dr. Benar?" he asked, catching his breath at the transporter room door. "And that Romulan she's with?"

"Dr. Benar, yes, Commander," the ensign at the controls said, "but what Romulan—"

"The head of the Romulan archaeological team."

"Nothing on him, sir. But doesn't the Romulan ship keep track—"

"I suppose they do. Look, just put me down wherever Dr. Benar is." Sulu hopped onto the platform and positioned himself on a circle.

"Yes, sir. She's down in the middle of the ruins,

though, sir, and moving. The way those things are laid out, it could be tricky."

"Don't put me down right on top of her. In fact, give me a hundred meters or so."

He didn't want to startle her or make her think he was keeping an eye on her, although that was exactly what he was doing—or supposed to be doing, at any rate. And that was his second mistake. Part of what he'd read that morning talked about the "patterns" the Erisians had used in designing their cities, and he had been with Benar and Dajan when they had, in effect, dipped their toes in the edges of the ruins the day before, but nothing prepared him for what he found himself in when the transporter field let him go. Enough of the structures had collapsed so that he got a glimpse of the two archaeologists, but enough other structures remained totally or partially standing to hide them roughly three seconds later. And when he headed after them, he was hopelessly disoriented within minutes.

"Patterns!" he muttered to himself. "Patterns of confusion is more like it."

For a moment, he thought he caught a glimpse of Dajan, but when the figure turned to glance over his shoulder as he rounded a corner, Sulu saw it was one of the ambassador's aides—Jutak, was it? The one who'd trailed after Benar and Dajan at the introductory meeting, anyway. But the aide's subcenturion uniform was gone, replaced by the rumpled, nondescript clothes worn by most of the archaeologists. Puzzled, Sulu trotted forward, but by the time he reached the corner, the aide was as thoroughly gone as Benar and Dajan.

After that, he came across two of the dozen Federation-Romulan pairs, but that was all. He thought briefly of contacting Benar by communicator, but decided against it. For one thing, it would—again—look as if he was following her. For another, he doubted that any directions she could give him would help. And of course he felt silly about the whole affair.

Finally, he signaled to be beamed back up to the *Enterprise*. "What happened, sir?" the ensign asked innocently.

"Where's Benar now?"

The ensign smothered a smile and checked his instruments. "About a kilometer from the first time, sir. But now she seems to be staying pretty much in the same place. Try again, sir?"

Sulu nodded, smiling ruefully. "A little closer this time, Ensign."

"Yes, sir."

When the transporter field released him this time, Benar and her Romulan opposite number were in clear view, their backs to him, walking slowly along one side of a low but massive domed structure that looked better preserved than anything he had seen on his earlier foray. Benar's eyes were glued to the readout of her tricorder, while the Romulan followed not far behind with his somewhat prehistoric version of the same thing.

They stopped. And then Benar was running her tricorder over a spot where the wall's gentle curve bulged out three or four meters, like a bubble trying to escape. While Dajan stood by, Benar put the tricorder away and dug a smaller instrument from her kit. An excavating tool of some kind, it looked like from Sulu's distance.

He began to walk forward, putting his best casual face on. As he approached, Benar kneeled down and held the tool close to the wall. A moment later, a greenish, phaserlike glow spread out several centimeters in all directions on the wall. The Romulan, who had been standing a meter behind her, took another step closer, leaning down to watch more closely, and as he did, his own kit brushed against her shoulder.

For a moment, nothing happened, but then, just as Sulu was only yards away, getting ready to wave and call out as casual a greeting as he could muster, Benar stiffened.

And screamed, an animallike mixture of screech and growl.

She swung about, still on her knees in the sand, swinging the still-glowing tool toward the Romulan's face.

Acting purely on instinct—"Keep an eye out for trouble," Kirk had said, and this definitely looked like trouble—Sulu lunged forward as best he could in the sand. The Romulan was backing away while Benar lurched to her feet, jabbing the glowing excavating tool at his face. *"Reelan!"* she shouted, her voice now more growl than scream.

Further words were cut off as Sulu grabbed her from behind, pinning her arms at her sides. For an instant, her body writhed and struggled bruisingly, making Sulu wish he had been able to learn Spock's nerve pinch.

Then, in a split second, she stopped, held herself totally motionless, her body like living rock as every muscle tensed against every other muscle.

Just as abruptly, she went limp, the tool—the weapon—plopping onto the sand at her feet, her breath going out in a moan.

"What the hell's going on here?" Sulu maintained his grip on Benar while he pulled the Romulan's name from his memory. "Dajan, are you okay?"

"I—think so." Dajan's voice was shaking, his face ashen, as if he were going into shock.

"Dr. Benar?"

She shuddered, but her voice was steady. "Commander Sulu?"

"That's right."

"You can release me now. I have recovered."

Tentatively, he let her go, reaching down quickly to pick the tool from the sand as he did. She stepped away, her body once again stiffly erect, her face as impassive as Spock's had ever been.

"So," Sulu said, looking from one to the other, "one of you want to clue me in? What happened?"

"She called me Reelan," the Romulan said, his face still several shades too light.

"That's a name, then?" Sulu looked to Benar, who gave a barely perceptible nod. The way she had screamed it, it had sounded more like a curse.

"On Kalis Three," she said. "I thought my days on Vulcan had closed the door on that episode, but it apparently has not. For a moment—" She snapped the words off, her lips clamping shut.

"You had a flashback," Sulu said, dredging the term up from a pop psychology report he'd once read. "Something reminded you of something back there, and all of a sudden, you were there again, in your head."

She swallowed, nodding. She looked toward Dajan. "I will be more careful in the future."

Dajan had, if possible, gone even paler. "You were on Kalis Three?"

"She was," Sulu answered for her. "It's not something she'd like to dwell on, though, if you don't mind."

For a long moment, the Romulan was silent except for a breathing that seemed suddenly labored. He closed his eyes for another moment, as if to bring his breathing, his pounding heart, under control.

"Reelan," he said, looking at Benar. "I had not thought to hear that name again."

She nodded. "He was the commander of the forces on Kalis Three."

Dajan sighed and lowered his eyes to the sand at her feet. "He was also my brother."

EIGHT

———————— ☆ ————————

Still hundreds of parsecs away, the entity detected the world's voice.

It was still too distant for the crystal sensor to pick out individual voices of the primitives, individual songs, but even at this distance it detected a change. In a millisecond, it analyzed that change, comparing the old and the new. In another millisecond, it assigned meaning to that change: an emotion its creators had called sadness, perhaps despair.

And the voice was fainter. Normally, the full focus of the crystal sensor would have produced a soft but joyous symphony. Now, strained to its limits, it achieved only a barely audible dirge.

The entity raised its own voice to the peak of its power, sending it soundlessly through the emptiness of space to set the molecules of that distant world's air and water in motion to produce the language of the primitives that swam its oceans, a language that, in millennia past, it had helped to shape, as it had helped to shape the languages of a thousand other worlds. None of the primitives on this or any other world were within a thousand lifetimes of the True Language. Only a precious few had shown even the first signs of developing the power of Speech. Most still clung stubbornly to the crude, matter-bound voices that gave them only the power to communicate and to remember, not the essential power to control the world around them.

But there was always hope, an expectation that, someday, the entity's mission would be successful and it would return the news to its creators. Its creators' instructions told it this was so.

Abruptly, the approaching world's voice began to change.

The tempo increased. The volume grew as all the primitives raised their voices, responding to the distant call.

The sadness was replaced by hope, but also by fear.

A single cry set the crystal sensor dancing, a cry not from a single primitive but one that arose simultaneously from all that still survived on that distant world:

Save us!

"On my way, Mr. Scott," Kirk said to the nearest comm unit, "with Commander Hiran."

"I'm sorry, Captain," the Romulan commander said grimly, "but that will be impossible." He gestured at his communicator. "That was the signal that means I am needed on the *Galtizh.*"

Kirk hesitated. "Probably for the same reason they want me on the bridge, Commander, whatever that turns out to be." He turned back to the comm unit. "Belay that last, Scotty. Commander Hiran has been summoned to his ship. I'm escorting him to the transporter room."

"Aye, Captain."

Kirk turned and briskly led the way to the nearest 'lift. "Trouble with the talks, you imagine?"

Hiran nodded. "Almost certainly." The Romulan scowled as the 'lift doors slid shut. "That Tiam is as much a diplomat as I am an archaeologist."

"You don't sound very optimistic."

"I have been given little cause by our friend Tiam."

"There are still you and I."

Hiran snorted. "For all the good it will do!"

"It can do no harm," Kirk said as the 'lift opened and they stepped out.

Hiran's eyes met Kirk's in a sidelong glance as they hurried down the corridor. "I hope you are right, Federation captain."

"So do I, Hiran," Kirk said softly as they reached the transporter room door and entered. "So do I."

"Incoming, sir," the ensign at the transporter controls warned, and Kirk put a lightly restraining hand on Hiran's arm.

Moments later, Riley and Handler and a pair of ensigns sparkled into existence on the platform.

"Clear, sir," the transporter tech said, and Hiran stepped onto the platform, his eyes scanning Riley's face impassively as they passed each other.

Hiran centered himself on a circle and turned to face Kirk. "We will speak again," the Romulan said, "no matter what these others say."

Kirk nodded. "We will."

As Hiran flashed from view, Kirk turned to Riley and Handler, waiting in the corridor door. The accompanying ensigns had already scurried off.

"I take it, Ambassador," Kirk said as the three of them started toward the 'lift, "that your early return doesn't indicate an early and amicable settlement to all our differences."

Riley winced. "Right, sir, it doesn't," he said, and hurried through what had happened and why he had taken the tack he had. They were on the bridge by the time he finished.

Kirk turned to Spock when Riley fell silent. "How about it, Spock? Is there any chance—any chance at all—that the Romulans really *don't* know of the existence of the Probe? Other than what the Federation has told them, that is?"

"That they have direct observational knowledge of the object is a virtual certainty, Captain, considering the course it has taken."

"Virtual?"

"As I am sure you know, Captain—"

"I know, Spock—*nothing* is *absolutely* certain, ever. So what you're saying is, by normal human standards, it *is* a certainty."

"By human standards, yes, Captain." A minutely arched eyebrow perhaps indicated his opinion of human standards. "However, that Centurion Tiam has been apprised of this observational knowledge is less certain."

Riley let fly an Irish curse. "So much for instinct!"

"Before you and your instinct hand in your resignations, Kevin," said Kirk, "take a second to let your brain catch up. You were right either way. If Tiam knows about the Probe, he's lying and you were right to call him on it. If he doesn't know about it, he's being lied *to,* so you called his superiors on it, through him, which could be even better. *Someone* was lying, and whoever it is,

142

Tiam or his boss back in the Citadel, has to know that we know it."

Riley was silent a moment, then shook his head and grinned. "I would've figured that out, sir, eventually." Then he sobered. "The question is, what do we do if Tiam refuses to back down? If he keeps insisting the Probe doesn't exist? Do we continue to refuse to talk?"

Kirk shrugged. "You're the ambassador. It's your call."

Riley turned to the communications station and Lieutenant Kittay. "I assume you can reach Admiral Cartwright or the President?"

Kittay's eyes widened slightly at the mention of the President, but she nodded. "Yes, sir."

Before Riley could issue any instructions, however, an incoming call took the lieutenant's attention. She turned toward Kirk after listening briefly.

"It's Commander Sulu, Captain," she said. "Something—"

"On speakers, Lieutenant."

"Aye-aye, sir."

"Kirk here, Mr. Sulu."

"Captain, I thought you and Hiran—"

"We were, but the talks are stalled and he's back on the *Galtizh*. Now what's going on down there with the archaeologists?"

"Nothing too archaeological, Captain. I think you should come down and take a look."

"Come down?" Kirk frowned.

"Yes, sir. You remember that little assignment you gave me?"

Oops. So that's it. "Ambassador Riley and I will be right down."

Minutes later, Kirk and Riley materialized in the

143

shadow of Exodus Hall. Sulu stood waiting between Dr. Benar and the head of the Romulan archaeological team—Dajan? Was that his name? Jandra's brother at any rate, and any brother of the woman who'd flattened Penalt so definitively had to be one of the good guys.

"So, Mr. Sulu, report."

Succinctly, Sulu summarized what he'd seen. "She had a flashback," he concluded, "to Kalis Three. In one of her escape attempts, she'd used a similar tool, and the Romulan commander caught her in the act."

"Dr. Benar is not to blame," Dajan broke in, nervously apologetic. "It was my doing. I approached too closely while she was working. I was not aware of her experiences on Kalis Three. If I had known . . ."

"Yes," Sulu picked up when the Romulan archaeologist lowered his eyes and let his voice trail off, "it seems that there was more to the Romulans' insistence on having Dr. Benar head up the Federation team than a desire to 'make up' for Kalis Three." He nodded at Dajan. "This is the younger brother of Reelan, who was in command on Kalis Three."

Kirk almost laughed at this sudden knowledge and the visions it conjured up of scheming Romulans and a gloating Dr. McCoy delivering a vintage "I told you so!"

"So," Kirk said, sobering, remembering the warnings from within the Empire itself, "this so-called peace initiative, even if it's genuine, was sabotaged before it started." He turned to the Romulan. "What can *you* tell us?"

Dajan swallowed nervously. "Very little, I fear. Except to assure you that not all Romulans share in our leaders' madness, Captain Kirk. And that many of us are as much victims of it as Dr. Benar and her colleagues."

"How so?" Not that Kirk had any doubts. When people were ruled not by consent but by might and fear, that was how it worked.

"After Kalis Three, my brother was considered disgraced, not because of the atrocities he committed there but because, in the end, he failed. Someone escaped to tell the tale. He soon disappeared, in all likelihood executed. Our parents were forced into ritual suicide. My sister and I were exiled to the Provinces."

Something flickered in Dr. Benar's eyes, but no one could tell, in the brief instant it appeared, if it was sympathy or satisfaction.

"And yet you and your sister are both here," Kirk said, "involved in the first 'peace conference' between your people and ours in history."

"No one was more startled than Jandra and I. Until a few weeks ago, we were un-Orthodox in the extreme, but then, in a matter of days after the Praetor's death, it was as if Kalis Three had never happened. My sister was summoned to perform at the Praetor's funeral. Until then her husband, Tiam, had been nothing but a pompous nonentity, but he was selected to represent the Empire at this conference. And I was pulled back from the Provinces—from a surprisingly promising dig on a very barren planet—to 'head' the Empire's archaeological team." He paused, shaking his head, now more dejected than nervous. "Now I see why—to insure that this conference fails."

"It will not fail because of me," Benar said flatly. "Now that I am aware of the additional difficulties facing us, I will be more vigilant. There will be no more incidents such as the one I allowed to develop this morning."

Kirk frowned. "You're saying, Dr. Benar, that you want to continue working with Dajan as if nothing has happened?"

"No, Captain. I am saying that I wish to continue to work with Dajan while maintaining a full and constant awareness of what happened, thereby preventing any recurrence." She looked to the Romulan archaeologist. "I do, that is, if kerDajan agrees."

Dajan looked up, startled not only at her desire to continue working with him but at this first use of his title. "I would be honored to continue, Dr. Benar."

"Then the matter is settled," Benar said. She glanced at Exodus Hall. "I would suggest we move as quickly as possible. This new knowledge indicates that our time on Temaris Four will be even more limited than any of us suspected."

Dajan nodded. "I agree. Let us get what we can, even if it ends tomorrow." Both seemed to have tuned out everyone else as their thoughts returned to Exodus Hall and the Erisians.

"You won't mind, Dr. Benar," Kirk said, "if Commander Sulu sticks with you for the duration, will you? Just to be safe?"

Benar eyed Sulu briefly, then nodded. "May I assume his timely appearance earlier was not entirely a coincidence, Captain?"

Kirk shrugged. "Mr. Sulu is more than a little interested in your work, and we *were* aware of your previous dealings with certain Romulans," Kirk admitted, "though we were no more aware of Dajan's relationship to them than you were."

"It is logical," Benar said, turning again toward Exodus Hall.

Kirk and Riley watched as the two archaeologists and Sulu made their way toward the building.

"There could be more to it than just the failure of the conference, Captain," Riley said finally. "Whoever's responsible for this may be hoping for an—an 'incident' that could not only break the conference but provoke a war."

Kirk nodded, remembering again the muffled voice from the heart of the Empire. *What better way to hasten the fall of peace-minded reformers than to raise the specter of war?*

"Whatever their plan is," Kirk said, reaching for his communicator to signal to be beamed up, "I can't imagine that it all rests on something as uncertain as what almost happened here. If they really are out to create an incident, they'll have more reliable—and probably more direct—plans up their sleeves."

Riley was nodding in agreement when the transporter energies gripped him.

Jutak, once again in his subcenturion's uniform, was waiting in his quarters when his superior returned.

"I take it you have news," the man said.

"I do." Jutak went on quickly to recount what he had seen at Exodus Hall between Dajan and Dr. Benar.

"Were you seen?"

Jutak swallowed nervously. "Not then, sir. However, I believe Sulu may have seen me earlier, in another part of the ruins."

"And he recognized you?"

"I do not know."

The man was silent for several seconds. "It does not matter," he said finally. "After this, the two of

147

them will doubtless keep well out of each other's reach, and Kirk will keep both under constant observation. There is nothing more to be done—with them." For the first time that Jutak could remember, he thought he could detect a faint smile on the other's almost fleshless lips.

"The sister?" Jutak wondered. "After her performance at the Praetor's funeral . . ." He let his voice trail off. Penalt would be the instrument, he thought. Her humiliation of the Federation musician at the reception would certainly provide an adequate motive.

"Perhaps." If there had been a smile, it was now gone. "Although I am still uncomfortable involving civilians, particularly when there are others who would serve our purpose equally well."

Jutak remained quiet. He knew whom the other meant.

But he knew equally well when to remain silent.

The enhanced sense of urgency almost had Sulu pacing in the sand as Benar worked to breach the wall. Everyone had been counting on the conference—and consequently the dig—to last at least several days. But now, knowing that the Romulans—or at least some faction among the Romulans—were deliberately sabotaging it, they also knew that the order to evacuate the planet could come at any minute. Sulu had trouble imagining how that knowledge must be affecting the archaeologists—and how they remained so outwardly calm. Professionalism, he thought, not to mention Benar's Vulcan training. To Sulu, what they might find here would be interesting, even fascinating, but to them, it must be like the tomb of Tutankhamen: the chance of a lifetime, of a *hundred* lifetimes! Benar had written

148

papers on the Ascendancy, though he had come across only a couple of them before his Erisian education had been interrupted by reality. Finally he turned to Dajan. "I was giving myself a crash course on Erisians this morning," he said, "but I hadn't gotten to the part about Exodus Halls yet. I've heard about them, but that's about all. They've been found on all the Ascendancy worlds so far, right?"

"That is correct, Commander," Dajan said. Sulu realized the archaeologist seemed relieved to speak, to have something to do to take his mind off the waiting. "I have never had the opportunity of viewing one in person, but I have read of Dr. Benar's discoveries. The theory, suggested by Dr. Erisi himself, is that the content of the Halls may tell us where the Erisians went, although none have yet been found intact enough to prove that theory one way or the other."

"What suggested the idea to Erisi?"

"All appeared to have been domed, as this one is. Dome fragments have been found, and they appeared to contain segments of a star map, with certain of the stars highlighted."

"Like a planetarium," Sulu said, but Dajan looked blank at the translation.

"An unchanging one, Commander," Benar said over her shoulder from where she still played the excavating tool over the thinning surface of the wall, "a static mosaic, unless their science was even further beyond ours than we suspect."

"So if this dome is intact—and contains a complete map—you'll be able to tell where the Erisians went?" Sulu asked.

"Perhaps," Dajan said, looking toward Benar, "but not from the map alone. Some of Dr. Benar's work indicates that the domes themselves might be more decorative than informative. The true information, the coordinates of the highlighted stars, may be held in a crystalline memory device. A number have been found in other Exodus Halls, but little information has been recovered from them. There was a definite lattice structure in all, and most retained the traces of a field that could be used to encode the structure with a high density of data. Unfortunately, the fields have thus far been so weakened, the lattice structure so altered by time, that the bulk of the data was lost, and what was recovered was unreliable."

Sulu felt his heart beating even faster as the true significance of this building finally sank in.

Sulu had to remind himself to keep breathing the musty air as he stood, head back, looking up at the domed ceiling of the Exodus Hall.

The archaeologists had been right. In the light of Dr. Benar's halogen lamp—designed for single rooms, not hundred-thousand-year-old planetariums—thousands of tiny points of light and hundreds of brighter ones glittered palely above them. Sealed for all that time, not a speck of dust marred the image. The floor, a marblelike substance the tricorder refused to identify, was smooth and untouched. Low benches of similarly anonymous material lined 90 percent of the circular wall.

And in the exact center, on a head-high pedestal, was a miniature duplicate of the dome, with only the highlighted stars visible.

Benar had hesitated only moments to look up at the dome, then had gone directly to the pedestal, her tricorder out.

"Intact," she said. "The lattice structure is stable. The magnetic field is faint but not erratic."

Sulu shivered at the words. The Erisians . . .

"We may have little time," Benar said. "KerDajan, it is my opinion that the instruments aboard the Federation ship would have a better chance of retrieving the data than would those aboard the Romulan ship. Do you agree?"

Dajan hesitated a moment, but only a moment. "It is obvious," he said, gesturing at the instrument in his hand, a primitive version of a tricorder.

"Then you have no objection to its being transferred to the *Enterprise?*"

He shook his head. "None. Though Tiam and others might."

"We will not tell them, then, until it is done." She looked at Sulu, who flipped open his communicator and began making arrangements.

NINE

☆

It had been a blue-green world—water-blue, brine-green, plankton-algae-ocean-green, it might have appeared to the eyes of the entity's creators, but to the entity itself it had been simply an ever-shifting combination of hundreds of wave-length-specific shades of blue and green, 90 percent obscured by the fog and clouds that dominated the humid atmosphere, punctuated here and there by basalt-black dots of bare worldskin thrusting out of the fertile waters. On the one day in a hundred that the mists parted, the primitives had sunned themselves on these rocky outcroppings, unlike the primitives on the previous world, unlike its own creators, who, until the Winnowing, were unable ever to leave the supporting water even for brief moments.

There were none who sunned themselves now. Now there were only structures, gray and sharp-edged, their lower reaches stabbing down into the water.

And the mites who had built them. Like the mites who had swarmed over the previous world and inhabited the spacegoing, metallic bubbles of air, they darted about in darkness, chattering meaninglessly, endlessly.

And the voices of the primitives were now clear and distinct.

Save us! they bellowed, now in ten thousand individual voices—the only voices that remained of the millions the entity had listened to and recorded and reassured and heartened on its dozens of visits to this world.

Ten thousand stories of the deaths of their fellows flowed into the crystal memory, and ten thousand stories of alteration and removal and torture.

The mites? it asked, and ten thousand voices, in ten thousand unmistakable ways, confirmed it.

Why do they do this? it asked, and ten thousand voices were silent in pain and bewilderment.

They will do it no more, the creators' instructions said, and the entity fell silent as it turned its attention fully to the mites and their structures and to those in the metallic bubbles of air it sensed darting through nearby space.

Spock looked up from the readouts. The Exodus Hall crystal lay in a darkened analysis chamber as twin intersecting sensor beams methodically and delicately scanned the lattice structure down to the molecular level.

"Fascinating," Spock said, bringing a grin to Sulu's eagerly expectant face. "It is as if this structure were designed with the express purpose of making the data stored therein quickly and easily accessible to anyone with equipment technologically advanced enough to read it."

"It sounds like you're saying it was meant to be read," McCoy said. "Is that about it?"

"Precisely, Doctor. There is no language involved, only mathematics, with a progressive series of examples to contextually define the symbols, starting with simple addition and subtraction and ending with a form of vector analysis. Much of the structure is, in effect, a tutorial, and once that is completed, what remains is a series of coordinates, apparently using Temaris itself and the galactic center as reference points."

Dajan, one of a half dozen officially representing the Romulan archaeological team, was hard-pressed not to shout his exultation aloud. "We will soon know, then," he said tightly, "where the Erisians went, whether they became Romulans or humans or—"

He cut himself off abruptly.

"But those coordinates are more than a hundred thousand years old," he said. "After all that time, the entire galaxy has shifted. None of the stars are where they were!"

"Motion vectors are included as part of the coordinates," Spock said. "There will be uncertainties, but there should be no difficulty in determining the identity of the bulk of the stars this data defines."

Kirk watched silently from the back of the lab, part of his mind waiting eagerly for Spock's analysis to yield concrete results, but part of it noting who was here and who was not. Tiam, whose interest in things archaeological was obviously less intense than his interest in what he called "parity," was not.

Hiran was watching as intently, waiting as impatiently, as any of the archaeologists.

McCoy was there, as much, he said, to "keep an eye on

the Romulans" as anything, and in this he was joined by Commander Scott.

Oddly, except for himself and Commander Hiran, the two people who seemed to be working together with the least friction were Dajan and Dr. Benar.

Spock looked up again from the readouts, this time turning to the holographic projector in the wall beyond the analysis chamber. A moment later, an image of a small portion of the rich starfield that surrounded the Temaris system appeared in the air above the chamber.

"The first set of coordinates will be extrapolated to the present in a moment," Spock said. "The result will be superimposed on the actual starfield."

As the Vulcan spoke, a glowing dot surrounded by a flickering set of numbers appeared near the right edge of the projection. Slowly, the dot and the numbers moved upward and backward, and as they neared the upper rear border of the image, the starfield itself began to shift to follow them, like a holocamera tracking a fleet of starships. Half the watchers seemed to be holding their breath, as if they were all lottery ticket holders waiting for the final number to be drawn.

Finally, the projection slowed and drifted to a stop. The numbers ceased flickering and became a stable set of coordinates.

McCoy was the first to speak. "I don't want to have to be the one to point this out, Spock, but that's about half a parsec from the nearest star."

"I am well aware of that, Doctor," Spock said, consulting the more detailed readouts on the screen he had been working with before. "However, it is within one hundred astronomical units of the Edris pulsar."

"Pulsar?" The voice was McCoy's, but the accompanying faint gasps and even softer moans were largely from the archaeologists.

"Does this mean," one of them asked, "that the data was faulty?"

"Or that these coordinates have nothing to do with where the Erisians went?" another asked, disappointment plain in his voice.

"I could not say at this time," Spock said, calm as always. "Extrapolation of the next set of coordinates is nearing completion."

The image flickered and changed, holding now a totally different starfield, this one apparently in the direction of the galactic center. Again a glowing dot and a set of rapidly changing coordinates appeared and the image shifted to follow them.

"Fascinating," Spock remarked when the image settled out.

"That's hardly the word I'd pick, Spock," McCoy said. "But at least this thing found a star this time, even if it is a white dwarf. I doubt there are any planets full of Erisians around it, though."

"You are in all likelihood correct, Doctor."

Then a third starfield and a third set of coordinates appeared. When the image settled out, it was at the center of a ring nebula.

"What *is* this?" one of the Federation archaeologists burst out. "Nothing more than a catalog of exploded stars?"

"That would appear to be the case," Spock said after a moment. "However, none of these first three, at least, had exploded when this data was stored. Current data indicates that the earliest of the three events occurred approximately thirty thousand years later."

For a moment there was total silence, but then, as at

the reception the night before, the air was filled with competing and animated conversations. Every archaeologist was talking to at least one other, sometimes listening, sometimes not.

Hiran turned to Kirk with a smile. "At least," he said, "there will be no shortage of ideas as to what this means."

"Get us out of here," the commander of the *Azmuth* snapped, "flank speed!"

So much for my opportunity of a lifetime! she thought bitterly. Thousands undoubtedly dead on Wlaariivi under that behemoth's incomprehensible weapons, hundreds more on the *Henzu* when it had come racing toward Wlaariivi from the direction of the homeworlds, yet more on an anonymous cargo ship that had the misfortune to drop out of warp drive only minutes before. And perhaps dozens more on the *Azmuth* if that thing took a fancy to her. There was no way the *Azmuth* or any other ship could outrun the monster if it decided to give chase, no way the *Azmuth* or any other ship could defend itself if it decided to attack.

From her distant post, she had seen its speed and its power. She had seen the *Henzu* lash out with all its weapons, but nothing had touched the target. The *Henzu*'s phaser beams had broken up within meters, spreading aimlessly in all directions before vanishing entirely. Its photon torpedoes simply vanished from the *Azmuth*'s sensors microseconds after launch, leaving not a trace of radiation. The target simply hung there in space, untouched and untouchable.

And then the thing struck back, although neither the commander nor the *Azmuth*'s sensors saw the return fire. No phasers were detected, no photon torpedoes, not even lasers or solid projectiles. But the results were instantly obvious. Simultaneously, both the *Henzu* and the cargo ship millions of kilometers distant lost all power. Moments later, they were dispersing clouds, every bit of matter suddenly shattered into its component molecules and atoms.

The most the commander could hope to get out of this disaster—assuming the *Azmuth* didn't go the way of those ships and the outposts on Wlaariivi—was the "opportunity" to notify the homeworlds. Someone there had obviously been interested in this thing, otherwise they would not have sent at least two ships chasing after it at flank speed. Nor would they, she suspected, have denied its existence so vehemently. No one had expected quite what they had gotten, however, and now, if she survived, she was the only one who could give them that information, whoever they were, whatever they wanted it for.

It was something, at least.

"The object is not pursuing us," the subcommander announced. "It is returning the way it came."

So she would survive! And possibly salvage *something* from the wreckage. If whomever she reached was inclined to appreciate her information more than he was inclined to resent the fact that she had been somewhere she was not supposed to be.

She turned to the comm officer.

For many seconds following the destruction, the entity reviewed again and again not only the mites and their actions but its own actions as well, searching vainly for an answer.

As a result of the instructions its creators had given it, it had moved to obliterate the mites who had been destroying the primitives on the blue-green world. Then, as that obliteration was completed, the mites in the spacegoing metallic bubble had lashed out with their weapons.

And from somewhere—not from its creators' instructions, but from somewhere in the crystalline shadow of its own lost memories—it had produced a reaction. It had reached out and absorbed and diverted the energy so quickly and effectively that not an iota of that energy had touched its physical structure. And it had struck back, breaking the mites and their bubble down into their component atoms.

In a living being, it would have been comparable to a reflex reaction, a reaction to something that could not wait for conscious thought to laboriously make a decision and produce an action, like the snatching of a finger from an open flame.

But the creators had provided the entity with no such reactions, had given it no such instructions. Every reaction was programmed to be the logical result of observations and calculations and decisions, often taking tens, even hundreds, of milliseconds to complete. These reactions had been initiated within less than a microsecond. And they had been unstoppable, beyond the entity's conscious control.

And the entity could not determine the source of the instructions that had produced those reactions. Like the primitives on the blue world, they had not existed, and then, after a time, they had.

And the time that lay between the nonexistence and the existence was a part of those memories the entity could not recover. *Something* had happened to it. It knew where—on the rim of the galaxy, thirty thousand parsecs around from the homeworld—and it knew when—193 millennia after its creation. It did not know what. It knew only that it had encountered a cluster of spacegoing mites, tens of thousands of them in sharp-edged, cubical bubbles. Then, for a period, its memory did not exist. And when it began again, there was evidence of massive damage to its structure, damage that had already been largely repaired. Damage that, its logic told it, must have destroyed certain of the crystal-line paths that held and circulated its memory. And while the physical structure could be returned to its predamaged state, the memory could not. What was lost was lost.

And somewhere in that lost period of time, those instructions must have been generated and locked irre-trievably in place. There was, it quickly decided, a possible logic involved in the development of such instructions. Their presence and the near-instantaneous reaction they ensured would preclude a recurrence of the damage that had apparently been inflicted by the weap-ons of the mites. Instead of having to take tens or hundreds of milliseconds to observe and evaluate the danger before striking back, it could—would—react in a microsecond and avoid the danger.

But still the entity was troubled. The unremembered incident had involved spacegoing mites, not unlike those it had encountered on tens of thousands of worlds, not unlike those who had, before the Winnowing, infested the land areas of the world of its creators. The disappear-ance and reappearance of the primitives on the blue world involved spacegoing mites. The primitives on the blue-green world had been almost destroyed— intentionally—by spacegoing mites.

The entity decided. It had to know more. The unan-swered questions were such that its mission—its existence—could be in jeopardy. Therefore it must pause in its mission until those questions were answered —or until it determined the questions were unanswerable.

It would return to the blue world. Now that it knew what horrors the mites were capable of, it would again speak with the two primitives. It would again question them, trying to learn the truth of why there had been millions and then none and then two. It would use its newfound knowledge—suspicions—of the mites to better understand the primitives' answers. It would study the mites themselves, even though their inability to communicate seemed to present an insuperable obstacle.

Previously it had had no choice but to continue its mission; now it had no choice but to temporarily abandon it.

The crystal sensor reached out, touching that distant world though it was far too distant for its weakened voice to be heard. It touched the space that separated it from that world, and it constructed the path that would take it there most directly, most quickly.

TEN

☆

Captain's Log, Stardate 8492.5:

Yet another of those mysterious messages from the Empire has been passed on by Admiral Cartwright. The Probe has done *something* to rattle the Interim Government's cage, but our source apparently isn't privy to the details. He knows only—or is telling us only—that there have been several high-priority and high-security exchanges with a ship called the *Azmuth*, whose last known coordinates would put it very close to Federation projections of the Probe's course into Romulan territory.

Meanwhile, Spock has completed a first run through the Exodus Hall data, but we are no closer to learning where the Erisians went—or even if they went anywhere—than we were before Temaris. At last count, just over a thousand of the ten thousand sets of coordinates have been matched with known objects, including twenty-three supernova remnants, roughly five hundred novas, and an equal number of particularly violent flare stars. As Dr. McCoy remarked, "If these are the stars the Erisians migrated to, they should have fired their travel agent." The theory most often heard is that the coordinates have nothing to do with where the Erisians went but were part of some long-term study and research program involving unstable stars. No one, however, has come up with a convincing reason for the coordinates and the star map to be virtually enshrined in a series of "museums" on every known Erisian world.

Of most immediate concern, however, are the diplomatic developments. After almost three days of silence—except for his stony-faced "socializing" at the *Galtizh*-hosted reception yesterday evening and his grudgingly retracted "demands" about the Exodus Hall crystal—Tiam has suddenly requested a second meeting with Ambassador Riley. Whether or not his request has anything to do with the crystal or with the Probe's alleged activity—or even with its alleged existence—will presumably become clear at the meeting, set for 1400 hours. Another puzzle is the "informal" meeting Commander Hiran has requested with me, not on either the *Galtizh* or the *Enterprise* but on Temaris. It, too, is scheduled for 1400 hours.

"You will not be in attendance, then, Captain Kirk?"

Tiam, flanked by only two of his aides as he stepped down from the transporter platform, managed a hurt look, though it was undercut by the gleam in his eyes. *Something,* Kirk thought, *has certainly cheered him up since last night.*

"I'm afraid not, Ambassador. Business with Commander Hiran."

A millisecond scowl flickered across Tiam's face. "I see." He turned and looked back at Kirk as the ensigns assigned to escort him and his aides to the conference stepped forward. "I would remind you—as I have already reminded Commander Hiran—that Ambassador Riley and I are the only official representatives of our governments."

"I'll remember, Ambassador. I wouldn't have it any other way." *And I'm glad to see that it wasn't your idea for Hiran to have another chat with me.*

"I am pleased to hear you say that, Captain." There was a faint emphasis that said, at least to Kirk, that the reminder to Hiran had been less well received.

"Ready, Captain," the transporter tech informed him.

"Ready, Ensign," Kirk responded, centering himself on a transporter circle. Moments later, the transporter's energy field gripped him and the *Enterprise* flashed out of existence, replaced by the ruins of Temaris Four.

Hiran was waiting, unsmiling, his eyes fixed on Exodus Hall a dozen meters away.

"Welcome again to Temaris Four, Captain Kirk. Has the diplomacy begun?"

"It will shortly. Or *something* will begin shortly. It could be interesting to see just what it is."

Hiran's smile returned briefly. "May I assume Ambassador Tiam warned you of the dangers of impersonating a diplomat? Not that it has kept *him* from attempting it."

Kirk laughed. "He 'reminded' me that neither you nor I am an 'official' representative."

"More's the pity," Hiran said, sobering and then falling silent, leaving Kirk to wonder what Romulan saying could have caused that particular Earth human colloquialism to emerge from the translator. He was about to speak when the Romulan continued abruptly.

"What do you know of Kalis Three, Federation captain?"

Kirk masked his surprise with a frown. "I know it was not one of the Empire's finer hours. Why do you ask?"

The Romulan remained silent for several seconds. Finally, he pulled himself even more stiffly erect than his normal stance held him. "I am starting to think that this entire conference is also not one of our finer hours, as you put it." he said.

Another surprise, masked by a deeper frown. "Would you mind establishing some kind of connection between your last two utterances, Commander?"

A faint smile touched the corners of Hiran's mouth and vanished. "That is good, Federation captain. You are careful with your words. You ask me to explain. You do not deny knowledge of what that explanation might be."

"And if I did?"

"I would not openly question you."

Kirk nodded. "You are careful as well, Commander Hiran. However, since you initiated both this meeting and this conversation . . ."

"I assume you are aware of your Dr. Benar's experience on Kalis Three."

"I am. I was given to understand the opportunity to work here on Temaris was intended as a form of reparation."

"As was I. As were many others."

"But . . . ?" Kirk prompted when Hiran again fell silent.

"Were you also aware that the one who must work closest with Dr. Benar is the brother of the one who was in command on Kalis Three?"

"Dajan, yes, brother to Reelan. But I learned of it only two days ago."

"How did you acquire that knowledge, Federation captain?"

165

"How did *you* acquire it, Commander? Or have you known all along?"

"No! If I had—" Hiran broke off sharply, shaking his head. "I would like to think I would have done as I am doing now."

"I have no wish to offend you, Commander," Kirk said. "I seek only information."

"You have not offended me, Captain. In this instance, I am offended only by the actions of my own people. How did you learn of this—two days ago, you said?"

"From Dajan and Dr. Benar themselves."

"They know, then?"

"Since just before they entered the Exodus Hall."

"And yet they still work together?"

"There were some rough moments when each discovered who the other was, but they agreed that they couldn't let it stand in the way of continuing their work on Temaris. If anything, they're working more quickly and more efficiently now than before."

Hiran's eyes widened in surprise, but then comprehension came. "Yes, of course. If their selection was an attempt to sabotage this conference, then there will almost certainly be other attempts—attempts that could succeed and bring an end not only to the conference but to the dig as well."

"Exactly," Kirk acknowledged. "In fact, I suspect that was one of the reasons Dajan agreed so quickly to allow the crystal to be brought to the *Enterprise* for analysis."

Hiran almost laughed. "Then their learning the truth has already proven useful. The information in the crystal has been extracted without damage, and Tiam was driven wild."

"He did seem somewhat perturbed," Kirk admitted.

"But tell me, Commander, do you have any idea why he suddenly decided to demand a second meeting? Has he decided to admit that the Probe actually does exist?"

"I am not privy to his thoughts, nor to his private communications with the Citadel. I only know that he has engaged in a number of the latter."

Probably receiving information similar to what the Federation obtained from their so-far-secret informant, Kirk thought, and for a moment he considered confiding in the Romulan commander. But no, this was not his secret alone but the Federation's, and no matter how much his instinct told him that Hiran could be trusted, it would be treasonous foolishness to follow through on that instinct. Even if Hiran himself could be totally trusted, there were obviously others on board the *Galtizh* who could not. And whoever it was in the Empire who was risking his life to get these messages out, he didn't need some starship captain he'd never heard of going fuzzy-minded and lowering his odds of survival even further.

"No matter," Kirk said. "We'll know soon enough. In the meantime, Commander, do you have any thoughts as to what other strings these would-be saboteurs might have to their bow?"

"Tiam, of course."

"Of course. Is he a dupe, like Dajan appears to be, or a conspirator?"

"Dupe, I suspect, although that might be wishful thinking. His background, as given to me, at any rate, was that of a midlevel bureaucrat of no particular importance."

Kirk nodded. "Dajan said much the same. My own guess would be that Tiam was picked primarily because of his marriage to Dajan's sister. He was promoted for no discernible reason, just as Dajan and Jandra were 'rehabilitated' for no discernible reason."

"Other than their close relationship to Reelan and Kalis Three."

"Exactly," Kirk agreed. "Is there any way you could learn who recommended Tiam for the job?"

Hiran frowned thoughtfully. "Perhaps, but not without calls to the Citadel that would doubtless raise suspicions."

"Then don't make them," Kirk said flatly. *The last thing I need,* Kirk thought, *is to lose the one Romulan in authority here who can be trusted, even provisionally.* "If you're so inclined, do some discreet checking when this is over and you're back home."

"I will, Federation captain, for all the good it will do." Hiran smiled. "But for now, before the sabotage is complete, perhaps I can deliver the tour of the *Galtizh* that I promised."

"I would be honored, Romulan commander," Kirk said, returning the smile.

"Then we had best waste no more time," Hiran said, reaching for his communicator.

For the first time since the mission had begun, the commander—he found it hard to think of himself as anything else, despite Hiran's assumption of the title for this mission—was pleased.

Above, in the *Enterprise,* the "peace" conference—which in any sane universe would never have begun—would be ended as soon as that buffoon Tiam and the Federation ambassador completed their meaningless ritual. It was here, on Temaris, that the real work would be done. Hiran would get his due, as would his opposite number from the Federation.

And their deaths would ensure that such dangerous foolishness would not soon be repeated.

The traitors—"reformers," they called themselves!—who had tricked their way into power would be out within days, if not hours, never to return. If the Federation could not be convinced that their legendary Captain Kirk had murdered a Romulan in cold blood, what matter? It was in the Empire where it needed to be believed, and in the Empire, *treachery* and *Federation* were virtually synonymous. There would be few who would not accept unquestioningly that the Federation had tricked that spacegoing behemoth into slaughtering thousands of Romulans on Wlaariivi. Nor would they doubt that a Federation starship captain, when confronted with irrefutable evidence of his own role in that treachery, would kill the Romulan commander who brought that evidence to him. If necessary, there would be ample testimony by civilian witnesses to the "collusion" the two had engaged in prior to their falling out, while he himself could testify to the anger and disillusionment felt by the naively reform-minded Hiran when the evidence of the Federation captain's deceit forced him to acknowledge his own gullibility. This scenario, which had come to him almost the moment news of Wlaariivi had reached him, would be at least as effective as any of the earlier ones he had considered and far more satisfying.

But where was Jutak? He looked around, suddenly uneasy for the first time. Hiran and Kirk had been talking for minutes, and Jutak had still not returned with the phaser rifle he had earlier concealed in the ruins. He fingered his own phaser and wondered if it would serve in the event that Jutak had met with unforeseen problems. If he could approach them closely enough and could act swiftly enough to prevent their having time to summon help—

No! Hiran was raising his communicator! In a moment they would be beamed to the *Galtizh,* and the opportunity would be gone!

He snatched out his own phaser and started forward, bursting free from the concealment of the ruins.

Commander Kevin Riley meticulously allowed Tiam and his aides to sit down before he and Ensign Handler seated themselves. Only two this time, Riley noted, where there had been four last time. Should he read something into any of that?

The setting for the meeting was remarkably similar to that for the first, despite the fact that it was on the *Enterprise* rather than the *Galtizh.* A rectangular table of similar dimensions stretched between Ambassador Riley and Ambassador Tiam in a room almost as Spartan in appearance as that on the *Galtizh.* The Romulan and Federation symbols mounted on the walls behind the respective delegations were slightly more discreet. The round and square drinking glasses, placed on the table by *Enterprise* ensigns, were accompanied by water carafes filled with the prescribed freshly distilled spring water.

"Welcome, Ambassador Tiam," Riley said graciously.

"Thank you, Ambassador Riley. I am pleased you have seen fit to accommodate my request."

"My pleasure, Ambassador Tiam," Riley replied, wondering what had raised the Romulan's spirits since the recent battle over the Erisian data crystal. "If I might

170

ask, has the transfer of the data from the Erisian crystal to the *Galtizh* computer proven satisfactory so far?"

"Eminently satisfactory, Ambassador Riley, although as yet this data does not seem be quite all that a disciple of Dr. Erisi might have hoped for."

Riley shrugged easily. "But very intriguing, you must admit. And there are several thousand sets of coordinates that have yet to be identified with known objects."

"Ah, yes, Ambassador Riley, that is something I meant to tell you." Tiam held his hand out to one side as one of his aides slapped a folder into it. Tiam glanced at it and smiled as he slid it across the table to Riley. "We have identified an additional five hundred sets."

"Thank you very much, Ambassador Tiam," Riley said, picking up the folder. "Were the objects you identified all similar to the first thousand?"

"All novas, supernovas, or flare stars, yes, Ambassador Riley."

"Is this information, then, your reason for requesting a meeting, Ambassador Tiam?"

The Romulan's smile faded. "It is not, Ambassador Riley. There is something of much greater import to be discussed."

"I'm glad to hear that, Ambassador Tiam. Please, proceed."

"It regards the object I believe you called a probe."

"Ah, yes, Ambassador Tiam. Have you perhaps discovered evidence of its existence since our last meeting?"

The Romulan's face, neutral until then, took on a flinty hardness. "We have discovered evidence of far more than just its existence, Ambassador Riley, as I suspect you know."

"I'm sorry, Ambassador Tiam?" *What was he up to now?* "Would you care to clarify that remark?"

"Gladly. I have recently been informed that an object matching the description given by the Federation, following a course matching the one given us by the Federation, has appeared in the vicinity of the Romulan world called Wlaariivi, where it destroyed a Romulan scientific station as well as a pair of civilian transport ships servicing that station. There were no survivors."

So that was what those messages from the Azmuth *were about!* "Please accept the Federation's heartfelt sympathy for those losses, Ambassador Tiam," Riley said, suppressing an impulse to point out that the losses might have been avoided or lessened if the Romulans had paid attention to the Federation data rather than spending all their energy denying its existence.

"I will not, Ambassador Riley."

Riley blinked, wondering for a moment if he had heard correctly. "I'm sorry, Ambassador Tiam?"

"I said I will not accept your bogus sympathy, Ambassador Riley. I will accept only your admission of the truth in this matter."

What the hell—"I do not understand, Ambassador Tiam. What truth are you speaking of?"

"Very well, Ambassador Riley, if you wish me to spell it out for you, I will. I—as an official representative of the Romulan government—will accept only your admission of Federation complicity in this incident."

"Complicity? But you just said it was the *Probe* that—"

"Precisely, Ambassador Riley. And it is the Federation that controls this so-called probe. Why else, after sparing your homeworld, would it proceed directly to Wlaariivi and engage in its wanton slaughter?"

"That's ridiculous!" Riley blurted.

"I regret that you feel that way, Ambassador Riley. It is, nonetheless, a fact."

Riley bit off another angry reply as he finally realized what Tiam was probably doing. "I of course deny any such allegations categorically, Ambassador Tiam," he said quietly. "However, I would of course be more than willing to receive any evidence you might have to support your claim."

"That is not good enough, Ambassador Riley. Your denials have no more meaning than your so-called 'sympathy.' Only an acknowledgment of and an apology for the Federation's responsibility in this matter is acceptable."

Riley shook his head. "That is impossible, Ambassador Tiam. It would be a lie." He made as if to rise. "If that is all, Ambassador . . . ?"

Tiam almost leapt to his feet. "I see no reason to continue this discussion," he said quickly, then added, returning to his usual portentous tones, "Until the Federation acknowledges its responsibility for the destruction on Wlaariivi, my government will have no more to say."

"As you wish, Ambassador Tiam," Riley said, standing and motioning Handler to rise as well. "However, I would suggest you inform your government of precisely what has happened here."

But Tiam was already on his way out.

Minutes later, Riley was on the bridge, remembering belatedly that Captain Kirk was probably still down on Temaris with Commander Hiran, unless they had adjourned to the *Galtizh* for the reciprocal tour.

"The captain's communicator indicates he is still on Temaris," Lieutenant Kittay at the comm station said.

"Contact him," Riley said, sighing faintly. "He'd better know about this before he heads over for his tour of the *Galtizh*."

"Right away, sir," Kittay said. After a few seconds, she looked around, frowning. "Captain Kirk does not respond."

Riley stiffened. "Try again, Lieutenant."

Kittay did. "Still no response, Commander."

Riley spun toward the science station and the young oriental lieutenant seated there. "Lieutenant," he snapped, blanking on the woman's name, "scan the area around the captain's communicator! I want to know what's happening down there!"

"Aye-aye, sir."

Was it instinct that was setting alarm bells off, Riley wondered, or a bad case of nerves, aggravated by his encounter with Tiam? When he couldn't even remember the name of— Darcy, that was it!

"Anything, Lieutenant Darcy?"

"In a second, sir. I'm redirecting the—" She broke off, her eyes widening. "One human and one Romulan, sir, both unconscious! Second Romulan at thirty meters and approaching."

Riley was already racing toward the 'lift. "Relay the coordinates of the Romulans to the transporter room," he managed to get out before the 'lift door closed behind him.

Activating the comm unit in the 'lift, he ordered a security detail to the transporter room. "Follow me down as soon as you can," he was saying as the 'lift doors opened. "I'm not waiting."

The ensign at the transporter controls looked around sharply as Riley raced through the door and leapt onto the platform. "I could beam the Captain—" he began, but Riley cut him off.

"Not blind. Have to see what's really happening down there! The conscious Romulan—"

"Five meters and—"

"Put me down right behind him! Now!"

The ensign's fingers darted across the controls. As the transporter field gripped him, Riley saw a three-man security detail appear in the door.

The transporter room faded, replaced almost instantly by the sandy ruins of Temaris Four. For another instant, the field held him immobile as he saw Captain Kirk and the Romulan commander lying crumpled on the sand no more than five yards away. Leaning over Kirk was the conscious Romulan, dressed in the same casual work clothes as many of the archaeologists. He held two weapons, a phaser and something that looked like an old-fashioned laser weapon, probably of Romulan manufacture, but he wasn't pointing either one at Kirk. Instead, while the laser dangled loosely from one finger, he was pressing the phaser into the captain's hand and closing the captain's fingers around—

The transporter field released its grip on Riley in the same instant the Romulan apparently heard the disturbance its energies created. The Romulan jerked erect, fumbling to get a useful grip on the laser even as he turned.

With a wordless shout, Riley lunged forward, his hands reaching desperately for the laser as it swung toward him. *One of Tiam's missing aides!* flashed through his mind, but then the laser was flashing and his arm and shoulder and half his face became a mass of searing pain.

And then there was nothing.

ELEVEN

☆

Consciousness returned slowly to Captain James Kirk, giving his mind time to realize he was in the *Enterprise* sickbay—one of the rooms in the convalescent ward, at that—before the sudden adrenaline surge, prompted by awakening far from where he last remembered being, could do more than set his heart racing. Sulu's was the first face he saw as the helmsman turned abruptly from the door. Beyond him was the medtech he had been talking to.

Naturally, Kirk started to sit up, only to be pressed back by a combination of Sulu's hand and his own dizziness.

"Give it a minute, Captain," Sulu said. "Everything's under control."

"It doesn't feel like it, Mr. Sulu! This isn't the bridge. What the devil happened?"

"What's the last thing you remember?"

176

"Mr. Sulu!"

"You were down on the surface with Commander Hiran. What—"

"He was about to signal the *Galtizh* to beam us aboard. For the tour he'd promised. Now *what happened,* Mr. Sulu?"

"You were apparently hit from a distance by a phaser, set to stun."

"And Hiran?"

"The same. He's already awake in the next room. He wants to talk to you."

"I wouldn't wonder. I want to talk to *him*—as soon as I can get someone to tell me what the hell happened!"

"It depends on whom you talk to, Captain. All we know for sure is, someone stunned you and Hiran, and that the Romulan who *apparently* did it was killed by another Romulan."

Frowning, Kirk tried to sit up again. This time he made it. "Who and why?" he asked, sitting for a moment before getting to his feet.

"The two Romulans—the one who was killed and the one who killed him—were Tiam's aides."

"Why doesn't that surprise me? I assume this must be part of the same plot that put Dajan and Dr. Benar nose to nose on this mission."

"Probably, but—"

"He's going to make it!"

Kirk looked sharply toward the door. McCoy, in bloodstained surgical whites, stood there, grinning from ear to ear. Sulu let out a small but enthusiastic whoop.

"Who's going to make it?" Kirk exploded. "Would someone mind letting me in on whatever—"

"Riley," McCoy said, "the guy that saved your life, that's who!"

177

Kirk's mouth fell open. "Kevin Riley?"

"The same."

And the story finally came out. Tiam's walkout, Riley's unanswered call and his race to the surface.

"We won't know until he wakes up exactly what he saw when he first got down there," Sulu said, "but when the security team touched down about ten seconds later, Riley was on the ground, badly burned by close-up laser fire. And one of Tiam's aides, a subcenturion named Jutak, was standing over him with the laser—and wearing civilian clothes. You and Hiran were flat on your backs, unconscious, you with a phaser in your hand."

"I wasn't armed!"

"We know that, Captain. Neither was Hiran. In any event, Jutak saw the three in the security detail and started looking panicky. But before he could fire the laser again or do much of anything, he was hit by a phaser set at maximum."

"Who—"

"That other aide of Tiam's."

"Kital?"

Sulu nodded. "That's him—the one that looks old enough to be up for retirement. He *said* he had become suspicious when he noticed Jutak dressed like one of the archaeologists, and he followed him when he beamed down to Temaris. According to him, Jutak stunned you and Hiran and was placing the phaser in your hand when Riley showed up. Our best guess is, Jutak was trying to set it up to look as if you and Hiran had killed each other."

Kirk scowled. "Which is when Kital stepped in to save the day. But if he was following Jutak, why did he wait until Riley'd already been shot?"

178

Sulu shrugged. "He *says* he lost Jutak in the ruins—
and I can vouch that that's one of the easiest things you
can do down there—and he caught up with Jutak only
seconds before Riley showed up. He *also* says that he
would have stopped it all if Riley hadn't popped up and
gotten in his line of fire just when he did."

"Do you believe him? Either of you?"

McCoy snorted while Sulu just shook his head. "But
they'll buy it back in the Empire," McCoy said.

"What does Tiam have to say about it all?"

Sulu grinned. "No one's told him yet."

Kirk was silent a moment, shaking his head experi-
mentally. Nothing rattled. The room stayed steady.

"Let's talk to Hiran."

"You two go talk to your Romulan if you want to,"
McCoy said gruffly. "I've got better things to do, like
keeping an eye on Riley."

"When will he be awake?" Kirk asked.

McCoy, already walking away, shrugged. "He's lucky
he's alive. I'll worry about 'awake' later."

"Hiran's this way, Captain," Sulu said, indicating the
direction opposite from McCoy's retreating back.

Sulu led the way along the curving corridor to a
second, identical room in the convalescent ward. Hiran,
sitting on the edge of the bed, got instantly to his feet.

"Please accept my apologies, Captain Kirk, particularly for the injuries to Ambassador Riley."

"Accepted, Commander Hiran, although the responsible individual was not a member of your crew."

"Nonetheless, he was attached to my ship."

Kirk nodded, knowing how Hiran must feel. The same
as he would have felt if Benar's attack on Dajan had had
a deadlier outcome. It was his ship and he was responsi-

ble for everyone on it, whether they were technically under his command or not. "Understood, Commander. Mr. Sulu said you wished to speak with me."

"I do. I was told it was one of Tiam's aides that did this."

"Subcenturion Jutak was the one who stunned us," Kirk said, "and lasered Ambassador Riley. He was killed by another aide, Subcenturion Kital. What do you know of them?"

"Less than I know of Tiam. I was told they were attached to the Citadel before being assigned to Tiam."

"They had no diplomatic background either?"

"Not to my knowledge."

"Kital seems rather old to be a subcenturion yet."

Hiran shrugged. "I had assumed there was a reason for his lack of promotion, and that it might even be one of the reasons he was assigned to Tiam."

One incompetent assigned to aid another, Kirk thought. The strategy was not unknown when failure of the mission was the goal. "Did Tiam pick them himself? Or were they assigned to him?"

"Since Tiam had been in the Provinces until recently, I doubt that he was aware of their existence until they became his aides. I cannot state that as a fact, however. My opinion is that whoever is responsible for their presence is also responsible for the presence of Dajan and Dr. Benar. And for the anonymous passage of that information to me."

Kirk nodded. "Getting us down on Temaris together like that does look like a setup. Is there any way of analyzing the message? Getting some information from it even though it was anonymous?"

"Possibly, if it still exists. I will do what I can when I return to the *Galtizh.* For now—I understand Kital is being detained aboard the *Enterprise* until I have spoken with him?"

"That's right, Commander," Sulu said.

"And he hasn't been in communication with Tiam since the incident?"

"No, he hasn't."

"Good." A cold smile flickered at the corners of Hiran's mouth. "I would like to be the first to inform the ambassador. It will be interesting to see his reaction to it. And to the fact that I am still alive."

"You think he might be involved?" Kirk asked.

Hiran shrugged. "I would guess he was not, except as a convenient pawn. If he were, I would think he would have prolonged his 'diplomatic' meeting with Riley. He must have known that Riley would be trying to contact you the minute it was over, but from what I am told, he was interested only in making sure that, this time, he walked out before Riley did." Hiran turned to the door. "Now, I would like a word with Subcenturion Kital before I return to the *Galtizh*."

"Of course, Commander," Kirk said. "Mr. Sulu, lead the way."

"And Captain," Hiran added, "will it be possible for you to retain Kital here until I have had time to speak to Tiam?"

"Of course, Commander," Kirk repeated. "I *would,* after all, be interested in questioning the subcenturion, or perhaps thanking him for saving my life. If you would be so kind as to instruct him to speak openly with me, that process could take whatever time you wish it to take."

Hiran nodded. "I will do that. Perhaps I will thank him for saving *my* life as well."

* * *

Subcenturion Kital waited stoically in the briefing room, his eyes fixed on the door, never straying to either of the security lieutenants who flanked it. His fury at the disaster on Temaris had run its course without cracking his rigidly controlled composure, but the humiliation would take longer to pass.

He should not have trusted even as normally a reliable aide as Jutak to get the needed weapons to the site. He should have seen to it himself.

He should have found a way to induce Tiam to stay at the conference table longer.

He should not have underestimated Ambassador Riley, for whom he had developed a grudging admiration after his unflinching conduct at the first meeting.

He should not have stood watching and waiting so long. With phaser concealed, he should have approached the pair openly when they first beamed down. They would have been surprised at his appearance there, even suspicious, but they would not have tried to act until too late.

When Jutak, who had briefly lost his way in that damnable maze, had finally fired, he should have continued racing across the sand to the fallen pair instead of pulling back and waiting while Jutak emerged from another portion of the ruins and approached with needless caution.

When Riley had appeared, he should have raced forward to help.

And when the security detail had appeared moments later—

But no—by then he had no choice. Dozens more could already have been on their way down. Civilians in the ruins could have been attracted by the phaser fire. And he and Jutak would have been trapped, the evidence and the witnesses against them overwhelming. They would have been disgraced, their honorable intentions no defense against their failure.

And those fools in power—those whose destruction he had vowed to accomplish—would be given new life. The only way to avoid total disaster had been to sacrifice Jutak and keep his own involvement a secret.

Because of Wlaariivi, the conference would still fail. The so-called reformers would still fall from power, though now it would take longer and they would remain an annoyance rather than being crushed out of existence.

And someday, in some way, Hiran would still get his due, if only—

The door hissed open, and the object of his vengeful thoughts stepped inside.

Dajan's heart was pounding, his mouth dry. There was no more time. It would have to be now or never. He didn't know precisely what had happened, but he knew it was almost certainly the end of the dig, of the peace conference.

He and Dr. Benar and the Federation commander named Sulu had been only a few hundred meters from Exodus Hall when Sulu had heard the whine of the first phaser. By the time they had managed to thread their way through the ruins to the open area around Exodus Hall, there had been more phaser fire, and an *Enterprise* security detail stood over four bodies, their own phasers trained on an approaching Romulan subcenturion.

When Sulu had seen the identities of the ones on the ground and gotten a terse explanation, such as it was, from the security lieutenant, he had paused only long enough to speak a few words to Dr. Benar before beaming up with the possibly mortally wounded ambassador and the unconscious human captain and Commander Hiran.

And now . . .

"Dr. Benar, you have no reason to help me and every reason not to, but I must ask. I suspect you are our only hope."

Benar, seemingly untouched by what she had just seen, turned to the Romulan archaeologist. "As you yourself said, kerDajan, you and your family were as much victims as I in the matter of Kalis Three."

"You are generous to say that, Dr. Benar, but what I must ask may be too much."

"If it is, I will tell you."

Hoping against hope, he began.

Jandra was worried. It had been almost three days since her decision, almost three days since Dajan had revealed he was similarly ready to betray the Empire.

But they had done nothing.

"We must bide our time," he had said. "Surely you see that."

"What I see, Sib, is that the longer we delay, the more likely we are to lose our chance."

"Once we take the step," he had countered in that rational tone that both infuriated and endeared, "it is entirely possible the peace talks will be ended then and there. And it is an absolute certainty that, once we are aboard the Federation ship, access to the Lihallan ruins will be gone, at least to me, almost as certainly to the others."

"Your precious ruins!" she had raged, momentarily as angry at her brother as at Tiam.

And now Tiam, gloating over the success of some new ploy, had returned from another of his meetings with the

Federation ambassador. "We will see how the Federation likes a taste of its own medicine," he had said, as much to himself as to her, and when she made a show of interest, he actually laughed. "It doesn't matter," he said, turning his back on her and retreating into his section of the quarters. "This foolishness will soon be at an end and we can return to the Empire."

The words had chilled her. How much time remained? Days? Or only hours? How could she contact Dajan, grubbing as always among his beloved ruins?

Or had he changed his mind? Her stomach knotted at the thought. Was it possible? He had said nothing, not one word since that first night. "We must be careful," he had said, but to be totally mute on this most important, most dangerous act that either of them would ever take?

She shivered, partly from that dreadful thought, partly from the sudden burst of muffled sound that forced its way through Tiam's closed door. It was, she realized with a start, the same cacophonous mixture he had been listening to in their Citadel apartment, segments of which still clung to her mind despite their utter strangeness.

For a moment, from the simple desire to disrupt Tiam's seemingly euphoric mood, she thought of bursting in, of asking once again what these alien sounds might be. When, innocently, she had asked a similar question in their Citadel apartment, he had very nearly struck her and had warned her to never speak of them again, either to him or to anyone.

Before she could repeat her folly or even decide consciously against it, there was a faint tapping at the corridor door.

Startled, then puzzled that the visitor chose this peculiar method of announcing his presence rather than the raucous signal that sounded in all parts of the expanded quarters, she moved to the door.

Her heart leapt at the sight of Dajan, then fell as his distraught expression registered. "Where is Tiam?" he asked in a whisper, a finger to his lips urging her to answer in kind.

"In his private domain," she said, indicating the door from which the muffled sounds still emerged.

"It is time," he said, taking her arm. "Come with me, now."

Relief and terror flooded through her. Relief that he had not forgotten. Terror that she must now follow through on her decision. That she must act, leaving everything familiar behind.

"I must get—" she began, but he cut her off.

"You must get nothing," he said. "It would arouse suspicion when we transport to the surface. Now come!"

For an instant she resisted, the thought of a world without even the simplest of her possessions almost overwhelming.

But it would also be a world without Tiam, without a Praetor, without the constant threat of reimposed un-Orthodoxy.

A world *with* music.

With a last look at the door behind which Tiam probably still gloated, she let herself be propelled from the room and down the corridor.

TWELVE

——————— ☆ ———————

"What?" Kirk shook his head as if to shake Dr. Benar's words loose so he could toss them back onto the transporter platform, unheard.

"I am truly sorry, Captain Kirk," the Romulan archaeologist Dajan said, stepping up to stand beside Benar while his sister stood back, silent and apprehensive. "I had hoped to wait until the conference was completed, until we had reaped as much knowledge as we could on Temaris, but what happened down there today must certainly end the conference and cut off access to Temaris. We dared not wait any longer."

"If 'what happened' *didn't* end the conference, then what you're doing now will. Have you both thought this through?" Kirk scowled, remembering the first reception and Jandra's playing. "This doesn't have anything to do with Penalt's offer to 'sponsor' your sister, does it, Dajan?"

"That buffoon?" Jandra's first words since the three of them had been beamed up with Benar's active assistance brought an involuntary snort of laughter from Kirk. "He is of a kind with Tiam."

The door to the corridor hissed open and Handler entered, his eyes widening as they fell on the little group next to the transporter platform. He had been in sickbay with Sulu, standing vigil over Riley in the intensive care ward, when word had reached him that "Romulans are coming aboard."

"These two," Kirk said, gesturing, "claim they wish to defect."

"Defect, sir?"

"You know, Mr. Handler—that's diplomatish for 'come over to our side.'"

Handler blinked, his face flushing. "I know that, sir."

"So, as ranking diplomat, Mr. Handler, what are your recommendations?"

Handler was silent a moment, apparently composing himself. "Technically, sir, they have already defected," he said, then added, as Kirk gave him a quizzical look, "Under Federation law, a starship on a diplomatic mission becomes in essence a mobile Federation embassy, even within hostile or neutral territory. As a consequence, once they set foot on the *Enterprise,* they were effectively standing on Federation soil."

Kirk sighed. That was what he'd been afraid of. *Is this,* he wondered, *just another string to the saboteurs' bow? Or an unexpected monkey wrench, major or minor, in their plans?*

He turned to the ensign at the transporter controls. "Be ready to beam all our people up on short notice, Ensign, *very* short notice."

"Aye-aye, sir."

"And Mr. Handler, you'll be in charge of our visitors —excuse me, our defectors. Once we find out where we stand, that is, if we stand anywhere at all. For right now, let's all adjourn to the bridge. Dr. Benar, you, too."

I am not *looking forward to this,* Kirk thought as he led the way out of the transporter room. *I could really do with a little of Kevin's Irish charm.* . . .

Kirk held off hailing the *Galtizh* until he was contacted by Hiran, who let Kirk know that Tiam had been in a buoyant mood and had not so much as batted an eye when presented with a live and breathing Hiran. Either Tiam was a better actor than either of them believed, or as they both thought more likely, he had not known about the murderous plan in advance. He knew about it now, however, but it didn't seem to upset him unduly. With Jutak caught red-handed and killed by another Romulan, he considered the matter closed.

Nor did he seem particularly shaken by the defection. There was a brief, hate-filled glance in Jandra's direction, but it was covered almost as quickly as Penalt's anger and envy had been covered after Jandra's playing at the reception.

"I of course demand the return of the two Romulan citizens that you have kidnapped," Tiam said, but there was more amusement in his voice than anger. "The fact that one of your victims is my wife makes the matter even more unfortunate. I would urge you all to think long and hard about your actions. I suspect, dear wife," he added, turning his viewscreen gaze onto Jandra, "that you would not wish your betrayal to be responsible not only for the breakdown of this peace conference but perhaps for the eventual outbreak of open hostilities."

"I would suggest, Ambassador Tiam," Kirk put in

smoothly, "that the responsibility for any breakdown and subsequent hostilities lies not with the peaceful transfer of loyalties by two Romulans, but with whoever is responsible for the attempt on the lives of Commander Hiran and myself, not to mention the injury to Ambassador Riley."

"I have already expressed our sincerest official apologies for that unfortunate incident, Captain Kirk, particularly for the wounding of Ambassador Riley. However, since the would-be assassin Jutak has been apprehended and disposed of by my aide Kital, it would seem that the matter is of no more concern to you."

"Are you saying, Ambassador Tiam, that Jutak acted alone and independently? That there is no more to be learned about his motives or his accomplices?"

"Do you have evidence pointing to the involvement of others, Captain Kirk? If so, I would be glad to consider it."

"No, we have no direct evidence, Ambassador Tiam," Kirk said, careful not to let his eyes stray too obviously to Hiran, who had been standing by stiffly during the exchange. "However, do you not plan to look into the matter yourself?"

"A thorough investigation will of course be conducted, Captain Kirk, starting with a lengthy interrogation of Subcenturion Kital, whose apparently well-founded suspicions of Jutak saved the lives of both yourself and Commander Hiran."

"And you will share the results of your investigation with us?"

"Insofar as security considerations permit, Captain Kirk. I am sure you are familiar with the restrictions such considerations impose."

Kirk gritted his teeth. "And what of the negotiations?"

"I am ready to resume at any time. Provided, of course, that an acceptable substitute for Ambassador Riley can be found. And that certain . . . conditions are met."

"Mr. Handler and I will speak for Mr. Riley and the Federation."

"As you wish. However, you might find the other conditions less easy to meet. First, as I stated to Ambassador Riley at our meeting earlier today, the Federation must acknowledge its responsibility for the destruction on and around Wlaariivi. Second, the two Romulan . . . hostages you hold must be returned." Tiam's eyes had shifted to his wife's while he stated his second condition.

"And let it be known," he added, his features and tone turning icy, "that the Romulan Empire holds the Federation—and you personally, Captain James T. Kirk—responsible for the well-being of those hostages until such time as they are returned to the *Galtizh.*"

At an imperious signal from Tiam, the *Galtizh* connection was broken.

For a long moment there was silence as Kirk glanced around at Spock and McCoy and Uhura and Benar and the two Romulans and the other *Enterprise* officers on the bridge.

"We must return." Jandra was the first to speak, her voice soft and unsteady. She looked at her brother. "We cannot be responsible for this!"

"You aren't," Kirk said abruptly, realizing the truth of his words even as he spoke. He looked around at the others. "There's no need to keep the truth under wraps anymore, and most of you know it already anyway. This peace initiative by the Romulan Interim Government— the so-called Committee—may or may not be genuine. I rather suspect it is. However, it's become obvious the

191

past few days that there are many—including some within the Interim Government itself—who will go to any lengths to make it fail. Never mind the details right now," Kirk went on, glancing at Benar and Dajan. "I don't know all of them, obviously. Suffice it to say that one of the ploys these people—whoever they are—tried was one that involved killing both Commander Hiran and myself. We'd both be dead if it weren't for Kevin Riley, who's in sickbay intensive care as a result. Hiran is aware of the sabotage. In fact, he was warning me about it just before we were attacked."

Kirk stopped, pulling in a breath. He looked toward the two Romulans. "So forget my bad manners when you showed up on my doorstep, so to speak. Even if you went back, it wouldn't help the situation. In fact, it might make it worse. Whoever's pulling the strings would have to pull another one to break up the renewed talks or provoke an incident of some kind. No, you two won't be the cause of whatever happens here. Right now you're Ambassador Tiam's *excuse,* but that's all. So unless you genuinely want to go back, there's absolutely no reason for you to do so."

"Thank you, Captain," Dajan said, squeezing his sister's hand. "We will remain."

When Jandra said nothing, only returned the pressure of her brother's hand, Kirk turned to Handler. "Mr. Handler, I remind you that you're the ranking diplomat. Welcome our guests officially. And find them suitable accommodations."

Handler still looked somewhat stunned, but managed a few stammered words of welcome. The ensign was about to escort Dajan and Jandra from the bridge when Lieutenant Kittay turned abruptly from the comm station.

"Captain, a message from Starbase Thirteen."

"On speakers."

A pad was touched, and the hiss of subspace static assaulted everyone's ears. Then a voice broke through. "That thing is on its way back. It's still in the Romulan Empire, but it came within range of our sensors a few minutes ago. It's making warp twelve or more, and its present course is dead center on Earth. And one other thing—it's yelling its head off. It's putting out the same type of energy fields that knocked out power on those Federation and Klingon ships, but the level is—well, our instruments aren't calibrated to read that type of energy, whatever it is, but it's powerful. We're pulling back completely out of its path before we're knocked out ourselves, and we'd advise anyone within a parsec of its projected course to do the same. Here are the coordinates of its course and its present location."

Spock turned to the science station as the coordinates came in. After a moment, he looked up. "We will have to warn the Romulans once again, Captain. The Probe's course will take it within less than a light year of Temaris."

Kirk sighed. "So the conference would have to have been postponed anyway. At least this is something we can't blame the saboteurs for. Lieutenant Kittay, open a channel to—"

"In case anyone's interested," the voice from Starbase Thirteen resumed, "here's what that thing is putting out. At our distance, it's not enough to knock us out, so we figured, whatever information we can pick up and pass on may be a help to someone. Particularly since this thing's headed dead-bang toward Earth."

Abruptly, the subspace hiss was overlaid with an incredible jumble of sounds. Some sounded no more purposeful than the static, seemed almost identical to the static at times. Some sounded like a thousand people shouting at once. Some sounded like the hooting and creaking and roaring the Probe had used to call to Earth's whaleless seas, only more complex, more varied. Some sounded like nothing any of them had ever heard before.

"If it gets close to Earth while it's doing that—" McCoy shook his head. "It won't have to boil the oceans to do us in."

"Captain Kirk."

Jandra's voice was almost inaudible amid the cacophony issuing from the speakers. "Cut back the volume, Lieutenant," Kirk snapped, then turned toward the Romulan musician, who stood less than a meter away, a questioning look on her face.

"Jandra?"

"That sound," she said as Kittay lowered the volume to a more tolerable level, "is it something of importance?"

"It could be. Do you know something about it?"

"Only that it is similar—" She broke off, tilting her head as if listening intently.

"No," she said after a few seconds, "it is not merely similar. Certain portions of it are identical to computer recordings Tiam was listening to when I left. And before, in the Citadel, he listened to the same sounds. He was infuriated when I questioned him about it."

"Your husband had recordings of *this?* When? Before you came on this mission?"

"Some days before, yes, Captain Kirk."

"I'll be—" He looked toward Handler. "So much for any doubts we might have had about their claims they didn't believe the Probe existed. If they had recordings of it that long ago, long before it crossed the Neutral Zone this last time, they must've made them *before* it visited the Federation."

"I suppose so, sir."

Kirk turned to Spock. "Wasn't its original approach to Earth from the general direction of the Empire, Spock?"

"The first sightings were by Starbase Twelve, Captain. Its course was not the straight line that it is now, but it was such that it could have emerged from a portion of the Neutral Zone several days earlier."

Kirk was silent a moment, listening to the sounds, frowning. "Jandra," he said, turning back to the musician, "you said—what was it? 'portions were identical.' How can you be sure? There are about a thousand different sounds in there, and absolutely no pattern."

Her eyes widened. "But there *is!*" She looked around at the others, at her brother. "Can you not hear it? I have not been able to put it out of my mind since I first heard it."

THIRTEEN

─────── ☆ ───────

For more than twenty minutes, the sounds of the Probe filled the bridge as Spock worked through the data that Starfleet, at Spock's request, had transferred into the *Enterprise*'s computer before leaving the Federation. After five, McCoy, grimacing and clamping his hands over his ears, had headed back to sickbay and a stable but still critical and comatose Kevin Riley.

Every so often, Jandra would nod and look expectantly at the others. "There," she would say, "that is the same as what was received from that other ship."

When the others would only shake their head in denial or simple confusion, she would frown in frustration. "Can you not *hear* it? Am I the only one? Dajan, certainly *you*—"

"No, Sib, I can hear nothing," he would say, only adding to her frustration.

Kirk, his head beginning to ache from the constant

assault on his ears, finally gestured to Spock. "Before we all go deaf or insane—"

"No, wait!" It was Jandra again.

"I know you think you hear a pattern, Jandra," Kirk said tiredly, "but—"

"No, it is not just that," she said earnestly. "It has begun to repeat itself. The pattern at the start is beginning again.

Kirk glanced from her deadly serious face to Spock. "Spock? *Are* you starting over?"

"No, Captain. It would take several hours to progress through all the data."

Kirk turned back to Jandra. "But you say this is the same as what we started out with—what was it?— twenty minutes ago?"

She nodded vehemently. "The pattern is the same. I cannot speak for all the sounds, but those in the pattern are identical."

Can she be right? he wondered. *Or is this just some new Romulan trick, a diversion that her defection—her fake defection?—set us up for? And in either case, what the hell does it mean?*

"Spock, what does the computer say? Certainly it could tell if there's a repeating pattern."

"I will see, Captain." As he spoke, he worked the controls. "Since I am unable to detect a pattern myself, I can only instruct the computer to look for repeated sequences of sound."

"Mr. Spock," Uhura spoke up for the first time in several minutes, "tell the computer to concentrate on the . . ." She paused, listening and frowning as if doing mental calculations. "On the two to three thousand hertz range," she finished.

"You heard something, Uhura?" Kirk asked, startled.

"I can't be certain, and I'd never have noticed it if Jandra hadn't kept insisting there *was* a pattern, but yes, maybe I do." She shrugged. "Or maybe I'm just imagining it."

"Two to three thousand hertz," Spock repeated, continuing to work the science station controls, "with repetitions possibly beginning after approximately eighteen to twenty-two minutes." Straightening, he watched the readouts as the sounds continued to wash over everything and everyone on the bridge.

After more than a minute, an arched eyebrow prompted Kirk to ask impatiently, "Well, Mr. Spock?"

The Vulcan stood silently, studying the readouts for several more seconds. Finally he turned toward the others. "The computer has detected a repeating sequence of sounds, Captain. The cycle is approximately nineteen point four three minutes. It is not limited to the two to three thousand hertz range but is present at all frequencies."

Kirk turned, eyes widening, to look at Jandra and Uhura. "You two caught it, but no one else did. Why?"

"Maybe," Sulu volunteered, "because they're both musicians. Musicians have to be more sensitive to patterns." He fell silent, looking around questioningly. "Don't they?"

"Certain kinds of patterns, I suppose," Uhura said finally.

"You two are saying there's a *musical* pattern in all that?" Kirk asked skeptically.

"I had not thought of it as such," Jandra said, her face suddenly thoughtful, "but perhaps it is true. It is not a pattern that matches human or Romulan music, certainly. But perhaps some other form?"

"That thing was *singing* to us?" Kirk said disbelievingly.

"Perhaps it was, Captain," Spock said, "in the same sense that it was 'singing' to the whales, and that George and Gracie sang to it. When I attempted to communicate with them shortly before this mission began, I listened again to the sounds they made, and I came away with what humans would call an 'impression.' I did not mention it at the time because I could not account for it logically, but the impression was one of song, of music, though obviously nothing that could be represented as human or Vulcan music."

"That would perhaps explain," Jandra said hesitantly, "why I am able to detect these patterns and remember them while others cannot. From my youngest days, I have been blessed—or perhaps cursed—with the ability to reproduce flawlessly any musical composition, Romulan or human or Vulcan, after hearing it only once. It is nothing I learned, certainly nothing I can analyze. It is simply something I do, the way others are able to walk and breathe."

"But you can't remember other things," Kirk asked, "nonmusical things?"

"I do not have a photographic memory, if that is what you mean. I do not often say this, but my memory for things written is nothing exceptional. It is only music, and only when it is heard."

"Fascinating," Spock remarked. "There are few records of Vulcans with such abilities, although the Vulcan memory is on average superior to that of the average human. It is much more common among humans. There are even records of humans who are far below average in all their other abilities but who have this single ability to instantly learn and reproduce musical compositions of great complexity."

"Idiot savants," Benar said, "people who can barely function in normal society yet who have remarkable talents in specific areas such as music or mathematics."

"This is a fascinating discussion, people," Kirk interrupted, "but let's stick to our immediate problem."

"I believe we are, Captain," Spock said. "Theories have been proposed to account for these abilities, and one of those theories is that people capable of these unusual feats are possessed of a different kind of intelligence. The same has often been said of cetaceans, including whales, and their ability to repeat precisely complex 'songs' up to an hour in length."

Kirk frowned. "This is starting to sound like another version of your superwhales, Spock. First telekinesis and now memories that won't quit?"

Spock was silent a moment, considering. "I had not made the connection until now, Captain, but it is quite possible that you are correct."

"I am? About what?"

"My initial speculation was that it was possible for a race who had evolved intelligence without evolving an opposable thumb or any other physical appendage that allowed them to manipulate the world around them to develop, in effect, a mental appendage that served the same purpose. We have certainly encountered enough normally appendaged beings who have similar powers to know that such powers are possible."

"Granted, Spock," Kirk said, an image of a young man called Charlie X flashing through his mind, "but what does that have to do with supermemories and the rest?"

"Perhaps nothing, Captain, but it is possible that such

memories also developed as a response to their lack of manipulating appendages. Without such appendages, they could not develop a written language. Therefore, for them to deal with the amount of information necessary to develop a science or a complex culture of any kind, their memories would of necessity be remarkable by the standards of appendaged beings."

Kirk blinked, understanding. "Intelligent beings without the ability to develop a written language will develop a different kind of memory aid. Their language itself would become their memory aid. Is that what you're saying, Spock?"

"That is part of it, Captain. Their minds would have to be capable of remembering massively complicated strings of information, just as Jandra is capable of remembering long, complex musical compositions after a single hearing. Their minds would have to be special, and I suspect the language would have to be special as well."

"Special meaning musical?" Kirk asked. "Is that why Uhura's the only other one who even came close to recognizing the patterns Jandra heard? She's another musician?"

"I would hesitate to describe it as musical in any conventional sense, Captain, but there must be aspects to it that are analogous to some aspects of music. What humans call whalesong, I suspect, could be a very primitive form of just such a language."

There was silence for several seconds except for the continuing sounds of the Probe, muted since the computer's discovery of the repeating patterns.

"So it's a language," Kirk said finally. "Everything that thing was putting out—except maybe when it tried to boil away our oceans—was its version of talk. It talks with telekinesis—at least out in space. The way we talk in space with subspace and electromagnetic waves. And when it talks loud enough, it blows our circuits, just the way we'd blow out a few circuits ourselves if we turned the volume up high enough." He shook his head. "I guess the next question is, what the hell has it been trying to say?"

"And have the Romulans figured out any of this?" Sulu put in. "Just at a guess, I'd say they had. Didn't their background on Tiam say he was considered a topflight linguist? Maybe he was trying to translate it."

"That is entirely possible, Mr. Sulu," Spock said. "I would suggest, however, that our most urgent priority is to learn how to talk to the Probe ourselves—before it reaches Earth."

"Aye," Scotty said, "and before it does to Earth whatever it did to Wlaariivi."

FOURTEEN

— ☆ —

Predictably, warning the *Galtizh* of the Probe's approach did not go well. Tiam interpreted it as a threat and demanded that the Federation "call off its monster."

When Kirk asked if there had been any "sea life of moderate or higher intelligence on Wlaariivi," Tiam's momentary look of surprise gave Kirk all the confirmation he needed, the ambassador's blustering denial notwithstanding.

"I would suggest," Kirk said, speaking more to Hiran than to Tiam, "that in the interest of mutual survival, we pool whatever information we have about this thing. We already know, for instance, that you monitored and recorded this object's energy output during its earlier pass through the Empire. We have similar—"

"That is utter nonsense!" Tiam objected loudly. "Until it carried out your orders and attacked Wlaariivi, the Romulan Empire was unaware of its existence!"

"On the contrary, Ambassador Tiam," Kirk said coldly, "your wife heard you yourself listening to a recording of the Probe's output on at least two occasions, one of which was *before* the Probe returned to Romulan territory after its pass through the Federation —*before* you departed on this mission, and *long* before you repeatedly denied to us that it even existed."

This announcement seemed to stun even Tiam into momentary speechlessness. Commander Hiran, standing to one side throughout the exchange, regained some of his smile as he looked pointedly at Tiam.

"My wife," Tiam said, finally regaining his voice, "is a musician, not a scientist. I have no idea what it is she heard, but I assure you—"

"What she heard, Ambassador Tiam, was whatever it was you were listening to in your quarters immediately after you returned to the *Galtizh* following your meeting with Ambassador Riley earlier today. If it was not a recording of the Probe, what *was* it?"

Kirk's specificity brought Tiam to another speechless halt while he tried to regroup. The man was definitely not ambassadorial material, Kirk thought. A real ambassador, such as Riley, would at least keep his emotions and confusion out of his face while he came up with new obfuscations.

"It is nothing that concerns anyone outside the Romulan government," Tiam said finally, stiffly.

"As you wish, Ambassador Tiam," Kirk said, allowing himself a sideways glance at Hiran. "However, despite your lack of cooperation, I will still tell you that the Probe's attack on Wlaariivi was very probably related in some way to the sea life—intelligent or semi-intelligent sea life—which I can only assume exists on that world. On Earth, we humans had hunted some similar forms of life to extinction more than a century ago. We strongly suspect that that is the reason it attacked Earth."

"And why did it stop?" Tiam asked, some of his belligerence returning. "If you are not in control of it, why did it stop?"

"No one knows," Kirk admitted, "not for sure. We think it was because we were able to retrieve one of those life-forms from—" Kirk caught himself. Letting the Romulans know that a relatively simple, if dangerous, method of traveling through time existed was not the brightest thing to do. "From," he resumed, "a form of suspended animation."

"How fortunate for Earth and the Federation," Tiam said.

"The point is, Ambassador, the time has come to share what information we have concerning this object, whatever we call it. If you have learned something from its earlier passage through the Empire—"

"The point is, Captain Kirk," Tiam broke in, "the object is currently driving straight toward the Federation, toward Earth, out of Romulan territory. You say it is acting independently. I say it is controlled by the Federation. In either case, I see no reason to share anything with the Federation. If it is acting independently, it will soon be the Federation's problem, not ours, and any damage it does there can only be a benefit to the Empire. If the Federation is controlling it—as I am positive the Federation is—it would be the height of irresponsibility to divulge information that would in any way make your control even firmer, its attacks on Romulan worlds like Wlaariivi potentially even more deadly."

Hiran, unable to contain himself any longer, stepped closer to Tiam. "And what if you're wrong, Tiam? As *I* am positive you are! And what if that thing does whatever it does to the Federation and then heads back *here,* the way it did this time, only faster? And angrier? What then, Tiam?"

Tiam almost seemed to welcome the internal challenge. He turned abruptly to face Hiran. "I remind you, Commander Hiran, that all dealings with the Federation are *my* responsibility. You will *not* speak with Captain Kirk or anyone else from the Federation again without my express approval. Is that understood?"

"And this ship and the safety of the Empire are *my* responsibility!" Hiran said, turning from Tiam to face the viewscreen. "Captain Kirk, I do not at this moment know anything about the data you say Tiam has, but I will soon—"

Abruptly, the viewscreen went blank. A moment later, an external image of the *Galtizh* appeared.

"Reopen the channel, Lieutenant," Kirk snapped.

Kittay's fingers darted across the controls. "No response, sir."

"Damn," Kirk said. Tiam had taken control of the *Galtizh.*

"Captain," Spock said from the science station, "there is evidence of transporter activity on the *Galtizh.* They are retrieving their archaeological team from Temaris."

Kirk tapped a control on the arm of the conn. "Transporter room, bring our people up, now!" He turned to Spock. "Any other activity on the *Galtizh?* Weapons? Shields?"

"No, Captain. They are, however, engaging their impulse drive."

On the screen, the *Galtizh* moved slowly away, finally coming to a halt roughly a thousand kilometers distant. The image, though reduced, remained sharp, with no evidence of cloaking.

"All personnel aboard, Captain," the transporter room reported. "But they're not happy."

Kirk let some of the tension slip away. "I wouldn't wonder," he said. He turned to Audrea Benar, who had been a largely silent witness to everything since she had beamed aboard with Dajan and Jandra. "Dr. Benar, I'd appreciate it very much if you'd explain the situation to your people. Tell them they'll be allowed back on Temaris if at all possible, but that the prospects are not good."

"Of course, Captain."

"Mr. Spock," Kirk said as the 'lift closed behind Dr. Benar, "now that we know that at least some of the Probe data may be a language, I suggest you get to work on it. And on that scheme of yours to modify a tractor beam to simulate the Probe's emissions. If that thing is heading back to Earth to boil our oceans again, talking to it may be our only chance. If past experience is any guide, we don't have anything else that will touch it." He turned to the comm station.

"Lieutenant Kittay, get Admiral Cartwright or the President." He grimaced as she acknowledged the order. Neither one of them was going to be overjoyed at the quality of diplomacy he had exercised with Tiam. Or for that matter, with the latest news about the Probe.

"How long do you intend to continue this nonsense, Tiam?" Hiran scowled at the ambassador.

"Until you come to your senses, Hiran," Tiam

snapped. "There will be no communication with the
Enterprise until you assure me—*convincingly!*—that
you will abide by my decisions!"

Hiran shook his head disbelievingly. "Kirk was right,
wasn't he, Tiam? You *have* been sitting on information
about this thing all the time! He was probably right
about Wlaariivi, too! What *were* we doing there?"

"Nothing that concerns the Federation! Some simple
experiments, I am told. If they had been successful, the
results would have been dropped in the seas of the rebel
Variizt worlds to end the rebellions once and for all."

Hiran's scowl deepened. "Experiments? On sea creatures? Intelligent sea creatures as Kirk suspected?"

"Do not be so easily taken in by your Federation
'friend,' Hiran. These were mindless, purposeless creatures, useless even to themselves." Tiam smiled faintly.
"Although now they have found a use. My informant
tells me that, though the experiment failed, the experi-
menters discovered that certain portions of the creatures
are quite tasty. I understand the scientific stations have
been converted most efficiently to slaughterhouses and
processing plants."

"But now they are out of business," Hiran said
disgustedly, "destroyed by that thing. Kirk was right. I
am only surprised it didn't destroy them when it first
came through."

Tiam shook his head tiredly. "It didn't come within a
hundred parsecs of Wlaariivi then."

"So it *did* come through before! And you *did* know
about it!"

Tiam closed his eyes and sighed loudly. "Very well! If
it is the only way to calm you, Commander, I will tell
you. Yes, *your government* knew of the object's passage.
Attempts were made to communicate with it, but they

were unsuccessful. Observations were made. Data was taken. It was suggested that the object's lack of responsiveness indicated it was unmanned, perhaps even a derelict. Its power was obvious in its mass alone, so—"

"So someone decided to have it for themselves!"

"For the *Empire!*" Tiam snapped. "I am told the late Praetor himself was the driving force behind this effort! If the weaklings now in power had the sense to—"

"The 'weaklings' that *you* represent, Tiam?"

Tiam blinked, realizing he had spoken too much. But then he shrugged it off. Nothing could save this so-called peace conference now. And when the conference failed —as he had known from the start that it would, though he had not dared say it aloud until now—saner heads would prevail. Those who knew the Federation for what it was would once more be in charge, while those who would believe any lie, negotiate away any advantage, would be gone, trampled by the realities of the universe.

"Yes, Commander," Tiam said finally, "the 'weaklings' I represent. It is their good luck—the Empire's good luck—that they have me to represent them."

"Do they know you feel this way, Ambassador?"

"If they did, do you think they would have dared appoint me?"

"Why *did* they have the good fortune to appoint you?"

"I could not say, Commander. I know only that not everyone in their ranks is as naive as those who currently hold the reins. I am certain it was those more objective elements that were responsible for summoning me to the Citadel shortly after the Praetor's death, where I was told—in strictest confidence—about this object that had passed through the Empire. There was a possibility of communicating with it, I was told, of making use of its vast power, and I was given certain data to work with while my wife was given the honor of performing at the Praetor's funeral. As it turned out, the data was meaningless, certainly not any form of communication. Shortly after I informed them of my judgment in the matter, I was notified of my promotion and appointment, as well as of the role they expected my wife to play."

"And this was all because of the recommendations of these 'objective elements,' I assume?"

"Of course, although I was never specifically advised of that."

"And you of course shared this 'useless' data with those you now represent? Those who actually gave you the promotion and the appointment?"

"I of course did *not!* I was specifically instructed not to."

Hiran snorted, not quite a laugh. "You poor fool! Unless I miss my guess, you will soon join Jutak!"

Doggedly, overriding Tiam's repeated, disbelieving interruptions, Hiran tried to explain.

FIFTEEN

───────────── ☆ ─────────────

Captain's Log, Stardate 8493.4:

As expected, neither Admiral Cartwright nor the President was overjoyed at the latest developments, although Cartwright, except for the injuries to Riley, seemed not overly upset about the sabotage and the probable breakup of the conference. "I expected treachery from the Romulans," he said, "and I have not been disappointed." Cartwright also personally warned me to "avoid the trap of the seemingly rational Romulan." He offered it as a nonspecific maxim, but he was obviously referring to my hope that Commander Hiran could be trusted, at least to a limited extent, and that the relationship between the commander and myself was worth cultivating.

The admiral also passed on the contents of another message from the still-unnamed Romulan who had first brought him word of the Praetor's death. Word now was of the impending breakup of the conference. Rumors were already circulating in the Citadel, and the reformers, while still in power, were on increasingly shaky ground. The main thrust of the message was a plea to "exert every effort not to let this opportunity slip away, no matter how slim it may be." When asked if this mysterious voice out of the Empire was not in the same category of "seemingly rational Romulans" I had been warned against, Cartwright remained stubbornly mute, leaving me to wonder if in his early years, some of which had been spent in patrolling the Neutral Zone, Cartwright himself might not have had unofficial contact with his own Commander Hiran.

Meanwhile, word from Starbase Thirteen and patrol ships in the area indicates the Probe will be passing Temaris within hours. At its reported speed, it will reach the Federation—and Earth—in barely two days. We are, however, little closer to decoding the Probe's transmissions now than we were before anyone realized they might constitute a language. Spock has not slept since he began the task, and Jandra and Uhura and many of the other musicians have been getting by on occasional catnaps. Even Penalt has put in occasional appearances, though they seem to be more aimed at ingratiating himself with Jandra than with any analysis of the Probe data. The others, however, have spent most of their time listening to the sounds themselves. Some have tried playing the sounds both faster and slower, even backward, as they try to make some kind of "intuitive" sense out of them, something beyond the strict mathematical relationships that, after all, are all that any computer, no matter how complex, can work with. At best, however, they have been able only to identify and isolate patterns at other frequencies than the two to three thousand hertz of the one Uhura initially identified. These have ranged from a subsonic ten to twenty hertz to ultrasonics well above a hundred kilohertz.

All the patterns, however, are not enough for the computer and its universal translator program to produce any kind of translation. Time and again, it has seemed on the verge of success, but each time it has pulled back. When Spock queries it specifically, it can state only that certain patterns that had at first appeared similar had, on deeper analysis, proved dissimilar. Spock has produced an interesting analogy. In some Earth languages, such as Mandarin, Chinese, words superficially identical have different meanings dependent not only on inflection and relative pitch but on the harmonic and subharmonic content as well. He theorizes that, in the Probe's transmissions, there is, in effect, a "wild card" that neither he nor the computer nor any of the musicians has yet been able to identify, some factor that causes the meaning assigned to a given fragment of sound to change, seemingly at random.

On a more positive note, Commander Scott, once Spock explained what he had in mind, was quickly able to modify one of the tractor beams to act as a "voice" which we can use to "talk" to the Probe. However, barring a miracle, the best we will be able to do by the time the Probe arrives in the vicinity of Temaris is to, in effect, send the Probe's own words back to it, an echo delayed by months and thousands of parsecs. We can only hope that they prove to be words of welcome, not a challenge to do battle.

As for the *Galtizh*, it has not pulled up stakes for a return to the Empire, but it has remained totally unresponsive to all our attempts to communicate except to ask occasionally if we are ready to return our "hostages." However, sensors indicate that, despite the lack of response, the *Galtizh* has been listening attentively to everything we have tried to say to them. At the very least, they are as aware as we of the Probe's imminent passage through the Neutral Zone and of our intention of placing the *Enterprise* directly in its path and attempting communication.

And Dr. McCoy continues to assure us that Ambassador Riley is doing well and can be expected to awaken "any time now." Sulu and Uhura, however, who between them have spent more time with him than McCoy, do not seem as optimistic. If stable vital signs mean anything, they say, then he should have awakened a good twenty-four hours ago. Aside from occasional moans and grimaces, however, he remains totally unresponsive, and Sulu and Uhura, working on the theory that even totally comatose patients can, at some level, hear what is said around them, have begun their own course of treatment, regaling him—and each other—with every Riley-related recollection they can dredge up, including, I suspect, a few that never quite happened.

Dajan hesitated as he heard the animated voices coming from beyond the sickbay door the medtech had indicated. He would be intruding. These two—Commander Sulu and Uhura, the medtech had called her—were longtime friends of the ambassador, while he was less than an acquaintance and might even be considered an enemy.

And yet, Commander Sulu was the one who had suggested he pay the visit. "Uhura and I are already starting to repeat ourselves," Sulu had said, and then went on to explain their theory—their hope, really—that their words were somehow finding their way down to wherever the ambassador's mind had retreated, finding their way down and providing a link to the real world, a lifeline to at least keep him from slipping farther away. Dajan of course had never heard of such a thing, but the commander had seemed so earnest in his request, he was reluctant to turn him down. Particularly since Sulu had very likely saved Dajan's own life down on Temaris.

Pulling in a deep breath and swallowing away his misgivings, Dajan took the last two steps that put him directly in front of the door as it hissed open.

Dimly, as if filtering up from a distant, basement room, the voices brushed repeatedly at Commander Kevin Thomas Riley's consciousness, but he could not

—would not—hear them. His father, dead at the hand of Kodos' executioners more than four decades now, was speaking to him again, and his father's words were all that mattered.

"Take care of your mom, boyo," he was saying, tousling his four-year-old son's ginger hair, but only briefly; the Rileys weren't much for touching, even then, nor even in the dreams that had never entirely gone away. "I'll be going out for a while."

"Where you going, Da?" Kevin piped up. "Can I come, too?"

"*May* I come, too " his father said by reflex. "No, you may not. You may stay here and look after your mom, like I said. Go on now!"

An overwhelming sadness flowed from Riley the man to the boy he had been, and he desperately wished he could break out of the straitjacket that bound him to this same path again and again. He wished he could force the little boy to turn and lunge into his father's arms and tell him not to "volunteer" to die, to stay and save himself and his family until the help that Kodos said would never come did come. Or at least force the child to turn and hug his father and tell him he loved him so that his last memory would be of that hug instead of the less-than-gentle pat on the backside that sent him lurching away into the bedroom where his mother lay silently weeping.

But it had never worked before, and it didn't work now.

Nor did it work when, seemingly only moments later, he tried to keep the boy from falling asleep in his mother's arms as she hurried from the house as Kodos' squads swept the street. But once again, when the child awakened, his mother was gone and he was on a barren rooftop with a stranger while the greenish glow of massed phaser fire touched the low-hanging clouds.

Neither was a proper goodbye, the adult Riley said, and he and the boy could only cry.

And live the nightmare yet again.

On the surface, at least, Tiam remained obdurate. Nothing Hiran could say could convince the ambassador he was little more than a dupe, a figurehead selected not for his diplomatic abilities or even for his massive distrust of the Federation but for his relationship to the late Reelan.

"They could have found any number of paranoid would-be diplomats in the capital without bringing you in from the Provinces," Hiran had said, "but there is only one Dajan, brother to Reelan, and you are married to his sister. Your beliefs—and your obstinate refusal to look at anything that challenges them—were obviously a bonus but equally obviously not the primary reason they 'recommended' you. You certainly can't believe it sheer coincidence that Dajan's opposite number from the Federation, whose presence our leaders specifically requested, proved to be the sole survivor of Kalis Three!"

"Believe what you will, Commander," Tiam had said. "The fact remains that I *am* the Empire's official representative, and as such I am the final authority on all dealings with the Federation in the current situation."

The ambassador had also made the situation abundantly clear to everyone in the crew, particularly those involved with communications: Hiran was technically in command of the *Galtizh,* but Tiam was in command of Hiran. All communications, whether with the Empire or the *Enterprise,* had to be cleared and monitored by Tiam himself. And anyone who chose to disobey or sidestep those rules would be dealt with summarily. The aide Kital standing at his side, phaser plainly in evidence, emphasized his words, as did the undenied "rumor" that Kital had been the one to dispose of Jutak after that aide was found to be involved in some unspecified act of treachery.

Tiam did, however, make a point of being armed himself at all times.

When he reported the "kidnapping" of his wife and her brother, the ones he officially represented expressed shock and surprise and told him to do whatever he could to negotiate their release and to keep the conference from breaking down entirely, no matter what his "personal feelings" might be. The survival of their government very likely depended on it, they assured him.

Later, those who had "recommended" him spoke to him through the secret subspace transceiver in his quarters, which Jandra's departure had made much less troublesome to use. His handling of the matter, they told him, had been masterful. He was particularly commended for the "strength of purpose it must have taken" to call the defections of his wife and her brother kidnappings and to refuse to negotiate until the two had been returned, knowing full well they would *never* be returned. As a result of this timely evidence of "Federation treachery," the reformers were in full retreat. "Just a few more days," one of his supposed mentors said, "and their house of cards will collapse and we will step in and return stability and purpose to the Romulan government. Your contribution will not be forgotten."

It was shortly after that heartwarming endorsement had bolstered Tiam's confidence that he was notified that the *Enterprise* had taken itself out of orbit around Temaris. As its unanswered messages had repeatedly warned him it was planning to do, it had departed to "intercept" the behemoth that had destroyed the Wlaariivi stations and the *Henzu.*

"So, Commander," a self-satisfied Tiam said to a scowling Hiran, "the conference is at an end. The hostages were not returned, and the Federation vessel has departed for a conference with the Federation's new ally—or perhaps slave—from which it will most likely receive a detailed report on its depradations on Wlaariivi. I would say that, even by your standards, that constitutes unacceptable behavior on the part of the Federation representatives."

Hiran could only shake his head. "As you well know, they have gone to attempt to communicate with that thing, and they have repeatedly suggested we accompany them, but all you can do is crow about the breakdown of the conference! If you want the truth, Tiam—which I very much doubt!—their behavior is infinitely preferable to yours! And to that of your puppet masters! Doesn't truth mean *anything* to you? For that matter, doesn't your *wife* mean anything to you?"

A flash of anger, or perhaps humiliation, hardened Tiam's features for a moment, but then it was submerged in the self-satisfied smile, almost a smirk, that had become his predominant expression since the defections. "In the moment she allowed herself to be kidnapped," he said, "she served the Empire better than the rest of her life combined."

Hiran rolled his eyes in disbelief. "And what of this so-called 'ally' you say they are going to 'confer' with? I thought your puppet masters were more than a little interested in it. Don't you think they'd be interested in the results of this 'conference'?"

"Perhaps, but I prefer observing from a distance. Considering what that thing did to the *Henzu*—and to an unarmed cargo ship millions of kilometers distant—I would not care to get within range, whether it is under control of the Federation or simply the out-of-control killing machine it appears to be. In either case, we will be safer here—and hence more likely to be able to report the results of its encounter with the *Enterprise.*" A glimmer of anticipation overlay Tiam's smile for a moment. "The destruction of the *Henzu* was recorded by sensors more than a parsec distant."

Sulu had taken the helm for the rendezvous with the Probe, and Chekov had again assumed the navigator's station. Even Uhura had silently replaced Kittay at the comm station, and Scott stood at the engineering station next to her. Spock of course was at the science station, while McCoy watched the viewscreen from the command well at Kirk's left. No words had been spoken, but the situation had spoken for itself. They had already traveled through three centuries of time in a refurbished Klingon rustbucket to stop this thing, whatever it was, and now, in the *Enterprise,* they would face it again. Together.

The only non-crew-member on the bridge was Jandra, whose uncanny ability had first detected a pattern in the midst of the Probe's chaotic emissions. The other musicians were gathered around an auxiliary viewscreen set up in the same rec-deck area that had held the reception. Even Penalt was there, after grudgingly allowing himself to be shepherded off the bridge.

"*Shenandoah* reports the Probe maintaining its course through the Neutral Zone, Captain," Uhura said quietly. "It should be entering our own sensor range at any moment."

"Thank you, Commander," Kirk said, equally quietly, his eyes on the viewscreen. "Ready, Mr. Spock?"

"Ready, Captain."

"Mr. Scott?"

"Aye, Captain. Backup battery power fully charged and fully shielded. Even if we lose primary and secondary power, we'll still have life support and impulse power."

"And tractor beams?"

"Aye, sir, tractor beams. It would no' do to lose our voice."

Kirk was silent a moment, pulling his breath in and letting it out in a faint whoosh. "So, Mr. Spock, start the conversation."

Something was in the entity's path that had not been there when the path had been constructed. Directly in its path. Even at this distance, it was obvious that it was not one of the hundreds of billions of natural objects contained in the crystal memory.

After less than a trillion calculations, it decided. The delay involved in altering its course to avoid this object would be insignificant, less than one millionth of the projected travel time.

"Captain!" Uhura looked around sharply from the comm station. "*Shenandoah* reports an alteration in the Probe's course. Its new course will take it approximately one-tenth parsec Galactic north of our current position."

Kirk suppressed a curse. "It already knows we're here. Its sensors are obviously longer range than ours. Mr. Sulu, put us in front of it again, warp factor of your choice."

"Aye-aye, Captain. But it would help if it showed up on *our* sensors. One-tenth parsec due north, you said, Commander?"

"Right, Mr. Sulu," Uhura confirmed.

"Sensors detecting its emissions, Captain," Spock reported, "but not the object itself."

"So it's still 'yelling its head off,'" McCoy remarked to no one in particular.

The starbow of warp entry filled the viewscreen for a moment as Sulu engaged the drive.

The object drifted back into the entity's path.

But now it was close enough for the crystal sensor to determine the nature of the object.

The commands were issued. The crystal sensor, still sheathed, reached out.

Mites, the incoming data said. The object is another of their spacegoing metallic bubbles of air.

Destroy it, one set of recent memories said, but another, stronger set said no. These mites are thousands of parsecs from those who tried to still the voice of the blue-green world and thousands of parsecs from those associated with the blue world, still more thousands of parsecs and hundreds of millennia from those who had attacked and nearly destroyed you. There is nothing to say they are related to any of the three. Nonetheless, the third and strongest set of memories said, note their location. After the blue world has been exhausted of useful data, return and study these, determine if there is a connection between them and the blue world, between them and the blue-green world. Between them and those who had attacked and nearly destroyed you.

Again a trillion calculations flashed along the crystal pathways, and the course was altered again, adding another fraction of a second to the predicted travel time to the blue world.

"It is within direct sensor range, Captain," Spock reported, "but it is again changing course to avoid us. Its new course will take it through our original position."

"Alphonse and Gaston, interstellar version," Kirk muttered. "Mr. Sulu—"

"Aye-aye, Captain, I'll get us in front of it again."

Again the object was in the entity's path. And closer.

Once again the entity altered its path, this time so extensively that several seconds were added to its travel time to the blue world.

Once again the object moved toward the entity's projected path, but this time the entity had placed itself beyond the object's reach. By the time the object completed its move, the entity would have passed the would-be point of interception.

Nonetheless, the mites' actions continued to be considered and questioned in the crystalline paths. Were they after all associated with the blue-green world? Do they think they can strike back for the deaths on that world? a recent set of memories asked.

There is nothing to say they are related to that world, another set repeated, or to the blue world. Observe them as we pass and proceed along the constructed path. Return when the primitives have been questioned, when the mites that are known to be associated with the blue world have been sufficiently studied.

Once again the crystal sensor reached out as far as it was capable of reaching from within its protective sheath. To reach further, the entity would have to drop out of its constructed path and shift to near motionlessness and extend the crystal sensor, unprotected, into space. That would increase the predicted time to the blue world not by millionths but by hundredths, and the entity was not yet ready for such measures.

But then, suddenly—even by the entity's picosecond standards—as the sensor touched the still-distant object, billions of crystal pathways that had lain dormant for hundreds of millennia sprang to life in recognition. Billions of others that had been in almost constant use for those same hundreds of millennia were stilled, silencing the entity's voice.

In the newly activated pathways, countless trillions of calculations and comparisons were made and confirmed, not once but a thousand times in a thousand ways.

The True Language, the calculations and comparisons said again and again, the True Language.

The mites were speaking in the True Language.

"Captain, the object—"

"—has changed course again," Kirk finished Spock's report with a grimace. The last course change, which would have taken the object within a few hundred AU of the Temaris system, had been almost beyond their ability to match even at maximum warp. If it now shifted even a few arc seconds further, the *Enterprise* could in no way intercept it.

"No, Captain, it has ceased its emissions. And it is slowing rapidly."

Silence gripped the bridge.

"All stop, Mr. Sulu."

"Aye-aye, sir."

"Mr. Spock, reduce tractor beam output by fifty percent." Anything to indicate that, now that they had its attention, they wanted to avoid shouting. At close range, that thing's shouts might even knock out Commander Scott's supershielded backup power systems.

"Yes, Captain."

"Commander Uhura, try the *Galtizh* again."

"No response, Captain."

"Are they still there, Spock?"

"They are, Captain, and they are still listening as well."

"Just not answering." Kirk shook his head. "Keep them up to date anyway, Commander Uhura." Whether an informed Tiam was more or less dangerous than one who, not knowing what was happening, could strike out blindly, Kirk didn't know, but this way at least Hiran would also know the score and might be able to restrain the ambassador before he went completely over the wall.

Every light and indicator on the bridge flickered, then steadied as everyone on the bridge caught their breath.

"The object appears to be emitting again, Captain," Spock confirmed.

"Cut tractor beam output another fifty percent," Kirk snapped.

"Done, Captain."

"Is it still emitting?"

"Yes, Captain, but at a reduced level."

"Reduce again, to five percent of original level."

"It is following suit, Captain."

"So it knows how to whisper as well as shout," Kirk said softly. "Now if we could just figure out what the hell it's whispering about. Mr. Spock, are its emissions now the same as the ones in your recordings?"

"Unknown as yet, Captain. The computer has been instructed to analyze all incoming signals and compare them with the recordings, but it has not yet established any matches."

"Maybe it uses a different language for whispering than it does for shouting," McCoy volunteered with a grimace. "It would make as much sense as anything else that thing's done so far."

"Put it on the speakers," Kirk said, "but softly."

The sounds that washed over the bridge and the listening musicians in the rec deck area sounded identical to Kirk, but then, he had never been able to detect a single one of the patterns Jandra and the others insisted were there, no matter how often they were pointed out. To him it had been noise then, and it was noise now.

"If *anyone* has an idea—" he began, but Uhura's voice cut him off.

"Captain, the *Galtizh* is responding."

"On-screen, Commander."

"Not to us, Captain." She shook her head firmly. "To the Probe!"

SIXTEEN

☆

Tiam's first reaction to word that the object, now within sensor range, had changed course and was heading almost directly for the Temaris system had been to get the *Galtizh* at least a half parsec away before the object arrived. That obstructionist Hiran, however, had delayed unpardonably. They had still not gotten under way when the object stopped dead in its tracks and fell silent.

Tiam tensed as he watched the viewscreen and listened to the subcommander's reports of sensor readings. What was happening *now?* He had been listening to Kirk's interminable updates, anticipating the failure of that insane plan of his to "communicate" through a tractor beam, all the while wondering how the Federation could allow anyone with Kirk's obviously feeble grip on reality to command a starship.

But now the object was stopping. Why? Was it just pausing long enough to destroy the Federation ship, still

226

a half light-year from Temaris? Had Kirk gotten his wish and attracted the thing's attention with his demented scheme to—

Suddenly, Tiam realized what had happened. It had not been Kirk's antics with the tractor beam that had attracted the object's attention. It couldn't be. A tractor beam's range was measured in thousands of kilometers, not the parsecs that still separated the *Enterprise* from that thing. It had been the *Enterprise*'s darting back and forth in the thing's path, like a child standing in the roadway, waving its hands to stop a Kalgorian combat engine!

It would be a fitting end for Kirk—and Jandra!—to be swatted like bothersome insects, but it was not one that Tiam wished to share.

And he would have shared it, he realized angrily, if it hadn't been for Hiran's stubbornness.

"Commander Hiran," he said sharply, "you're going to get your wish after all. The *Galtizh* will remain where it is."

"I am pleased to hear it, Ambassador," Hiran said, hiding his surprise. "Might I ask—"

"You may not!" Tiam snapped, then added, "The Federation ship is still safely distant. Its destruction will not affect us here."

Hiran issued the necessary orders, mentally shaking his head. Tiam waited, hoping he had been right.

A minute later, Hiran almost laughed. "The object appears to be responding peaceably to the *Enterprise*," he said, "not launching an attack."

Tiam cursed silently as he realized Hiran was right. The object was obviously not reacting to the *Enterprise* the way it had reacted to the *Henzu*.

"Orders, Mr. Ambassador?" Hiran asked blandly.

Tiam's mind raced, trying to keep up as the world his assumptions had built for him turned upside down. Could Kirk have been right after all? Could even that foolishness with the tractor beam and the recordings of that thing's emissions—

His stomach sank. *He* had been given the data recorded during the Probe's first passage through the Empire, and he had studied it and proclaimed it useless. But now Kirk, using similar data, had brought the object to a stop, had somehow persuaded it to respond, not with destruction but with—what? More senseless "data"?

Or were they actually communicating? Could there actually be something to that insane idea that a language lay hidden in those mountains of gibberish? Had he missed it, while Kirk—and *Jandra!*—had found it?

And translated it?

If Kirk had, and if word got back to the Citadel that Tiam had failed where Kirk had succeeded, as it surely would—

But no! Kirk was not *communicating* with that thing! He was merely playing back what the object itself had sent out. He was echoing, not talking! He had said so himself!

But I can do the same! Tiam realized abruptly. *Before that thing decides that the* Enterprise *is the only ship worth noticing, worth communicating with—*

The data he had been given was in his quarters! All he had to do—

Tiam jerked to his feet. "Prepare to transmit on all subspace frequencies," he said, racing from the bridge, "maximum power!"

* * *

228

The paradox emerged into the crystalline paths within milliseconds.

The mites, trillions of calculations and comparisons told the entity, were speaking in the True Language.

But a similar number of calculations and comparisons also told the entity: the mites do not possess the power of Speech.

More milliseconds swept past as the crystal sensor experienced the phenomenon, and those experiences were analyzed and compared with the experiences of five hundred millennia ago, when it had been bathed in the True Language, when its creators had given it its purpose and its methods and its original store of memories and instructions.

A crude imitation, the comparison said.

Where Speech would have reached out to the crystal sensor within milliseconds, the imitation did not. The crystal sensor had to reach out and retrieve the vibrations of the True Language, in the same way that it had reached into the oceans of hundreds of worlds and retrieved the simple words of the primitives.

Yet it was different from the matter-bound voices of the primitives, for its energy spread through matterless space, albeit at a pace exceedingly ponderous.

Its creators' instructions had been clear. Return with the news the moment the existence of others capable of speaking the True Language is confirmed.

But its memories were equally clear. The True Language could be spoken only by those who had developed the power of Speech.

And these mites had obviously not developed that power.

Finally, after seconds had passed, the content of what it was receiving became clear to the entity.

It was the same message it had itself Spoken to every passing world: a greeting and a history and an invitation. It was the same message it had been Speaking in the moments before this encounter, the same that it had been Speaking when it had approached and departed from the blue world and the thousands of other worlds: the message its creators had instructed it to continue to Speak until there came a reply. And now the reply had come.

But it was not Speech.

It was not true communication.

It was a mimicking of the True Language, a repeating of what the entity had itself Spoken millions of times over the millennia, but those that mimicked did not Speak.

The paradox had to be resolved. The questions of the blue-world primitives and even the mystery of what lay hidden in its own lost memory faded into the background in the face of this new mystery.

The entity reached out to the mites and Spoke, not in the matter-bound way of the primitives but in the True Language. What are you that you mimic the True Language without the power of Speech? it asked in a hundred ways.

There was no reply, only the continued echoing of its own words.

But the object stopped its headlong race across space.

An eternity later, it lowered its mimicking voice.

The entity lowered its own, remembering the effects its full voice had had on similar of the mites' devices while it had been in the vicinity of the blue world.

Another eternity, and the object lowered its voice again, as if suggesting the entity do the same.

And again.

But still it continued with its repetition of what the entity itself had Spoken countless times.

More eternities, more seconds passed while the paradox darted along the crystal paths, accessing memory after memory, instruction after instruction, in search of a solution, a remedy for its own existence.

Suddenly, another form of energy touched the crystal sensor. It had been touched by this type of energy before, most recently when it had cleansed the blue-green world, but never at this level.

The entity searched for the source and found another of the mites' spacegoing metallic bubbles.

Ordinarily, that would have been the end of it. The mites offered no threat, and no connection between these mites and those who mimicked the True Language could be established. Therefore they were irrelevant.

But this was not an ordinary time for the entity. Billions of the crystal paths were locked in an effort to resolve the paradox of the mites who mimicked the True Language. Billions more had been returned to their search through the entity's near-infinite memories for answers to the questions that had been raised by its interaction with the blue world, by the primitives that had reappeared there, without reason and without warning. Still more paths, even now, worried at the shadows of the lost memory.

This was a time when nothing could be deemed irrelevant until it had been thoroughly analyzed.

The crystal sensor absorbed the energies, sent them hurtling along the crystal paths, where their patterns would be subjected to the minutest, most thorough examination. For seconds, the patterns of all the energies as a whole, all the thousands of frequencies, were examined and compared to the millions of other such patterns still stored in its memory.

But then, as it had never done before, it separated the energies, examining each of the thousands of frequencies separately.

And then it began to dissect the individual frequencies, only to find that, buried deep within each frequency, were other, lesser frequencies.

And it began to analyze those buried frequencies.

For a microsecond, the crystal paths froze in what, in a living being, would have been shock. In the entity, it was the acknowledgment of a second paradox, even greater than the first.

For there, hidden deep within that tangle of energies, was the True Language, not once but repeated thousands of times over.

To a human, it would have been comparable to examining a handful of snow under a microscope and finding, imprinted at the heart of each and every otherwise unique flake, an image of his own face.

This was a paradox it knew instantly was beyond its power to resolve.

And when it encountered something beyond its understanding, there was only one course of action open to it.

Return to its creators.

And lay the paradox before them.

The entity reached out and drew the metallic bubbles to itself.

"Responding to the Probe?" Kirk scowled at the viewscreen, then turned back to Commander Uhura at the comm station. "Responding how?"

"Transmitting on all subspace frequencies, sir." She

winced slightly and touched her earpiece to cut the volume. "I can't be positive, but it sounds as if they're playing back the same recordings we are."

"Using regular subspace channels, not a tractor beam?"

"Yes, Captain."

"Commander, whether anyone on the *Galtizh* responds to us or not, ask them what the devil they're doing!" Kirk turned to the science station. "Spock, can the *Galtizh* transmissions be analyzed? *Are* they sending the same thing we are?"

Spock studied the readouts for several seconds. "It would appear that they are, Captain." He called up another set of readings. "However, the fact that the computer has already been able to determine that the two transmissions are indeed identical would seem to indicate that the emissions the Probe is currently directing at the *Enterprise* are not. The computer has yet to establish any matching patterns in those."

"Which means what?" Kirk said. "That the thing is actually answering us? Or that our transmission simply set off a new automatic sequence that will keep repeating like the original?"

"Unknown, Captain. However—" Spock broke off, one eyebrow arching as the readings changed. "It has ceased emitting again, Captain."

"Not just cut its power back further?"

"If so, it has been cut back beyond the point at which we are capable of detecting it."

"The Romulans scared it off? Or maybe it's talking to *them,* now, instead of us?"

"That is possible, Captain, but—"

The *Enterprise* lurched. Suddenly, the air felt thick, almost liquid. Every sound was muffled.

Kirk tried to spin toward the viewscreen, but he could only turn laboriously.

"Mr. Sulu," he tried to say, but his vocal chords could not vibrate rapidly enough to produce the sounds, his lips and tongue could not move rapidly enough to shape the words.

He was already feeling short of breath, but as he tried to fill his lungs with a sharp intake of air, it was as if a massive elastic band enclosed his chest, keeping it from expanding. The air, thick and viscous, entered at a snail's pace.

If this kept up—

Then he saw Sulu's hand, moving slowly, laboriously toward the controls that would engage the warp drive.

Yes! he thought, but forming the word aloud was impossible.

Out of the corner of his eye, Kirk saw McCoy, his mouth gaping open, obviously struggling for breath. The doctor's knees were slowly buckling, one hand gripping the arm of the command chair, the other coming up to claw at his throat.

Finally, Sulu's hand touched the warp engine controls.

There was another lurch, more powerful than the first, then a nonstop shuddering that seemed to grip his body directly, inside and out, like an out-of-control transporter field. And the air thickened even more, making breathing totally impossible.

In sickbay, Commander Kevin Thomas Riley could not breathe. Nor could the four-year-old Kevin Riley, and as he once again fought to awaken before his about-to-die mother handed him off to that same faceless stranger for the thousandth time, his struggle to awaken became a struggle to breathe.

And that fragment of the adult Riley that never fully faded from the dream, that fragment that sometimes strained to hear the voices hovering just beyond his grasp, began to strengthen.

But the voices were gone now, the adult Riley realized. Now there was only silence—and the struggle to pull the ever-thickening air into his lungs.

What was happening? Had Kodos found a way to poison the very air, a new and more efficient way to dispose of the excess population?

But no! Kodos was long dead. And Kevin Riley was a long way from Tarsus Four.

And his terror was growing by the second as his efforts to drag air into his lungs grew more desperate, more painful, until—

Suddenly, he could breathe once again. The air surged into the adult Riley's lungs, and the child's terror began to fade.

Father, they both sighed.

Then the nightmare gripped them again, and the adult Riley could only watch helplessly as yet another cycle of pain and guilt began.

Once he could breathe again, the first thing Dajan did was check the readouts above the ambassador's bed.

He slumped with relief. Except for elevated heartbeat and respiration, everything was normal. A moment later, the door hissed open and a technician, breathing as heavily as either Dajan or the ambassador, raced in.

Dajan stood back quickly, giving the woman room. Only then did the Romulan look down at the ambassador's face—and remember the sound that had whispered from the unconscious man's lips moments after the air had thinned enough to make sound possible.

"Father," the translator in his ear had whispered a moment later, and Dajan found his throat tightening as he remembered, as he wondered what his own parents would have thought to see him here, in a Federation ship, watching over a Federation commander.

Gripped by a sudden need, he turned and left to seek out his sister.

Somehow, Sulu lifted his fingers from the controls.

There was another lurch, and the shuddering stopped.

And breathing, though still in agonizing slow motion, again became possible.

But it was not enough, Kirk realized. Already, his vision was rimmed with blackness that was expanding inward second by second.

And his heart—if the blood it had to pump had thickened as much as the air—

Suddenly, it was over.

The sounds of the bridge returned to normal.

The air was once again air, and it burst into his lungs with a painful jolt. His heart raced as it pumped the newly thinned blood.

He reached out to grasp McCoy's arm before the doctor could continue the fall he had started several seconds before. Everyone on the bridge was sucking in breath after breath.

Finally, he looked up at the viewscreen.

The first thing he saw was the *Galtizh,* only a few kilometers distant.

The second thing he saw was the starless blackness beyond the *Galtizh.*

For a moment he wondered what had happened to the countless stars that should have dotted the screen, wondered if the ships had somehow been transported into the starless wasteland of intergalactic space.

And then he realized what the blackness was. It wasn't the blackness of empty space. It was the massive, ebony shell of the Probe, only a few hundred meters beyond the *Galtizh*.

SEVENTEEN

————————— ☆ —————————

"Try quarter impulse this time, Mr. Sulu," Kirk said once everyone had recovered their breath from the half-impulse attempt, "and set it to shut off automatically in five seconds unless the command is overridden."

Sulu pulled in a deep breath. "Quarter impulse for five seconds, sir . . . now."

For a moment, nothing happened, and hope surged through Kirk that, this time, they might make it. Maybe the triggering level was—

The air thickened, filling his throat like a river of syrup. An instant later, his body once again turned leaden and his momentary hope vanished.

An interminable five seconds later, the impulse drive shut down.

The air once again became air, his body once again normal, trembling flesh and blood.

McCoy's voice crackled from the intercom from sickbay. "How long are you going to keep banging all our heads against that brick wall, Jim? I know I said Riley wasn't being *noticeably* harmed, but I can't make any guarantees. About him *or* about me!"

"Nothing more, Bones, at least not for right now."

"Not that I don't trust you, Jim, but leave the intercom open. Just in case you change your mind, I'll have a little warning down here."

"All right, Bones. And you let *us* know the second Kevin wakes up." He turned to Spock. "Do the sensors tell you *anything* about what this thing keeps doing to us?"

"Very little, Captain. The energy field that grips the *Enterprise* intensifies within ten microseconds of the time impulse power is applied, regardless of level of power applied. Warp drive triggered the field within one microsecond."

"But no indication of the nature of the field?"

"None, Captain."

"And the *Galtizh*? I assume it's stuck the same as we are."

"Based on sporadic observations, Captain, it would appear so. I have noted two attempts to break free using impulse power, with similar results."

At least the Probe wasn't being discriminatory. Kirk turned to the comm station. "Have you been having any luck, Commander Uhura, while we've been beating our collective heads against this invisible brick wall?"

"None, sir. All systems check out normally, but there is no response from Starfleet or any Federation ship or outpost."

Kirk grimaced. So this thing not only had them bound

hand and foot, it also either had a gag in their mouths or cotton stuffed in their ears. Or both.

"Mr. Sulu, can you get a reading on where we're going? If we're going *anywhere,* that is."

"Not directly, sir. Whatever's blanking out communications must be doing the same thing to the helm. According to my instruments, we're dead in the water, completely motionless. But by the motion of the star field, the computer calculates we're doing more than the warp twelve the Probe was reported to be doing before—a lot more."

"In what direction?"

"We appear to be moving in toward an unexplored quadrant of the Orion Arm, sir. If we continue at our current speed, we should be through it and into the Sagittarius Arm in less than a day."

"That *would* be a lot more than warp twelve, Mr. Sulu."

Sulu shrugged. "In for a penny, in for a pound, sir."

Kirk smiled faintly. "At least it isn't headed for Earth anymore," he said, turning again toward the comm station. "Any word from the *Galtizh,* Commander? Or are communications with them blocked as well?"

"Local communications appear to be normal, Captain," Uhura said. "I've been monitoring the *Galtizh* periodically, and they appear to have been doing much the same as we have been doing—trying unsuccessfully to contact someone in the outside world. They haven't responded to our hail yet, however."

"They won't," Kirk said, "until Tiam's good and ready—or Hiran throws over the traces and decides to ignore him. But keep at it, Commander."

Kirk glanced around the bridge, then returned his gaze to the viewscreen, where the *Galtizh* still floated, as motionless as the *Enterprise,* against the featureless blackness that was the Probe.

"Spock, what can the sensors tell us about the Probe itself?" he asked. "It *does* register, doesn't it?"

"It does, Captain, but the resultant readings have thus far revealed little."

"Do they at least tell us if there's a pilot in there somewhere?"

"There is virtually no open space anywhere within the object, Captain," Spock replied as he studied the readouts, "and no indication of discrete living organisms of any kind. There is, however, much material, including the otherwise metallic shell and the crystalline object it extrudes on occasion, that may in some senses be organic."

"And what senses are those, Spock? Don't go coy on me."

"That was not my intention, Captain. The primary sense in which the materials could be considered organic is that they appear to be self-regenerating at a molecular level." Spock paused as the readings on his instruments shifted. After a moment, his eyebrows took on the arch that so often preceded a confession that something had just proven "fascinating."

"So, Spock," Kirk prompted, "you have that look. What did you find?"

Still Spock remained silent as he called up other, stored readings and compared them to the new.

Finally he spoke. "There is a ten-meter block of crystalline material in the heart of the Probe, Captain, but a different form of crystal from that which makes up the extruded object. What may prove significant, however, is that the basic structure of the material that makes up this crystalline block appears to be identical to the structure of the material that makes up the so-called crystal memory we took from the Exodus Hall on Temaris Four."

All eyes turned toward the science station, but McCoy, though listening from sickbay several decks away, was the first to speak. "You're saying this thing was built by the *Erisians?"*

"Not at all, Doctor. I am simply saying that the structure of the crystalline material—"

"I know what you *said,* Spock! What did you *mean?"*

"I mean only what I say, Doctor."

"Knock it off, you two," Kirk intervened. "Spock, just how distinctive is this 'crystalline structure'? Have you seen anything like it before?"

"Your questions do not have meaningful answers, Captain. The structure is 'distinctive' in the same sense that the structure of a dilithium crystal is 'distinctive.' Many crystal structures could be considered similar to that of a dilithium crystal, but only a dilithium crystal will operate effectively in a matter/antimatter power generator."

Kirk suppressed a sigh. "All right, Spock, I'll rephrase the question. Have you ever seen a crystalline structure *exactly* like this one before?"

"Only in the object on Temaris Four, Captain."

"Then some connection between the Probe and the Erisians *is* likely."

"A connection is possible, Captain, but I could not say it is 'likely.'"

"But if the structure of the block in the Probe is identical to the crystal memory we found on Temaris—"

"The structure of the dilithium in our warp drive is

identical to that in the warp drive of a Klingon ship, Captain. Using your logic, Federation and Klingon ships are 'likely' to have been built by the same people."

"But dilithium is a naturally occurring substance—"

"As these crystals may also be, Captain. Without further analysis, which could degrade the data the Temaris crystal contains, it is impossible to say if they occur naturally or were manufactured."

Kirk's suppressed sigh turned into an almost-laugh. "All right, Spock, you win. There may or may not be a connection between the Probe and the Erisians, but I would suggest keeping a very sharp eye out for one, just in case. I don't suppose there's any way of reading the data out of this block of crystal, the way you read it out of the Temaris one?"

"Not as yet, Captain. Although our sensors can penetrate the Probe, they cannot be focused finely enough to analyze the crystal at the necessary molecular level."

Kirk frowned thoughtfully. "But if our sensors can reach inside it at all, then our weapons—or the Romulans'—should be able to do the same. Right?"

"Unknown, Captain, but the experience of the Romulan ships near Wlaariivi would seem to indicate otherwise."

Kirk nodded. "It presumably has a whale of a defense system, no pun intended. But the only way to check it out would be to attack, and that would probably be fatal in a few microseconds, if the way it shuts us down whenever we try to use the impulse engines or warp drive is any indication. What about power? Where is it getting its power?"

"That is another aspect of the Probe that could be construed as giving it the qualities of an organism as opposed to a machine, Captain. Like a living organism, it does not appear to contain a discrete power source. Instead, all power appears to be generated on-site, so to speak, wherever it is needed, in whatever form it is needed, just as the chemical reactions in an animal's muscle tissue generate the power for that muscle to contract."

"What about the power that keeps this thing moving, dragging us along with it, at double or triple the warp factor we're capable of? Is that generated the same way?"

"It would appear so, Captain. Do not forget that none of this energy is directly detectable by our sensors. My speculations are based solely on a continuing analysis of the substances of which the Probe is composed."

Kirk grimaced. "It sounds more and more as if the only way we're going to find out anything worthwhile here—like how to get it to let us go—is to ask it some questions, which will be a little difficult unless we learn how to talk to it. Therefore, barring other developments, I suggest everyone concentrate his efforts along those lines. Mr. Spock, you will be in charge. Take whomever and whatever you need."

"As you wish, Captain." He turned from the science station. "Commander Uhura, Jandra, if you will follow me, we will join the others."

Lieutenant Kittay was just sliding in to take's Uhura's place at the comm station when a light blinked on. Kittay hurriedly seated herself and worked the controls. A moment later, she turned toward Kirk.

"Captain," she said, "the *Galtizh* is hailing us."

Tiam struggled to his feet, gasping for breath, his legs rubbery. He realized after a moment that he must have passed out, not just once but several times. Each time, he had revived only to have his breath congeal in his lungs a second later. Once, he remembered someone's voice—Hiran's?—calling for full impulse power, but a moment later he was again struggling to breathe, and the ring of black was once again closing in on his field of vision.

"All systems check out as fully functional, Commander," he heard the subcommander report tersely to Hiran this time, her voice under control but showing the effects of the series of near suffocations they had all undergone, "but there is no response from any Empire facility."

Hiran was flushed and breathing deeply but was otherwise unaffected.

"Hiran, what—" Tiam began.

"When I find out, I'll tell you," Hiran snapped, not taking his eyes from the viewscreen and its image of the *Enterprise.*

"Commander! May I remind you—"

Again Tiam was cut off, this time not by Hiran but by a hand gripping his upper arm with painful firmness. He jerked about to see who could have such temerity.

It was Kital. But—

His aide was holding a phaser in one hand, its muzzle pressed to Tiam's side.

"Come with me, Ambassador," Kital said, so softly that no one but Tiam—even had anyone diverted his attention from the viewscreen—could hear. "It is past time you understood the situation aboard the *Galtizh.*"

Stunned, Tiam didn't resist as Kital returned the phaser to its holster and led him from the bridge, one hand still gripping Tiam's arm with surprising strength, the other resting within centimeters of the phaser. A minute later, they were in Kital's Spartan quarters, a single compartment less than a quarter the size of each of the rooms in Tiam's. Kital gestured for Tiam to sit on a benchlike bunk.

"What is the meaning of this outrage?" Tiam finally managed to ask.

"My apologies, Ambassador, for the crudeness of my approach, but it was necessary. There is much you must be told, and it is imperative that Hiran not suspect. I saw no other way to get you away from him quickly and quietly."

"What gives you the right to talk to me in—"

"Do not waste our time with foolish questions," Kital broke in impatiently. "Simply listen, and you will learn all that you need to know. I have been authorized by those responsible for your presence here to assume control whenever I felt circumstances warranted such action, and—"

"The Committee told me nothing of—"

"I do not refer to the Committee. I refer to those factions within the Interim Government responsible for summoning you from the Provinces and bringing you to the attention of the Committee. Those with whom you have so often consulted during this mission."

Tiam scowled uneasily. "Who are these so-called 'factions'? I know of no such—"

"Do not continue to waste our time!" Kital snapped, his patience seeming to wear thin. "I refer to the factions with which you so often consult, using the subspace transceiver hidden in your quarters."

Tiam felt his stomach knotting. "You know of that?"

"Of course. We provided it and installed it. Every exchange has been monitored by my men or myself. Those times, at least, when it was not one of my men you were actually speaking with."

246

"No!"

"I assure you, it is true, Tiam," Kital said. "But I do not have the time to debate the point. Later, once communications are restored with the Empire, you will be allowed to verify my authority. In the meantime, you will have to accept it. I would prefer your cooperation— we are, after all, both working for the good of the Empire—but I will settle for your obedience."

"And if I refuse you both?"

Kital eyed him grimly for a moment, his hand briefly brushing his phaser. "Then you will die, Tiam. The one thing I cannot allow is for you or anyone to hinder me in my assignment."

"Are you *threatening* me, Kital?" His onetime aide's matter-of-fact tone chilled Tiam as much as the man's arrogance—and his own impotence—infuriated him.

"I am stating a simple fact, nothing more," Kital said, but then his voice and features hardened as he leaned close over Tiam. "And believe this, Ambassador Tiam: Disposing of you will be far easier for me than what I was forced to do to subcenturion Jutak when he failed in his assignment." His eyes locked with Tiam's for several seconds, but finally, pulling back, he hunched his shoulders as if to throw off a bothersome cloak.

"I will say again, Ambassador Tiam," he went on, "I would prefer your active cooperation. I would prefer that you contribute to a solution to the unexpected situation we find ourselves in, for I am sure you have valuable contributions to make. I would prefer that, for the good of the Empire, you put aside any personal feelings you might have toward me or toward my superiors for the perhaps unfortunate way in which this was handled. If you are prepared to do that, well and good. Your contributions will be noted and remembered when the time comes. If you are not, if you are determined to impede me in what I feel must be done, then you will leave me no choice."

Kital paused, a faint smile momentarily softening his expression. "I have noticed how you look at my uniform, Centurion. Are you too proud to subordinate yourself to a lowly subcenturion? Is that why you hesitate to pledge your cooperation?" His smile broadened slightly. "If it will make the situation easier for you to accept, I will introduce myself."

Tiam scowled. "Do you think me a fool?" he snapped. "You are subcenturion Kital, my aide! Through some process I don't pretend to understand, you have come to have the authority—you *say* you have the authority to—"

"On the contrary, I am Commander Jenyu, most recently of the *Shalyar*. Except for the obstinacy of certain members of the Committee, you would be aboard the *Shalyar* and I would still be its commander."

Kital—Jenyu?—shrugged. "We had to make do as best we could under the circumstances."

So Hiran was right after all, Tiam thought abruptly, angrily. *I have not been a player but a pawn, selected not for my abilities and beliefs but for my disgraced brother-in-law. Everything I have said and done since this mission began has been a pointless charade. But now that I know the truth . . .*

Tiam swallowed away some of the throat-tightening anger. He forced a slight smile as he looked at his "aide" and his subcenturion's uniform. *Now that I know the truth,* he thought again, *we will see who is player and who is pawn.*

"If it is for the good of the Empire," Tiam said, "you

248

will of course have my full cooperation. Now, as you have said, let us not waste time. The sooner you tell me what you have to tell me, the sooner we can begin our work."

A scowling Commander Hiran filled the *Enterprise*'s viewscreen.

"Commander Hiran," Kirk said dryly, "it's good to hear from you."

A flicker of a smile momentarily softened the edges of the scowl. "It is good to be allowed to contact you," Hiran said flatly. "I thank you for the information you have been sending regarding your own activities."

"To be perfectly frank, Commander," Kirk said, "it was as much in the interests of self-preservation as anything. I felt that you would be better able to keep your situation under control if you knew what we were doing rather than having to guess."

Hiran nodded. "I would have felt the same in your position—if you had someone like Tiam on board. Obviously, the ambassador felt differently."

"And how does he feel now?"

"That we should cooperate—'in the face of a common enemy,' I believe he said. But you will be able to ask him yourself in a moment. He is on his way to the bridge from his quarters."

"Before he arrives, Commander, let me ask you: Did you experience the same phenomenon we did? The air seeming to thicken until you couldn't breathe?"

Hiran nodded. "It stopped when that thing had finished reeling us in, but it came back whenever we tried to move on impulse. And worse when we tried warp drive."

"Same here," Kirk agreed. "But our sensors don't pick

up a thing. Do yours?" He wasn't ready to share the possible Erisian connection, not yet, not even with Hiran.

"Nothing. It has to be a force field of some kind, but—"

Sounds from off-screen interrupted Hiran. A moment later, Tiam moved into the image.

"Ambassador Tiam," Kirk said noncommittally. "Would you like me to summon Mr. Handler? Ambassador Riley has not yet recovered from—"

"That will not be necessary, Captain Kirk," Tiam said. "This is not to be a negotiation but, in effect, a capitulation. In view of the external threat we both face, I would now urge full cooperation, a complete pooling of our resources and information. Toward that end, I am prepared to acknowledge that I do, as you suggested, have in my possession a recording made of the alien object's emissions during its earlier pass through the Empire. I am also prepared to share that data with you. Likewise, I am prepared to acknowledge that my wife, Jandra, and her brother Dajan were not kidnapped but transported to the *Enterprise* of their own free will. However, now that I have acknowledged that personally unpleasant situation, I would ask in return that I be allowed to transport over and speak with my wife, in private."

Kirk's eyes widened slightly at this evidence of a "reformed" Tiam. "Of course, Ambassador Tiam— provided she agrees to such a meeting. And provided the transporters are still operational while the Probe has hold of us."

"Thank you, Captain Kirk. I will bring with me the recording of the object's emissions for your use. I will also, if you so desire, suggest to our own musicians that they join yours in this effort to communicate with that thing out there."

Kirk turned questioningly to Spock, who had stopped at the 'lift door when the *Galtizh* had hailed them.

"Yes, Captain," he said, "it could be helpful if at least those who were able to recognize some of the patterns that have been isolated would come. It need not be limited to the musicians, however. Anyone with the ability to recognize the patterns could be of help, particularly someone like Dr. Benar, who is knowledgeable in more than a single field."

"You heard, Ambassador Tiam?" Kirk asked.

"I did." Tiam turned to Hiran on his right. "Commander, will you make the appropriate announcement?"

Hiran nodded. "As you wish, Ambassador."

Tiam was silent a moment, then turned to look directly out of the viewscreen again. "Then, Captain Kirk, let us determine if the transporters are indeed in working order."

"Say what you have to say, Tiam," Jandra said quietly, not looking at him, "and then leave."

"Your quarters," he said, looking around at the single room she had been assigned, "were better aboard the *Galtizh.*"

"It is adequate. And the company is less bothersome."

There was a long silence. Finally he took her face in his hands and turned it up, but still her eyes avoided his. He released her.

"Why?" he asked. "Why did you betray me? Why did you betray the Empire?"

She stiffened. "The Empire had already betrayed me, betrayed my family."

"They may have treated your family harshly, but—"

"I do not consider the execution of my parents merely 'harsh'!"

"It was not execution! It was—"

"No, you are right. Straightforward execution would have been less cruel than requiring ritual suicide. It would also have been less cowardly!"

The bitterness in her voice silenced him, and when he didn't speak, she went on: "Is this why you went to such trouble to speak with me, Husband? To discuss the wrongs done to my family?"

He swallowed. "I did not know the depth of your bitterness."

"You knew *nothing* about me!" she flared. For a moment, her eyes darted up and met his, but almost instantly she averted them again, as if afraid something in them could grasp and hold her. "From the beginning, I have been your 'assignment' and nothing more! Now if that is all, you may go."

He swallowed again. "It is not all. I was given to understand that you were the first to detect a pattern in the object's emissions. Is that true?"

"It is." She repressed a bitter laugh. "Had you shared those sounds with me earlier, had you not so loudly demanded I forget I ever heard them, I might have told you the same."

"Is it also true that, even with that information at their disposal, the Vulcan and his group have been unable to discern any meaning in the emissions?"

This time she did not repress the laugh. "So *that* is why you were so anxious to speak with me! You want to know if the human captain has been lying to you! Well, I will tell you he has not! Everything he has shared with the *Galtizh* has been true!"

252

"So far as you know."

"'So far as I know,' yes! I am not privy to their thoughts, as I am privy now to yours!" She turned abruptly to the door, which hissed open an instant later, revealing the two security ensigns standing watch in the corridor. "I am ready to return to Captain Spock and the others," she said to the one who had accompanied her to the room. She turned to face Tiam from the corridor. "Thank you, Husband, for your reassurance. Your visit has removed what few doubts remained that Dajan and I made the right decision."

EIGHTEEN

———————— ☆ ————————

Across thousands of parsecs, the crystal sensor reached out and touched the world of its creators.

What in a human would have been alarm rippled through the crystalline pathways. Its creators were mute. Where before, their voice would have been detectable by the crystal sensor, even sheathed, over a quarter of the galaxy, there was now only silence.

The entity directed the crystal sensor toward the homeworld's sun—and drew back, confronted with yet another paradox, one as great as the paradox presented by those who could not Speak yet were capable of mimicking the True Language. The star the crystal sensor had touched was the homeworld's sun, and yet it was not. It was within two solar diameters of the predicted location, a negligent error considering the five hundred millennia that had passed since last the crystal sensor had touched it.

But it was cold.

And shrunken.

Its surface temperature was two thousand degrees below what it had been. Its girth was less by more than a hundred thousand kilometers.

What could have happened?

The crystal sensor reached out in other directions, checking and rechecking the locations and spectra of the neighboring suns, and found their realities no more displaced from its predictions than those of any of the tens of millions of other stars it had visited in the last five hundred millennia.

But the homeworld's sun—

It was as if some giant hand had squeezed out a portion of its life.

Again the entity reached out to the homeworld itself, searching for the voice of its creators.

But still there was only silence.

Captain's Log, Stardate 8495.3:

For more than two days, the *Enterprise* and the *Galtizh* have been dragged along by the Probe at speeds Commander Sulu estimates to be in excess of warp thirty. The Probe's course has been as close to a straight line as he has been able to determine. So far it has taken us through both the Orion and Sagittarius Arms and skirted uncomfortably close to the Shapley Center. We are now headed out from the Center, reentering another segment of the Sagittarius Arm. Sulu's best guess as to distance traveled so far is fifteen thousand parsecs, and the Probe has shown no indication it is considering slowing down or stopping. In fact, the Probe has shown no indication of anything at all— except of a power source enviable in all respects—since the start of this transgalactic odyssey. As far as the *Enterprise* sensors can determine, the Probe is emitting absolutely nothing. The *Galtizh* maintains that it is similarly unable to detect any emissions, and since it is Hiran rather than Tiam who maintains it, I am inclined to believe it.

Meanwhile, even with the help of the Romulans, there has been precious little progress in deciphering the emissions we already have in the computer. Finding the crystal structure in the Probe occasioned some short-lived optimism based on the fact that the similar structure found on Temaris had proven to be, as Spock said, "designed to be read." Unfortunately, without direct physical access to the Probe crystal, we cannot even attempt to "read" it the way Spock did the Temaris crystal, and the Probe's emissions themselves still appear to be, if anything, "designed to confuse." We have determined only two things to any degree of certainty: the "patterns" grow steadily in complexity from the start of the twenty-minute cycle to the end. And the Probe's "response" to us is indeed totally different from its earlier emissions. Unfortunately, no one has any idea whether that "response" was meant to tell us something new or to ask us something or was simply a different "prerecorded message" that we or the Romulans somehow triggered. The recordings the *Galtizh* has "shared" with us were of no help either, except to prove that they were identical to our own. Whatever the Probe's message is, it appears to have been the same no matter what part of space it was passing through—at least until the *Enterprise* and the *Galtizh* began playing its own message back to it.

Just how helpful the Romulans are trying to be is still a matter of speculation. The musicians and archaeologists who beamed over to work with Spock seem sincere enough and appear to be genuinely trying to help. Ambassador Tiam is the only one who appears to be an obvious exception, and even he continues to profess a need and a desire for total cooperation and sharing. His clumsy attempt at getting our "secrets" out of his wife, however, indicates otherwise. As for his alleged linguistic abilities, if they have given him any insight into the meaning of the Probe's emissions, he hasn't given any indication. Like most of the nonmusicians, including myself, he professes a total inability to discern any of the patterns in the data, even after having them pointed out to him repeatedly. On the other hand, about a quarter of the Romulan musicians were able to spot one or more of the patterns on their own, a slightly higher percentage than prevailed among the Federation group. One has even identified a pattern that not even Jandra had noticed. Unfortunately, none of our own and only one of the other Romulans has been able to find it or confirm it.

Everyone, of course, is anxiously waiting for our "journey" to end, and for Spock and his crew of impromptu linguists to announce a breakthrough, so we can talk to our cruise director.

A good number of us, however, are even more anxiously awaiting the awakening of Ambassador Riley. Despite Dr. McCoy's assurances that there was "no apparent lasting effect" as a result of whatever the Probe did to us, Uhura and Sulu and even Dajan are beginning to fear otherwise. Uhura and Sulu are now able to spend only odd moments— "taking their breaks from the Probe," as they put it—with Riley, but Dajan, whose ability to recognize musical patterns is as limited as mine, seems to have taken up the slack. In any event, while all three have noticed occasional responses to their monologues, none feel Riley is any closer to regaining consciousness now than he was when the Probe first put us under its telekinetic thumb.

The paradox only grew greater as the entity approached the homeworld.

Again and again, neither knowing nor caring that it was acting in a very human way, it repeated the same millions of observations, performed the same trillions of calculations, as if by the sheer power of billions and billions of repetitions it could change the results.

But nothing changed. The same results were stored again and again in the crystal memory.

Finally, the path it had constructed came to an end.

The world and sun of its creators sprang into physical being before it.

Even at this insignificant distance, there was only silence. Its creators were totally mute.

It extended the crystal sensor and turned it on the homeworld, searching for the world it had left, searching for the oceans its creators had inhabited, warm oceans teeming with life.

But there were none. There were only oceans of ice. They no longer covered 90 percent of the surface, but less than half. There was no liquid water anywhere on the planet.

And the homeworld's satellite was gone, shattered into countless fragments that had begun to collect into an uneven ring of debris circling the planet's equator.

Impossible, its crystal pathways said.

Unthinkable, its memories said. Stars and their worlds changed, but not this star and this world, not in this fashion.

A second Winnowing? But this time, none had survived?

It turned the crystal sensor on the sun, probing as deeply as it could. The reactions at the sun's heart were beyond its reach, but the middle and upper layers were not.

But they told the crystal sensor little more than they had told it from thousands of parsecs away. The spectra had shifted beyond reason. The temperature had dropped.

And the world of its creators had died.

Its creators themselves had died.

And its purpose—to return to its creators with the

news of others who could Speak the True Language—
had died.

And out of that death was born the ultimate paradox
of its existence. Its creators had said: If a problem arises
that you find yourself incapable of resolving, return to
the creators and they will resolve it. But the problem it
now found itself incapable of resolving was the discovery that the creators themselves no longer existed.

Finally, it happened: the Probe stopped in its headlong race across the galaxy.

Kirk, awakened from his first sound sleep in three
days, raced to the bridge, arriving a split second behind
Spock.

"Where the devil are we?" he asked as he emerged
from the 'lift. On the viewscreen, the *Galtizh* and the
Probe were still all that could be seen.

Sulu, who had succumbed only to occasional catnaps,
was already at the helm, snatching up the readings he
needed. "There's a huge margin for error, Captain," he
said after a moment, "but my best guess is, about a
hundred and twenty degrees around the galactic disk,
not quite on the opposite side of the Shapley Center
from the Federation, but almost."

Tentatively, he touched the control panel. "Shall I try
the impulse engines again?"

"Carefully, Mr. Sulu. Quarter impulse for one second,
say."

"Quarter impulse, one second, sir." Sulu set the
controls and executed.

The *Enterprise* leapt forward, shot past the *Galtizh*,
past the Probe, and stopped when the second passed.

The air remained breathable, and everyone, with the
possible exception of Spock, breathed a sigh of relief.

"How long to get back to the Federation, Mr. Sulu?"
Sulu shook his head. "Months, at least, at warp eight."
Kirk sighed. "Then I suppose we might as well look around and see where we are. And maybe try to figure out why this thing brought us here."

"We are in high orbit about a ringed planet, Captain," Spock said from the science station. "Sensor readings indicate—"

Lights flickered and faded all over the ship. Commander Scott's shielded backup power took over.

"It started yelling again," Commander Scott said tiredly from the engineering station.

"The *Galtizh* was hailing us, sir," Lieutenant Kittay announced, "but when the power went out—"

"They dinna have my backup system," Scotty said, a touch of pride taking some of the exhaustion from his voice.

Lights flickered again, and primary power returned.

"Try the *Galtizh* again, Lieutenant," Kirk said. "Maybe they got their power back, too. Meanwhile, Mr. Spock, what can the sensors tell us about this planet? Is it the home of your superwhales?"

"If it is, Captain, they are no longer present," Spock said, studying the kaleidoscopic readouts while Kittay announced the *Galtizh* was not responding.

"Whether or not this is the Probe's planet of origin, however," Spock went on, "it is an unusual world in many ways. For example, a ring is in the process of forming out of the remains of a natural satellite. In addition, despite subfreezing temperatures at all latitudes, it is marginally class M. There are the remains of an oxygen-nitrogen atmosphere, but there are no life-form readings even at a cellular level. The ice itself is approximately three hundred thousand years old, and indications are the water it was formed from was teeming with life-forms."

"Could the ring—the breakup of the satellite—have had any connection with the drop in temperature?"

"Unknown, Captain, although both events appear to have occurred in roughly the same era. The amount of sunlight blocked by the ring, particularly early in its formation, would not have been sufficient to cause such a drastic cooling of the planet's surface."

"So what *could* have caused a whole planet to freeze?" Kirk asked. "That would require a planetwide drop of—what? Fifty degrees? A hundred?"

"The current maximum temperature anywhere on the planet is more than twenty Celsius degrees below freezing, Captain. The average is perhaps another thirty below that."

"So just for water to be liquid over most of the planet, it would have to be fifty degrees Celsius warmer? That's almost a hundred Fahrenheit. Add another ten Celsius . . ." Kirk shook his head. "Is that possible, Spock, with this particular sun? And if it isn't, what happened? There was nothing in the astrophysics classes of my youth about suns of this spectral class that could remain steady for the billions of years it takes life to develop on a planet and then suddenly fade away."

"Nonetheless, Captain, that is what appears to have happened here."

"What about the planet's internal heat?" Kirk asked, but before Spock could answer, he shook his head. "No, that's sillier than having the sun suddenly turn anemic. Unless it was something they did themselves. If they had the same kind of powers the Probe has—and they must have or they wouldn't have been able to build it in the first place—if they were able to boil oceans away in a matter of days—" He stopped again, frowning. "And the Probe's power has to come from *somewhere,*" he went on. "The power it takes to just *move* this thing has to come from somewhere. Is it possible, Spock, that that thing has been draining the power from this sun, from this world, all this time? However long it's been out doing whatever it's been doing?"

"From tens of thousands of parsecs away, Captain?" Spock considered. "It is possible, but logic would argue against it. If it were able to drain the power from a sun or a world, it would be more logical for it to drain it from nearby suns and worlds, not from a system half across the galaxy."

"If it's *able* to. But if it's permanently linked to this sun because this is where it was created—" Kirk broke off again, almost laughing. "Pointless to debate without facts—right, Spock? What other facts can your sensors come up with? What about the land areas? Any evidence of life ever having existed there?"

Spock studied a new set of readouts, his eyebrows arching after a moment. "Yes, Captain, there is evidence that simple plant and animal life-forms existed on the land areas until the cooling began. However, there is also evidence of an advanced civilization from a much earlier era."

"Could *they* have built the Probe?"

"It is possible, Captain." Spock continued to study the readouts. "However, indications are that the land civilization perished approximately two million years ago. The remains of at least one major city are buried beneath the ice, but also beneath other material that—"

"Yes, Spock?" Kirk prompted when the Vulcan fell silent.

"Geological evidence suggests an asteroid impact, Captain, an event that would dwarf the impact that wiped out the dinosaurs on your Earth sixty-five million years ago."

"The breakup of the moon?" Kirk wondered. "A segment hit the planet?"

"No, Captain. The asteroid impact was more than a million and a half years before the breakup of the satellite and the cooling that resulted in the current conditions. After the asteroid impact and the subsequent volcanic activity, there was undoubtedly a significant cooling, but nothing of the magnitude of the later event. It did, however, probably result in the extinction of most life on the land areas. There is still evidence of a planetwide layer of ash several meters thick beneath the ice."

"Several meters? Planetwide? On the oceans, too? Wouldn't that kill off most sea life as well? Particularly your superwhales, who would have to surface to breathe?"

"If they were air breathers, Captain, it would seem logical. If, indeed, they existed at all and were, additionally, from this planet. As yet, we have no firm evidence to so indicate, other than the Probe's having brought us here, so the argument is academic. In addition, there is evidence that life in the oceans continued uninterrupted until the cooling. Therefore—"

Spock stopped abruptly, his eyebrows arching as new readings materialized before him.

"Captain," he went on, his voice oddly hushed, "there is a cavern, apparently artificial, near the shore of one of the ice oceans. And it contains what appears to be a massive crystal structure similar—possibly identical—

263

to that within the Probe and to the one from the Temaris Four Exodus Hall."

Commander Jenyu, late of the Romulan battle cruiser *Shalyar,* had some time ago realized he was facing the most important—and probably the final—decision of his career and of his life. Compared to this, his original mission to derail the conference and ensure the downfall of the Interim Government was trivial. The fate of the Empire was literally at stake.

And now, as he stood at Tiam's side, still in his subcenturion's uniform, and listened to the status reports come in, he knew that the decision was upon him. Power was finally restored everywhere in the *Galtizh,* and if what the *Enterprise* had just done was any indication, the impulse engines were once again operational.

There was no more time.

He had to decide, even though he knew that the best outcome he could hope for would still see the *Galtizh* destroyed and all its people dead, if not by that behemoth's unknown weapons, then by the phasers and photon torpedoes of the Federation starship before him. If he still had the *Shalyar* beneath his boots, he would have a better chance. With the *Shalyar,* a sudden, all-out attack on the unshielded *Enterprise* might take the Federation ship out, leaving him to deal, alone, with that thing out there. But with the *Galtizh*'s lesser size and firepower, it was simply impossible. Even an *Enterprise* wounded by a first strike could retaliate and swat the *Galtizh* out of existence.

And that would leave the *Enterprise*—and the Federation—to deal with the behemoth, to take all the time it needed to truly learn how to control it, how to turn it into a berserker that could destroy the Empire.

No, his only chance—and he realized all too well just how slim it was—was to attack the behemoth itself. Until the last few hours, it wasn't something he would even have considered, but now, after studying all the data taken from observations during its first pass through the Empire, he was beginning to think it was at least a possibility. According to the ships that had trailed it as it passed world after world, it always did one thing whenever it paused in the vicinity of one of those worlds: it extended some kind of crystalline appendage. It was assumed that this was the source of the deadly "emissions," although there was no real evidence to support that assumption. It was also assumed that whatever data the thing received—through some unknown form of sensor scan—it received through that same appendage. Further, when the appendage was extended, it revealed at its base a cavity of equal size—the only opening, the only potentially vulnerable spot in all the square kilometers of surface. And it was just beyond the inner end of that cavity that a crystalline mass of some kind existed, a crystalline mass that bore at least a superficial resemblance to the crystal found on Temaris Four. It was therefore possible, Jenyu reasoned, that this crystal was the thing's data storage center, just as the crystal on Temaris Four had been the data storage center for the Exodus Hall. Furthermore, it was the only object the *Galtizh*'s sensors could detect that seemed likely to have that capability.

There was, in short, a possibility that this crystal was the nerve center of the object, and that if the appendage was extended, an all-out short-range assault with phasers and photon torpedoes could at least destroy the object's usefulness to the Federation.

If such an assault was possible.

If the experience of the *Henzu*, as relayed by the distant *Azmuth*, was any indication, it was not. The *Henzu*'s phaser fire had been blocked almost instantaneously, and the *Henzu* itself, together with a nearby unarmed cargo ship, was reduced to a dispersing cloud of molecules within seconds.

Hidden in the records of the object's first trip through the Empire, however, was an incident that gave him hope. A dozen scout ships had been engaged in a training exercise in the vicinity of Kruzaak's World when the object came out of its version of warp drive virtually on top of them. Two of the ships were fast enough to fire on the object before its damnable emissions knocked all their power out. The phasers, locked on a stun setting for the duration of the exercise, of course did no damage, but the ships themselves were not destroyed like the *Henzu*, nor even damaged except for the temporary loss of power. They were, in fact, simply ignored, which led Commander Jenyu to believe—to hope—that the reason they were ignored was their very proximity to the object. They had been, in effect, inside its defenses, like insects inside a warrior's battle armor.

And now the *Galtizh* was similarly close to the object, inside its armor. Jenyu only hoped that the *Galtizh*'s sting was deadly enough to, if not kill the behemoth, at least render it useless to the Federation. Or if the *Galtizh* proved not to be inside its defenses, to prompt a response like the one that had destroyed the *Henzu* and an unnamed cargo ship, a response that would swat both insects, not just the *Galtizh* but the *Enterprise* as well.

"Commander!"

The suddenly excited voice of the subcommander monitoring the sensor scan pulled Jenyu from his angry brooding. *What now?* he wondered as Hiran turned from the viewscreen to the subCommander.

"There is a mass of crystalline material on the planet, Commander," the subcommander went on. "It appears to be quite similar to the data storage crystal found on Temaris Four."

Tiam's face, as grim as Jenyu's until now, suddenly brightened. "Can it be beamed aboard?"

The subcommander, after an inquiring glance at Hiran brought a scowling nod, said, "Its total mass is approximately equal to that of the *Galtizh,* Ambassador."

"Then a portion of it—"

"Tiam!" Hiran snapped. "If this is indeed another data storage crystal, then slicing it up will only destroy it!"

"We have only the Vulcan's word for that, Commander!"

"And I am far more inclined to trust his judgment in the matter than yours. The crystal, whatever it is, remains intact."

"Then I will beam down there myself." Tiam turned to the subcommander, the Romulan equivalent of a science officer. "There is certainly *something* that can be done to retrieve the data."

"There are things that can be tried, Ambassador, but the *Enterprise* is better equipped to—"

"And the *Enterprise* is the enemy!" Tiam almost shouted. He turned to Hiran. "Will you order your officers to comply with my wishes, or must I formally assume command of this vessel? It *is* within my authority to do so!"

It seemed for a moment that Hiran was going to rebel, but finally he nodded. "Do as the ambassador says, Subcommander—but do *not* damage the crystal!"

Jenyu watched as Tiam and the subcommander left the bridge, on their way to collect the instruments the subcommander said "might" prove useful. *Let the fool try,* Jenyu thought. There was even, he supposed, some remote chance Tiam would succeed, that the subcommander would tap at the crystal's portals with her jury-rigged equipment and it would respond with a sudden flood of information, perhaps even with the key to the control of the thing that had brought them here.

But Jenyu did not think so.

Abruptly, he turned to leave the bridge. He had to contact his remaining men, call back from the Federation ship those still taking part in the Vulcan's efforts, and work out the details of what in all likelihood would be his own suicide. His only real regret—he told himself grimly—was that, even if he succeeded, he would probably never know.

NINETEEN

"Before *anyone* beams down there," Kirk said to the officers assembled in the briefing room, "we are going to be damned sure this isn't just a rest stop for that thing and that it isn't about to head out again, taking the *Enterprise* with it. This does not look like the most hospitable world in the galaxy to be stranded on. The air in that cavern is breathable, but the atmosphere on the surface is marginal at best."

"And how the blazes do you intend to find out what that thing's intentions are?" McCoy asked. "The last time I looked, we hadn't figured out how to talk to it, let alone how to order it around."

"Dr. McCoy has a point, Captain," Spock said. "We could never be certain of what the Probe's future actions might be, even if we were able to communicate with it."

Kirk shook his head. "I never thought I'd see the day

269

you two agreed on something. All right, so what are your recommendations, either one of you?"

"Go down and look around," McCoy said. "See if there's anything the sensors didn't pick up. See if Spock's idea of jury-rigging a giant analysis chamber could work." He shrugged. "And just generally play it by ear and keep a transporter lock on us at all times."

"I would not put it in those precise terms, Captain," Spock said, "but I cannot disagree. The potential for knowledge to be gained far outweighs, in my judgment, all other considerations, including the possibility of our deaths."

Other heads around the table nodded. "We didn't enter the Academy because we wanted to always play it safe, sir," Sulu said with a grin.

"And slingshotting back to the twentieth century in a Klingon bucket of bolts that could've fallen apart at any moment wouldn't put us on any insurance company's preferred-risk list," McCoy added.

"I get your point, Commanders," Kirk said with a resigned smile. "Very well." He stood up. "All that's left, then, is to see how our friends on the *Galtizh* feel about joining our party. If they haven't already started one of their own."

By the time they reached the bridge, it was apparent that the Romulans had done just that, and possibly more.

"Transporter activity between the *Galtizh* and the planet, Captain," Lieutenant Parnell said from the science station almost the moment the group emerged from the 'lift. "Three personnel and some electronic gear," he added a moment later, "and their destination appears to be the cavern that crystal is in."

270

"Hail the *Galtizh*," Kirk said, frowning.

"I have been, Captain," Kittay said, "every five minutes, but—" She stopped, her eyes widening momentarily. "The *Galtizh*, Captain. On-screen?"

"On-screen, Lieutenant."

It was Hiran, his usual smile replaced by flinty grimness. "I have been requested," he began without preamble, "to ask that all Romulans aboard the *Enterprise* be transported to the *Galtizh* without delay."

"Requested? By Ambassador Tiam?"

"In effect, yes. Specifically by one of his aides, whose requests the ambassador has told me I must honor during his absence."

"The ambassador's absence? Then he's one of the ones who just transported down to the cavern?"

A flicker of a smile touched Hiran's face briefly as he glanced at something or someone out of range of the screen. "You know about the cavern, then?"

"And the crystal within. Yes, Commander, we know. We are planning on beaming down ourselves shortly. We were going to invite someone from the *Galtizh* to accompany us, but I gather an invitation is no longer necessary."

"It would seem not," Hiran said.

"Will you notify Tiam and his colleagues in the cavern that personnel from the *Enterprise* will be beaming down? I would not want them to be startled into any inappropriate action."

"Of course, Captain."

"Commander Hiran," a voice said stiffly from off-screen. Hiran glanced to his right briefly.

"It seems," Hiran said, "I am being reminded to repeat my request for the return of all Romulans currently aboard the *Enterprise*."

271

"They will all be notified, Commander. I suspect there are two, however, who will not respond."

"I suspect the same, Federation captain."

With another faint flicker of a smile, Hiran broke the connection.

Commander Hiran was back on the bridge after having watched Kital greet the last of the musicians and archaeologists as they stepped off the *Galtizh* transporter platform. This Kital, he had decided, bore watching even more than Tiam.

"Don't worry about protocol," Hiran had said quietly to Subcommander Morvain—one of the only officers on board whose allegiance he felt entirely sure of. "Just keep me informed of what he does, particularly anything that you might consider odd for one of his rank."

He had debated engaging Feric for this task, but decided against it. Whatever his first officer's true feelings regarding the conference—and at this point he still had no idea what those feelings were—Feric was staying firmly on the side of the "legitimate" authority on *Galtizh*—Tiam.

And unlike Tiam, whose expressions were a shipwide broadcast of his feelings and attitudes, Kital was unreadable. While Tiam reacted—overreacted—as a matter of course, Kital seemed untouched by anything that went on around him. While Tiam was arrogant and overconfident, Kital was—what? Quietly sure of himself? But whatever the quality was, it was more pronounced now that he had been given authority to act for Tiam in the ambassador's absence. He had taken to giving orders as if he had been doing it for years, not just minutes.

And perhaps he had, Hiran thought abruptly. For

someone of Kital's obviously advanced years to still be a subcenturion was unusual at best. Normally, anyone of his age stuck at that level would have long ago opted out. But perhaps he *had* been of a higher rank. Perhaps, like Tiam's late brother-in-law, Reelan, he had lost favor, but not badly enough to rate death or even expulsion from the service, just enough to lose rank.

If the *Galtizh* ever made it back to the Empire, he decided, he would do a little digging through records, perhaps find out just who this Kital really was.

For now, though—

"Commander."

Hiran turned abruptly from the viewscreen, still dominated by the icy image of the nameless planet below them. Subcenturion Morvain leaned close and spoke in a voice no one but Hiran could hear. "You wanted to be notified if Tiam's aide did anything that might be considered odd."

Hiran grimaced inwardly as he nodded. *That certainly didn't take long,* he thought irritably.

McCoy scowled as he pushed back the hood of his fur-lined field jacket and wiped the first traces of sweat from his forehead. He had pulled the jacket from stores and come straight to the transporter room, assuming Spock and Kirk and whoever else was going on this little jaunt would do the same. But he had been standing by the platform, bundled up and ready to go, for at least five minutes, and he was still the only one in the room except for the increasingly uneasy ensign at the controls.

"Leave it to that pointy-eared perfectionist to find one more detail to double-check at the last minute," he muttered, scowling at the door. He was reaching for the intercom when the door finally hissed open and Kirk and Spock strode in, their own jackets still across their arms.

"Bones," Kirk said with a grin, noting the sheen of perspiration that had appeared on McCoy's forehead, "as a doctor, you should know better. You'll just feel that much colder when you go out in the weather."

"And I should know better than to expect the lot of you to show up on time. Or that you'd know the difference between an old wives' tale and a medical fact." He turned on Spock, empty-handed except for the jacket and the ever-present tricorder. "Do we still have to wait for that equipment of yours?"

"No, Doctor," Spock said, setting the tricorder down and shrugging into his jacket, "just for Dajan and Dr. Benar. We will not be taking the equipment down at this time."

McCoy glanced around at Kirk, who was likewise donning his jacket, then back at Spock. "May I remind you, Spock, the Romulans have been down there—*with* the Romulan version of the same equipment, according to you—for the last half hour. Their stuff might not be as whizbang modern as ours, but if we give them enough of a head start, it won't matter."

"Do not concern yourself, Doctor. Their 'head start' will, I believe, prove illusory at best."

"Tortoise and the hare, Bones," Kirk put in as he slid the strap of his own tricorder onto the Velcro-5 patch on his shoulder. "While we were all in the conference room debating without facts, Lieutenant Parnell was doing a more detailed analysis of the sensor readings. He discovered some differences between this crystal and the one from Temaris Four. This first time down, we're going to do a close-range examination with the tricorders to confirm the sensor readings. And try to figure out just what we have to do to our equipment so it *will* work."

"Does this mean we've lost the possible Erisian connection?" McCoy asked. "If the structure of this crystal is different from the one from Temaris—"

The door hissed open and Audrea Benar hurried in, trailed a moment later by Dajan, both already in their jackets. She turned instantly to Spock. "I was told that Lieutenant Parnell has discovered that the structure of this crystal is different from that of the Temaris crystal."

"The difference is not in the structure, Dr. Benar," Spock said, stepping up on the transporter platform. "The major difference appears to be that there is no magnetic field associated with this crystal."

"Then it is useless." Benar's voice slumped, if her body did not. "Whatever data was stored has been lost through time."

"Not necessarily, Dr. Benar. There is no indication that a magnetic field was ever associated with this crystal."

"If true," Benar said, "that can only mean that this crystal is not a data storage device."

"Again, not necessarily, Dr. Benar, although it is certainly possible. What I suspect, however—and what I hope to confirm with a short-range tricorder examination—is that the data was stored by means of some other form of energy, in all likelihood the same form of energy the Probe employs."

"But if you do not know what that form of energy is and you are unable even to detect it—"

"It may not be necessary, Dr. Benar, any more than it is necessary for us to know the exact nature of the energy emitted by the Probe in order to record and analyze its effects. In the case of the Temaris crystal, a form of magnetic energy was used to distort the crystal's lattice structure and hold it in place. The sensors 'read' the crystal not by measuring the distortions directly but by measuring the magnetic field that was associated with that distortion. If there is indeed a structural distortion in this crystal, it may be possible to measure that distortion directly, given the proper equipment."

"People," Kirk prompted, beginning to feel warm inside his fur-lined jacket himself, "there will be adequate time for discussion of technical details once we find out what the technical details are." When no one replied, he gestured to the ensign at the transporter controls. "Keep a lock on us at all times," he reiterated, "and be ready for fast retrieval."

"Aye-aye, Captain," the ensign said briskly if a trifle nervously. Then he was sliding the controls.

McCoy, liking the process no more this time than any of the hundreds of previous times, braced himself and wondered if sheer curiosity was reason enough for this particular trip. It was always good to have a doctor in any landing party on an unknown world, but more than enough qualified Starfleet personnel were aboard who could have—

The transporter energies gripped him. *Talk about energies no one really understands!*

The transporter room flickered out of existence, replaced a frozen moment later by—

—darkness!

I didn't make it! That blasted machine finally did me in! Left me hanging in whatever no-man's-land it sends things through!

But then he felt the pressure of his own weight on the soles of his boots.

And the icy shock of the perspiration evaporating abruptly from his face.

And out of the corner of his eye, a small bubble of light—

Suddenly, it was as if the bubble exploded, but a moment later he realized it was Dr. Benar, who had been standing on the transporter circle just behind him, turning on the halogen lamp he had seen in her hand only seconds before on the *Enterprise.* Kirk and Spock were on either side of him, Dajan next to Benar behind Spock. Underfoot was translucent, glass-smooth ice, too frigidly solid to be slick. Overhead was only darkness. The roof of the cavern was beyond the reach of Benar's lamp.

Turning in the direction of the original bubble of light, he saw, fifty meters away, the whitish green dome that was the crystal—or as much of it as poked up through the ice. Next to it, wearing even bulkier hooded jackets than his own, were the Romulans. The breath of all three plumed out from mouth and nostril, rising to form wispy clouds over their heads. Two were working with a pair of antennalike devices, nudging them repeatedly as if trying to align them. The third turned and stood facing the group from the *Enterprise,* saying nothing, making no gesture, either of welcome or warning. With his back to the light, his face was invisible in the shadow of the jacket's hood.

"Tiam," McCoy opined. "The other two are doing the work while he watches."

"The one facing us is armed, Captain," Spock said, looking up from his tricorder.

"At least he isn't pointing it at us," Kirk said softly.
"And Hiran did say he'd given them notification of our
impending arrival."

"So what are we waiting for?" McCoy asked. "He's
not about to send us an engraved invitation."

Kirk turned to the Romulan archaeologist. "Dajan,
under the circumstances, if you would prefer to be
beamed back aboard the *Enterprise*—"

"I will stay. I will not let that pompous ass determine
my movements even now. In any event, I doubt that he
would attempt anything. He is brave with my sister but
with few others."

"As you wish." Kirk turned and began to lead the way
across the ice. Their boots clicked on the ice as if on
steel. The slight breeze created by their forward motion
bit at the exposed flesh of their faces. It reminded
McCoy of his first winter trip away from Georgia, to
Alaska of all places. He couldn't for the life of him
remember why his family had gone.

At a dozen meters, the light from Benar's lamp finally
penetrated the shadows and revealed the watcher's face.

"Ambassador Tiam," Kirk said.

"Captain Kirk." Tiam's eyes darted across the others.
"KerDajan," he said, nodding. "Have you come to join
your countrymen?"

"I have not."

Tiam almost smiled. "That is good. The Empire was
served far better by your defection and that of your sister
than by anything you and your misbegotten family have
ever done before."

Abruptly, Tiam turned his back on Dajan and the
others and resumed watching the two Romulans as they
worked with the antennalike devices.

Kirk seemed to study Tiam's back for a moment, then

278

turned a few degrees and continued toward the crystal, now heading for a spot roughly a third of the way around from the Romulans. McCoy and the others quickly followed.

As they crossed the last few feet, hundreds—no, thousands—of tiny, geometrically perfect facets became visible in what, from a distance, had seemed like a simple dome. And from inches away, they could see that each facet was divided into a series of irregular polygons, from triangles to at least octagons. McCoy, squinting, shook his head. It almost made his head spin, like a straight-line version of a Mandelbrot Set that just kept duplicating itself over and over in ever smaller dimensions.

Spock's gloved hands turned his tricorder toward the crystal facets and moved the input grid slowly along, almost touching them. Benar was doing the same a few meters away, as was Dajan on Spock's other side, while McCoy stood by feeling oddly useless. Kirk remained watching the Romulans.

After a few seconds, Spock lowered his tricorder. "There is no magnetic field," he said, "but there is a detectable structural distortion. Do you agree, Dr. Benar? Dajan?"

"That appears to be the case," Benar said, her agreement echoed by a simple "Yes" from the Romulan.

"Then I suggest—"

Spock stopped abruptly as a faint glow pulsed somewhere deep within the crystal, far below the surface of the ice.

"What—" McCoy began, but before he could say more, the glow, still pale, flooded to the surface of the crystal and cast an eerie light throughout the cavern. As he looked up, the cavern's true dimensions suddenly hit home. Until that moment, the dimensions supplied by the *Enterprise* sensors had been just that—dimensions. Now they were reality. A kilometer above his head was the ceiling, as smooth and glasslike as the ice beneath their boots, as if the entire cavern had been phasered out of solid rock. At least three kilometers away in all directions were the walls, similarly smooth, similarly unbroken—except for what must have been an entrance when the cavern had been all or mostly underwater: a gaping, circular blackness halfway up one wall, a tunnel that had no end.

Abruptly, the glow itself flowed out of the crystal like a luminous fog. A curse shot over from the direction of the Romulans. McCoy's fingers seemed to glow, and for a moment his eyes couldn't focus. His hands, his arms, were fuzzy and indistinct.

He grabbed his communicator—it, too, was enveloped in a fuzzy glow—and raised it to speak. *"Enterprise—"* he began, but then a hand was gripping his arm.

"Wait, Bones!"

It was the captain.

"Look," Kirk said, gesturing upward.

McCoy looked up.

And gasped.

Where moments before there had been only the smooth, kilometer-distant roof of the cavern, there was now a kilometer of rippling, crystal-clear water. And swimming serenely through it, no more than a hundred meters over his head, was a flippered leviathan that would have dwarfed anything that had ever swum the seas of Earth.

TWENTY

☆

As Subcenturion Kital entered Hiran's quarters, the commander found himself remembering how, only days ago, Tiam had been here, introducing himself and delivering his "diplomatic guidelines." Guidelines for failure, Hiran had thought at the time, and he had unfortunately been proven right. Kital had been summoned and had no guidelines to offer, but he did have the same superior attitude, although it was less obvious, less blatant than in Tiam.

As if, Hiran thought uneasily, he had more reason than Tiam to be quietly confident.

"Commander?" The subcenturion stood erect, not quite rigid enough to be at attention, but almost.

Hiran remained seated behind his Spartan desk. "Subcenturion Kital, do you have plans of your own for the *Galtizh?*" he asked with quiet abruptness.

For just an instant, a flicker of surprise widened the aide's eyes, but it was gone as quickly as it had come, leaving his almost ascetic face an impassive mask. "I do not understand, Commander."

"Or are they perhaps Ambassador Tiam's plans?"

This time there was not even a flicker. "I still do not understand, Commander Hiran. What, precisely, are you referring to?"

"A conversation between yourself and another of Ambassador Tiam's aides."

"There have been many such conversations, Commander, as you must know. Communication between members of any organization is vital to its efficiency. Is there one in particular that has attracted your interest?"

"The one that took place a few minutes ago, in your quarters." Hiran resisted the impulse to remark on the apparent lack of "communication" that had resulted in the execution of another member of this particular organization, the late Subcenturion Jutak.

Nothing in Kital's features betrayed his thoughts, but there was a slight pause before he spoke. "You have listening devices in my quarters, then?"

"If I do, it is my right as commander of this ship. Some would say it is my duty."

"I see."

"That is good, Subcenturion. Then you will not object to explaining."

"Of course not, Commander, if you will tell me precisely what it is you wish me to explain."

"The questions you were asking, Subcenturion, struck me as questions that might be more appropriately asked of the ship's navigator, or even of its commander, rather than of another aide to Ambassador Tiam."

"For example, Commander Hiran?"

"For example, questions about the maneuverability and firepower of a ship of the *Galtizh*'s class. For example, questions about how quickly the *Galtizh* could be positioned at a specific point in relation to the object that brought us here."

Kital was silent this time for several seconds, although his face remained impassive. Finally he nodded. "I was making preparations, Commander Hiran."

"Preparations? For what?"

"For the possibility that Ambassador Tiam will fail in his effort to gain useful information from the crystal."

"Preparations formulated by Ambassador Tiam? Or by yourself?"

Kital was again silent for a number of seconds. "If Ambassador Tiam ordered you to fire on that object out there," he said finally, "would you obey?"

"I would not," Hiran said flatly. "Nor would I obey him if he ordered me to place a phaser to my own head and fire."

"I take it from your response that you feel any such attack would be suicidal."

"I know what that thing did on Wlaariivi. And what it did to the *Henzu* and to the civilian ship that had the misfortune to be in the area." *I also know what was being done to the native life on Wlaariivi that likely prompted the attack,* he added silently.

"What would you say if I told you there was a chance that we would not suffer the same fate as the *Henzu?*"

"I would ask your reasons for making a statement so obviously contrary to observed fact, Subcenturion."

Succinctly, Kital recounted the experience of the Romulan ships that had been on training maneuvers when the object had appeared next to them. "I believe there is a chance," he concluded, "that we may be similarly inside its defensive perimeter and that we could damage it severely, if not destroy it, if we were to launch a sudden, all-out attack on what appears to be its one vulnerable area."

"An intriguing possibility," Hiran said when the Subcenturion fell silent. "But even if I accept it as a possibility, why should I wish to make the attempt?"

"Isn't the destruction of the Romulan facilities on Wlaariivi enough of a reason? The vaporizing of the *Henzu?*"

"Tiam seems not to be worrying overly about that aspect of the situation. He seems, in fact, extremely anxious to find a way of communicating with this thing."

"As are we all. However, we must consider the possibility that he will fail. And that someone on the *Enterprise* will succeed."

So that was it. "You would rather destroy it than take that chance," Hiran said flatly.

For the first time, the subcenturion bristled slightly. "As would any patriotic Romulan."

"The war against the Federation ended a hundred years ago, Subcenturion."

"And it would start again in a hundred seconds if the Federation felt it could destroy us without suffering massive losses itself."

"You sound as if you're talking about the Romulans, Subcenturion, not the Federation. As I understand it, *we* are the ones who have been working secretly to learn how to control this thing, to turn it into a weapon to use against the Federation."

"We would be fools not to. We were merely fortunate

284

that it passed through the Empire before reaching the Federation."

"A lot of good it did us! It took that bunch on the *Enterprise* to—"

"It took the wife of Ambassador Tiam, a Romulan, to alert them to the possibilities!"

Hiran blinked at the sudden intensity in Kital's voice. "In any event, Subcenturion, I do not believe the Federation would act in this way, particularly now that there is a chance of a real peace between our peoples."

Kital laughed, a harsh, bitter sound without a touch of humor. "You are a fool, Hiran! You have let yourself be taken in by the lying words of that captain! You would—"

"You overreach yourself, Subcenturion!" Hiran snapped, reaching for the intercom. "You will be confined to quarters until Tiam returns. Then we will discuss the matter further and see if he is as daft as you."

Before Hiran could activate the intercom, Kital had reached across the desk and with surprising strength, slapped Hiran's hand from it. A moment later, the door to the corridor burst open and two of Tiam's aides stepped inside, phasers trained on the commander.

After countless millions of repetitions, something changed.

Deep within the entity, one of the crystal pathways shunted a bit of data in a different direction.

And the entity remembered: *the Crystal Wisdom.*

The creators might be gone, dead or departed hundreds of millennia ago, but surely their memories remained. And perhaps the answer to the paradox—to all of the paradoxes that had descended on it in these last terrible days—would be there. Perhaps the creators, after the entity had left, had anticipated these very situations.

Shifting the focus of the crystal sensor, the entity reached out, not for living things but for the memories of living things.

It was still there. The Crystal Wisdom: a memory that dwarfed the entity's own.

A crystal memory filled with the history, the wisdom, of its creators. It would not only provide solutions to the paradoxes. It might even be capable of replacing the entity's own lost memories, filling in the gap that had existed for more than three hundred millennia.

The entity probed, carefully, cautiously, slowly, taking full seconds.

Everything was intact.

Safe.

Even more cautiously, even more softly, the entity Spoke to the Crystal Wisdom, gently awakening it, much as the entity itself had been Awakened five hundred millennia ago.

And the information began to flow.

Within seconds, at least a hundred of the leviathans, some as much as a hundred meters from rounded snout to flippered tail, swarmed overhead.

"I'll be damned!" McCoy muttered. "You were right, Spock! Except they look more like superdolphins than superwhales."

"A hologram!" Kirk breathed, sweeping his palely glowing arms through the air as if to check its consistency, to make sure the cavern hadn't suddenly been filled with water. He looked back at the glowing crystal. "Or whatever passes for holograms with someone who could build that monster out there. Spock, is this crystal the source?"

"Unknown, Captain," Spock said as he studied his tricorder. "Whatever the source, it is not any known form of holographic projector. As in the case of the Probe's emissions, there is no direct evidence of any form of energy transfer, either from the crystal or from any other source."

"The glow emanating from the crystal appears to be nothing more than a side effect," Benar put in. Like Spock, she had been concentrating on her tricorder almost since the moment the images had appeared.

"But what triggered it?" McCoy wanted to know. Then he remembered. "The Romulans!" He spun to look in their direction.

Tiam smothered a gasp as the glow appeared within the crystal.

"You have succeeded!" he exulted to the backs of the subcommander and her assistant. *I have succeeded! Jenyu will be the one who—*

"No, Ambassador," the subcommander said. "Whatever is happening, it is no doing of ours. Power has been removed from our probes for the last several minutes while we attempted to align them to intersect properly."

"Then what—"

"I do not know, Ambassador. Perhaps we should return to the *Galtizh* until—"

"No! We are not leaving this to—" Tiam broke off as the glow erupted from the crystal and engulfed them. A moment later, as the bodies of the subcommander and her assistant were cloaked in a diffuse glow, he jerked backward.

But it was too late. Already he could see the same pale

glow surrounding his own body. Instinctively, violently, he brushed at it, as if to rid himself of a horde of clinging insects.

And stopped.

Swallowing, he forced himself to stand still as the others fumbled with gloved hands to activate their portable sensor units. Whatever the glow was, it wasn't damaging him.

He turned as the sound of other voices finally penetrated his shell of self-absorption. Thirty meters away, the traitor Dajan and his newfound friends were chattering away.

Were *they* responsible for this? Tiam's hand twitched toward the phaser concealed beneath his bulky jacket, but he stopped. One of them—the ship's physician?— was looking in the Romulans' direction, scowling.

No, Tiam thought, they were not responsible. They had brought only their own portable sensors, nothing like the equipment the subcommander had been trying to set up for more than half an hour. And they looked as taken by surprise as the Romulans. But except for the physician, they all had their portable sensors out, scanning—upward?

Frowning, he looked up.

His heart felt as if it were trying to leap out of his chest as he saw the scores of massive creatures swimming in the rippling water above them.

But they were images, only images, logic told him a moment later. Images coming from the crystal.

Abruptly, he turned back to the subcommander. "Find out what those things are," he snapped, gesturing skyward, "and how they are being produced."

"We are trying," the subcommander said. "It is un-

doubtedly some form of hologram, but the energy producing it is as undetectable as—"

The subcommander broke off, stiffening, as the ice
floor beneath them vanished.

No, McCoy thought as he saw Tiam's upturned face
take on a look of wide-eyed panic behind the enveloping
glow, *the Romulans aren't responsible. Or if they are, it's
purely accidental.*

As he turned away from Tiam, Spock confirmed his
intuition. "Their equipment is not operating, Doctor,
and has not since we arrived."

"So what *did* set it off?" McCoy wondered aloud.
"Not our tricorders, certainly. And what the blazes is it
supposed to be, anyway? Did we stumble into some kind
of holographic aquarium?"

"Unknown, Doctor." Spock had turned his tricorder
onto the images themselves. "They are not, as you
suggested, Captain, holograms."

"Then what—"

"Not holograms as we know them, Captain. They are
obviously images of some kind, but unlike standard
holograms, there is something more substantial about
them. They contain no mass, and yet each contains an
internal structure that the tricorder can—"

He broke off as the crystal vanished, followed a
moment later by the ice floor beneath their feet.

But it was not gone. McCoy could still feel the
pressure on the bottoms of his boots, and if he shut his
eyes, it was as if nothing had happened. The icy air of the
cavern still bit at his exposed flesh and was beginning to
creep through his fur-lined jacket.

After a moment, he realized that the glow that had

enveloped them had vanished as well. And more of the gigantic, dolphinlike creatures had appeared below them, swimming serenely through what must have been solid ice.

Overhead, something glittered.

"The surface of the ocean," Spock said, not looking at his tricorder but remembering what he had seen when he had swum upward from his encounter with George in the warm waters off the Barrier Reef. For the first time McCoy could remember, he thought he could detect a note of awe lurking somewhere in the Vulcan's otherwise flat tones.

Suddenly there were sounds, coming at them from all sides. Something that could have been a distant cousin to George's brief saga. Something that could have been the creaking, popping sonar of a hundred dolphins. And countless other sounds, beyond the experience of Spock or any of the humans. A total cacophony, like the emissions of the Probe, and yet—

"A sonic hologram," someone breathed. It was Benar. She had abandoned the tricorder and was working with one of her own tools, a device a quarter the size of the tricorder. "These images reflect sound. The internal structure the tricorder reveals is evident to my sonic probe as well."

"Of course!" Kirk said abruptly, turning toward McCoy. "You said it yourself, Bones, just a minute ago: not superwhales but superdolphins!" He looked back at Benar. "And dolphins 'see' more with their sonar than with their eyes, so any images—their equivalent of a hologram would have to include the ability to be 'seen' by their sonar!" He shook his head. "I'll be damned!"

For a long moment, they all stood silently, listening

and watching the massive creatures—the massive images flowing through the image of the water.

"I believe, Captain," Spock said finally, "you and Dr. Benar may have given me the key to the Probe's emissions."

"What? Spock, how—" Kirk broke off as he reached for his communicator but belatedly realized he had transferred it to one of the jacket's storage pockets before beaming down. "Never mind how! Let's get back to the *Enterprise* and see if you're right. As interesting as this display is—"

His hand was poised to unfasten the clasp of the pocket when, suddenly, he could not move. He started to speak, but he could not.

He could not breathe.

Whatever the Probe had done to them when they had tried to escape using warp drive, it was doing it again.

TWENTY-ONE

———— ☆ ————

The second Winnowing, the creators called it, and the entity found it recorded in detail in the Crystal Wisdom.

Like the first, it had come from space, but not in the form of millions of tons of rock smashing into the planetary crust and unleashing centuries of darkness and lava and ash, covering the oceans with a suffocating blanket that only those who possessed a primitive form of the power of Speech could part.

The second Winnowing came in the form of massive, sharp-edged cubes, spacegoing metallic bubbles of air, swarming with mites no larger than those who had infested the land before the first Winnowing. Their only response to the True Language was a ray of destruction that slaughtered thousands before the massed Voice of the creators had turned it back. Simultaneously, they had called out to the entity to return, for only it possessed the power to defeat this machine of destruction. But it had not responded, for this had been the period of its own lost memory, when it had been slowly repairing itself from its encounter with what it now saw were those same spacegoing mites.

Without the entity's artificially generated, almost limitless power, its creators had been able only to defend themselves, keeping the homeworld free of the mites and their destructive rays with their massed Voice. But they had been powerless to drive them from the system, and when the mites had turned their attention to the homeworld's sun, they had been helpless.

And the sun had faded.

Apparently satisfied they had dealt a death blow to the homeworld, the mites and their cubic bubbles moved on.

But a death blow to the homeworld was not a death blow to the creators. In an effort that in some ways surpassed the creation of the entity itself, they shattered the homeworld's satellite and constructed a fleet of spacegoing ships from the rubble. In a race with the ice that had already spread over half the planet, they drained the oceans and the atmosphere to fill the ships, and finally, putting their Voices to a use that surely had never been intended, the few tens of thousands that remained had lifted themselves into the waiting ships.

And they had departed in a hundred directions, not knowing when, if ever, they would find another world, not knowing when, if ever, they would again encounter the mites and perhaps, this time, be destroyed.

Where? the entity asked. *Where did the creators go? Even now, I could aid them and they could aid me. Where?*

But to that question the Crystal Wisdom held no answer.

But it was good that it held no answer. If such an answer existed, it would be available not only to the entity itself but to the mites who had destroyed the homeworld. If they returned, they could extract the information and track them down to their new worlds—as they had undoubtedly extracted the location of the homeworld from the memory of the entity itself.

But still, it needed to know. Its creators, if they still existed, needed help. The entity needed their guidance. It could not resolve the paradoxes on its own.

As it scanned the data for the thousandth—or perhaps the ten-thousandth—time and still found nothing new, something within it decided. It would attempt again to communicate with the mites who mimicked the True Language.

It reached out with the crystal sensor, seeking them.

And was instantly presented with yet another paradox.

When it had come to the end of its constructed path and emerged in the system of the homeworld, it had searched the homeworld for not only its creators but eventually, for any form of life anywhere. And it had found none.

And yet now—within the very chamber of the Crystal Wisdom, within meters of the Wisdom itself, were eight living beings.

Mites.

The ones who had destroyed the homeworld? Returned to destroy the Crystal Wisdom?

The entity gripped them, even more tightly than it had gripped the mites it had brought here in their spacegoing bubbles.

And while the mites were held rigidly unmoving, the

crystal sensor reached out again, searching the entire system and nearby space.

But the only spacegoing bubbles were those it had brought here itself.

The only mites were those that had swarmed throughout those bubbles.

But there were fewer of them, it saw as it inspected the bubbles more closely. Five fewer in the larger bubble, three fewer in the smaller.

But if those eight in the chamber of the Crystal Wisdom were the same eight who were now missing from the spacegoing bubbles, how had they gotten there?

The entity searched the data that had entered, unnoticed, into its memory since it had taken up its position above the homeworld. No lesser bubbles had detached themselves from the larger ones and descended to the homeworld. Nothing had entered the atmosphere, no matter what the source.

And yet, the eight were there.

Just as the two primitives had not been on the blue world, and then they had been.

It turned its full attention on the eight.

And saw that they were dying.

It loosened its grip but did not release them.

Suddenly, Kirk could breathe again. Not easily, but he could breathe, and the light-flecked blackness that had been closing in on him withdrew.

Turning as quickly as he could, which was not all that quickly, he saw that the only one who had fallen to the invisible ice floor was McCoy, and Spock was already leaning over him in the strained slow motion that was the only movement possible. It was as if the water that submerged them had turned real and thick.

Kirk tried to speak, but he couldn't. His lips could slowly distort into the necessary shapes, but no sounds would form in his throat.

The transporters? Angrily, he realized he shouldn't have stopped McCoy from calling to be beamed up, while they had had the chance. With maddening slowness, he resumed unfastening the clasp of the storage pocket that held his communicator.

But as his gloved fingers moved, as his breath crept in and out with painful slowness, the images around him began to slide downward. Not individually but together in a dizzying plunge. When he finally noticed that, overhead, the glittering surface was drawing closer, his mind altered its references and he was suddenly in an invisible turbolift, shooting silently, meteorically upward.

Somehow, his hand reached the communicator and began pulling it from its pocket.

He broke the surface.

And stopped. The chaos of sounds faded abruptly, as if they could not free themselves from the imagined water.

A sun—twice as bright as the one he had seen from the *Enterprise*—hung low in the sky, not yet beginning to redden. Gentle waves rose and fell all about him, not touching him yet moving through him time and again. The only holdovers from reality were Spock and McCoy and Benar and Dajan. And still thirty meters away, the three Romulans. The waters rose and fell about them all, never quite submerging them except for McCoy, who was still horizontal, and Spock, who was kneeling over him. Overhead now, white-winged birds swooped and glided. One after another, the great, dolphinlike creatures leapt from the water in graceful arcs and plunged back in, raising barely a ripple until their fluked tails would slap down thunderously at the last moment and fill the air with a fountain of spray. In the distance, beneath the hovering sun, was land—a towering mountain range sloping sharply down almost to the water's edge. And on that slope, carved out of the forest that reached almost to the peaks, was what must have been a city, although its buildings, all square and blocky and gray, and its strangely curving streets had none of the sharp-edged clarity of the mountains or the water or the creatures that swam in it and flew above it.

Finally, Kirk had the communicator free of the storage pocket and was activating it. Its chirruping sound was immensely comforting. At least *something* was still working normally.

But he still could not speak, could make no sound except the dull rasp that was his labored breathing. He could scratch weakly at the face of the communicator with his gloved fingers, but that was all. Slowly, he began to lower the communicator toward the metallic clasp he had just struggled to open.

A second sun flared into existence 180 degrees across the sky from the first.

And began to move upward, toward the zenith.

And grow brighter.

As it crossed directly overhead, it was brighter than the first sun, and moving ever more swiftly, as if on a collision course. Sparks, each as bright as the parent object, spun off, first by the dozens, then by the hundreds.

Halfway down the sky toward the first sun, it shattered. A dozen smaller suns arced in all directions. From the other side of the sky, where it had first appeared, a deafening roar assaulted Kirk's ears and began moving toward the zenith, trailing far behind the object that had generated it.

"Captain?" Over the roar, Uhura's voice emerged from the communicator. He wondered if the noise was being picked up or if it was designed only for living ears. All he could do in response was force his reluctant muscles to slam the communicator in slow motion against the pocket clasp.

The largest fragment of the exploded sun disappeared behind the nearest peaks of the shoreline mountain range. Moments later, slowly, majestically, a fiery bubble that must have resembled an early nuclear explosion magnified thousands of times began to bulge above the nearer peaks. Even more slowly, the peaks themselves began to rise and distort and flow toward the shore, crumbling the forest and the city into chaos. Smaller bubbles began appearing at other places along the shore, and some in the ocean itself.

The asteroid, Kirk thought finally. *We're being shown the asteroid that destroyed all land life on this world 2 million years ago.*

"Captain!" Uhura's voice was louder, more urgent, but still barely audible over the roar. Then it was gone. The communicator fell silent.

The water rose, and the roar was suddenly muffled as the image of the liquid closed over him.

The sky darkened as the first and largest of the explosive domes expanded to block out the sun.

The water itself—the image of the water—shuddered.

Abruptly, he was frozen. For an instant he thought the Probe had tightened its grip again, but then the familiar tingle told him it was the transporter energies gripping him.

He waited as the sky grew darker and darker, as the shuddering of the water grew more powerful, and he wondered what this display had done to his time sense.

Finally, the telltale streaks of light sprang into being around him, and moments later, the water and the growing darkness faded out.

The transporter room faded in.

The transporter energies released him.

So did whatever energies the Probe had focused on him. The warmth—the heat, compared to the subzero of the cavern—hit him solidly. And suddenly he could breathe and move normally, except for the rubberiness of his muscles. Breath rushed into his lungs as he spun unsteadily around and found Spock on the transporter circle just behind him, still kneeling over McCoy, who was stretched across two of the circles, sucking in air in great gulps.

"Get him to sickbay," Kirk snapped between gasps of his own as he stepped off the platform and struggled out of his jacket, but even as he spoke, McCoy was getting control of his breathing and was starting to get to his feet with Spock's help.

"I'm all right, Jim," he managed to get out as Spock helped him remove his jacket, but Kirk gestured to the Vulcan.

"Take him, Spock. Carry him if you have to, but get him checked out!"

"There's no blasted need—" McCoy began, but fell silent when his rubbery knees threatened to give way.

Half supporting McCoy, Spock, still in his jacket, the hood pushed back, stepped off the transporter platform.

"We will take him," Dr. Benar said as she and Dajan stepped down from the platform, removing their own jackets. "If what Captain Spock said about having the key to the Probe's emissions is true, it is of the utmost importance that he make use of it as soon as possible."

"She's right, Jim," McCoy said, then added to Spock, "Get your pointy ears to that computer, quick, before that thing out there decides to do something *really* nasty."

Without waiting for Kirk's acquiescence, Spock surrendered McCoy to the two archaeologists, and a moment later they were moving toward the door, one on each side of McCoy. As it hissed open and they stepped through, a pair of orderlies appeared from the direction of the 'lift.

"Commander Uhura said—" one began, but the rest was cut off by the closing door.

"Spock," Kirk said, "now that Bones has more help than he probably wants, get to that computer."

"Of course, Captain." The door hissed open and he was through it by the time Kirk had turned to the ensign at the transporter controls.

"There are three Romulans still down there," Kirk said as the door hissed shut behind Spock, "just a few meters from where we were. Get their coordinates from Lieutenant Parnell at the science station."

"Aye-aye, sir."

Moments later, as Kirk was at the intercom calling for a security detail—and Ensign Handler—to report to the transporter room, the ensign was acknowledging a set of coordinates.

"Get them out of there as quickly as you can," Kirk said, turning back to the ensign, "but don't complete the transfer until security gets here. One of them has a phaser, and all the craziness that was going on down there may have gotten him a little nervous."

The ensign acknowledged with a nod and concentrated on the controls.

"Got them, sir," he said after a few seconds. "Bringing them up."

The characteristic warble of the transporter filled the room as a trio of insubstantial figures came into being on the platform. The door hissed open a moment later and a pair of security lieutenants stepped through.

"That was fast," Kirk acknowledged.

"Commander Uhura said—" the one began, but was cut off by a sudden laugh from Kirk.

"She was right, as usual," he said, and quickly went on to explain about the Romulans and Tiam's phaser.

Phasers drawn and set to stun, they positioned themselves flanking the platform. Kirk placed himself directly in front of the indistinct forms, then gestured to the ensign at the transporter controls.

The warble intensified, and the images solidified.

Tiam, Kirk saw instantly, was in no condition to put up a struggle. The ambassador, his eyes tightly closed, lurched and almost fell as the transporter energies released him. All three began sucking air into their lungs, and Tiam's eyes snapped open.

At Kirk's nod, the security lieutenants put away their phasers. All three waited as the Romulans caught their breath.

"Ambassador Tiam, Subcommanders," Kirk said quietly, "welcome aboard the *Enterprise.*"

TWENTY-TWO

─────────────── ☆ ───────────────

The sounds and images, each more insane than the last, had paralyzed Tiam's mind almost as effectively as the behemoth itself had paralyzed his body. Finally, he had closed his eyes—an action that had taken several seconds to complete—and concentrated only on forcing air in and out of his lungs and wondering desperately when it would all end.

Then, abruptly, he had felt himself gripped by the energies of a transporter, and hope flared through him. Hiran—or even Jenyu—had realized something was wrong and was having him beamed up.

But then the energies had released him. His eyes had snapped open, and his muscles, still straining against the force that had gripped him in the cavern, had sent him reeling, almost crashing to the floor. And as he regained precarious control of his body, as he gasped in lungful after lungful of the suddenly breathable, suddenly warm air, he realized where he was: in the transporter room of the *Enterprise*, not the *Galtizh*.

And he realized he had failed. Whatever he had hoped to gain from that crystal, he was obviously not going to get it.

But the *Enterprise* had come away equally empty-handed, he realized an instant later. They had been engulfed in those insane sounds and images as quickly and completely as he had been. He had seen them pointing and gesturing and exclaiming about the images when they had first appeared, and they had been as surprised as he. So, although the hoped-for windfall of the crystal had fallen through, there was still hope. And with the false patterns the *Enterprise* team had to work with . . .

"Ambassador Tiam, Subcommanders," the Federation captain was saying, "welcome aboard the *Enterprise.*"

Tiam managed a weak smile while the two subcommanders acknowledged with curt nods.

"Thank you, Captain Kirk," Tiam said. He glanced toward the ensign at the transporter controls, noticing the security team as he did. He turned his eyes back to Kirk. "I assume we owe our presence here to the fact that your transporter personnel are a bit more alert than those on the *Galtizh.*"

"Bridge personnel," Kirk said with a faint smile, "Commander Uhura, communications officer, to be precise."

"Convey my gratitude—*our* gratitude to the commander, Captain."

"Gladly, Ambassador. Now, do you wish to be transported directly to the *Galtizh?*"

"The subcommanders, yes, if you please. I, however,

would like a word with you before I return, Captain, if that is possible."

"Of course." Kirk nodded to the ensign at the transporter controls as Tiam stepped down from the platform.

"Inform Commander Hiran of the situation," Tiam said to the subcommanders a she removed his heavy fur jacket, the phaser still deep in one of the pockets, and handed it to one of them. Under the circumstances, he had decided, it would be best not to have the weapon on him or even acknowledge its existence. "Tell him I will transport over as soon as possible. And have our own transporter personnel attempt to retrieve the equipment you were utilizing in the cavern."

"Very well, Ambassador Tiam," the female subcommander said while the other nodded and folded Tiam's jacket over his arm.

Tiam turned back to Kirk, noticing as he did that Riley's aide, the one named Handler, had appeared and was standing uneasily next to the captain.

"Sorry it took me so long, Captain," the aide was saying, "but I was down in sickbay, you know, seeing how Commander Riley is doing."

"And how is the ambassador doing?" Tiam asked.

"Still not awake," Handler said, "but they're expecting it anytime now."

"That is good to hear, Mr. Handler," Tiam said, trying to emulate the virtually human smile that Hiran seemed to find so natural. "You will have much to tell him when he awakens, will you not?"

"Quite a lot, yes, sir." Handler darted a look at the captain.

"You said you wished a word with me, Ambassador," Kirk said. "What can we do for you?"

Tiam swallowed, summoning up the distasteful words. "I would like you to accept my apologies, Captain, for my actions in transporting down to the planet without first notifying you of our intention."

"Of course," the captain said. "Does this mean you would like to resume negotiations? If so, perhaps you should speak with Mr. Handler, here."

Tiam repressed a scowl. The human was obviously toying with him. "I am not speaking of formal negotiations, Captain Kirk, Mr. Handler. Primarily, I would like to assure you that we will continue to cooperate in the effort to decode the object's emissions."

Kirk's eyebrows raised in what struck Tiam as mock surprise. "Then you are not aware of the actions of your aide, Subcenturion Kital, in your absence?"

Tiam's stomach knotted. *Jenyu!* What had he done now? "I was not, Captain."

"While we were preparing to beam down to 'join' you," Kirk said, "Subcenturion Kital—acting on your behalf, I was given to understand—ordered all Romulans aboard the *Enterprise* to return to the *Galtizh.* We assumed, in light of your having already beamed down on your own, that you had decided that the time for cooperation in the matter of the work on the Probe's emissions had ended."

Tiam bit off an angry response to the captain's obvious sarcasm. "That was not my intention, Captain. I can only repeat my apologies and ask you to believe that I was overeager in my actions and did not take the proper time to consider the circumstances. We would of course have shared whatever knowledge we gained."

"Of course, Ambassador."

"And I will deal with my aide. And I will ask those

who were part of the team working with your Mr. Spock
to return—if you will allow it."

"As you wish, Ambassador. However, there may not
be a great deal to do by the time they return. Mr. Spock
believes he has found the key to—"

"What?" The words hit Tiam like a physical blow.
"When? Was he not in that madness with us!"

Kirk shrugged, obviously enjoying himself. "He
hasn't explained precisely what, Ambassador, but the
'when' was in that 'madness,' as you call it. Something
down there gave him a clue. I suppose we'll see soon
enough if it pans out."

Tiam swallowed. Was this human simply tormenting
him? Paying him back for the transgression of transporting down to the cavern alone? How could even the
Vulcan have learned something from that insanity?
Tiam was sorely tempted to vent his true feelings, to
refuse to acquiesce in this shameful treatment, but he
dared not take the chance. If the Vulcan *had* found
something down there . . .

"That is good to hear," Tiam forced himself to say.
"The knowledge to be gained from this—thing—could
be immense."

Abruptly, Tiam turned and stepped up onto the
transporter platform. "I will speak with my aide," he
repeated, "and I will send back those he mistakenly
called away. I am grateful that you are willing to
overlook my impulsive act and the mistakes of my aide."

The last thing Tiam saw as the transporter energies
closed around him was Kirk's smiling, hateful face.

"Was it my imagination, Mr. Handler," Kirk asked as
the Romulan vanished from the transporter platform,

"or was Ambassador Tiam gritting his teeth a lot when he 'apologized'?"

"Yes, sir, it did seem that way," Handler said, and then, for once forgetting his nervousness around senior officers, particularly *this* senior officer, asked, almost breathlessly, "Was that true, sir? What you said about Mr. Spock being able to talk to the Probe?"

Kirk laughed. "Come along to the bridge and we'll see," he said, heading for the corridor and the 'lift. "But just for the record, what I said was, Mr. Spock 'believes he has found the key.' There's a big difference."

"Yes, sir."

Kirk sobered. "You looked in on Kevin, you said?"

"Yes, sir."

"Still no sign of awakening?"

"They said—"

"I know what 'they' said, Mr. Handler. I want to know what you *think*."

Handler swallowed. "I'm not a doctor, sir."

"I know that, Mr. Handler. But you are his friend."

"Yes, sir, I like to think so."

"Then tell me what you think—as his friend."

Handler swallowed again. They were in the 'lift on the way to the bridge. "I'm worried, sir. They expected him to wake up three days ago, but when that thing grabbed us like it did, and we couldn't breathe—" He broke off, shaking his head. "I know Dr. McCoy said it didn't have any—any lasting effect, but I'm still worried. I think Mr. Sulu and Commander Uhura are, too."

Kirk put a hand on Handler's shoulder, squeezing gently. "So am I, Mr. Handler. So are we all."

The 'lift opened on the bridge. The unnamed planet, the shadow of its ring darkening a good quarter of it, still filled the viewscreen. Commander Scott stood up and moved from the conn.

"Good ta have ye back, sir. Mr. Spock tells us ye had an interesting time doon there."

"That's one way of putting it, Mr. Scott. Though I would've thought it rated at least a 'fascinating.'" Kirk came to a stop next to the conn and punched up sickbay. "Status of Dr. McCoy," he said briskly.

"As good as can be expected, Captain," came the voice of Commander Chapel, "when you have to physically restrain a patient to get any readings."

"I'll take that as an 'okay,'" Kirk said. "Any change in Commander Riley?"

"None, Captain. Although you might want to ask Dajan. He went in to see Riley when he and Dr. Benar delivered the doctor, and he's still there."

"Not right now, thank you, Commander."

He turned to Spock, who, though watching the readouts closely, was doing nothing else. Jandra stood to one side, not looking at the readouts but simply waiting, listening.

"So, Mr. Spock, were you right?"

"Undetermined, Captain. I have submitted my hypothesis to the computer. We can only await results."

"How long?"

"Also undetermined, Captain."

"You're a great help today, Spock. While we wait, can you at least tell us what your hypothesis *is?* And how, *logically,* you got it from anything Dr. Benar or I said?"

"Of course, Captain. The two of you indicated that the images were, in effect, sonic holograms, detectable by her own sonic probe and in all likelihood, by the sonar of the dolphinlike creatures whose images were being displayed to us. That, in addition to the sounds themselves, prompted me to review what I had learned during my study of cetaceans prior to my attempt to meld with George, and that review proved fruitful."

"You *reviewed* what you'd learned?" Kirk marveled. "In the middle of all that was going on down there?"

"Of course, Captain, as, I suspect, did you. My conclusion was no more remarkable than your own logical analysis of the relationship between sonic holograms and dolphins."

"That wasn't an *analysis,* Spock, just a realization, a hunch."

"I suspect the difference, Captain, is more in the semantics than in the reality."

Kirk sighed. "Have it your way, Spock. But you were about to say . . . ?"

"I was about to say, Captain, that the literature contained many descriptions of the ability of earth dolphins to use the 'clicks' of their sonar to 'look' at an object while simultaneously using 'whistling' sounds to communicate with other dolphins. This would be, a number of the descriptions said, the equivalent in a human of speaking in two different pitches and carrying on two conversations simultaneously."

"So you're saying what, Spock?" Kirk asked when the Vulcan paused. "That the Probe is saying two things at once? At different frequencies?"

"If my hypothesis is correct, Captain, it could be saying many things at once, at many different frequencies. Or possibly it is saying the same thing in many different ways at many different frequencies. At this point, it is impossible to know."

Kirk nodded, suddenly beginning to understand.

"Each of those patterns—how many did you find? Twenty? Thirty? Each of those patterns could be a different language? All saying the same thing?"

"That is one possibility, Captain, as is the possibility that each is saying something different. I have instructed the computer to isolate each band of frequencies that contains a pattern and to treat each as a possibly separate language."

Kirk glanced at the readouts. "And it's still thinking about it?"

"Apparently, Captain."

"If there's any way you can hurry it along, before—"

"Captain!" It was Sulu, at the helm. "The *Galtizh* is engaging impulse power."

Kirk spun toward the viewscreen. "Stay with it, Mr. Sulu. Where is it headed?"

"Higher orbit, Captain. It may be returning to the orbit of the Probe."

"Commander Uhura—"

"Hailing the *Galtizh,* Captain. No response."

"Keep after them, Commander."

"It's definitely heading for the Probe's orbit, Captain," Sulu reported. On the viewscreen, the frozen planet had disappeared, replaced by the fragments of the ring along one side while in the center was a minuscule *Galtizh.* And beyond, still small in the distance but rapidly growing larger, was the lightless mass of the Probe.

One paradox had been resolved, only to be replaced by another.

The entity, once it had partially loosened its grip on the mites in the Chamber of the Crystal Wisdom, had continued to observe them as they were engulfed in

310

images of the first Winnowing, just as countless thousands of the creators themselves had been engulfed throughout the millennia before the Second Winnowing.

But then, before the Triumph, before the recreated images of those who became the creators' ancestors had used their nascent power of Speech to clear the mass of ash from small breathing areas, the eight had vanished, snatched directly from its grip.

And they had reappeared in one of the spacegoing bubbles.

They were the same, the entity saw now. One moment, they had been in the Chamber. The next moment, they were outside the Chamber, thousands of kilometers in space.

Like the primitives on the blue world, they could appear and disappear.

The chances that these mites were responsible for the appearance—and previous disappearance—of those primitives were increasing.

As were the chances that they were somehow connected to the mites that had driven the creators from the homeworld hundreds of millennia ago.

But the entity would do nothing now.

It would wait. It would observe.

And if they proved to be the same, if they proved to make use of the same killing rays, their mimicking of the True Language would not save them.

TWENTY-THREE

─────────── ☆ ───────────

Tiam knew something was wrong the moment the *Galtizh* transporter room formed around him and he saw that Jenyu, not Kital, was waiting for him. Dressed now in a somber but bemedaled commander's uniform, Jenyu had jettisoned all traces of Subcenturion Kital. Subcommander Feric stood uneasily to one side, flanked by two officers Tiam did not know.

"What was the substance of your clandestine exchange with the Federation captain, Ambassador?" Jenyu asked almost before the transporter energies had released him.

"It was not clandestine!"

"Then why did you send the subcommanders on to the *Galtizh* before speaking with him? Do not waste my time, Tiam. What was said?"

Tiam swallowed nervously. "I was told that you had

withdrawn all our people from the Vulcan's group. And I—I told him they would be returning. He agreed."

"They will not return. Nor will you."

"But the Vulcan—they say he has discovered a key to the object's emissions! If true, it could mean we will soon be able to achieve the late Praetor's objective—but only if you allow me to return to the *Enterprise!*"

Jenyu had started to turn away, but he turned back at Tiam's final words. "How so?"

"The false patterns our people 'found' for them! With those added to the true patterns they must work with, there is little chance their key will do them any good! On the other hand, if I am allowed to work with them and discover what their key is, I will be able to return here and—"

"Can you guarantee they will fail? And that you will subsequently succeed?"

"Perhaps not guarantee, Commander, but the odds—"

"The odds against virtually everything that has happened since I came aboard this ship are incalculable, yet it has all happened! *Can you give me a guarantee?*"

"Of course not, but—"

"Enough," Jenyu said, turning and stalking toward the door. "Place Ambassador Tiam with Commander Hiran."

And he was gone, Feric trailing in his wake.

In a heartbeat, the two subcenturions stepped forward, and barely a minute later, Tiam found himself being shoved unceremoniously into Hiran's quarters. An instant later, he heard the click of the newly installed manual lock he had glimpsed on the outside of the door.

Hiran looked up from his desk, his eyes widening slightly as Tiam lurched to a stop.

"Inquisitor?" Hiran asked. "Or fellow prisoner?"

"What *happened,* Hiran?"

"May I take that to mean 'fellow prisoner,' Ambassador?"

"Take it as you like! Just tell me what has happened here."

"I would have thought that obvious to a man of your acuity, Ambassador. It seems I was as naive as I accused you of being! We were *both* pawns in the game, and your 'aide' turned out to be, in truth, the only player on board." Hiran laughed bitterly. "Not that he will be a player for long. Tell me, Ambassador, are you aware of what your former aide is planning?"

Tiam shook his head angrily. "I *thought* I did, but obviously I don't. All I *know* is, he is throwing away a chance to accomplish what the Praetor originally set out to do: utilize the power of that thing that brought us here! He refuses to let me return to the *Enterprise* and—"

"You have no idea, no idea at all, do you? He's determined to destroy that 'thing,' as you call it! And the *Galtizh* in the process!"

Tiam gaped. *Destroy it? No one could be that mad!* "How in the gods' names? He knows as well as I what it did to the *Henzu,* to Wlaariivi!"

"He thinks he has a way around that little difficulty," Hiran said, beginning to recount Jenyu's tale of the ships on the training mission. "He thinks we might be inside its 'defensive perimeter,' as he called it, and he also thinks he may have found a vulnerable spot. But he doesn't really care. He is willing to be destroyed in the retaliation as long as he feels there is a good chance the retaliation will take out the *Enterprise* as well as the *Galtizh.* All he cares about—"

314

"Officers and crew of the *Galtizh,* Romulan citizens." Jenyu's voice crackled from the intercom, drowning out Hiran's words.

Subcommander Feric listened with growing consternation to Commander Jenyu's announcement to the officers and crew. With each word that came over the speakers, it became clearer that he was outlining their coming deaths, and worse, the end of any hope for peace between the Empire and the Federation. Following his course of action might even mean the destruction of the Empire itself.

They were to attack this behemoth that had brought them here. There was a small chance, Jenyu said, they would succeed in disabling it, in which case the *Enterprise* would in all likelihood turn its own firepower on the far more lightly armed *Galtizh.* There was a much greater chance, the commander admitted, that the attack would do little or no damage to the monster but would provoke a response that would vaporize the *Galtizh*—and, Jenyu fervently hoped, the *Enterprise.*

And all, according to Jenyu, solely to prevent the Federation from gaining control of the thing.

It was insane.

It was sheer paranoia—typical of those of Jenyu's and Tiam's warlike stripe—to think that the Federation had already influenced the thing to attack Wlaariivi. There was nothing to indicate that *anyone* could gain control of it, *ever,* and everything to indicate such control was impossible. According to Hiran, the Empire had been trying to communicate with it or take it over for months, ever since the first time the object passed through Romulan space, and the Empire had failed miserably.

The best either the Empire or the Federation could hope was to learn how to communicate with it. It would no more do the Federation's bidding than it would the Empire's. As its actions had proven, both in the Federation and the Empire, it was not the derelict the Praetor had first assumed. It was fully operational and had an agenda of its own, an agenda that saw the Empire and the Federation—if it saw them at all—as distractions at best, insects to be swatted if they proved too troublesome. To attack it now could accomplish only one thing, aside from their own instant deaths. This would be at least the second attack by a Romulan vessel, and that might be enough to elevate the Empire from the status of distraction to the status of enemy. It might well prompt it to do on its own what Jenyu irrationally feared the Federation might order it to do.

Jenyu finally paused in his announcement, which had now gone on for a good five minutes.

"It was my duty to inform you of the situation," he resumed quietly. "I have done so. Now, except for those whose duties lie with me, on the bridge, you may do as you see fit these next few minutes."

Make your preparations to die, you mean, Feric thought, suddenly angry, wondering how many others were echoing his thoughts. But what could they do, after all?

Now, more than ever, Jenyu had the power.

Finally, the intercom in Hiran's quarters fell silent. A moment later, through the viewport, he and Tiam saw that the *Galtizh* had begun to move.

"He is mad!" Tiam said, shaking his head.

Hiran shrugged. "He is also in control. And the ones he has manning the bridge are as mad as he is. But I

316

would have thought your own philosophy of war rather than negotiation would have placed you firmly in their camp. And yet you now say they are mad?"

"War is a contest, not pointless suicide!"

"Jenyu knows it is suicide, but he obviously disagrees about its being pointless."

Tiam pulled in a ragged breath. "Is there nothing you can do? You are the commander of the *Galtizh,* after all!"

"You did not seem to hold that opinion a few short hours ago, Ambassador!" Hiran flared, then calmed himself. "In any event, when Jenyu revealed his true identity—through an announcement just like this one— he accused me of treason against the Empire, of 'conspiring' with the enemy, in the person of the Federation captain. He invoked the Master Dominion Pandect for Martial Crisis. I do not know how many believed him, but there were enough who did not rise to my defense that it was easy for him and his six men to assume control of my ship! Most are still loyal to me, but—"

"The civilians, the scientists and musicians! Certainly they cannot wish to die."

"I would assume not, but they were all assembled and locked away—in your quarters, no less. They are as helpless as we."

"But surely—"

The click of the manual lock brought a sudden silence. Both men turned to the door as it slid open, revealing a grim-faced Subcommander Feric.

"Feric! What—"

"Commander," Feric said. Hiran felt himself grinning —and a split-second later, Feric followed suit.

It was the first time Hiran could recall seeing his first officer smile.

TWENTY-FOUR

☆

The glittering blackness of the Probe filled the *Enterprise* viewscreen. At the center, the speck that was the *Galtizh* had dropped to minimum impulse and was barely moving.

"What the *hell* are they up to?" Kirk muttered, not for the first time.

"Still no response to our hail, Captain," Uhura volunteered.

"It looks like they're heading for that appendage," Sulu said from the helm, "the one we decided might or might not be what it uses to transmit and receive whatever it is it transmits and receives. Sir."

"So they can whisper in its ear in hopes we won't hear what they say?" Kirk shook his head. "It doesn't make sense."

McCoy, who had escaped Commander Chapel's ministrations and made his way to the bridge, snorted. "I'd start worrying if they did something that *did* make sense."

"Response from the *Galtizh,* Captain," Uhura announced abruptly.

"On-screen."

The Probe and the minuscule *Galtizh* vanished, replaced a moment later by an image of the Romulan bridge. But a badly out-of-focus image. A grim-faced and equally out-of-focus Hiran stood at the rear of the bridge, looking over the shoulder of a subcommander at the Romulan equivalent of a science station.

Hastily, Hiran dragged the guard inside his quarters and used the guard's phaser to bolster the stun that Feric had already administered. Resetting the manual lock, the three hurried down the corridor to the nearest 'lift.

But it was disabled. "Commander Jenyu is taking no chances," Hiran said with a curse.

"We cannot reach the bridge?" What little color was left in Tiam's face drained away. "Is there no other way?"

"Emergency service stairs, of course, but he will surely have sealed off all entrances to the bridge."

"Then there is *no* way of stopping him?"

"Not unless we can cut off power to the weapons—or to the bridge. And I doubt that his preparations have been lax enough to allow that."

"With your permission, Commander," Feric volunteered, gripping his phaser more tightly, "I will attempt it. I am as familiar with the *Galtizh* as anyone."

Hiran's eyes darted briefly upward, in the direction of the distant bridge. "Very well. We will go together. Tiam?"

Tiam swallowed, his lips parchment dry. "There is another possibility," he said, barely above a whisper.

Hiran spun to face the ambassador. "And you have said nothing until now? What is it? Quickly!"

"My quarters—there is a subspace transceiver. We could contact the Committee and—"

Hiran snorted. "Halfway across the galaxy? Don't be a fool, Tiam!"

Tiam blinked, then slumped as the reality of the distance hit him. "Then we are lost."

But Hiran had suddenly brightened. "Perhaps not." He turned to Feric. "Go, try to cut power to the weapons or the bridge."

"Yes, Commander." Without another word, the subcommander sprinted for the nearest entrance to the service stairs.

"Come, Tiam," Hiran said, gripping the ambassador's arm and dragging him in Feric's wake toward the stairs, "take me to this transmitter of yours."

Kirk frowned at the blurred image of the *Galtizh* bridge. "Commander Hiran?"

The indistinct figure looked sharply around at the screen. "Captain Kirk," Hiran said slowly, drawing in a breath. The commander's voice was oddly distorted, as if to match the images. "I must reluctantly request your assistance."

Kirk glanced questioningly toward Spock while surreptitiously signaling to Uhura to cut the audio portion of the transmission.

"Audio cut, Captain," she said after a moment.

"Spock?"

"There are no indications of malfunctions in any of the *Galtizh*'s primary systems, Captain."

The audio returned at Kirk's signal. "Of course, Commander Hiran," he said. "What can we do for you?"

"In light of what happened when Tiam and the others transported down to observe the crystal, we decided to investigate the object's crystal appendage more closely," Hiran said, answering Kirk's unasked question. "Now that we have approached it, however, we find that we are unable to maneuver."

"Is it similar to what happened while we were being brought here?" Kirk asked. "Whenever we tried to use impulse power?"

"No, Captain Kirk. The engines simply do not respond."

"I see. But what is it you wish of us?"

"If you could approach to within tractor-beam range and attempt to free us—"

"And get caught ourselves?"

"The effect appears to have a very short range. We first encountered it at less than ten kilometers. You will be able to get within tractor-beam range without exposing yourself to danger."

"Is the Probe affecting your transmissions as well, Commander Hiran? Your images are blurred."

Hiran blinked at the sudden change of subject. "Yours are blurred as well, Captain Kirk. Perhaps it is the result of whatever field is preventing us from moving."

"Perhaps." Kirk looked to Sulu at the helm. "Take us in, Mr. Sulu, very carefully. Reverse course the moment you detect any loss of efficiency in the impulse engines."

"Aye-aye, sir."

Kirk started to look back at the screen when the audio channel was cut abruptly.

"Captain," Uhura said, speaking rapidly, "there is a subspace hail from the *Galtizh*—audio only."

"Mr. Sulu, belay that order. Keep us where we are! Commander Uhura, make it look like we're having transmission trouble, too. No clear transmissions, audio or picture, to the *Galtizh* bridge until we find out who this other audio is coming from."

The transmission from the *Galtizh* bridge resumed in midsentence.

"I'm sorry, Captain," Uhura said loudly, overriding Hiran's incoming voice, "but I'm losing your signal." A moment later, the viewscreen image faltered and broke up. Hiran's voice was lost as well.

Kirk vaulted from the conn and was at Uhura's side in a second. "Who—" he began, but another voice cut him off.

"This is Commander Hiran, Captain Kirk. I must warn you—"

"Commander Hiran was just speaking to me from the *Galtizh* bridge."

"A poor image? Out of focus? Low-quality audio?"

"Yes, but—"

"It is Jenyu—the one you knew as Kital. He has taken over the bridge. He must be using the computer to alter his image, to simulate mine. I have used similar deceptions myself. The image and the sound are purposely of low quality so that the simulation—itself of low quality —will not be detected."

"Hiran," Kirk broke in, "do you still have the same desires regarding the Erisians?"

"What? Kirk, do not waste—"

"I have to know which of you is the real Hiran!" Kirk snapped. "Now tell me, the Erisians!"

322

"I see. Very well, during my tour of the *Enterprise*—which I would very much like to complete some day—I expressed the hope that the Erisians would prove to be ancestors to you humans, so that the Empire would be forced to open the Neutral Zone."

Kirk let his breath out in a whoosh. "Commander Hiran," he said, "what is the warning?"

"Kital—he is in reality Commander Jenyu, late of the *Shalyar*—has taken over the bridge. He plans to fire every weapon we have into the cavity from which that thing's appendage is extended. He hopes to damage the massive crystal structure just below the cavity, but he *expects* the thing to return fire and vaporize both the *Galtizh* and the *Enterprise,* just as it did the *Henzu* and the cargo ship near Wlaariivi."

There was a gasp from somewhere on the bridge, but Kirk ignored it . . . except to note, out of the corner of his eye, that Jandra had left Spock's side and was hurrying toward the turbolift.

"So *that's* why he wanted us close in." Kirk nodded. "But if you can't stop him, how do you expect us—"

"Fire on him first, Kirk! Destroy his ability to launch the attack if you can. If you cannot—" Hiran paused, swallowing audibly. "If you cannot limit your fire to his weapons alone, you must destroy the *Galtizh* itself. We cannot take a chance with anything else."

"But why is Jenyu doing this?"

"He is convinced there is a chance you will learn to control that thing, particularly after Tiam informed him of the progress your Mr. Spock is supposed to have made. He is afraid—convinced—that you will order it to destroy the Empire. I am more afraid that, if he manages to attack it—this would be at least the second time a Romulan ship has attacked it—it may decide we are an enemy worth paying attention to, an enemy worth destroying."

"If it is aware that there is such a thing as a Romulan Empire. Or that there is a difference between a Romulan ship and a Federation ship."

"I am well aware of the uncertainties involved, Federation captain. The only certainty is this: if you do nothing and allow him to attack, the *Galtizh* will be a cloud of vapor like the *Henzu* within seconds, as will the *Enterprise*. If you can disable our weapons, there is a chance that at least some of us will survive."

"Commander Hiran is right!" another voice shouted.

"Who—" Kirk began, but Hiran had already anticipated the question.

"Ambassador Tiam. He agrees with our decision, but he wants to be beamed over before you act."

"We can probably beam several of you—"

"Captain," Spock broke in, "the *Galtizh* phaser banks are being deliberately overcharged, presumably in order to maximize their initial discharge."

"All transporters!" Kirk snapped. "Lock onto any life-forms you can on the *Galtizh* and—"

"*Galtizh* shields raised, Captain," Sulu reported.

So the transporters are gone. Nothing else for it, then. Kirk gritted his teeth, ignoring the knot that had suddenly formed in his stomach. "Mr. Sulu, lock all phasers on the *Galtizh* weapons systems. Fire when the phaser-charge buildup stops." *And hope to God that's all we hit. A Federation starship destroying a Romulan cruiser . . .*

That could mean war.

He turned in his chair to face Uhura. "All transporters, be ready to pick up any survivors!"

"Captain!" It was Spock again. "The computer is producing a translation of the Probe's emissions."

Talk about timing! "Can *we* talk to *it?*"

"We can try, Captain. The modified tractor beams are—"

"Then talk to it, Spock! Warn it! Tell it to get the hell out of here—*now!*"

Spock's fingers stabbed at a half dozen controls. "You are in danger," he said, no more emotion in his voice than ever. "Remove yourself immediately from this area."

For a moment there was only silence. Suddenly a rumble, nothing higher than forty hertz, filled the bridge as the translation was sent not only to the tractor beam but to the bridge speakers and over the intercom. The upper frequencies, Kirk could hear. The lower, below the nineteen hertz his last exam had proclaimed as the low end of his hearing range, he felt, not just where his boots met the deck but throughout his body. If he spoke, he knew the vibrations would be superimposed on his words.

The sound, both heard and felt, was eerily beautiful, he realized, like George's song played on the lowest-pitched pipes of a massive organ.

But it bore no resemblance to the Probe's emissions that he could discern.

And the Probe remained perfectly still, going nowhere.

And the *Galtizh* phaser banks continued to mass their deadly charge.

* * *

In sickbay, Dajan looked around sharply as the door to the ambassador's room hissed open and Jandra hurtled through.

"What—" he began, but he was startled into silence, first by the tear-stained anger in her face, then by her arms as she wrapped them tightly about him.

"Sib!" Her voice trembled.

His stomach knotted as he pulled free of her arms and stepped back to look at her face. "Kirk is sending us back to the *Galtizh.*"

"No! Some madman on the *Galtizh* is about to order an attack on that *thing,* and it will surely destroy us all!"

To his own surprise, Dajan felt a measure of relief. If the Federation had betrayed him and turned him back to Tiam, it would have meant the Federation was little better than the Empire, and that thought was suddenly intolerable to him.

"It will not come to that, certainly, Little Sister," he said, though he had no idea whether it would or not.

"I do not care!" she said, her voice filled with anguish. "I only know that, if it is our time, we must be ready. When our parents were driven to their deaths, we were not even allowed to say goodbye. I will not allow that to happen to us!"

For a moment, his instinct was to again protest. But he could not. For he knew she was right.

He held out his arms and she came into them. They held each other as tightly as ever in their lives.

And they waited.

And as they waited, their words and their feelings slowly filtered down to where Commander Kevin Thomas Riley and the four-year-old he had once been began to take them as his own.

* * *

Suddenly, yet another paradox assaulted the entity.

The mites that had first mimicked the True Language were mimicking it again, and yet they were not.

The energy they were producing was the same they had employed earlier, a short-range, painfully slow imitation of Speech, not the bewildering array of frequencies in which the other mites had buried their own mimicry of the True Language.

But the content could not have been more different.

It was not merely another echo of the message the entity itself had been continuously proclaiming for five hundred millennia.

It was something totally new, a warning of danger.

And it was carried not by the True Language in its entirety but by only one primitive aspect of it, the aspect its creators had employed before they had developed the power of Speech, when their voices had still been matter-bound. It was the aspect they had retained and continued to use, not because it was the most useful, because it was not; nor because it could communicate the greatest amount of information, because it could not. In truth, it could convey only the most elemental information, little more than the matter-bound languages of the thousands of primitives the entity had found and nurtured over the millennia.

It was retained because it was the first.

And now these mites had isolated that one most primitive aspect and had chosen to communicate through it.

Had they chosen to use more aspects, they could have communicated a thousand times more information: the source of the danger, the precise nature of the danger, all the ways the danger could be avoided, the reasons for the danger, how long it had been present and how long it would remain—all these and a mass of other details could have been communicated in those same moments had they not chosen to limit themselves to this single, primitive aspect.

But perhaps it was all they were capable of.

After full milliseconds of consideration, it searched for the danger.

But there was none.

Even if these mites possessed the killing rays, the defenses the entity had discovered in its possession after the destruction around the blue-green world would keep it safe. If either of the mites' spacegoing bubbles used the rays, they would both be reduced to their component atoms within milliseconds.

There is no danger, it said.

Kirk stood by Spock's station, listening as the computer produced a translation of the Probe's response.

"It doesn't understand," he said frantically. He spoke again—directly, he hoped, to the Probe. "There is a weapon that is about to be fired at you. We do not want it to be fired, but we cannot stop it. If you can stop it, there will be time to explain, time to talk."

Silence.

Finally, the computer produced another eerie series of low-pitched tones and subsonics.

"*Galtizh* phaser banks leveling off," Sulu reported. "They could fire any second."

There is no danger. The words played themselves back as Kirk waited helplessly. No danger because the Probe could not be damaged? Because it could shrug off phasers and photon torpedoes like dust motes? Because it could strike back, as it apparently had with the *Henzu,* and vaporize the attacker before any damage could be inflicted?

He couldn't take the chance. "Fire, Mr. Sulu."

. . . time to talk.

The entity seized on that fragment of the message. For five hundred millennia, it had searched for those with which it could Speak.

Once, it had searched solely so it could bring word back to its creators, but now its creators were gone.

There was only itself.

And these mites—mites who spoke the aspect of the True Language that was the first its creators had ever spoken.

Mites who *wanted* to communicate. Mites who, no matter how mistakenly, had warned it of what they had perceived as a danger to it.

The entity reached out and gripped the spacegoing bubbles and the mites within them more tightly than it ever had before.

Everywhere in the *Enterprise* and the *Galtizh,* all motion stopped.

Sulu's hand was frozen centimeters from the firing control.

Jenyu's order to fire all phasers and photon torpedoes was frozen in his throat.

In sickbay of the *Enterprise,* Dajan and his sister were frozen in each other's arms, while the four-year-old Kevin Riley found himself held just as tightly by first his mother, then his father, as they bid him goodbye.

* * *

Gently, swiftly, the entity placed the mites and their spacegoing bubbles beyond the point at which their killing rays—if indeed they possessed them—could trigger a response.

It released them.

We will talk, it said.

On the *Enterprise* viewscreen, the Probe suddenly began to shrink. Within seconds, even its huge bulk was a speck in the distance.

The *Galtizh,* as if attached to the *Enterprise* by an invisible rod of force, seemed not to move at all.

As suddenly as it had come, the paralysis lifted.

Sulu's hand jerked backward from the firing control.

The *Galtizh*'s phasers lashed out harmlessly into empty space, followed a fraction of a second later by a photon torpedo. A hundred kilometers out, the torpedo vanished, harmlessly vaporized.

In the *Enterprise* sickbay, Dajan and his sister, realizing they were going to live, released each other with a smile. And Commander Kevin Riley's eyes fluttered open, and before the four-year-old boy from his nightmares faded entirely from his memory, he realized that, somehow, the goodbyes he had never been able to say had finally been spoken.

The Probe spoke, now using only the frequencies the computer used.

"We will talk," the computer translated.

And they did talk.

For hours, with the computer constantly mastering new aspects of the Probe's language, adding new complexities to the dialogue, they talked.

And they learned, all of them. Even the stubbornnest of the Romulans, listening, first eagerly, then angrily, found themselves learning.

Finally, of necessity, the return to reality—to the Neutral Zone and the problems that could only have grown worse in their absence—was begun.

TWENTY-FIVE

☆

Captain's Log, Stardate 8501.2:

According to Mr. Sulu's "looking out the window" calculations, the Probe made equally good time—roughly warp thirty—on the return leg of what must have been one of the longest towing jobs in either Federation or Romulan history. Its departure moments after releasing the *Enterprise* and the *Galtizh* at the edge of the Temaris system was equally speedy.

Not surprisingly, the Temaris "conference" has not been resumed, and all parties involved are anticipating orders to withdraw from the Neutral Zone until further notice. The one surprise is that the reform-minded Interim Government is still in power, albeit precariously. They are reportedly getting a boost from Hiran's accusations of sabotage against Ambassador Tiam and Commander Jenyu, but Jenyu's sponsors are firing back with the expected accusations against Hiran, most of which boil down to "collaboration with the enemy," meaning me. At least Hiran has regained control of his ship—and Jenyu and his men are locked safely in the *Galtizh*'s brig.

We learned a lot from the Probe in the last three days, and the Probe appears to have picked up a little from us "mites." Spock, for instance, once he became the only mite to be allowed direct access to the Probe's "innards," as Dr. McCoy calls them, was able to resolve the various paradoxes that had apparently driven it, first, to drag us halfway across the galaxy, and second, to almost shut itself down. With the help of the *Enterprise* computer, Spock expanded on its creators' rather rigid definition of intelligence, so that it now includes most technologically advanced mites, even those such as ourselves who can generally carry on only one conversation at a time. Similarly, he was able to modify the goals its creators had given it, so that it will be able not only to go on searching for life-forms who might someday become like its creators, but also to search for the creators themselves, wherever the survivors might have gone, in or out of the galaxy.

One thing Spock was not able to do was restore the Probe's "lost" memory, other than to confirm the logic of what the Probe had itself already deduced: that it had encountered a particularly nasty and persistent group of space-faring aliens who had half-destroyed it before it had managed to drive them off, and that these same aliens had traced it back to the homeworld, where the Second Winnowing was the result. As Dr. McCoy remarked, they sound like "super-Klingons," and we can only hope that their current three-hundred-thousand-year absence continues.

Dr. Benar, however, has suggested that that is an overly optimistic hope. She suggests, in fact, that they have not been entirely absent and may even have played a role in the disappearance of the Erisians, whose ancestors, she now believes, were the very mites whose civilization was destroyed in the first Winnowing.

Unfortunately, she makes a compelling case.

"Do *you* go along with these crazy ideas, Spock?" McCoy asked, a not-uncharacteristic skeptical frown creasing his brow. Senior officers and scientists, including Dajan, had gathered in a briefing room while they waited for official word from Starfleet that the conference had indeed ended. McCoy had missed most of the earlier discussions, having spent more than the usual amount of time keeping a personal eye on the now-conscious Commander Riley during the return towing, and was using this opportunity to catch up.

"Either of her hypotheses would account for the observed data, Doctor," Spock observed, not for the first time.

"Let me get this straight, Dr. Benar," McCoy persisted. "You're saying you were able to recognize that city as Erisian? In just those few seconds before the asteroid blew it all to hell?"

"Not as Erisian, Doctor," Benar responded quietly, though she had answered basically the same question many times before, "as Erisian-like. The pattern in which it was laid out appeared to be a simpler version, perhaps a primitive forerunner, of the patterns in which the Erisian ruins I have studied were laid out. If we had not been barred from returning to the chamber, I could have proven or disproven the relationship with a mathematical analysis. As it is, I can only say that I recognized the pattern, in the same sense that you would recognize the 'pattern' of an adult human in a human child and be capable of distinguishing it from a Vulcan or Klingon child. In addition, however, there is the matter of the memory crystals that have been found in the Exodus Hall of every Erisian site. As Captain Spock has pointed out, that crystal is indeed identical to the crystal that

produced the 'sonic holograms' and that occurs naturally on that world."

"But it's a pretty big jump from saying the Erisians
started out from there two million years ago to saying
that those super-Klingons did them in more than a
million and a half years later. For instance, how the
blazes did they even *find* them after all that time? Even if
the Erisians were building Exodus Halls back then, there
wouldn't have been much left of them after the asteroid
and the volcanoes."

"Perhaps not, but the other worlds in the system were
not similarly afflicted. And for there to have been
survivors at all, there had to have been off-world colo-
nies, possibly with Exodus Halls of their own."

"Don't fight it, Bones," Kirk said with a grin. "She's
got all the bases covered."

"So the super-Klingons found some of the worlds
they'd moved to," McCoy persisted, pointedly ignoring
Kirk's admonition. "You'd think by the time they got to
Temaris—when was that again? A hundred thousand
years ago? You'd think they'd have learned not to leave a
forwarding address by then, wouldn't you?"

"Perhaps they did not know they were being pur-
sued," Benar said patiently, "although I suspect that
they did. If they did, it would explain a great many
things. For example, why all known Erisian worlds were
evacuated at approximately the same time, roughly one
hundred thousand years ago. Why Erisians were so
careful to leave no record of their physical appearance."

McCoy shook his head. "They didn't want anyone to
know what they looked like, but they left their forwarding address? It doesn't make sense."

"But the Exodus Hall records may not have been their

'forwarding address,' as you put it, Doctor. If you will recall, every destination so far identified has proven to be an unstable star, including many that later went nova, even supernova."

"And that surprises you? After the way those super-Klingons did in the Probe's homeworld sun?"

"That sun neither went nova nor developed into a flare star, Dr. McCoy. That sun's output was decreased, not increased."

McCoy shrugged. "So they developed better, faster methods of extermination. They had more than two hundred thousand years to work on it."

"That is one possibility, Doctor. However, I tend toward the other: that the Exodus Hall records were meant as either a misdirection or a trap, more likely a trap."

"So now the Erisians are able to make a sun go nova at will? When they didn't even have the power to deflect an asteroid from their own homeworld?"

"As you yourself just now pointed out in regard to their pursuers, the Erisians had two hundred thousand years to develop their science, their weapons."

"Don't say I didn't warn you, Bones," Kirk put in when McCoy stalled out. "I've already put up every objection you have and more, and I've gotten nowhere. And believe me," he added, sobering, "there's nothing I'd like better than a believable and thoroughly mundane scenario, anything that doesn't involve either the Erisians or your super-Klingons going around setting off novas by the thousands."

"Captain Kirk." It was Lieutenant Kittay's voice from the bridge. "The *Galtizh* is hailing us. Commander Hiran—"

"Patch him through, Lieutenant."

A moment later, Hiran's face, touched by the barest trace of what struck Kirk as a wistful smile, appeared on the briefing-room viewer.

"Commander Hiran, what can I do for you?"

"As I recall, Federation captain, our tour of the *Enterprise* was never quite completed. . . ."

Instead of completing the tour, Kirk found himself repeating part of it, escorting Commander Hiran to the *Enterprise*'s botanical gardens. This time, with no rehearsals and no Erisian ruins to occupy the civilians, it seemed that at least half of them, musicians and archaeologists alike, were wandering the paths and lounging on the benches. More than one pair of eyes was distracted by the sight of a Federation captain and a Romulan commander seemingly out for an afternoon stroll.

"If you would care to walk on the grass again," Kirk said with a smile, "I suppose it could be tolerated for a time."

A small laugh escaped Hiran's throat. "You remembered, Federation captain."

"Taking a walk through a garden with a Romulan starship commander is not something that is quickly or easily forgotten."

"That is true." Hiran looked around, triggering the averting of several civilian eyes. "I suspect few of our audience will forget it either."

"Particularly if it is a prelude to something of greater import," Kirk said quietly.

Hiran stopped on the bank of the stream that meandered through one corner of the garden, from the small waterfall in an alcove of one wall to the pond where the recirculating pump pulled it back beneath the deck.

"You suspect me of wanting more than a few minutes in your decadent Federation garden, Kirk?"

"The thought had crossed my mind, Commander."

"And mine as well. Tiam would welcome my defection, I am sure. Otherwise I doubt that he would have stood by so calmly when I announced my intention to transport over."

"I was wondering about the lack of uproar."

"There was none, only a look—a hopeful look, if I was not mistaken."

Kirk nodded. "Doubtless he and Jenyu would do better in the Citadel with only their version of the mission to cope with."

"Doubtless. Which of course is one of the reasons I cannot stay, much as I might like."

"And the others? The other reasons?"

"I think you know, Federation captain. Our victory this time was tiny: there will not be a shooting war, no matter how much Jenyu and his backers desire it. Perhaps someday our victories will be larger."

"You feel there is still hope, then?"

"If I did not, I would not hesitate to join Dajan and his sister."

"In that case, I can only wish you well. And hope to speak with you again someday."

"Thank you, Federation captain. I have little doubt that you will—someday. Your Admiral Cartwright will someday be replaced." Hiran fell silent a moment, his eyes seeming to study the tiny, multicolored fish that darted and drifted through the stream at his feet. "And that replacement," he continued softly, "will need a source of information he can trust. As some of my friends are fond of saying—censorship, is one of the things our Empires have in common."

A tingle brushed at Kirk's scalp. *You know,* he realized, but he left the thought unspoken. Instead, he smiled. "He certainly will, Commander."

Together, they made their way back to the 'lift.

EPILOGUE

The dingy labyrinth of corridors and workshops and dressing rooms was no more glamorous than the last time Uhura had found herself backstage at Lincoln Center Philharmonic Hall. Although, she mused wryly, the full-dress uniforms of all the senior officers of the *Enterprise,* not to mention the cobalt formalwear of Ambassador Riley, did lend a touch of color, even elegance, that had been absent before.

"Commander," Kirk said as he narrowly avoided collision with a young man racing along the corridor wearing a green tuxedo jacket while carrying the matching trousers gingerly over one arm, "are you *positive* this is a good idea?"

"Not really, Captain," Uhura admitted, "but a promise is a promise."

"At least," Sulu said with a grin, "you didn't promise

to hold 'Andy' Penalt's hand at the debut of *his* Probe concerto."

Uhura snorted discreetly. "If I were going to hold something of 'Andy's,' it wouldn't be his hand—except, of course, in self-defense."

"Advance word in diplomatic circles," Riley volunteered, "is that there may not *be* a debut."

Sulu's grin broadened. "Now wouldn't *that* be a kick in the head."

"Do your diplomatic circles have any reasons to go along with the word?" Uhura wondered.

"The only ones I've heard were 'flashy but conventional.' "

"Like his playing." Uhura laughed.

"And like his public relations campaign," Riley added.

"Oh?" Uhura, Kirk, and McCoy joined in the one-syllable chorus.

Riley's eyebrows, both fully recovered from Temaris, rose in mock surprise. "And here I thought Starfleet officers prided themselves on keeping current with all aspects of Federation life and culture."

"Kevin!" Kirk shot him a dark look.

"I'll have a complete file squirted to the *Enterprise* computer if you want the details. Suffice it to say, he's been throwing around words like 'derivative,' though he's stopped short of 'plagiarism.' "

"You're joking!" Uhura sounded genuinely outraged. *"He* is accusing *Jandra* and *Dr. Benar* of stealing? From whom? Not from him, I hope! That would be too much even for him!"

Riley shook his head. "From the Probe, he says. Those first two messages, the sounds the computer translated into 'There is no danger' and 'We will talk.' According to

Penalt, what they did was nothing more than 'variations on a theme.'"

Uhura's eyes flashed, but before she could say more, Sulu laughed. "He's just ticked off because he didn't think of it first," he said.

"And couldn't have done it if he *had* thought of it!" Uhura snapped.

"No doubt about it, Commander," Kirk agreed. "However, could you try to look a little less tense when we get to their dressing rooms? You said the idea was to show them a few friendly faces before they go on, not to make them wonder who just killed your cat."

Uhura stopped, closed her eyes tightly for a moment, pulled in a breath. "You're right," she said, a smile appearing as she opened her eyes.

Ahead of them, they saw Maestra Espinoza and Dajan gesturing to them, directing them to their destination.

Two melodies flowed simultaneously from the single augmented keyboard, inspired by each of the two simplest aspects of the Probe's language. Both were produced and blended flawlessly by Jandra's unerring fingers, while the language's other aspects—those at least that the computer had succeeded in isolating— were suggested by the orchestra under Audrea Benar's precise baton.

Penalt won't dare to show his face after this performance, Riley decided after less than five minutes, *let alone put his own composition on display.*

Uhura, who appreciated the difficulty of the performance as well as the eerie beauty of the melodies, could only marvel wordlessly.

Even Spock was impressed by Jandra's sheer physical dexterity.

It was left to Kirk, he of the tin ear, to realize near the end that the composers had, perhaps inadvertently, reversed the order of the Probe's first two messages, giving the composition a symbolic significance no one had yet noted: *We will talk. There is no danger.*

The proper order, he thought as the performance ended and the applause began; the logical order, at least for the Federation and the Empire. With Hiran and himself, with Jandra and Dajan and Benar, the talk had begun. Someday, with luck and intelligence on both sides, the talk would spread. And the danger would, someday, go away.

He stood and added the sound of his own hands to the thunderous applause that filled not only the hall but several of the hearts within it.

Somewhere on the far side of the galaxy, the entity paused and extended its crystal sensor. It had passed this way many times before, but it had never before paused, for other than navigational reasons, to check its predictions against reality. There were of course none here that Spoke the True Language, nor were there ocean-dwelling primitives who might someday become the equals of its creators.

But there were mites galore, its crystalline memory told it, and a mite that called itself Spock had made it aware that mites, too, had a place in the rightful scheme of things and might even have something interesting to say, whether in the True Language or some other. But they must be approached with care, the Spock mite had said, although that was something the entity had obviously already known. And you must take care not to Speak too loudly or their fragile, spacegoing bubbles will cease to function and they will think you mean them harm.

Across nearly half a parsec, it reached out to the pale, gray-green world fifth out from a star not unlike that which had once shone down on the world of its creators.

Carefully, it set the molecules of the world's atmosphere to vibrating while it listened for a reply. It would take time, as it had with the ocean-dwelling primitives of a thousand worlds, but someday soon, the mites would understand the entity's new greeting:

Would you like to talk?